J. M. G. Le Clézio

THE PROSPECTOR

Translated from the French by
C. DICKSON

Atlantic Books
LONDON

First published in France in 1985 as *Le chercheur d'or* by Éditions Gallimard.

First published in Great Britain in 2016 by Atlantic Books, an imprint of Atlantic Books Ltd.

This paperback edition published in 2017 by Atlantic Books.

10 9 8 7 6 5 4 3 2 1

A CIP catalogue record for this book is available from the British Library.

Paperback ISBN: 978 1 84887 378 0
E-book ISBN: 978 1 84887 385 8

Set in Carré Noir by Tetragon, London

Atlantic Books
An Imprint of Atlantic Books Ltd
Ormond House
26–27 Boswell Street
London
WC1N 3JZ

www.atlantic-books.co.uk

Printed and bound by CPI Group (UK) Ltd, Croydon, CR0 4YY

Contents

to my grandfather Léon

Boucan Embayment, 1892

As far back as I can remember, the sound of the sea has been in my ears. Mingled with that of the wind in the needles of the she-oaks, the wind that never stops, even when you leave the coast behind and cross the cane fields, it's the sound of my childhood. I can still hear it now, deep down inside of me, it accompanies me wherever I go. The slow, tireless sound of the waves breaking out on the coral reefs in the distance and then coming up to die on the sand of Black River. There's never a day I don't go down to the sea, nor a night that I don't wake up, sit up in my cot, back damp with sweat, pull aside the mosquito net and try to hear the tide, fretful, filled with a yearning I don't understand.

I think of the sea as a person and – in the darkness – all of my senses are alert to better hear it coming, better welcome it. The giant waves leap over the reefs, come crashing down into the lagoon, and the noise makes the earth and the air quake like a blast furnace. I can hear it, it's moving, breathing.

When there's a full moon I slip silently out of bed, being careful not to make the worm-eaten floorboards crack. Even though I know Laure isn't sleeping, I know her eyes are open in the dark and that she's holding her breath. I climb over the windowsill and push open the wooden shutters — I'm outside in the night. The white moonlight is shining on the garden, I can see the silvery trees whose crowns are whispering in the wind, I can make out the dark flowerbeds planted with rhododendrons, with hibiscuses. Heart racing, I walk down the pathway that leads out to the hills where the fallow lands begin. Right next to the crumbled-down wall stands the tall chalta tree, the one Laure calls the tree of good and evil, and I climb up on the main branches to look at the sea and the vast stretches of sugar cane over the treetops. The moon rolls around between the clouds, throwing out flashes of light. Then maybe I suddenly catch sight of it, out over the leaves to the left of the Tourelle de Tamarin, a large inky pool where a shiny patch is glittering. Do I really see it, do I hear it? The sea is inside my head and it's when I close my eyes that I can see and hear it best, listen to every rumble of the waves being parted on the reefs, then merging once again to come washing up on the shore. I sit clinging to the branches of the chalta tree for a long time, until my arms grow numb. The sea breeze blows through the trees and the cane fields, makes the leaves shimmer in the moonlight. Sometimes I stay until dawn, just listening, dreaming. At the other end of the garden the large house is dark, closed up, like a shipwreck. The wind makes the loose clapboards bang, makes the frame creak. That too is the sound of the sea along with the creaking of the tree trunk, the whimpering of the she-oak needles. I'm afraid, all alone up in the tree, and yet I don't want to go back to the bedroom. I struggle against the chill of the wind, the weariness making my head feel heavy.

It's not really fear. It's like standing at the edge of a chasm, a deep ravine, and staring down intently with your heart beating so hard that your neck throbs and grows painful, and yet you know you have to stay there, that you're finally going to understand something. I can't go back to the bedroom as long as the tide is rising, it's impossible. I have to stay clinging to the chalta tree and wait while the moon slides over to the other side of the sky. I go back to the bedroom and duck under the mosquito net just before dawn, when the sky is turning grey over in the direction of Mananava. I hear Laure sigh, because she hasn't been able to sleep either the whole time I was outside. She never talks to me about it. She just looks at me the next day with those dark, questioning eyes and I regret having gone out to listen to the sea.

I go down to the shore every day. You have to cross the fields, the cane is so high that I move along blindly, running down the harvest paths, sometimes lost amid the razor-sharp leaves. There, I can't hear the sea any longer. The late winter sun burns down, smothering the sounds. I can sense it when I'm very near the shore, because the air grows heavy, still, laden with flies. Up above, the sky is blue, taut, birdless, blinding. I sink up to my ankles in the dusty red earth. To avoid damaging my shoes, I take them off and, tying the laces together, carry them strung around my neck. That way my hands are free. You need to have your hands free when crossing a cane field. The stalks are very tall. Cook, the cook, says they're going to cut them next month. They've got leaves as sharp as cane knives; you have to push them aside with the palm of your hand to get through. Denis, Cook's grandson, is out ahead of me. I can't see him any more. He's always gone barefoot. Armed with his pole, he walks faster than I do. To call to one another, we decided to squeak a grass harp twice, or else to bark twice, like this: woua! The men do that, the Indians, when they walk through the tall cane stalks at harvest time with their long knives.

I can hear Denis far out ahead of me: Woua! Woua! I answer with my harp. There is no other sound. The tide is at its lowest this morning, it won't rise before noon. We're moving as fast as we can to get to the tide pools where the shrimp and octopuses hide.

In front of me, in the middle of the cane, is a stack of lava stones. I love to climb up there to see the green fields stretching away and, far behind me now, lost in the jumble of trees and thickets, our house like a shipwreck, with it's odd, sky-blue roof and Capt'n Cook's little hut, and still further off, Yemen's smokestack and the high red mountains bristling towards the sky. Pivoting at the top of the pyramid, I can see the entire landscape, the smoke from the sugar mills, the Tamarin River winding through the trees, the hills and, finally, the dark, shimmering sea that has drawn back to the other side of the reefs.

That's what I really love. I think I could stay up on top of this stack of stones for hours, days, not doing anything, just looking.

Woua! Woua! Denis is calling me from the other end of the field. He too is on top of a stack of black stones, marooned on a small island in the middle of the ocean. He's so far away I can't make out anything about him. I can just see his long insect-like silhouette atop the stack of stones. I cup my hands around my mouth and bark in turn: Woua! Woua! We go back down at the same time and start walking blindly through the cane again towards the sea.

In the morning the sea is black, closed. It's the sands from the Big Black River and the Tamarin that do that, lava dust. When you head northward or go down towards the Morne in the south, the sea is more limpid. Denis is fishing for octopuses in the lagoon, shielded by the coral reefs. I watch him walk away on his long stork-like legs, pole in hand. He's not afraid of sea urchins or stonefish. He walks through the pools of dark water in such a way that his shadow is always behind him. As he goes further and further from the shore he disturbs flights of mangrove herons, of cormorants, sea larks. I watch him, barefoot in the cold water. Often I ask permission to join him, but he doesn't want me to. He says I'm too young, he says he's the keeper of my soul. He says my father entrusted me to him. That's not true, my father has never spoken to him. But I like the way he says 'the keeper of your soul'. I'm the only one who goes with him out to the seashore. My cousin Ferdinand isn't allowed to, even though he's a little older than I am, and neither is Laure, because she's a girl. I like Denis, he's my friend. My cousin Ferdinand says he isn't a friend because he's black, because he's Cook's grandson. But that doesn't matter to me. Ferdinand only says that because he's jealous, he too would like to walk through the cane fields with Denis all the way out to the sea.

When the tide is very low like this, early in the morning, the black rocks appear. There are large dark pools and others so luminous you'd think they were emitting the light. Urchins make purple balls at the bottom, anemones fan out their blood-red corollas, brittle stars slowly wave their long downy arms. I examine the bottom of the tide pools, while Denis is searching for octopuses with the point of his pole in the distance.

Out here the sound of the sea is as beautiful as music. The waves come in on the wind, break on the coral barrier, very far away, and I can hear the vibrations in the rocks and then reverberating through the sky. There's a sort of wall out on the horizon that the sea is pounding, hammering away at. Sprays of foam go shooting up at times, fall back down on the reefs. The tide has begun to rise. This is the time of day when Denis catches octopuses, because they can feel the cool water from the open sea with their tentacles and they come out of their hiding places. One after another, the pools fill with water. The brittle stars wave their arms in the current, clouds

7

of alevins swim up the cascading tide water and I see a boxfish go by looking hurried and stupid. I've been coming here for a very long time, ever since I was a little boy. I know every pool, every rock, every nook and cranny, the place where whole communities of urchins can be found, where large holothurians creep, where the eels, the sea centipedes hide. I stand there, not making a move, not making a sound, so they'll forget me, not see me any more. That's when the sea is beautiful and so very gentle. When the sun is high up in the sky, over the Tourelle de Tamarin, the water grows light, pale blue, the colour of the sky. The rumbling of the waves on the reefs booms out with all its might. Blinded by the light I blink my eyes, searching for Denis. The sea is coming in through the pass now, its slow waves are swelling, covering the rocks.

When I reach the beach at the mouth of the two rivers I see Denis sitting on the sand high up on the beach in the shade of some velvet soldierbushes. Hanging from the end of his pole like rags are some ten octopuses. He's sitting very still, waiting for me. The hot sun is burning down on my shoulders, on my hair. Suddenly, I throw off my clothes on the spot and dive naked into the water, right where the sea meets the two rivers. I swim against the freshwater current until I can feel the sharp little pebbles against my belly and knees. When I've made my way completely into the river I grab hold of a large rock with both hands and allow the water of the rivers to run over me, cleanse me of the burn of the sea and the sun.

Nothing exists any more, everything stands still. This is all there is, what I'm feeling, seeing, the sky so blue, the sound of the sea struggling against the reefs and the cold water flowing over my skin.

I get out of the water, shivering in spite of the heat, and get dressed without even drying myself off. There's gritty sand in my shirt, in my trousers, rubbing my feet raw in my shoes. My hair is still matted together with salt. Denis has been watching me. His smooth face is dark, impenetrable. Sitting in the shade of the velvet soldierbushes, he's remained very still, both hands resting on the long pole where the octopuses hang like tatters. He never bathes in the sea, I don't even know if he can swim. When he does bathe it's at nightfall, upstream in the Tamarin River or in the brook in Bassin Salé. Sometimes he goes far up near the mountains in the direction of Mananava and washes himself with plants in the torrents in the gorges. He says his grandfather taught him to do that, to grow strong, to have a man's penis.

I like Denis, he knows so many things about the trees, the water, the sea. He learned everything he knows from his grandfather and his grandmother too — an old black woman who lives in Case Noyale. He knows the name of every fish, every insect, he knows all the edible plants in the forest, all the wild fruit, he can recognize a tree simply by its smell or else by chewing a bit of its bark. He knows so many things that you never get bored with him. Laure likes him a lot too, because he always brings back little presents for her, a fruit from the forest or a flower, a shell, a piece of white flint, of obsidian. Ferdinand calls him 'Friday' to make fun of us, and he nicknamed me the Wild Woodsman, because one day Uncle Ludovic said that when he saw me coming back from the mountains.

One day — already a long time ago, in the very beginning of our friendship — Denis brought home a little grey animal for Laure, it was so cute with its pointy snout and he said it was a muskrat, but my father said it was just a shrew. Laure kept it with her for one day and it slept in a little cardboard box on her bed; but in the evening when it was time to go to bed it woke up and started running all around and making so much noise that my father came in in his nightshirt, holding a candle, and he got angry and drove the little

9

animal outside. We never saw it again after that. I think Laure was quite upset about it.

When the sun is nice and high in the sky Denis stands up, steps out of the shade of the bushes and shouts 'Alee-sis!' That's how he pronounces my name. Then we walk quickly through the cane fields until we reach Boucan. Denis stops to eat at his grandfather's cabin and I run over to the big house with its sky-blue roof.

———————

When dawn breaks and the sky grows light behind the peaks of Trois Mamelles, I set out with my cousin Ferdinand along the dirt road that leads to the Yemen cane fields. We scale up high walls and enter the '*chassés*' or private hunting grounds, the dwelling place of the deer that belong to the big landowners of Wolmar, Tamarin, Magenta, Barefoot and Walhalla. Ferdinand knows where he's going. His father is very rich, he's taken him to all the estates. He's even been as far as the Tamarin Estate houses, as far as Wolmar and Médine all the way up north. It's forbidden to enter the *chassés*, my father would be very angry if he knew we were trespassing on these properties. He says it's dangerous, that there could be hunters, that we could fall into a gulley, but I think it's mostly because he doesn't like the people who have large estates. He says that everyone should stay on his own land, that one shouldn't go wandering about on other people's land.

We move along cautiously, as if we were in enemy territory. In the distance, amid the grey underbrush, we glimpse some quick shapes that disappear in the thick of the wood: they're deer.

Then Ferdinand says he wants to go down to Tamarin Estate. We come out of the *chassés* and walk down the long dirt road again. I've never been out this far before. Except one day with Denis I hiked all the way up to the top of the Tourelle de Tamarin, the place where you can see the whole lay of the land all the way out to the Trois Mamelles, even out as far as the Morne, and from there I could see the roofs of the houses and the tall chimney of the sugar mill belching out heavy smoke.

The day grows rapidly hot, because it will soon be summer. The cane is very high. They started cutting it several days ago. All along the road we pass oxen pulling carts, wobbling under the weight of the cane. They're driven by young Indians who look apathetic, as if they were dozing. The air is filled with black flies, with horseflies. Ferdinand is walking fast, I have a hard time keeping up with him. Every time a cart passes we jump aside into the ditch, because there's just room enough for the large, iron-rimmed wheels.

The fields are full of men and women working. The men have harvest knives, sickles, and the women are carrying hoes. The women are clothed in gunny cloth with old burlap bags wrapped around their heads. The men are bare-chested, streaming with sweat. We hear cries, people calling out woua! The red dust is churning up from the paths between the square patches of cane. There's an acrid smell in the air, the smell of raw cane juice, of dust, of men's sweat. Feeling a little light-headed, we walk, run down to the Tamarin outbuildings where the cartloads of cane are arriving. No one pays any attention to us. There's so much dust on the paths that we're already red from head to toe and our clothes look as if they're made of gunny cloth. Children are running with us along the paths, Indians, Kaffirs, they're eating pieces of sugar cane they've found on the ground. Everyone is going towards the sugar mill to watch the first pressings.

We finally reach the buildings. I'm a little frightened because it's the first time I've been here. The carts are stopped in front of a high, whitewashed wall and the men are unloading the sugar cane that will be thrown into the drums. The boiler is spitting out a thick, red smoke that darkens the sky and suffocates us when the wind blows it our way. There is noise everywhere, great jets of steam. Directly in front of us I see a group of men feeding bagasse from the crushed cane into the furnace. They're almost naked, like giants, sweat running down their black backs, faces grimacing against the heat of the fire. They aren't saying anything. They're simply scooping up the bagasse by the armful and throwing it into the furnace, grunting every time: hmph!

I don't know where Ferdinand is any more. I stand there, petrified, watching the cast-iron boiler, the large steel kettle bubbling like a giant's cooking pot, and the gearwheels turning the rollers. Inside the sugar mill men are bustling about, throwing the fresh cane into the shredder's jaws, gathering the already shredded cane to extract more juice. There is so much noise, so much heat and steam that my head is spinning. The clear juice streams over the rollers, flows towards the boiling vats. The children are standing at the foot of the centrifuges. I notice Ferdinand standing and waiting in front of the kettle that is turning slowly as the thick syrup finishes cooling off. There are large waves in the kettle and the sugar spills over on to the ground, roping down in black clots that roll through the leaves and straw covering the ground. The children rush up, shouting, gather the pieces of sugar and carry them off to one side to suck on them in the sunshine. I too am keeping an eye out in front of the vat, and when the sugar spills out, rolls on the ground, I dash forward, snatch the soft, scalding lump covered with grass and bits of bagasse. I take it outside and lick it as I squat in the dust, watching the thick, red smoke coming out of the chimney. All of the noise, the shouting children, the bustling men, fills me with a sort of fever that makes me tremble. Is it the noise from the machines and the hissing steam, is it the acrid red smoke enveloping me, the heat of the sun, the harsh taste of burned sugar? My vision grows blurry, I know I'm going to vomit. I call out to my cousin to help me, but my voice is hoarse, it rips through my throat. I call for Denis, for Laure too. But no one around me is paying any attention. The crowd of children is endlessly rushing up to the large rotating vat, waiting for the moment when – the valves having opened – the air goes whooshing into the vacuum pans and the wave of poppling syrup comes flowing down the troughs like a golden river. All of a sudden I feel so weak, so lost, that I lay my head on my knees and close my eyes.

Then I feel a hand stroking my hair, I hear a voice speaking to me softly in Creole: 'Why you cry?' Through my tears I see a tall, beautiful Indian woman draped in her gunny cloths stained with red earth. She's standing in front of me, very straight, calm, unsmiling, and the top part of her body is immobile, because of the hoe that she's carrying balanced on folded rags on her head. She speaks gently to me, asks me where I'm from, and now I'm walking with her on the crowded road, clinging to her dress, feeling the slow swinging of her hips. When she reaches the entrance to Boucan on the other side of the river she walks me to Capt'n Cook's house. Then she leaves immediately, without waiting for any reward or thanks, sets off down the middle of the long lane between the rose apple trees, and I watch her walking away, so nice and straight, the hoe balancing on her head.

I look at the large wooden house lit up in the afternoon sun, with its blue or green roof, of such a lovely colour that today I remember it as being the colour of the dawn sky. I can still feel the heat of the red earth and of the furnace on my face, I brush off the dust and bits of straw covering my clothing. When I'm near the house I can hear Mam helping Laure recite her prayers in the shade of the veranda.

Her voice is so gentle, so clear, that tears spring to my eyes again and my heart starts beating very fast. I walk towards the house, barefoot over the dry, crackled earth. I go over to the water basin behind the kitchen, dip the dark water from the basin with the enamel pitcher and wash my hands, my face, my neck, my legs, my feet. The cool water quickens the burn of the scratches, the cuts from the razor-sharp cane leaves. Mosquitoes, water spiders are skimming over the surface of the water, and larvae are bobbing along the sides of the basin. I hear the soft sound of evening birds, smell the scent of smoke settling on the garden, as if it were heralding the night that is beginning in the ravines of Mananava. Then I walk over to Laure's tree at the edge of the garden, the tall chalta tree of good and evil. It's as if everything I'm feeling, everything I'm seeing now is eternal. I'm not aware that it will all soon disappear.

There's Mam's voice too. That's the only thing I know about her now, the only thing I have left of her. I threw out all the yellowed photographs, the portraits, the letters, the books she used to read, so as not to dampen her voice. I want to be able to hear it for ever, like the people we love whose faces we're no longer familiar with, her voice, the gentleness of her voice, which encompasses everything, the warmth of her hands, the smell of her hair, her dress, the light, the late afternoons when Laure and I would come out on the veranda, our hearts still skipping from having run, and lessons would begin for us. Mam speaks very softly, very slowly, and we listen, believing we can understand in that way. Laure is more intelligent than I am, Mam repeats that every day, she says she knows how to ask questions at the right time. We read, each in turn, standing in front of Mam, who's rocking in her ebony rocker. We read and then Mam quizzes us, first on grammar, on verb conjugation, adjective and participle agreement. Then she questions us together about the meaning of what we've just read, about the words, the expressions. She asks questions carefully and I listen to her voice with both pleasure and misgivings, because I'm afraid of disappointing her. I'm ashamed of not catching on as rapidly as Laure, I feel as if I don't deserve these moments of happiness, the gentleness of her voice, her fragrance, the light at the end of day that turns the house and the trees golden, that comes from her eyes and her words.

For more than a year now Mam has been teaching us, because we no longer have any other schoolmistress. A long time ago — I can hardly remember it — there was a schoolmistress who would come out from Floréal three times a week. But with my father's progressive financial ruin we can no longer afford that luxury. My father wanted to put us in boarding school, but Mam was against it, she said Laure and I were too young. So she's in charge of our education every evening and sometimes in the morning. She teaches us everything we need to know: writing, grammar, some arithmetic and Bible History. In the beginning my father was doubtful about the worth of her teaching. But one day Joseph Lestang, who is headmaster at the Royal College, was astonished at the breadth of our knowledge. He even told my father that we were far ahead of other children our age, and since then my father has completely accepted Mam's teaching.

Still, today I wouldn't be able to explain exactly what that teaching was. At the time we — my father, Mam, Laure and I — lived closed up in our world in the Boucan Embayment, bordered in the east by the jagged peaks of Trois Mamelles, in the north by the vast plantations, in the south by the fallow lands of Black River, and in the west by the sea. In the evenings, when the mynahs chatter in the tall trees of the garden, there is Mam's young, gentle voice dictating a poem or reciting a prayer. What is she saying? I don't know any more. The meaning of her words has faded away, like the cries of the birds and the rumour of the sea breeze. All that's left is the soft, light, almost imperceptible music in the shade of the veranda blending in with the light in the leaves of the trees.

I listen to it tirelessly. I hear her voice vibrating in unison with the song of the birds. Sometimes I watch a flight of starlings very intently, as if their trajectory through the trees, out towards their secret places in the mountains, could explain Mam's lesson. From time to time she brings me back down to earth by slowly pronouncing my name, the way she does, so slowly that I stop breathing.

'Alexis . . . ? Alexis?'

She and Denis are the only ones who call me by my first name. Everyone else — maybe because Laure was the first one to have the idea — calls me Ali. As for my father, he never pronounces first names, except maybe for Mam's, as I heard him do once or twice. He was saying Anne, Anne very softly. And at the time I heard *'Ame'*, the French word for soul. Or maybe he really was saying *Âme*, in a deep, gentle voice that he used only when speaking to her. He really loved her very much.

In those days Mam was pretty, I wouldn't be able to say just how pretty. I hear the sound of her voice and I immediately think of the evening light under the veranda at Boucan, surrounded by reflections off the bamboo stalks, and of the clear sky traversed by small flocks of mynahs. I believe all the beauty of that moment stems from her, from her thick curly hair of a slightly reddish-brown colour that captures the slightest glimmer of light, from her blue eyes, from her still full face, so very young, from her long vigorous pianist's hands. There is so much peace, so much simplicity in her, so much light. I stare hard at my sister Laure, sitting up very straight on her chair, wrists resting on the edge of the table, facing the arithmetic book and the white notebook that she's holding open with the fingertips of her left hand. She's concentrating on writing, her head slightly tilted towards her left shoulder, her thick black hair covering one side of her Indian-like face. She doesn't look like Mam, they have nothing in common, but Laure looks at her with her black eyes, shiny as stones, and I know she feels as much admiration, as much fervour as I do. Then the evening draws out, the golden light of sunset recedes imperceptibly from the garden, drawing flights of birds along with it, bearing the cries of field workers, the rumble of ox carts on the sugar-cane roads off into the distance.

Every evening brings a different lesson, a poem, a fairy tale, a new problem, and yet today it seems as if it was always the same lesson, uninterrupted by the burning adventures of the day, by the wanderings out as far as the seashore or by dreams at night. When did all of that exist? Mam, leaning over the table, is explaining arithmetic by placing piles of beans in front of us. 'Three here, I take two away, and that makes two thirds. Eight here and I put five aside, that makes five eighths . . . Ten here, I take nine away, how much does that make?' I'm sitting in front of her, watching her long hands with the tapered fingers I know so well — each one of them. The very strong index finger of her left hand, the middle finger, the ring finger encircled with a fine band of gold, worn with water and with time. The fingers of the right hand, larger, harder, thicker, and the ring finger that she is able to lift up very high when her other fingers are running over the ivory keyboard, but that will suddenly strike a high note. 'Alexis, you're not listening . . . You never listen to the arithmetic lessons. You won't be able to get into Royal College.' Is that what she says? No, I don't think so, Laure is making that up, she's always so diligent, so conscientious about making piles of beans, because it's her way of showing her love for Mam.

I compensate for it with dictations. It's the moment of the afternoon I like best when, leaning over the white page of my notebook, holding the fountain pen in my hand, I wait for Mam's voice to begin inventing the words, one by one, very slowly, as if she were giving them to us, as if she were drawing them with the inflections and syllables. There are the difficult words that she's carefully chosen, because she makes up the texts for our dictations herself: 'wagonette', 'ventilator', 'half-hourly', 'cavalcade', 'equipage', 'fjord', 'aplomb', and, of course, from time to time, to make us laugh, 'beef', 'brief', 'leaf' and 'lief'. I write slowly, as best I can, to draw out the time that Mam's voice will resonate in the silence of the white page, waiting also for the moment when she'll tell me, with a little nod of her head, as if it were the first time she'd noticed, 'You have pretty handwriting.'

Then she rereads the dictation, but at her own rhythm, marking a slight pause for the commas, a silence for the periods. That cannot come to an end either, it's a long story she tells us, every evening, in which the same words, the same music is repeated, but jumbled up and arranged differently. Nights, lying on my cot under the veil of the mosquito net, just before falling asleep, listening to the familiar sounds — my father's deep voice reading a newspaper article or conversing with Mam and Aunt Adelaide, Mam's buoyant laughter, the distant voices of the black men sitting under the trees listening for the sound of the sea breeze in the needles of the she-oaks — that same interminable story comes back to me, full of words and sounds slowly dictated by Mam, sometimes the acute accent she pronounces a syllable with or the very long silence that makes a word grow larger, and the light in her eyes shining upon those beautiful and incomprehensible sentences. I don't believe I go to sleep until I've seen that light shining, until I've glimpsed that sparkle. A word, just a word that I carry off with me into sleep.

I like Mam's moral lessons too, usually early on Sunday mornings before reciting Mass. I like the moral lessons because Mam always tells us a story, always a different one, set in places we're familiar with. Afterwards she asks Laure and me questions. They aren't difficult questions, but she just asks them, looking straight at us, and I can feel the very gentle blue of her gaze penetrating deep inside me.

'The story takes place in a convent where there were a dozen residents, twelve little orphans just like I was when I was your age. One evening at dinner time, guess what they saw on the table? A large platter of sardines, which they were very fond of – they were poor, you see, and for them having sardines for dinner was a feast! And in that platter there were precisely as many sardines as there were little orphan girls, twelve sardines. No, no, there was an extra one – there were thirteen sardines in all. When everyone had eaten, the sister pointed to the last sardine that remained in the middle of the platter and asked, "Who will eat the last one? Does anyone among you want it?" Not a hand was raised, not one of the little girls answered. "Well then," said the sister gaily, "here's what we'll do: we'll blow out the candle and when the room is dark, whoever wants the sardine can eat it without being ashamed." The sister put out the candle, and do you know what happened then? Each of the little girls reached out her hand in the dark to take the sardine, and her hand found another little girl's hand. There were twelve little hands in the platter!'

Those are the stories Mam tells, I've never heard better or funnier ones.

But what I really like a lot is Bible History. It's a big book bound in dark-red leather, an old book with a cover embossed with a golden sun and twelve rays emanating from it. Sometimes, Mam lets Laure and I look at it.

We turn the pages very slowly to look at the illustrations, to read the words written at the top of the pages, the captions. There are engravings that I love more than anything else, like the Tower of Babel or the one that says: 'The prophet Jonah remained three days in the belly of the whale and came out alive.' Off in the distance, near the horizon, there is a large sailing vessel melting in with the clouds, and when I ask Mam who is in the vessel she can't answer me. I have the feeling that one day I'll know who was travelling in that large ship and saw Jonah when he came out of the whale's belly. I also like it when God makes 'armies in the air' appear amid the clouds over Jerusalem. And the battle of Eleazar against Antiochus, where we see an enraged elephant bursting into a group of warriors. What Laure likes best is the beginning, the creation of man and woman and the picture where we see the devil in the form of a serpent with a man's head coiled around the tree of good and evil. That's how she knew it was the chalta tree that is at the edge of our garden, because it has the same leaves and fruit. Laure loves to go out to the tree in the evening, she climbs up on the main branches and picks the thick-skinned fruit that we've been forbidden to eat. She doesn't talk about that to anyone but me.

Mam reads us stories from the Holy Scripture, the Tower of Babel, the city with the tower reaching all the way up to the sky. Abraham's sacrifice, or else the story of Joseph being sold by his brothers. It took place in 2876 BC, twelve years before the death of Isaac. I remember that date well. I also really like the story of Moses saved from the waters, Laure and I often ask Mam to read it to us. To prevent the Pharaoh's soldiers from killing her child, his mother put him in a 'little cradle of woven reeds', the book says, 'and she placed him in the water near the bank of the Nile'. The Pharaoh's daughter went down to the river 'to bathe, in the company of her many servants. As soon as she noticed the basket, she was curious to learn what was in it and sent one of her maidservants to fetch it. When she saw the infant crying in the cradle she was touched and, as the child's beauty caused her tender feelings to grow even deeper, she resolved

21

to save it.' We recite the story by heart and we always stop at the place when the Pharaoh's daughter adopts the child and names him Moses, because she'd saved him from the waters.

There is one story that I love above all, it's the one about the Queen of Sheba. I don't know why I like it, but after talking about it so much I succeed in getting Laure to like it too. Mam knows this and sometimes, with a smile, she opens the big red book to that chapter and starts reading. I still know every sentence by heart, even today: 'After Solomon had built such a magnificent temple for God, he built a palace for himself — which took fourteen years to finish — and gold glittered in every corner and the eyes of the world were turned upon the magnificence of the columns and sculptures . . .' Then the Queen of Sheba appears, 'who came from deep in the south to ascertain whether all that was said about the young prince was true. She came in magnificent circumstance and brought rich presents to Solomon, six score talents of gold' — which would be approximately eight million pounds — 'extremely precious pearls and perfumes the likes of which had never been seen.' It isn't the words I'm hearing, but Mam's voice that is drawing me into the palace of Solomon, who has risen from his throne as the extremely lovely Queen of Sheba leads in the slaves rolling treasures across the floor. Laure and I really like King Solomon, even if we don't understand why he forsook the Lord and worshipped the idols at the end of his life. Mam says that's just the way it is, even the most righteous and powerful men can commit sins. We don't understand how that can be possible, but we like the way he rendered his judgements and that magnificent palace he had built that the Queen of Sheba came to visit. But maybe what we really like is the book with its red-leather cover and the large golden sun, and Mam's slow, gentle voice, her blue eyes glancing up at us between each sentence, and the sunlight lying ever so golden upon the trees in the garden, for I've never read any other book that made such a deep impression upon me.

On afternoons when Mam's lessons finish a little early, Laure and I go exploring in the attic of the house. There is a little wooden stairway that leads up to the ceiling and you just need to push open a trapdoor. Under the shingled rooftops it is dusky and the heat is stifling, but we love being up there. At each end of the attic there is a narrow garret window, with no panes, simply closed with poorly joined shutters. When you crack open the shutters, you can see way out over the landscape as far as the cane fields of Yemen and Magenta, and the peaks of Trois Mamelles and Rempart Mountain.

I love staying up here in this secret place until dinner time and even later, after nightfall. My hiding place is the part of the attic that's all the way at the end of the roof, on the side where you can see the mountains. There's a lot of dusty, termite-eaten furniture — all that is left of what my great-grandfather had bought from the East India Company. I sit down on a very low seamstress chair and look out through the garret window towards the mountains jutting up from the shadows. In the middle of the attic there are large trunks filled with old papers, French reviews in bundles tied up with string. That's where my father has put all of his old journals. Every six or seven months he makes a packet that he puts on the floor near the trunks. Laure and I often come up here to look at the pictures. We're lying in the dust on our stomachs with stacks of old journals in front of us and turning the pages very slowly. There is the *Journal des Voyages* that always has a drawing on the front page representing some extraordinary scene, a tiger hunt in India or the attack of the Zulus against the English or still yet the Comanches making an attack on the railroad in America. Inside, Laure reads passages from *Les*

Robinsons marseillais, a serial she's fond of. The journal we like best of all is the *Illustrated London News* and, since I don't understand English very well, I look more closely at the illustrations to guess what the text says. Laure has already started to learn English with my father and she explains what it's about, the way to pronounce the words. We don't stay very long because the dust soon makes us start sneezing and stings our eyes. Sometimes though, we stay for hours, on Sunday afternoons when it's too hot outside or when a fever is keeping us in the house.

In the reviews that aren't illustrated I look at the advertisements, the ones for the Parisian Dry Cleaners, for the A. Fleury & A. Toulorge Pharmacy, the Coringhy Tobacconist, blue-black sumac ink, American pocket watches, the beautiful bicycles that we dream of having. Laure and I play at buying things and we get our ideas from the advertisements. Laure would like a bicycle, a real bicycle painted in black enamel with large wheels fitted with pneumatics and chrome handlebars like the ones we see when we go over to Champ de Mars or Port Louis. As for me, there are several things I would like to have, like the large drawing pads, the paints and the compasses from Magasin Wimphen, or the pocket knives with twelve blades from the gunsmiths'. But there's nothing I want more than the Favre-Leuba fob watch imported from Geneva. I always see it in the same place in the journals, on the next-to-last page, with the needles showing the same time and the second hand at twelve. I always read with the same delight the words of the advertisement describing it: 'unbreakable', 'waterproof', 'airtight', 'made of stainless steel', 'enamel face', 'amazing precision', 'sturdiness', 'ready to serve you for a lifetime'.

That's what we dream about up in our hiding place under the sun-baked rooftops. There's also the landscape, as I see it through the garret window, the only landscape I know and love, the one these eyes will never see again: out beyond the dark trees of the garden, the green stretch of the cane fields, the grey-and-blue patches of the aloes over by Walhalla, by Yemen, the smoking sugar-mill chimneys and, off in the distance, like a huge semicircular wall, the flamboyant red mountain range where the peaks of Trois Mamelles tower. The tips of the volcanoes standing against the sky are like needles, gracile, like the towers of a fairy castle. I gaze at them tirelessly through the narrow window, as if I were the lookout on a beached, motionless ship, watching for some kind of sign. Listening to the sound of the sea deep within me, behind me, borne along on the tide winds. And I truly am in a ship as the joists and struts of the roof timbers crack, floating eternally before the mountains. This is where I heard the sea for the very first time, this is where I can feel it best, when the tide rises, bringing in its long waves that force their way through the pass facing the estuary of the two rivers, casting spurts of sea foam high over the barrier reefs.

Back in the days of Boucan we never see anyone. Laure and I grow to be downright unsociable. Whenever we can, we escape from the garden and go walking through the cane, towards the sea. It's grown hot, a dry, 'stinging' heat as Capt'n Cook says. Are we even aware that we have such freedom? We don't even know the meaning of the word. We never leave the Boucan Embayment, the imaginary property bordered by the two rivers, the mountains and the sea.

Now that the long holidays have begun, my cousin Ferdinand comes over more often, when Uncle Ludovic goes down to his lands in Barefoot and Yemen. Ferdinand doesn't like me. One day he called me 'the Wild Woodsman', as his father had, and he also said something about Friday, because of Denis. He said 'all tar', black skin and soul to boot, and I got mad. Even though he's two years older than I am, I jumped on him and tried to get his neck in an armlock, but he quickly got the better of me and then he squeezed my neck under his arm until I could feel the bones cracking and my eyes filled with tears. He never came back to Boucan after that day. I hate him and I also hate his father, Uncle Ludovic, because he's tall and strong and he talks loudly and he always looks at us with those ironic, black eyes of his and that slightly tense sort of smile. The last time he came to our house my father wasn't in and Mam didn't want to see him. She had us tell him that she had a fever, she needed to rest. Uncle Ludovic sat down in the dining room anyway, on one of our old chairs that creaked under his weight, and he tried to talk to Laure and me. I remember him leaning over towards Laure and saying, 'What's your name?' His black eyes gleamed when he looked at me too. Laure was all white, sitting up very straight on her chair and she was staring straight ahead without answering. She sat there like that for a long time, very still, staring ahead, while Uncle Ludovic said teasingly, 'What? Have you lost your tongue?' Anger was making my heart beat very fast and I finally said, 'My sister doesn't want to answer you.' So then he stood up without saying anything more, he took his hat and cane and walked out. I listened to the sound of his footsteps on the steps of the veranda, then on the hard earth of the lane, and then we heard the sound of his coach, the jingling of the harness and the rumbling of the wheels, and we felt quite relieved. He never came back to our house.

At the time we thought it was some sort of victory. But Laure and I never talked about it and no one knew what had happened that afternoon. We hardly saw Ferdinand in the following years. As a matter of fact it was probably that very year, the year of the cyclone, that his father put him in boarding school at the Royal College. We had no idea that everything was going to change, that we were living our last days in the Boucan Embayment.

It was around that same time that Laure and I realized something was not right with my father's affairs. He didn't speak to anyone about it, I don't believe, not even to Mam, so as not to worry her. Yet we could sense what was happening perfectly well, we could guess. One day as we're lying up in the attic as usual, in front of the bundles of old reviews, Laure says, 'Bankruptcy. What does bankruptcy mean?'

She's not asking me the question, since she knows very well I have no idea. It's simply a word that is there, that she heard, that's echoing in her mind. A little later she repeats other words that are also frightening: mortgage, seizure, time draft. A large paper lying on my father's desk, which I hastily read, is laden with minute figures like fly specks. Two mysterious English words stand out: *assets* and *liabilities*. What does that mean? Laure doesn't know the meaning of these words either and she doesn't dare ask our father. They are menacing words, they hold a danger that we don't understand, like those series of underlined, crossed-out figures, some written in red.

Several times I awaken to the sound of voices, late at night. With my damp, sweaty nightshirt sticking to my skin, I creep down the hallway to the dining-room door. Through the open crack I can hear my father's deep voice, then other voices of strangers answering him. What are they talking about? Even if I listened to every word, I wouldn't be able to understand. But I'm not listening to the words. I hear only the gabbling of the voices, the glasses clunking down on the table, the feet scuffing over the floorboards, the chairs creaking. Maybe Mam is there too, sitting beside my father as she does at mealtimes? But the strong smell of tobacco enlightens me. Mam doesn't like cigar smoke, she must be in her bedroom, lying in her brass bed, also staring at the line of yellow light under the half-open door, listening to the strangers' voices, just as I am, crouching here in the dark corridor, while my father talks on and on for such a long time . . . Later I go back to the bedroom, slip under the mosquito netting. Laure doesn't budge, I know she isn't sleeping, that her eyes are wide open in the dark and that she's also listening to the voices at the other end of the house. Stretched out on my cot with canvas webbing, I wait, holding my breath, until I hear footsteps in the garden, the axles of the coach squeaking as it drives away. I wait even longer, until I can hear the sound of the sea, the invisible tide of night, when the wind whistles in the needles of the she-oaks and bangs the shutters, and the roof timbers groan like the hull of an old boat. Then I can drift off to sleep.

––––––––––

Denis's lessons are the most beautiful. He teaches me the sky, the sea, the caves at the foot of the mountains, the fallow fields where we run together that summer, between the black pyramids of Creole dead work. Sometimes we leave at the crack of dawn when the mountaintops are still caught in the mists, and the low tide in the distance is uncovering the reefs. We go through the fields of aloes along silent, narrow paths. Denis walks out in front, I can see his tall, slim, supple silhouette moving along as if he were dancing. Here he doesn't bark like he does in the cane fields. From time to time he stops. He looks like a dog that has caught scent of a wild animal, a rabbit, a tenrec. When he stops, he raises his right hand slightly, as a signal, and I stop too, listening. I listen to the sound of the wind in the aloes, as well as the sound of my heart. The first rays of dawn are shining on the red earth, lighting the dark leaves. The mist is tearing on the peaks of the mountains, now the sky is intense. I imagine the sea, azure-coloured out around the coral reef but still black at the mouth of the rivers. 'Look!' Denis says. He's standing still on the path and is pointing at the mountain over by Black River Gorges. I see a bird very high in the sky, gliding along on the air currents, head turned slightly to one side, its long white tail floating out behind. 'Tropicbird,' says Denis. It's the first time I've seen one. It circles slowly over the ravines, then disappears in the direction of Mananava.

Denis has started walking again. We're following the narrow valley of the Boucan, up towards the mountains. We walk over old cane fields that are now uncultivated, where nothing remains but short low walls of lava stone hidden under the bramble bushes. I'm no longer in my territory. I'm on foreign terrain, that of Denis and the black people on the other side, the people from Chamarel, from Black River, from Case Noyale. As Denis goes further away from Boucan and makes his way up towards the forest, towards the mountains, he grows gradually less wary, talks more, seems more relaxed. He's walking slowly now, his gestures are more casual, his face even lights up, he waits for me on the trail, smiling. He points to the mountains near us on the right. 'Le Grand Louis, Mont Terre Rouge.' We're surrounded by silence, the wind has fallen, I can't smell the sea any more. The underbrush is so dense we have to walk in the bed of a torrent. I've taken off my shoes, tied the laces together and slung them around my neck, as I usually do when I'm out with Denis. We're walking in a trickle of cold water that runs over the sharp rocks. Denis stops in the bends, scans the water in search of camarons, of crayfish.

The sun is high in the sky when we reach the source of the Boucan high in the mountains. The January heat is oppressive, I find it hard to breathe under the trees. Striped mosquitoes come out of their nesting places and dance in front of my eyes, I can see them dancing around Denis's woolly hair too. On the banks of the torrent, Denis takes off his shirt and begins to gather leaves. I draw nearer to look at the dark-green leaves covered with fine grey down that he's harvesting in the shirt, now converted into a sack. 'Dasheen,' Denis says. He splashes a little water into one of the curved leafs and holds it out to me. Caught in the fine down, the drop remains suspended, like a liquid diamond. Further on, he gathers other leaves: 'Dasheen wrap'. On the trunk of a tree he points to a vine: 'Mile-a-minute vine'. Palmate leaves open out in a heart shape: 'Faham tea'. I knew that Old Sara, Capt'n Cook's sister was a '*yangue*' — that she made potions and cast spells — but this is the first time Denis has taken me to look for plants for her. Sara is Malagasy, she came from Grand Terre with Cook, Denis's grandfather, back in the slave days. One day Cook told Laure and me that he'd been so frightened when he arrived in Port Louis with the other slaves that he'd gone and sat up in a tree at the Intendance and refused to come down again, because he believed they were going to eat him, right there on the wharves. Sara lives in Black River. She used to come and visit her brother and she liked Laure and me a lot. Now she's too old.

Denis continues to walk along the torrent towards its source. The thin trickle of water runs black, smooth over the basalt rocks. The heat is so muggy Denis splashes his face and chest with water from the stream and tells me to do the same to freshen myself up. I drink some cool, light water right from the stream. Denis is still walking out ahead, along the narrow ravine. He's carrying the bundle of leaves on his head. He stops at times, motions to a tree in the thick of the forest, a plant, a vine, 'Benzoin', 'hart's-tongue fern', 'Indian laurel', 'tall balm', 'mamsell tree', 'prine', 'glorybower', 'tambourissa'.

He picks a creeping plant with long, fine leaves and crushes it between his thumb and forefinger in order to smell it: 'verbena'. Still further along, he walks through the underbrush until he reaches a tall tree with a brown trunk. He removes a bit of bark, makes a cut with a flint: golden sap runs out. Denis says 'balltree'. I walk behind him through the brush, bent forward, avoiding the thorny branches. Denis moves agilely through the forest, in silence, senses on the alert. Under my bare feet the ground is wet and warm. I'm afraid, yet I want to go further, penetrate deep into the forest. Denis stops in front of a very straight tree trunk. He tears off a piece of bark and has me smell it. It's a smell that makes me dizzy: 'rosin'.

We walk on, Denis is moving faster now, as if recognizing an invisible path. I'm suffocating in the heat and humidity of the forest, I'm having trouble catching my breath. I see Denis stopped in front of a bush: 'coromandel'. In his hand a long, half-opened pod from which black seeds like insects spill. I taste a seed, it's bitter, oily, but it gives me strength. Denis says, 'This food for maroons with the great Sacalavou.' It's the first time he's talked to me about Sacalavou. My father told us once that he died here, at the foot of the mountains, when the white people caught him. He threw himself off a cliff rather than return to captivity. It makes me feel strange, eating what he ate, here in this forest with Denis. We're far from the stream now, already at the foot of Mont Terre Rouge. The earth is dry, the sun is burning down through the sparse acacia leaves.

'Ironwood,' says Denis. 'Blackcurrant.'

Suddenly he stops. He's found what he's been looking for. He goes straight to the tree standing alone amid the underbrush. It's a handsome, dark tree with low, spreading branches that have thick green leaves with copper reflections. Denis is squatting at the foot of the tree, hidden in the shadows. When I come over he doesn't look at me. He's laid his bundle on the ground.

'What is it?'

Denis doesn't answer right away. He's searching his pockets.

'Affouche,' he says.

There is something in his left hand. Still squatting, Denis hums a little, like Indians do when they pray. He rocks his body back and forth and hums, and in the shade of the tree all I can make out is his back, which is shiny with sweat. When he's finished his prayer, he digs down into the earth at the foot of the tree with his right hand. The left hand opens and I glimpse a copper coin cupped in his palm. It slides down, falls into the hole, and Denis carefully covers it over with earth and a little moss that he takes from around the roots. Then he stands up and, without paying any attention to me, gathers the leaves from the low branches and lays them on the ground next to his bundle. With his sharp flint he peels away pieces of bark from the smooth trunk. A light-coloured milk oozes from the wound. Denis puts the bits of bark and the leaves of the affouche in his shirt and says, 'We go.' Without waiting for me, he walks quickly away through the brush, goes back down the slopes of the hills towards the Boucan River Valley. The sun is already in the west. Over the tops of the trees, between the dark hills, I can see the fiery patch of sea, the horizon where the clouds are born. Behind me, the rampart of the mountains is red, heat is radiating from them as if from an oven. I walk hurriedly in Denis's footsteps until we reach the stream that is the source of the Boucan, and I feel as if I've been gone for a very long time, maybe for days, it makes me dizzy inside.

It was during that summer, the year of the cyclone, that my father threw himself back into his old project of creating an electrical power plant on Black River. When had it really all begun? I don't have a clear memory of it, because at the time my father had dozens of different projects that he dreamt of in silence, and about which Laure and I heard only faint echoes. I believe he had a project to build a shipyard at the mouth of the Black River, and also an aerostat project for transporting passengers between the Mascarene Islands and South Africa. But all of that was only pipedreams and we knew nothing about it except what Mam or the people who sometimes came to visit would say. The project for the electrical power plant was probably the earliest one, and it didn't begin to get underway until that summer, when my father was already hopelessly indebted. One day after class Mam talks to us about the situation. She talks about it for a long time, shiny-eyed, filled with excitement. A new era is to begin, we will at last know what it is to be prosperous, to not fear the future. Our father has had work done at Bassin aux Aigrettes, where the two arms of Black River flow together.

This is where he'd chosen to set up the power plant that will provide electricity to the entire western region, from Médine all the way to Bel Ombre. The generator he'd bought in London by correspondence has just been unloaded in Port Louis and it has come all the way in an ox cart down the coast to Black River. From now on the days of oil-lamp lighting and the steam engine are over and, thanks to our father, electricity will gradually bring progress to our island. Mam also explains electricity to us, its properties, its uses. But we are too young to understand any of that, except for experimenting, as we used to do every day back then, with the mysteries of the bits of paper magnetized by Mam's amber necklace.

One day, we all – Mam, my father, Laure and I – leave in the carriage to go out to the Bassin aux Aigrettes. It's very early, Mam wants to be back before noon because of the heat. At the second curve in the road to Black River we take the path that leads up along the river. My father has had the path cleared so that the ox cart carrying the generator could get through, and our carriage rolls along in a huge cloud of dust.

It's the first time that Laure and I have been up Black River and we're peering curiously at the surroundings. The dust from the path rises up around us, enveloping the cart in an ochre cloud. Mam has a shawl about her face, she looks like an Indian woman. My father is cheerful, he's talking as he steers the horse. I can still picture him, just as I'll never be able to forget him: very tall and thin, elegant, wearing his grey-black suit, black hair swept back. I can see his profile, his fine, aquiline nose, his neatly kempt beard, his elegant hands, which are always holding a cigarette between the thumb and forefinger, the way one holds a pencil. Mam is looking at him too, I can see the light in her eyes that morning, on the dusty road that runs along Black River.

When we near the Bassin aux Aigrettes my father ties the horse to the branch of a tamarind tree. The water in the pool is clear, sky-blue. The wind is making ripples that stir the reeds. Laure and I say we'd like to go swimming, but my father is already walking over to the structure that houses the generator. Inside a wooden shed he shows us the dynamo connected with wires and belts to the turbine. In the dim light there is an eerie gleam to the gearing that somewhat frightens us. Our father also shows us the water from the pool flowing down from a conduit back into Black River. Large spools of cable lie on the ground in front of the generator. My father explains that the cables will be strung up along the entire length of the river, all the way to the sugar mill. Then from there, up over the hills to Tamarin and the Boucan Embayment. Later, when the installation has been tried and tested, the electricity will go even farther north, up to Médine, to Wolmar, maybe as far as Phoenix. My father is saying all of this to us, to my mother, but his face is turned away, towards another era, another world.

So we're always thinking about electricity. Every evening Laure and I believe it's going to come, as if all of a sudden it will miraculously illuminate everything inside of our house, and will shine outside and light up the plants and the trees like Saint Elmo's Fire. 'When will it come?' Mam smiles when we ask her that question. We'd like to hasten the mysterious event. 'Soon . . .' She explains that the turbine needs to be installed, the dam consolidated, the wooden poles set in the ground and the cables attached to them. It will take months, maybe years. No, it's just impossible that we should have to wait so long. My father is even more impatient, electricity also means the end of his problems, the beginning of a new chance. Uncle Ludovic will see. He'll understand – he who never wanted to believe in the project – when electric turbines replace the steam engines in all of the sugar mills in the west. My father goes to Port Louis, to Rempart Street almost every day. He sees important people, bankers, businessmen. Uncle Ludovic doesn't come to Boucan any more. They say he doesn't believe in electricity, at least not in this type of electricity. Laure heard our father say that one evening. But if Uncle Ludovic doesn't believe in it, how will it get out this far? Because he owns all of the land in the surrounding area, he owns all of the streams. Even Boucan Embayment belongs to him. Laure and I spend that last summer, the long month of January, lying on the floor in the attic, reading. We stop whenever there is mention of an electric machine, a dynamo or even just a filament lamp.

35

Nights are oppressive, now there is a sort of expectancy between the damp sheets under the mosquito netting. Something is supposed to happen. In the darkness I wait for the sound of the sea, watch the full moon rise through the shutters. How do we know what is supposed to happen? Maybe it's in Mam's eyes every evening at lesson time. She tries not to let anything show, but her voice isn't the same, her words have changed. We can sense that she's anxious, impatient inside. At times she stops in the middle of a dictation and looks over in the direction of the tall trees as if she expected something to appear.

One day in the late afternoon, as I'm returning from distant expeditions with Denis in the woods over by the gorges, I see my father and Mam on the veranda. Laure is with them, standing a little off to one side. I feel a pain in my chest, because I know right away that something bad has happened while I was in the forest. I'm also afraid of being reprimanded by my father. He's standing near the stairs, looking gloomy, very thin in his baggy black suit. As always, he's holding his cigarette between the thumb and forefinger of his right hand.

'Where were you?'

He asks me that question as I'm coming up the stairs, and I stop. He doesn't expect an answer. He simply says, in a voice I've never heard him use, an odd, somewhat gruff voice, 'Very grave events are likely to occur . . .'

He doesn't know how to go on.

Mam begins talking in his place. She's pale, looks distraught. That's what hurts most. I would be so grateful not to hear what she has to say.

'Alexis, we'll have to leave this house. We'll have to go away from here, for ever.'

Laure doesn't say anything. She's standing up very straight on the veranda, she's staring out straight ahead. She has the same impassive, hard look as she did when Uncle Ludovic was asking her name in that ironic voice of his.

It's already twilight. Night is beginning to fall gently over the garden. Before our eyes, up over the treetops, the first star suddenly twinkles with a magical gleam. Laure and I look at it, and Mam also turns towards the sky, she stares at the star hanging over Black River as if it were the first time she'd ever seen it.

We stand still under the gaze of that star for a long time. Shadows settle under the trees, we hear the cracking, the swishing of night, the high-pitched song of mosquitoes.

Mam is the first to break the silence.

'How lovely!' she says with a sigh.

Then, cheerfully, walking down the steps of the veranda, 'Come along, let's try to find the names of the stars.'

My father has come down too. He's walking along slowly, slightly stooped, hands behind his back. I'm walking beside him, and Laure has put her arm around Mam. Together we make our way around the large house, as if it were a beached ship. In Capt'n Cook's hut there is a wavering light, we can hear muffled voices. He and his wife will be the last to leave the property. Where will they go? When he first came to Boucan, in the days of my grandfather, he must have been not more than twenty years old. He'd just been emancipated. I can hear his voice in the hut, he's talking to himself, or singing. In the distance, other voices echo out in the cane fields, it's the gunnies who are out gleaning or walking down the La Coupe track towards Tamarin. There's also the chirping of insects and the song of toads in the ravine at the other end of the garden.

Just for us, the sky lights up. We must forget everything else and think only of the stars. Mam shows us the lights, she calls my father over to ask us questions. I can hear her clear young voice in the darkness and it soothes, reassures me.

'Look, there . . . Isn't that Betelgeuse, up at the very top of Orion? And the Three Kings! Look north, you'll see the Big Dipper. What's the name of the little star at the very end of the Dipper, on the handle?'

I stare as hard as I can. I'm not sure I can see it.

'A tiny little star set right at the top of the Dipper, just above the second star?' My father asks that question very gravely, as if on this evening it is particularly important.

'Yes, that one. It's very small, I see it and then it disappears.'

'That's Alcor,' my father says. 'It's also called the Rider. The Arabs named it Alcor, which means "test", because it is so small only the sharpest eyes can make it out.' He falls silent for a moment, then says to Mam in a gayer tone of voice, 'You've got good eyesight, I can't see it any more.'

I too can see Alcor, or rather I imagine I can, as tiny as a small speck of cinder glowing above the handle of the Big Dipper. And having seen it makes all the bad memories, all the anxiety, vanish.

My father taught us to love the night. Sometimes in the evenings, when he isn't working in his office, he takes us by the hand, Laure on his right and me on his left, and walks us down the alleyway stretching south all the way down to the bottom of the garden. He calls it the 'alley of stars', because it leads out towards the most crowded region of the sky. As he walks he smokes a cigarette and we smell the sweet odour of tobacco in the night and see the tip glowing red near his lips and lighting up his face. I love the smell of tobacco in the night.

The most beautiful nights are in July, when the sky is glittering and cold and, up above the mountains of Black River, we can see all the most beautiful lights in the sky: Vega, Altair in the Eagle — Laure says that it looks more like a lantern on a kite — and the third one whose name I can never remember, like a jewel atop the great cross. They are the three stars my father calls the *Belles de nuit*, that shine in a triangle in the pure sky. There are also Jupiter and Saturn, far to the south, which are stationary lights hanging over the mountains. Laure and I often observe Saturn because Aunt Adelaide told us it was our planet, the dominant planet in the sky when we were born, in December. It's lovely, slightly bluish, and it shines out above the trees. But it's true, there's something frightening about it, a pure, steely light like the one that sometimes shines in Laure's eyes. Mars isn't far from Saturn. It's bright red and its light also attracts our attention. My father doesn't like what people say about the planets.

'Come with me, let's go have a look at the Southern Cross,' he says.

He walks out in front of us all the way to the end of the alley, over by the chalta tree. In order to be able to see the Southern Cross you need to be far from the lights of the house. We look up at the sky, almost without breathing. I immediately pinpoint 'The Followers' high up in the sky at the tail end of Centaurus. To the right, the Cross hovers palely, slightly tilted, like the sail of a pirogue. Laure and I spot it at the same time, but we don't need to say anything. We gaze up at the Cross without speaking. Mam comes out to join us and she doesn't say a word to our father. We just stand there and it seems as if we're listening to the sound of the planets in the night. It's so beautiful, there's no need to say anything. But I can feel that pain in my chest and throat growing tighter, because something has changed on this night, something says that it must all come to an end. Maybe it's written in the stars — that's what I think — maybe what needs to be done to keep things from changing and save us is also written in the stars.

There are so many signs in the sky. I remember all of those summer nights when we would lie in the grass in the garden trying to glimpse falling stars. One night we'd seen stars come raining down and Mam had blurted out, 'It's a sign of war.' But she'd said nothing more, because our father doesn't like us to say those kinds of things. We lay there for a long time, watching the incandescent trails streaking across the sky in all directions, some so long we could follow them with our eyes, others very brief, exploding immediately. We would look up at the sky so intently that it made our heads reel, made us teeter dizzily. I could hear Mam speaking softly with my father, but I didn't understand the meaning of their words. Even today, on summer nights, I'm sure that Laure still tries — as I do — to see those streaks of fire that plot people's destinies and make it possible for secrets to come true.

Back then my father teaches us all about the night sky. Beginning in the east and stretching all the way northward, the great pale river of the Galaxy forms islands around the Cross of the Swan and then flows on towards Orion. Slightly above that, in the direction of our house, I can make out the dim glow of the Pleiades, like so many lightning bugs. I know every part of the sky, every constellation. Almost every evening our father shows us the positions of the stars on a large map tacked to the wall in his office. 'A man who knows the stars well has nothing to fear from the sea,' he says. Whenever there's any mention of the stars, my father, who's normally so reserved, so quiet, will grow lively, chattering on, bright-eyed. That's when he says wonderful things about the world, about the sea, about God. He talks about the travels of the great mariners, those who discovered the route to India, discovered Oceania, America. Surrounded by the odour of tobacco hovering in his office, I'm listening, looking at the maps. He speaks of Cook, of Drake, of Magellan, who discovered the

South Seas on the *Victoria* and who later died in the Sunda Islands. He speaks of Tasman, of Biscoe, of Wilkes — who travelled all the way to the eternal ice and snow of the South Pole — and also of the extraordinary travels of Marco Polo in China, De Soto in America, Orellana, who sailed up the Amazon River, Gmelin, who went out to the far end of Siberia, Mungo Park, Stanley, Livingstone, Przhevalsky. I listen to those stories, the names of those countries, Africa, Tibet, the South Sea Islands. They are magical names, to me they are like the names of the stars, like the drawings of the constellations. At night, lying on my cot, I listen to the sound of the sea rolling in, the wind in the needles of the she-oaks. And I think of all those names, it seems as if the night sky opens out and I am on a ship with billowing sails on the infinite sea, sailing out as far as the Moluccas, as far as Astrolabe Bay, Fiji, Moorea. On the deck of that ship, before falling asleep, I see the sky as I have never seen it before, so vast, dark blue over the phosphorescent sea. I slip slowly over to the other side of the horizon and glide out towards the Three Kings, towards the Southern Cross.

———————

I remember the first time I went to sea. I think it was in January, because at that time of year the heat is already torrid long before dawn and there isn't a breath of wind in Boucan Embayment. At the first light of dawn I creep out of the room without making a sound. Outside all is silent still and everyone in the house is sleeping. A lone glimmer comes from inside Capt'n Cook's shack, but at this early hour he's paying no heed to anyone. He's looking at the grey sky and waiting for daybreak. Maybe the rice is already boiling in the big black pot over the fire. To avoid making noise I walk barefoot over the dry earth in the alley, all the way out to the end of the garden. Denis is waiting for me under the tall chalta tree and when I get there he stands up and starts walking in the direction of the sea without saying a word. He walks quickly across the cane fields without worrying about my having trouble catching my breath. Turtle doves scuttle about between the cane stalks, alarmed, but not daring to take flight. It's daylight when we reach the road to Black River. The earth is already hot under my feet and the air smells of dust. The first ox carts are already trundling along the paths in the fields and I can see the white smoke of the sugar-mill chimneys in the distance. I'm waiting for the sound of the wind to reach my ears. Suddenly Denis stops. We stand still in the middle of the cane field. Then I hear the murmur of the waves on the reefs. 'Rough sea,' says Denis. The tide wind is blowing towards us.

We reach Black River just as the sun is coming up from behind the mountains. I've never been so far away from Boucan and my heart is pounding as I run behind Denis's dark silhouette. We ford the river near its mouth and the cold water rises all the way up to our waists, then we walk along the black sand dunes. On the beach the fishermen's pirogues lie lined up on the sand, a few with their stems already in the water. The men push the pirogues into the waves, holding on to the rope of the sail that the wind is filling, making it snap. Denis's pirogue is at the end of the beach, two men are pushing it towards the sea, an old man with a wrinkled, copper-coloured face and a tall, athletic black man. There is a very beautiful young woman with them, standing on the beach, hair tied up in a red scarf. 'She mi sista,' says Denis proudly. 'And 'im har fiancé. Is 'im pirogue.' The young woman catches sight of Denis, calls him over. Together we push the pirogue into the water. When the wave lifts the back of the pirogue, Denis shouts, 'Get inna!' And he jumps in too. He runs up to the front, grabs the pole to guide the pirogue out to the open sea. With the pirogue sailing close-hauled, the wind fills the large sheet-like sail and the boat goes leaping through the waves. We're already a long way from shore. I'm drenched from the breakers and shivering, but I watch the dark coastline growing distant. I've been waiting so long for this day! Denis once talked to me about the sea and about this pirogue and I asked him, 'When will you take me out with you on the pirogue?' He looked at me without saying anything, as if he were thinking it over. I didn't tell anyone about this, not even Laure, because I was afraid she'd repeat it to my father. Laure doesn't like the sea, maybe she's afraid I'll drown. So when I went out barefoot this morning, to keep from making noise, she turned over in her bed, to face the wall, so she wouldn't see me.

What's going to happen when I go back? But I don't feel like thinking about that now, it's sort of like I might never go back. The pirogue plunges into the hollows of the waves, making bursts of spume shower into the light. The old man and the fiancé have secured the triangular sail to the boom and the heavy wind coming from the pass is causing the pirogue to heel. Denis and I are squatting in the front of the pirogue, against the quivering canvas, soaked with sea spray. Denis's eyes shine when he looks at me. Without saying a word he motions towards the dark-blue, open sea or else back behind us – already very far away – to the black line of the beach and the shapes of the mountains against the pale sky.

The pirogue is skimming over the open sea. I can hear the deep rumble of the waves, the wind fills my ears. I'm no longer cold or afraid. The sun burns down, makes the crests of the waves sparkle. I can see nothing else, think of nothing else: the deep blue sea, the bobbing horizon, the taste of the sea, the wind. This is the first time I've been out on a boat and I've never experienced anything more wonderful. The pirogue sails through the pass, runs alongside the reefs amid the thundering waves and the heaving bursts of spray.

Denis is leaning over the stem, looking at the dark water as if searching for something. Then he extends his hand, indicating a huge, blackened rock straight ahead.

'The Morne,' he says.

I've never seen it up this close before. The Morne rises from the sea just like a lava stone, with not a tree, not a single plant. Around it are stretches of pale sand, the waters of the lagoons. It's as if we are headed out to the end of the Earth. The seabirds are flying all around us, screeching, seagulls, sterns, white petrels, enormous frigates. My heart is pounding and I'm trembling anxiously, because I feel as if I've gone very far away, across the sea. The slow waves slap at the side of the pirogue and water floods into it. Denis ducks under the sail, picks up two gourds from the bottom of the pirogue and calls to me. We bail out the boat together. In the back, the tall black man – one arm enlacing Denis's sister – is holding down the sail rope, while the old man with the face of an Indian is working the tiller. They are soaked with seawater, but laugh when they see us bailing the water that keeps flooding back in again. Squatting down in the back of the boat, I'm throwing the water over the leeward side and from time to time I catch a glimpse of the huge black wall of the Morne and the whitecaps out on the breakers.

Then we change course and the wind sweeps the large sail over our heads. Denis points to the coastline.

'Over there, the pass. L'île aux Bénitiers, Clam Island.'

We stop bailing and crawl up to the front to get a better view. The white line of the breakers is fanning out before us. Borne along on the swell, the pirogue is heading straight for the Morne. The roaring of the waves on the coral reef is very near. The waves roll in diagonally, then break. Denis and I stare at the deep water, so very blue it is dizzying. Little by little the colour in front of the stem grows lighter. Green reflections, golden clouds can be seen. The bottom becomes visible, rushing past at top speed, patches of coral, the purplish balls of sea urchins, schools of silvery fish. The water is calm now and the wind has ceased. The sail hangs loose, flapping around the mast like a sheet. We are in the lagoon around the Morne, the place where the men come to fish.

The sun is high. The pirogue is sliding silently over the peaceful waters, punted along with Denis's pole. In the back the fiancé is helping — not letting go of Denis's sister — using a small paddle with one hand. The old man is inspecting the water with his back to the sun, looking for fish in holes in the coral. He's holding a long, weighted line that he sends whistling through the air. After the fury of the dark open sea, after the gusting winds and the bursts of sea spray, in this place it's as if I'm in a warm, light-filled dream. I feel the burn of the sun on my face, on my back. Denis has taken his clothes off to let them dry and I do the same. When he's naked, he suddenly dives into the transparent water, almost without making a sound. I can see him swimming underwater, then he disappears. When he comes back to the surface, he's holding a large red fish that he's speared and he throws it into the bottom of the pirogue. He dives again immediately. His body goes gliding down into the depths, reappears, dives again. Finally he brings back another fish with bluish scales that he also throws into the pirogue. The pirogue is very near the coral reef now. The tall black man and the old man with the Indian face throw out their lines. They haul in fish several times, groupers, emperors, spinefoot.

We fish for a long time as the pirogue drifts along the reefs. The sun is burning up in the centre of the dark sky, but the light is springing from the sea, a blinding, inebriating light. As I lean over the stem, motionless, staring into the shimmering water, Denis touches me on the shoulder and brings me out of my torpor. His eyes gleam like black stones, he breaks into an odd Creole chant, '*Lizié mani mani*. Eyes all adazzle.'

It's a dizziness that stems from the sea, like a kind of spell cast by the sun and the reflections that is befuddling me and draining my energy. In spite of the torrid heat I feel cold. Denis's sister and her fiancé help me stretch out in the bottom of the pirogue, in the shade of the sail that is flapping in the breeze. Denis cups seawater in his hands and wets my face and body. Then, punting with his pole, he steers the pirogue over to the shore. A little later we run up on the white beach, near the point of the Morne. There, a few small trees grow — velvet leaf soldierbushes. With Denis's aid I walk to the shade of one of them. Denis's sister encourages me to drink a sour substance from a gourd; it burns my tongue and throat and wakes me up. I already want to stand, walk back to the pirogue, but Denis's sister tells me I must stay in the shade until the sun has begun to go down towards the horizon. The old man has remained in the pirogue, leaning on the pole. Now they're moving away on the shimmering water to fish some more.

Denis has remained sitting next to me. He doesn't say anything. He's just here with me in the shade of the small tree, legs covered with patches of white sand. He's not like those other children who live in grand estates. He doesn't need to talk. He's my friend and his silence here beside me is a way of saying so.

Everything is lovely and peaceful in this place. I look at the green expanse of the lagoon, the ruff of foam along the barrier reef and the white sand of the beaches, the dunes, the sand dotted with spiny shrubs, the dark she-oak woods, the shade of the soldierbushes, the umbrella trees, and before us, the charred rock of the Morne, like a castle inhabited by seabirds. It's as if we've been castaways here for months, far from any dwelling, waiting for a vessel to appear on the horizon to retrieve us. I think of Laure, who must be on the lookout up in the chalta tree, I think of Mam and my father, and I wish this moment would never end.

But the sun descends towards the sea, turns it to metal, to opaque glass. The fishermen come back. Denis is the one who sees them first. He walks across the white sand, his gangly figure looks like the shadow of his shadow. He swims out to meet the pirogue, in the sparkling water. I go into the sea after him. The cool water washes away my fatigue and I swim over to the pirogue in Denis's wake. The fiancé holds out his hand and pulls us out effortlessly. The bottom of the pirogue is filled with all kinds of fish. There is even a small blue shark that the fiancé killed, jabbing it with a harpoon when it came up to eat one of the catch. Pierced through the middle of its body, the shark is stiff, mouth open, showing its triangular teeth. Denis says that the Chinese eat shark and that we'll also make a necklace with the teeth.

Despite the hot sun, I'm shivering. I've taken off my clothes and laid them out to dry near the stem. Now the pirogue is slipping out towards the pass, we can already feel the long rollers that are still coming in from the open sea crashing down upon the coral reef. All of a sudden the sea turns violet, hard. When we go through the pass near Clam Island the wind rises. The large sail next to me fills out tightly and hums, sea foam splashes up at the prow. Denis and I quickly fold our clothes and tuck them away near the mast. The seabirds are following the pirogue, because they've smelled the fish. At times they even try to snatch a fish and Denis shouts, waving his arms to scare them away. They're black frigates with piercing eyes that glide along on the wind next to the pirogue, cackling. Behind us, the large scorched rock of the Morne is growing distant in the veiled twilight like a castle being engulfed in shadows. Down flush with the horizon, the long grey clouds are streaking the sun.

Never will I forget this long day, so long it seems like months, like years, the day I discovered the sea for the first time. I'd like it to never end, to last even longer yet. I'd like the pirogue to keep skipping over the waves in the splashing sea foam, all the way out to the Indies, even out to Oceania, going from island to island, lit by the sun that would never set.

Night has fallen when we run up on the beach in Black River. Denis and I walk rapidly to Boucan, barefoot in the dust. My clothing and hair are stiff with salt, my face, my back are burning with the light of the sun. When I arrive in front of the house Denis walks away without saying anything. I walk down the lane, heart racing, and I see my father standing on the veranda. By the light of the storm lamp he seems taller and thinner in his black suit. His face is pale, drawn with worry and anger. When I'm in front of him he says nothing, but his eyes are hard and cold and my throat tenses, not because of the punishment that awaits me, but because I know I'll never go back out to sea again, that this is the end of it. That night, in spite of the fatigue, the hunger and the thirst, lying motionless in my bed which is burning my back, indifferent to the mosquitoes, I listen to every movement of the air, every breath of wind, every lull that brings me closer to the sea.

Laure and I live the last days of that summer — the year of the cyclone — even more closed up in our own world, secluded in the Boucan Embayment where no one comes to see us any more. Maybe that's why we have this strange feeling that there is some kind of impending threat or danger. Or maybe solitude has made us more sensitive to the signs portending Boucan's downfall. Maybe it's also the almost unbearable heat that weighs upon the shores, upon the Tamarin Valley, night and day. Even the wind from the sea cannot alleviate the heat bearing down upon the plantations, upon the red earth. Around the aloe fields of Walhalla in Tamarin the land is as hot as a furnace and the streams have dried up. In the evening I look at the smoke from the Kah Hin distillery mingling with the clouds of red dust. Laure tells me of the fire that God sent raining down on the accursed cities of Sodom and Gomorrah, and also of Vesuvius erupting in the year AD 79, when the city of Pompeii was drowned in a rain of molten ash. But here we search the heavens in vain and the sky over Rempart Mountain and the Trois Mamelles remains clear, barely flawed by a few inoffensive clouds. But deep down inside ourselves we can sometimes sense the danger.

Mam has been sick for weeks now and she's stopped her lessons. As for our father, he's sombre and weary, he stays shut up in his office reading or writing or smoking, gazing blankly out of the window. I think it's around this same time that he really speaks to me about the Mysterious Corsair's treasure and the documents he's kept concerning it. I've already heard about it once, long ago, maybe from Mam, who doesn't believe in it at all. But this is when he talks to me about it at length, as one would about an important secret. What does he say? I can't remember for certain, because it's all mixed up in my mind with everything I read and heard afterwards, but I recall how strange he looks that afternoon when he asks me into his office.

It's a room we never go into, except in secret, not that it is categorically off-limits, but there's something secretive about that office which intimidates, even frightens us a little. At the time, my father's office is a long narrow room all the way at one end of the house, wedged between the living room and my parents' bedroom, a silent room, facing north with a parquet and panelled walls of varnished wood and furnished simply with a large writing table that has no drawers, and one easy chair and a few metal trunks filled with papers. The table is up against the window so that when the shutters are open Laure and I can see – from our hiding place behind the bushes in the garden – the silhouette of our father reading or writing, wreathed in clouds of cigarette smoke. From his office he has a view of the Trois Mamelles and the mountains of the Black River Gorges and can watch the course of the clouds.

I remember going into his office then, almost holding my breath, looking at the books and journals piled up on the floor, the maps tacked to the walls. The map I prefer is the one with the constellations that he's already shown me to teach me astronomy. Whenever we go into the office we read the names of the stars and their formations in the night sky in awe: Sagittarius, led by the star named Nunki, Lupus, Aquila, Orion. Boötes, with Alphecca in the east, Arcturus in the west. Scorpius with threatening lines, with Shaula at the end of its tail like a luminous stinger and the red Antares in its head. The Greater Bear and each of the stars along its curve, Alkaid, Mizar, Alioth, Megrez, Phecda, Dubhe, Merak, Auriga, whose main star — Menkalinan — rings oddly in my mind.

I remember the Greater Dog that has the lovely Sirius in its mouth — like a fang — and down below it a triangle in which Adhara pulses. I can still see one perfect drawing, the one I love most, that I look for, night after night, in the summer sky over in the direction of Le Morne: that of the vessel Argo, which I sometimes draw in the dust on the paths like this:

My father is standing up, he's talking and I don't understand what he's saying very well. He's not really talking to me, the child with the too-long hair, the sun-browned face, the torn clothing from running through the underbrush and the cane fields. He's talking to himself, his eyes are bright, his voice a bit husky with excitement. He's talking about the immense treasure he's going to discover, for he knows at last where it's hidden, he's discovered the island upon which the Corsair stowed his hoard. He doesn't say the Corsair's

name, but just – as I will later read in his documents – the Mysterious
Corsair, and even today that name still seems to me to be more real
and filled with more magic than any other. He's talking to me for
the first time about Rodrigues Island, a dependency of Mauritius,
that takes several days to reach by boat. Tacked to the wall of his
office is a map of the island covered with signs and landmarks that
he's copied in India ink and painted in watercolour. At the bottom
of the map I recall reading these words: *Rodrigues Island*, and under
that *Admiralty Chart, Wharton 1876*. I'm listening to my father
without hearing him, as if from deep in a dream. The legend of the
treasure, the research that's been done over the last hundred years
on Amber Island, in Flic-en-Flac, in the Seychelles. Maybe it's the
feeling of being overwhelmed or the anxiety that's keeping me from
understanding, because I can tell it's the most important thing in the
world, a secret that can at any moment mean our salvation or our
downfall. Now there's no more talk of electricity or any other project.
The light of the Rodrigues treasure is dazzling me and dulling all
others. My father talks for a long time that afternoon, pacing around
the narrow room, picking up papers and looking at them, then laying
them back down without even showing me, while I remain standing
still near his table, looking furtively at the map of Rodrigues Island
stuck on the wall next to the map of the night sky. Maybe that's why,
later, I will always feel as if everything that happened after that, the
adventure, the quest, took place in ethereal lands, not down on the
real earth, as if my journey aboard the Argo had already begun.

———————

These are the last days of summer and they seem very long, filled
with so many events at all times of the day or night: they're more like

months or years, deeply changing the world around us and leaving us aged. Heatwave days when the air is dense, heavy and liquid down in the Tamarin Valley and one feels a prisoner of the circus of mountains. Beyond, the sky is clear, restless, the clouds scud along in the wind, their shadows hurrying over the burned hills. The last of the harvesting will soon be over and there are angry rumblings among the field labourers because they have nothing left to eat. Sometimes in the evening I see the red smoke of fires in the cane fields, then the sky turns a strange colour, a glaring, ominous red that hurts your eyes and makes your throat tighten. In spite of the danger I walk through the fields almost every day to see the fires. I go out as far as Yemen, sometimes as far as Tamarin Estate, or make my way up towards Magenta and Belle Rive. From high up on the Tourelle I see other clouds of smoke rising in the north over by Clarence or Marcenay on the outskirts of Wolmar. Now I'm alone. Ever since the journey in the pirogue my father has forbidden me to see Denis. He doesn't come to Boucan any more. Laure says she heard Denis's grandfather, Capt'n Cook, shouting at him, because Denis came to see him in spite of the restriction. Since then he's disappeared. It has made me feel as if there is an emptiness, a great solitude here, as if my parents, Laure and I are Boucan's last inhabitants.

So I wander out very far, farther and farther. I climb to the top of the high Creole walls and search for the smoke of the revolts. I run through the fields, devastated from the harvests. There are still labourers in places, very poor, old women dressed in gunny cloth, gleaning or cutting the couch grass with their sickles. When they see me, my face tanned and clothes stained with red earth, barefoot and carrying my shoes slung around my neck, they shout at me to drive me away, because they're afraid. No white person ever comes out this far. Sometimes the sirdars also insult me and throw stones and I run through the cane until I'm out of breath. I hate the sirdars. I despise them more than anything in the world, because they are unfeeling and cruel, and because they beat the poor people with sticks when the bundles of cane don't reach the cart fast enough. But in the evening they get paid double and then get drunk on arak. They're cowardly and obsequious with the field managers, they take off their caps when they speak to them and feign being fond of the people they've just mistreated. There are men in the fields who are almost naked, covered only with a tattered piece of cloth, pulling out the cane stubble with heavy iron pincers that are called '*macchabées*'. They carry blocks of basalt over to the ox cart on their shoulders, then go and pile them up at the end of the field, making new pyramids. They are the people Mam calls 'the martyrs of the cane'. They sing as they work and I really like hearing their monotone voices in the lonely expanse of the plantations as I'm sitting up on top of a black pyramid. Just for myself I like to sing the old Creole song Capt'n Cook used to sing to Laure and me when we were very small, the one that goes:

Mo passé la rivière Tanier	Mi guh dung a Tanier riva
Rencontré en' grand maman,	Mi si a ole grandmada
Mo dire li qui li faire là	Mi ax har weh shi a do deh
Li dire mo mo la pes cabot	She tell me seh shi a fish mullet
Waï, waï mo zenfant	Yeh, yeh mi pickney
Faut travaï pou gagn' son pain	Haffi wuk fi get yuh bread
Waï, waï mo zenfant	Yeh, yeh mi pickney
Faut travaï pou gagn' son pain . . .	Haffi wuk fi get yuh bread . . .

I see the smoke from fires over by Yemen and Walhalla, from up there on the heap of stones. On this particular morning they're very close, right next to the shacks of Tamarin River, and I realize something bad is happening. Heart racing, I rush down through the fields until I reach the dirt road. The blue roof of our house is too far away for me to warn Laure about what's going on. I can already hear the sounds of the riot when I reach the Boucan ford. It's a rumbling sound like that of a storm that seems to be coming from all sides at once, that is echoing through the mountain gorges. There are shouts, grumbling, shots too. In spite of my fear I run through the middle of the cane field, without taking care to avoid being cut. When I come up in front of the sugar mill, the noise is all around me, I see the riot. The mob of gunnies is thronging around the door, all of the voices shouting at once. Facing the crowd are three men on horseback and I can hear the sound of their hooves on the cobblestones when they rear their steeds. Behind them I can see the gaping mouth of the furnace, where sparks are whirling.

The mass of labourers moves forwards, then back again in a strange sort of dance while the shouting rises and falls in strident modulation. Men brandish cane knives, scythes, and the women hoes and billhooks. Panic-stricken, I stand frozen to the spot, while the crowd jostles around me, encircles me. I'm suffocating, I'm blinded by the dust. With great difficulty I make my way over to the wall of the sugar mill. Just then, without my understanding what is happening, I see the three horsemen start to gallop towards the throng that closes in around them. The withers of the horses are pushing the men and women back and the riders are striking out with their rifle butts. Two horses escape in the direction of the cane fields, pursued by the angry cries of the crowd. They pass so close to me I throw myself to the ground in the dust for fear of being trampled. Then I glimpse the third rider. He's fallen from his horse and the men and women have grabbed him by the arms, are shoving him around. I recognize his face, despite it being twisted with fear. He's a relative of Ferdinand's — a man named Dumont, the husband of one of his cousins — who is a field manager on Uncle Ludovic's plantations. My father says he's worse than a sirdar, that he beats the workers with sticks and if they complain about him he steals their pay. Now it's the field labourers who are mauling him, hitting him, insulting him, making him fall to the ground. For a moment, in the midst of the crowd that is shoving him around, he's so close to me that I can see the wild look in his eyes, can hear the hoarse sound of his breathing. I'm afraid, because I realize he's going to die. Nausea rises in my throat, strangles me. My eyes fill with tears, I strike out with my fists at the angry crowd that doesn't even see me. The men and women in gunny cloth pursue their strange dance, their shouts. When I'm able to get out of the crowd I turn around and see the white man. His clothing is torn to pieces and he is being carried, half-naked, at arm's length above the crowd over to the bagasse furnace. The man isn't screaming, isn't moving. His face is a white blotch of fear as the black people lift him up by the arms and legs and begin to swing him in front of the red door of the furnace. I stand there, petrified, alone in the middle of the dirt road, listening to the voices shouting louder and louder, and now it is like a slow and painful chant punctuating the swinging of the body over the flames. Then there is one movement of the crowd and a great wild cry when the man disappears into the furnace. Then the clamour suddenly ceases and I can once again hear the dull roaring of the flames, the gurgling of cane juice in the large shiny kettles. I can't tear my eyes away from the flaming mouth of the bagasse furnace into which the black men are now shovelling dried cane as if nothing has happened. Then, slowly, the crowd breaks up. The women in gunny cloth walk through the dust, veiling their faces with their head rags.

The men wander off towards the paths in the cane fields, knives in hand. There are no more clamours or noises, only the silence of the wind in the cane leaves as I walk towards the river. The silence is within me, is brimming up inside me making my head spin, and I know I'll never be able to talk to anyone about what I've seen today.

Sometimes Laure comes out into the fields with me. We walk down the paths through the cut cane and when the earth is too loose or when there are piles of harvested cane stalks I carry her on my back, so she won't ruin her dress and her ankle boots. Though she's a year older than I am, Laure is so light and fragile it feels as though I'm carrying a small child. She really likes it when we walk like that and the sharp-edged cane leaves open before her face and close behind her. One day in the attic she showed me an old edition of the *Illustrated London News* with an image depicting Naomi being carried on Ali's shoulders through the barley fields. Naomi is laughing gaily, tearing off the heads of barley that are whipping at her face. She tells me it's because of that picture that she calls me Ali. Laure also talks to me about Paul and Virginie, but I don't like that story, because Virginie was so afraid to undress before going into the water. I think that's ridiculous and I tell Laure it's surely not a true story, but that makes her angry. She says I just don't get it at all.

We walk over around the hills where the Magenta Estate and the rich people's '*chassés*' begin. But Laure doesn't want to enter the forest. So we go back down towards the source of the Boucan. Up in the hills the air is humid, as if the morning mists are still caught in the leaves of the bushes. Laure and I really like sitting down in a clearing when the trees are barely emerging from the night shadows and watching for the seabirds to pass. Sometimes we see a couple of tropicbirds. The beautiful white birds come out of the Black River Gorges — over by Mananava — and they glide leisurely above our heads, wings spread like crosses of sea foam, their long tails trailing out behind. Laure says they are the souls of sailors who've died at sea and of the women who await their return in vain. They are silent, graceful. They live in Mananava, where the mountains are dark and the sky is clouded over. We believe it's the place where the rain is born.

'One day I'll go to Mananava.'

'Cook says there are still maroons in Mananava. If you go there, they'll kill you,' says Laure.

'That's not true. There's nobody over there. Denis went very near to it and he told me that when you get there everything goes black, as if night were falling, so then you have to turn back.'

Laure shrugs her shoulders. She doesn't like hearing those kinds of things. She stands up, looks at the sky where the birds have disappeared.

'Let's go!' she says impatiently.

We head back towards Boucan, making our way across the fields. Amid the vegetation, the roof of our house shines out like a puddle.

Since she's been sick with fevers, Mam hasn't been giving us lessons any more, only a few recitations and a little Bible study. She's thin and very pale, she doesn't come out of her room any more except to sit in a lawn chair on the veranda. The doctor came from Floréal in his horse-drawn carriage, his name is Koenig. He told my father as he was leaving, the fever has fallen, but she mustn't go and have another attack, for it would be *irremediable*. That's what he said and I can't forget that word, it's always in my head, day and night. That's why I can't sit still. I have to move all the time, over mountains and valleys, as my father says, through the cane fields burning in the sun from early morning on, listening to the gunnies chanting their monotone chants, or else over to the seashore, still hoping to run into Denis coming back from fishing.

It's the threat that's hanging over us, I can feel it weighing upon Boucan. Laure can feel it too. We don't talk about it, but it's on her face, in her worried looks. At night she doesn't sleep and we both lie there motionless, listening to the sound of the sea. I can hear Laure breathing steadily, too steadily, and I know her eyes are open in the dark. I also lie still on my bed, not sleeping, the mosquito netting drawn aside because of the heat, listening to the dancing of mosquitoes. Since Mam has been sick I don't go out at night any more, to keep from worrying her. But in the wee hours of the morning, before dawn, I begin my excursions through the fields or else I go down to the sea, all the way to the outskirts of Black River. I think I still hope to see Denis appear upon rounding some bushes, or else sitting under an umbrella tree. Sometimes I even call him, using the signal we'd agreed upon, making the grass harp squeak. But he never comes. Laure thinks he's left for the other side of the island, around Ville Noire. I'm alone now, like Robinson on his island. Even Laure is quieter now.

So we read episodes of the novel *Nada the Lily* by H. Rider Haggard, which are published every week in the *Illustrated London News*, illustrated with engravings that are a little frightening and make you dream of adventure. The journal arrives every Monday, three or four weeks late, sometimes in packets of three or four issues, aboard the British India Steam Navigation ships. Our father leafs distractedly through them and then leaves them on the table in the hallway and that's where we watch anxiously for them to arrive. We take them up to our hiding place under the eaves to read them at leisure, lying on the floorboards in the baking dusk light. We read aloud, not understanding most of the time, but with such conviction that those words have remained engraved in my mind. Zweeke the witch doctor says, 'You ask me, my father, to tell you of the youth of Umslopogaas, who was called Bulalio the Slaughterer, and of his love for Nada, the most beautiful of Zulu women.' Every one of those names are deep within me, like the names of living people that we've met this summer in the shadows of the house we will soon be leaving. 'I am Mopo who slew Chaka the king,' says the old man. Dingaan, the king who died for Nada. Baleka, the young girl whose parents were killed by Chaka, and who was forced to become his wife. Koos, Mopo's dog, who goes to his master's side during the night while he is spying on Chaka's army. The dead haunt the land conquered by Chaka, 'We could not sleep for we heard Itongo, the ghosts of the dead, moving about and calling each other.' I shiver when I hear Laure reading and translating those words, and also when Chaka comes before his warriors.

'O Chaka, O Elephant! His justice is bright and terrible like the sun!' I look at the engravings in which vultures glide through the twilight past the disc of the sun already half hidden by the horizon.

There is also Nada, Nada the Lily, with her large eyes and curly hair, her copper-coloured skin, the descendant of a black princess and a white man, she was the last survivor of the kraal Chaka killed. She is beautiful, mysterious, draped in her animal skin. Umslopogaas, Chaka's son, whom she believes to be her brother, is madly in love with her. I remember the day when Nada asks the young man to bring her a lion cub and Umslopogaas slips into the den of the lioness. But here come the lions back from the hunt and the male 'roared so loud the earth shook'. The Zulus fight the lion, but the lioness carries Umslopogaas away in her mouth and Nada weeps over the death of her brother. How we love to read that story! We know it by heart. To us, the English language — that our father has begun teaching us — is the language of legends. When we want to say something extraordinary or secret we say it in English, as if no one else could understand.

I also remember the warrior who strikes Chaka in the face. 'I smell out the Heavens above me,' he says. And when the Queen of the Heavens, Inkosazana-y-Zulu, also appears, announcing Chaka's imminent chastisement: 'And her beauty was awful to behold . . .' When Nada the Lily walks up to the assembly, 'Nada's splendour was upon each of them . . .' Those are the sentences we repeat tirelessly up in the attic, in the murky light at the end of the day. Today I feel they're particularly meaningful — they encompass the unspoken anxiety that precedes metamorphoses.

We still daydream when we see the pictures in the journals, but now they seem inaccessible to us: the Junon bicycles or the ones from Coventry Machinist's & Co., the Lilliput opera glasses with which I imagine I could scour the depths of Mananava, the Bensons keyless watches or the famous nickel Waterbury watches with their enamel faces. Laure and I read the line written under the drawing of the watches as if it were Shakespearean verse: 'Compensation, balance, duplex escapement, keyless, dustproof, shock-proof, non-magnetic.' We also like the advertisement for Brooke soap that shows a monkey playing a mandolin on a crescent moon, and together we recite:

> 'We're a capital couple, the Moon and I,
> I polish the earth, she brightens the sky . . .'

And we burst out laughing. Christmas is already far behind us — a pretty sorry one this year, what with the financial worries, Mam's illness and the loneliness of Boucan — but we play at picking out presents for ourselves in the pages of the journals. Since it's only a game, we don't hesitate to pick the most expensive objects. Laure chooses an ebony Chapell practice piano, an oriental pearl necklace and a Goldsmith & Silversmith enamelled and diamond broach representing a chick coming out of an egg! And it costs nine pounds! I pick out a silver and cut-glass carafe for her, and for Mam I've got the ideal gift: the Mappin leather toiletry case with an assortment of small bottles, boxes, brushes, nail utensils, etc. Laure really likes the case a lot, she says she'll have one too, later, when she's a young lady. I choose a Negretti & Zambra magic lantern for myself, a gramophone with records and needles, and of course a Junon bicycle — they're the best. Laure, who knows my tastes, picks out a box of Tom Smith firecrackers for me and that gives us a good laugh.

We also read the news, already several months, sometimes several years old, but what difference does it make? The stories of shipwrecks, the earthquake in Osaka, and we pore over the illustrations. And there's the tea with Mongolian lamas, Eno's fruit salts with the light-house, and The Haunted Dragoon, a fairy alone, surrounded by a pride of lions in an 'enchanted forest', and a drawing for one of the episodes of *Nada the Lily* that makes us shiver: 'Ghost Mountain', a stone giant whose open mouth is the cave where the lovely Nada will die.

Those are the images that remain with me from back then, mingled in with the sound of the wind in the she-oaks up in the stuffy air of the baking-hot attic as the darkness creeps gradually into the garden around the house and the mynahs start their chattering.

We're waiting, without really knowing what we should be waiting for. In the evening, under the mosquito net before drifting off to sleep, I dream that I'm in a vessel with full sails that is clipping along over the dark sea and I'm gazing at the glinting of the sunlight. I listen to Laure's breathing, slow and even, and I know that her eyes are also open. What is she dreaming about? I think that we're all on a ship heading north, towards the Corsair's island. Then suddenly I find myself deep in the Black River Gorges somewhere around Mananava, where the forest is dark and impenetrable and where one sometimes hears the sighs of Sacalavou, the giant, who killed himself to escape the white men from the plantations. The forest is full of hiding places and poisons, it echoes with the shrieks of monkeys and up above my head the white shadow of the tropicbirds passes in front of the sun. Mananava is the land of dreams.

The days are long that are leading us up to Friday the 29 of April. They're welded one to the other as if there were but one long day, interspersed with nights and dreams, far from reality, a day that already vanishes into memory just as I'm living it, and I can't understand what these days hold, what burden of destiny they bear. How could I understand when I have no points of reference? Nothing but the Tourelle that I can see off in the distance between the trees, because it's my lookout post over the sea and, facing it, the jagged rocks of Trois Mamelles and Rempart Mountain that are the guardians of this world's frontiers.

There is the sun that burns down as soon as dawn breaks, that dries up the red earth along the furrows that the rains have dug after running down over the blue, sheet-metal roof. There were

thunderstorms in February, with that east-north-easterly wind blowing over the mountains, the rain that gullied the hills and the aloe
fields, and the torrents that made a huge stain in the blue lagoons.

So my father just stands under the veranda from early morning
on, watching the curtains of rain moving over the fields, eclipsing
the peaks around the Machabé and Brise-Fer mountains, where the
electrical generator is. When the soggy earth glimmers in the sunshine I sit down on the steps of the veranda and sculpt little statues
of mud for Mam, a dog, a horse, soldiers and even a ship with twig
masts and leaf sails.

My father often goes to Port Louis and from there he takes the
train to Floréal to see my Aunt Adelaide. She's the one who will take
me in next year when I enter the Royal College. None of that interests
me in the least. There's a threat weighing down upon us here in the
world of Boucan, like an incomprehensible storm.

I know that this is where I live, nowhere else. This is the landscape
I've been tirelessly studying for so long now that I'm familiar with
every hollow, every patch of shade, every hiding place. With the
dark chasm of the Black River Gorges, of Mananava, the mysterious
ravine always at my back.

There are also our evening hiding places, the tree of good and evil
where Laure and I go. We hoist ourselves up on the main branches,
legs dangling, and sit there without talking, watching the light fading
under the thick foliage. When the rain begins to fall around evening
time, we listen to the sound of the drops on the wide leaves as if it
were music.

We have another hiding place. It's a ravine at the bottom of which
runs a thin stream that later flows into the Boucan River. Sometimes
the women go there to bathe — a little lower down — or sometimes a
herd of goats driven by a little boy. Laure and I go to a place in the

ravine where there's a level shelf and an old tamarind tree leaning out in mid-air. Straddling its trunk, we shimmy up towards the branches and remain there, heads resting against the bark, daydreaming and watching the water rush over the lava stones down to the bottom of the ravine. Laure thinks there's gold in the stream and that's why the women come to do their washing, to trap gold dust in the cloth of their dresses. So we're always watching the water run past, searching for reflections of sunlight in the black sand, on the beaches. When we're up there, we don't think about anything else, we don't feel the threat any more. We don't think about Mam's illness or the lack of finances or Uncle Ludovic, who's buying up all of our land for his plantation. That's why we go to those hiding places.

———————

My father left for Port Louis in the horse-drawn carriage at dawn. I immediately went out into the fields and headed north first, to see the mountains I love, then turned my back on Mananava and now I'm walking towards the sea. I'm alone, Laure can't come with me because she's indisposed. She's never used that expression before, never talked about the blood that comes to women with the phases of the moon. Afterwards she never speaks of it again, as if she'd later grown ashamed of it. I remember her on that day, a pale, stubborn-looking little girl with long black hair and that very straight, handsome forehead with which she took on the world and something that had already changed, made her distant, foreign. Laure standing on the veranda, wearing her long pale-blue cotton dress, sleeves rolled up, showing her thin arms, and the smile on her face when I walk away, as if to say: I'm the Wild Woodsman's sister.

I run without stopping until I reach the foot of the Tourelle on the edge of the sea. I don't want to go to Black River beach any more, or the sandbar at Tamarin, because of the fishermen. Ever since the adventure in the pirogue, ever since they punished Denis and me by separating us, I don't want to go to the places we used to go any more. I go up to the top of the Tourelle or up to the Etoile, into secret places in the underbrush and watch the sea and the birds. Not even Laure knows where to find me.

I'm alone and I'm talking to myself out loud. I'm asking questions and giving the answers, like this:

'Come on, let's sit down there.'

'Where?'

'Over there on that flat rock.'

'Are you looking for someone?'

'No, no, my good man, I'm watching the sea.'

'Are you trying to catch a glimpse of the sea larks?'

'Look, a boat sailing by. Can you see its name?'

'I know that boat, it's the Argo. It's my ship, it's coming to get me.'

'Are you going away?'

'Yes I'll be going soon. Tomorrow or the day after, I'm going away . . .'

I'm up on the Etoile when the rain first comes in.

It had been a nice day, the sun was burning my skin through the clothing, the chimneys were smoking far away in the cane fields. I sat gazing at the expanse of dark-blue sea, choppy out beyond the reefs.

The rain comes sweeping over the sea, coming from Port Louis, a great grey curtain in a semicircle that is coming straight towards me at top speed. It's so sudden I don't even think of looking for shelter.

I just stand there on the rocky outcrop — heart racing. I love seeing the rain driving in.

At first there is no wind. All sounds are suspended, as if the mountains are holding back the breath of air. That's what's making my heart pound too, the silence that drains the sky, that makes everything stand still.

All of a sudden the cold wind hits me, blustering through the foliage. I can see the ripples running over the cane fields. The wind is whirling around me, with gusts that force me to squat down on the rock to keep from being blown over. Over in the direction of Black River, I see the same thing: the huge dark curtain that is rushing towards me, veiling the sea and the land. That's when I realize I need to get away from here as fast as I can. It's not just an ordinary rainstorm, it's a tempest, a hurricane like the one in February that lasted two days and two nights. But today there is that silence, like none I've ever heard before. And still I don't move. I'm unable to tear my eyes away from the huge grey curtain that is swooping so swiftly over the valley, over the sea, swallowing the hills, the fields, the trees. The curtain is already obscuring the breakers. Then Rempart Mountain, Trois Mamelles disappear. The dark cloud has passed over them, erased them. Now it's sweeping down the mountainsides towards Tamarin and the Boucan Embayment. I think suddenly of Laure, of Mam, who are home alone, and panic tears me away from the sight of the onrushing rain. I jump off the rock and make my way down the slope of the Etoile as fast as I can, charging unhesitatingly through the underbrush that scratches my face and legs. I run as if a pack of mad dogs were at my heels, as if I were a deer escaped from a 'chassé'. Without thinking about it I find all the shortcuts, clamber down a dry streambed leading eastward and in a second I'm in Panon.

Then the wind hits me, the wall of rain comes crashing down upon me. I've never felt anything like it. Water envelops me, streams over my face, into my mouth, my nostrils. I'm suffocating, I'm blinded, I'm staggering in the wind. Most terrifying of all is the noise. A deep, heavy noise that rumbles in the earth, and I think the mountains must be tumbling down. I turn my back on the tempest, crawl on my hands and knees through the bushes. Branches torn from trees go whipping through the air, shooting past like arrows. I wait, squatting at the foot of a tall tree, my arms over my head. A second later the blast has passed. Rain is pouring down, but I can stand up now, breathe, see where I am. The underbrush on the edge of the ravine is beaten flat. Not far from there a tall tree like the one that sheltered me has fallen to the ground with its roots still clinging to the red earth. I start walking again – haphazardly – and suddenly, during a lull, I see the buttress of Saint Martin, the ruins of the old sugar mill. No time to waste, that's where I'll go for shelter.

I know these ruins. I often saw them when I used to roam around in the fallow lands with Denis. He didn't want to go near them, he says it's the Mouna Mouna's house, that they beat the 'devil's drum' here. Inside the old walls I huddle up in a corner under what's left of the vaulting. My drenched clothing is clinging to my skin, I'm shivering with cold, and with fear too. I can hear the blasts of wind barrelling across the valley. It's making a sound like an enormous animal lying down on the trees, crushing the thickets and the branches, breaking the tree trunks as if they were simple twigs. The rainwater is flooding over the ground, surrounding the ruins, cascading down into the ravine. Streams appear as if they'd just sprung up out of the earth. The water swirls by, branches out, knots together, eddies. There is no longer sky or earth, only that mass of liquid, and the wind whipping trees and red mud up into the air. I look straight ahead, hoping to catch a glimpse of the sky through the wall of water. Where am I? Maybe the ruins of Panon are all that's left on Earth, maybe everyone's been drowned in the flood. I want to pray but my teeth are chattering and I can't even remember the words any more. All I can remember is the story of the great flood that Mam used to read us in the big red book, the one where water fell upon the Earth and covered everything up to the mountains and the large boat that Noah built to escape the Flood, and in which he put a pair of every animal species. But how could I build a boat? If Denis were here, maybe he would know how to make a pirogue or a raft with tree trunks. And why should God punish the Earth again? Is it because men have become hardened, as my father says, and they feed on the poverty of the labourers in the plantations? Then I think of Laure and Mam in the abandoned house, and I'm seized with such intense panic that I can hardly breathe. What's become of them? Maybe the raging wind, the great wall of water have engulfed them, swept them away, and I imagine Laure flailing in the river of mud, trying to grab hold of tree branches, being borne towards the ravine. In spite of the blasting winds and the distance I get to my feet, cry out, 'Laure! . . . Laure!'

But I realize it's no use, the sound of the wind and the water drown out my cries. So I squat back down against the wall, my face hidden in my arms, and the water streaming down over my head mingles with my tears, because I feel so immensely desperate – as if a dark void is swallowing me up and I'm falling through the liquid earth as I crouch here, helplessly, on my heels.

I remain motionless for a long time, while the sky changes above me and the walls of water sweep along like waves. Finally the rain subsides, the wind weakens. I stand up, walk, deafened by the sudden silence. The sky has rent in the north and I can see the shapes of Rempart, of Trois Mamelles appearing. They've never seemed more beautiful to me. My heart is beating very fast, as if they were human friends that I'd lost and just found again. They are unreal, dark blue among the grey clouds. I can see every detail of their ridges, every rock. The sky around them is still, has reached down into the hollow of Tamarin where other rocks, other hills are slowly emerging. Turning around, I can see islands of neighbouring hills out on the sea of clouds: the Tourelle, Mont Terre Rouge, Brise-Fer, Morne Sec. Far away, lit with incredible sunshine, Grand Morne.

It is all so beautiful I just stand there, motionless. Lingering, I contemplate the wounded landscape upon which tattered clouds are snagging. Out around Trois Mamelles, perhaps somewhere near Cascades, there's a magnificent rainbow. I'd love for Laure to be here with me to see that. She says rainbows are the roadways of the rain. The rainbow is very bright, it's resting on the base of the mountains in the west and stretching all the way over to the other side of the peaks around Floréal or Phoenix. There are still dark clouds roiling. But all of a sudden the ones just above me tear open and I see the sky is a pure, dazzling hue of blue. Then it's as if time takes a leap backwards, inverting its course. A few moments ago it was evening, the light was waning, yet an infinite evening, leading out to the void. And now I can tell it is barely noon, the sun is at its zenith and I can feel the heat of its light on my face and hands.

I run through the wet grasses, go back down the hill towards Boucan Valley. Everywhere the earth is sodden, streams are spilling over with water the colour of red ochre. There are broken tree trunks on the path. But I pay no attention. It's over with, that's what I'm thinking, it's all over with since the rainbow appeared to seal God's peace.

When I arrive in front of our house I'm so anxious the strength drains from my body. The garden, the house are intact. There are just leaves, broken branches strewn about in the lane, muddy puddles everywhere. But the sunlight is gleaming on the light roof, on the leaves of the trees, and everything seems newer, younger.

Laure is on the veranda, as soon as she sees me she cries, 'Alexis!' She runs to me, hugs me tightly. Mam is there too, standing in front of the door, pale, worried. Though I keep telling her, 'It's over, Mam, it's all over, there isn't going to be a flood!' I don't see her smile. Only then do I think of our father who went to town and something inside me hurts. 'But he's going to come now? He's going to come?' Mam squeezes my arm, says in a hoarse voice, 'Yes, of course he's going to come . . .' But she's unable to hide her worry and I'm the one who has to repeat, holding her hand as tightly as I can: 'It's over now, there's nothing to be afraid of any more.'

We remain huddled together on the veranda, clinging to one another, warily observing the far end of the garden and the sky where once more large black clouds are gathering. There is that strange silence again, weighing down upon the valley around us as if we were all alone in the world. Cook's hut is empty. He left for Black River this morning with his wife. In the fields, not a cry, no sound of a carriage to be heard.

It's that silence penetrating deep down inside us, that ominous silence, bearing the threat of death that I'll never be able to forget. There's not a bird in the trees, not an insect, not even the sound of the wind in the she-oaks. The silence is more powerful than the sounds, it swallows them up, and everything around us drains away and is annihilated. We stand still on the veranda. I'm shivering in my damp clothes. When we speak our voices ring out strangely in the distance and our words are immediately eclipsed.

Then the sound of the hurricane comes upon the valley, like a herd running through the cane fields and the brush, and I can also hear the sound of the sea, terribly close. We stand there frozen on the veranda and I feel nausea rising in my throat, because I realize that the hurricane isn't over. We were in the eye of the storm, where everything is calm and silent. Now I hear the wind coming in from the sea, coming in from the south — louder and louder — and the body of the huge enraged animal crushing everything in its path.

This time there is no wall of rain, the wind comes alone. I see the trees tossing in the distance, the clouds scudding like wisps of smoke, long sooty trails stained with violet patches. The sky is the most frightening. It is speeding past, opening, closing, and I feel as if I'm sliding towards it, falling.

'Hurry! Hurry, children!'

Mam has finally spoken. Her voice is hoarse. But she's succeeded in breaking the spell, our horrified fascination at the sight of the sky destroying itself. She's pulling, pushing us into the house, into the dining room with closed shutters. She blocks the door with the hooks. The house is filled with shadows. It's like the interior of a ship where we're listening to the wind bearing down upon us. In spite of the stifling heat I'm shivering with cold, with anxiety. Mam notices. She goes to her room, looking for a blanket. While she's gone the wind hits the house like an avalanche. Laure clings even tighter to me and we hear the boards squealing. Broken branches are flung up against the sides of the house, stones roll against the shutters and doors.

Through the cracks in the shutters we suddenly see the daylight blink out and I realize that clouds are covering the earth again. Then water falls from the sky, whipping at the walls under the veranda. It seeps in under the door, through the window frames, floods over the floorboards around us in dark, blood-red streams. Laure watches the water coming towards us, pooling around the big table and the

72

chairs. Mam returns and the look on her face frightens me so much that I take the blanket and try to plug up the space under the door, but the water quickly soaks through it and rushes in again. The howling winds outside are deafening and the sinister cracking of the frame of the house, the sharp snapping of the clapboards being torn away fills our ears. The rain is flooding into the attic now and I think of our old journals, our books, everything that we love that is going to be destroyed. The wind has shattered the garret windows and is rushing through the attic, howling, smashing the furniture. With a thunderous blast, it rips up a tree that comes crashing into the southern façade of the house, eviscerating it. We hear the sound of the veranda caving in. Mam pulls us out of the dining room just as a huge branch thrusts through one of the windows.

The wind enters the breach like a furious and invisible animal and for a moment I have the feeling that the sky has descended upon the house to crush it. I hear the clatter of furniture being overturned, windows breaking. Mam somehow drags us over to the other side of the house. We take refuge in our father's office and remain there, the three of us crouching against the wall where the large map of the night sky hangs alongside that of Rodrigues. The shutters are closed, but even so, the wind has broken the windows and the hurricane waters are running over the parquet, over the desk, over our father's books and papers. Laure clumsily attempts to put a few papers away, then sits back down, discouraged. Outside, through the cracks in the shutters, the sky is so dark you'd think it was night. And the incessant tumult of trees toppling all around us.

'Let's pray,' says Mam. She hides her face in her hands. Laure's face is pale. She's staring unblinkingly at the window, and I'm trying to think of the angel Gabriel. I always think of him when I'm afraid. He's tall, surrounded by light, armed with a sword. Could he have

73

condemned us, abandoned us to the raging sea and sky? The light is growing ever dimmer. The sound of the wind is shrill, high-pitched, and I can feel the walls of the house trembling. Pieces of wood fly away from the veranda, the shingles are torn off the roof. Branches are whirled up against the windows like blades of grass. Mam holds us tightly to her breast. She's not praying either. She's staring out with a steady, terrifying gaze, while the roaring of the wind makes our hearts quail. I'm not thinking about anything, I can't utter a word. Even if I wanted to talk, there's such a furore that Mam and Laure couldn't hear me. An endless sound of destruction that reaches down into the very depths of the earth, a wave that is slowly, inexorably unfurling upon us.

It lasts for a long time, and we're falling through the ragged skies, through the gaping earth. I hear the sea as I have never heard it before. It has gone over the coral reef and is coming up the estuary of the rivers, pushing the overflowing torrents out in front of it. I can hear the sea in the wind, I can't move any more: everything has come to an end for us. Laure, with her hands over her ears, is leaning against Mam in silence. Mam, wide-eyed, is staring fixedly at the dark shape of the window, as if to stave off the furious elements. Our poor house is shaking from top to bottom. On the southern end part of the roof has been torn off. The wind and gushing water are devastating the gutted rooms. The wooden partitioning wall of the office also splits apart. A little while ago, through the hole made by the tree, I saw Capt'n Cook's cabin being swept away in the wind like a toy. I also saw the tall bamboo hedge bending to the ground as if an invisible hand were holding it down. In the distance, I can hear the wind pounding against the rampart of the mountains with a thunderous rumble that joins in with the rushing sound of the unleashed sea surging up the rivers.

At what point do I realize that the wind is easing off? I don't know. Before the roar of the sea and the cracking of trees come to an end, deep within, I am convinced that something has been released. I breathe in, the tight vice around my temples loosens.

Then suddenly the wind falls and once again we are surrounded by a profound silence. We can hear water trickling everywhere, on the roof, in the trees, even in the house, thousands of rivulets trickling down. The bamboo is cracking. Daylight returns, little by little, and it is the soft, warm light of dusk. Mam opens the shutters. We just sit there, not daring to move, clinging tightly to one another, looking out the window at the shapes of the mountains emerging from the clouds, and they are like familiar, reassuring people.

That's when Mam begins to cry, because she has no strength left and when calm is suddenly restored she just can't hold up any more. I remember that Laure and I begin to cry too, I don't think I've ever cried that much since. Afterwards we all lie down on the floor and sleep, huddling together because of the cold.

We are awakened at dawn by the sound of our father's voice. Had he arrived during the night? I remember his distraught face, his mud-stained clothing. Then he tells us how, at the height of the hurricane, he jumped out of his carriage and lay down in a ditch at the side of the road. That's when the tempest passed over him, sweeping the carriage and the horse away God only knows where. He saw incredible things, boats hurled inland that landed in the branches of the trees of the Intendance. The swollen sea invading the river inlets, drowning people in their cabins. Above all the wind that tossed everything upside down, that tore the roofs off houses, that snapped the smokestacks off sugar mills and demolished the hangars and destroyed half of Port Louis. When he was able to get out of the ditch he took shelter for the night in one of the blacks' cabins over by Médine, because the roads were flooded. At daybreak an Indian had given him a lift to Tamarin Estate in his wagon, and to reach Boucan my father had to cross the river with the water up to his chest. He also talks about the barometer. My father was in an office in Rempart Street when the barometer fell. He says it was incredible, terrifying. He'd never seen a barometer go so low in such a short time. How can the fall of mercury be terrifying? It's something I can't comprehend, but the sound of my father's voice when he spoke of it rings in my ears and I'll never be able to forget it.

———————

Later on there's a sort of fever that heralds the end of our happiness. Now we're living in the northern wing of the house, in the only rooms spared by the cyclone. On the southern side the house is half caved in, devastated by water and wind. The roof has holes in it, the veranda no longer exists. Another thing I won't be able to forget is the tree that crashed through the wall of the house, the long black branch that came through the shutter of the dining-room window and remains there, immobile like the claw of some fantastic animal that struck with lightning force.

Laure and I have ventured up into the attic using the mangled staircase. The water gushed in furiously through the holes in the roof, devastating everything. Only a few soggy pages remain of the piles of books and journals. We can't even walk around in the attic any more, because the floor is torn up in several places, the roof beams are disjointed. The mild winds that come in from the sea every evening make the whole of the weakened structure of the house creak. A wreck, that's what our house truly looks like, the wreck of a sunken ship. We roam around the grounds to assess the extent of the disaster. We look for what was there yesterday, the handsome trees, the planted palmettos, guava trees, mango trees, flower beds of rhododendrons, of bougainvilleas, hibiscuses. We wander about, teetering as if we were recovering from a long illness. Everywhere we see the battered, defiled earth, strewn with crushed grass, with broken branches, and the trees with their roots turned skyward. Laure and I go down as far as the cane fields, over by Yemen and Tamarin, and everywhere the immature cane lies flattened in the fields as if it has been cut down with a gigantic scythe.

Even the sea has changed. From up on the Etoile I watch the large mud stains spreading out over the lagoon. There's no longer a village at the mouth of Black River. I think of Denis, was he able to escape?

Laure and I sit perched atop a Creole pyramid in the middle of the devastated fields almost all day long. There's a strange odour in the air, a stale smell wafting in on the wind. And yet the sky is cloudless and the sun is burning our hands and faces like it does at the height of summer. Around Boucan the mountains are dark green, sharp, they seem closer than before. We gaze at it all, the sea out beyond the reefs, the bright sky, the battered earth, just like that, not thinking about anything, our eyes stinging with weariness. There's no one in the fields, no one walking down the paths.

Silence fills our house as well. No one has come out since the storm. We eat just a little rice with some hot tea. Mam stays prone on a makeshift bed in my father's office and we sleep in the hallway, because those are the only places the cyclone spared. One morning I accompany my father out to Bassin aux Aigrettes. We walk in silence over the devastated land. We already know what we will find and it makes our throats tighten. At one point an old black gunny woman is sitting by the side of the path in front of what is left of her home. As we go by her plaint grows slightly louder and my father stops to give her a coin. As soon as we reach the pool we immediately see what remains of the generator. The lovely machine is lying on its side, half-submerged in muddy water. The shed has disappeared and all that is left of the turbine are unrecognizable pieces of bent metal. My father stops, says in a loud, clear voice, 'That's it.' He's tall and pale, the sunlight is shining on his black hair and beard. He draws nearer to the generator, paying no attention to the mud that comes up to his thighs. He makes an almost childish gesture to attempt to set the machine upright. Then he turns around and walks down the path. When he passes me, he puts his hand on my neck and says, 'Come on, let's head back.' That moment is truly tragic, at the time I feel as if everything is finished, for ever, and my eyes and throat fill with tears. Following rapidly in my father's footsteps, I watch his tall, thin, stooped figure.

Those are the days when everything moves towards its end, but we aren't yet certain of that. Laure and I sense a more precise threat. It begins with the first news from the outside, rumours spread around by the plantation labourers, the gunnies from Yemen, from Walhalla. The news reaches us reiterated, amplified, relating the island devastated by the cyclone. The city of Port Louis, my father says, has been wiped off the map, as if it had been bombarded. Most of the wooden houses were destroyed and entire streets have disappeared, Rue Madame, Rue Emmikillen, Rue Poivre. From Signal Mountain to Champ de Mars there is nothing but ruins. Public buildings, churches have collapsed, and people were burned alive in explosions. My father tells us that at four o'clock in the afternoon the barometer was at its lowest point and the wind was blowing at over a hundred miles an hour with gusts of up to a hundred and twenty miles, they say. The sea became alarmingly swollen, covering the shores, and boats were thrown as far as a hundred metres inland. At Rempart River the sea caused the already high waters to overflow the riverbanks and the inhabitants were drowned. The names of destroyed villages makes a long list: Beau Bassin, Rose Hill, Quatre Bornes, Vacoas, Phoenix, Palma, Médine, Beaux Songes. In Bassin, on the other side of Trois Mamelles, the roof of a sugar mill fell in, burying one hundred and thirty people who had taken shelter there. In Phoenix sixty were killed and still more in Bambous, in Belle Eau and in the north of the island, in Mapou, in Mont Goût, in Forbach. The number of victims increases every day, people swept away in the river of mud, crushed under houses, under trees. My father says there are several hundred dead, but the following days the figure is a thousand, then one thousand five hundred.

Laure and I stay outside all day, hiding in the battered thickets around the house, not daring to venture very far away. We go to see the ravine in which the torrent is still very angry, hauling mud and broken branches. Or else, from high in the chalta tree, we watch the devastated fields lit up in the sun. The women in their gunny sacks are gathering the immature cane and pulling it along on the muddy ground. Starving children come to steal the fallen fruit and cabbage palms around our house.

Mam waits silently inside the house. She's lying on the floor of the office, wrapped in blankets in spite of the heat. Her face is burning with fever and her eyes are red, with a painful sheen to them. My father sits on the ruined veranda, gazing at the tree line in the distance, smoking cigarettes, not speaking to anyone.

Later, Cook comes back with his daughter. He speaks briefly of Black River, sunken boats, destroyed houses. Cook, who is very old, says he hasn't seen anything like that since the first time he came to the island when he was a slave. There'd been the hurricane that had toppled the chimney from the residence and almost killed Governor

Barkly, but he says it wasn't as bad as this. We think that, since Old Cook isn't dead and that now he's come home, everything will go back to the way it was before. But he looks at what is left of his cabin, shaking his head, he nudges a few boards with his foot and, before we realize what is happening, he turns and leaves. 'Where's Cook?' asks Laure. His daughter shrugs her shoulders. 'He gone, Mamsell Laure.' 'But he's coming back?' There is a worried tone in Laure's voice. 'When is he coming back?' Cook's daughter's answer makes our hearts sink, 'God knows, Mamsell Laure. Might be never.' She's come to get some food and a little money. Capt'n Cook won't live here any more, he'll never come back, we're well aware of that.

So Boucan remains as it has been since the storm: lonely, abandoned by the world. A black man came from the plantation with his oxen to pull out the tree trunk that had ripped open the dining room. We helped my father clear away all the debris strewn about the house: papers, glass, shattered dishes mingled with branches and leaves, with mud. With the holes in its walls, the veranda in ruins, and the roof through which we can see the sky, our house looks even more like a shipwrecked vessel. And we are castaways, clinging to our ship in the hopes that everything will go back to the way it was before.

To ward off the anxiety that is mounting daily, Laure and I roam farther and farther away, across the cane fields, all the way out to where the forests begin. We go out every day, drawn by the dark valley of Mananava, the home of the tropicbirds who circle up so very high in the sky. But they too have disappeared. I think the hurricane must have carried them off, dashed them against the walls of the gorges, or else thrown them so far out to sea that they will never be able to come back.

We search for them every day in the empty sky. There is a dreadful silence in the forest, as if the wind will soon return.

Where can we go? There's no one around any more, you can't hear the sound of dogs barking on the farms any more or the cries of children near the streams. There are no more wisps of smoke in the sky. Perched atop a Creole pyramid, we search the horizon, over by Clarence, over by Wolmar. The chimneys have stopped. To the south, down by Black River, there isn't a trace in the sky. We don't talk. We just sit there, baking in the noonday sun, gazing at the sea in the distance until our eyes sting.

In the evening, we head back towards Boucan, feeling heavy-hearted. The wreck is still there, half-crumbled to the still damp earth in the ruins of the devastated garden. We slip furtively into the house, barefooted on the floorboards, where the dried mud has already left a layer of gritty dust, but our father hasn't even noticed our absence. We eat whatever we can find, starved from our distant wanderings: fruits we've gleaned from neighbouring properties, eggs, the 'lampangue' or the dry crust stuck to the bottom of the large pot of rice my father boils every morning.

One day when we're over by the forest, Koenig, the doctor from Floréal, comes to see Mam. Laure notices the tracks of his carriage in the muddy lane when we get back. I don't dare go any farther, I stand there, waiting, trembling, while Laure runs to the veranda, leaps into the house. When I go in afterwards, through the north entrance, I see Laure holding Mam tightly in her arms, her head lying against Mam's breast. Mam is smiling in spite of her weariness. She goes over to the cupboard upon which the alcohol stove sits. She wants to heat up some rice, make some tea for us.

'Eat, children, eat. It's so late, where have you been?'

She speaks rapidly with a sort of breathlessness, but her good cheer is genuine.

'We'll soon be going away, we're leaving Boucan.'

'Where are we going, Mam?'

'Ah, I shouldn't be telling you, it's not sure yet, I mean, the decision hasn't been completely made. We'll go to Forest Side. Your father has found a house, not far from your aunt Adelaide.'

She hugs us both tightly and we can feel nothing but her happiness, can think of nothing else.

My father has gone back to town, probably in Koenig's carriage. He must make preparations for our departure, for the new house in Forest Side. Later I learned of everything he did that day to attempt to fend off the inevitable. I learned of all the papers he signed for the usurpers in town, the acknowledgements of debts, the mortgages, the secured loans. All the arable lands of Boucan, the wastelands, the gardens around the house, the stands of trees, even the house itself, everything was pawned, sold. He was in over his head. He'd put his last hope into that crazy idea, that electrical generator for the Mare aux Aigrettes that was to bring progress to the entire western side of the island and that was now no more than a heap of scrap metal sunk in the mud. How could we, who were only children, have understood that? But at the time we didn't need to understand things. Little by little we were able to guess what we were not told. When the hurricane had stopped we knew very well that everything had already been lost. It was like the flood.

'Will Uncle Ludovic come to live here when we're gone?' asks Laure.

There is so much anger and grief in her voice that Mam can't answer. She turns her eyes away.

'He did this! He's the one who did all this!' says Laure. I wish she'd be quiet. She's pale and trembling, her voice is trembling too. 'I hate him!' 'Be quiet,' says Mam. 'You don't know what you're talking about.' But Laure doesn't want to let it drop. She stands up for herself for the first time, as if she were defending it all, everything we love, this house in ruins, this garden, the tall trees, our ravine, and even beyond, the dark mountains, the sky, the sound of the sea borne along on the wind. 'Why didn't he help us? Why didn't he do anything? Why does he want us to go away, so he can take our house?' Mam is sitting on the deckchair in the shade of the mangled veranda, like in the old days when she was preparing to read us the Holy Scriptures or begin a dictation. But today a lot of time has gone by in just one day and we know none of that will ever be possible again. That's why Laure is shouting and her voice is trembling and tears are welling up in her eyes, because she wants to express how much pain she's feeling, 'Why did he get everyone to turn against us, when he's so rich, he could have just said one word! Why does he want us to go away, to take our house, take our garden, and plant sugar cane everywhere?' 'Be quiet, be quiet!' shouts Mam. Her face is tense with anger, with distress. Laure has stopped shouting. She's standing in front of us, filled with shame, her eyes shiny with tears, and all of a sudden she turns around, jumps into the dark garden and runs away. I run after her. 'Laure! Laure! Come back!' I look for her hastily in vain. Then I think it over, I know where she is, as if I could see her through the underbrush. This is the last time. She's in our hiding place on the other side of the devastated palmetto field, up on the main branch of the tamarind tree above the ravine, listening to the sound of the rushing water. In the ravine the light is ashen, night has already begun. A few birds have already come back and some insects are humming.

Laure isn't up on the branch. She's sitting on a large rock near the tamarind tree. Her light-blue dress is stained with mud. She's barefoot.

When I arrive, she doesn't move. She's not crying. There's that obstinate expression that I love on her face. I think she's happy I came. I sit down next to her, put my arms around her. We talk. We don't talk about Uncle Ludovic or about our impending departure, none of that. We talk about other things, about Denis, as if he would come back, bringing strange objects, like in the old days, a turtle egg, a head feather from a bulbul, a seed from a dodo tree, or things from the sea, shells, stones, amber. We also talk about *Nada the Lily* and we have to talk about that a lot because the hurricane destroyed our collection of journals, blew it all the way up to the top of the mountains maybe. When night has truly fallen, we shimmy up the inclined trunk and lie there for a moment, suspended in the darkness, arms and legs dangling over the drop.

That night is long, like nights that precede a long journey. And it's true, leaving the Boucan Valley will be the first journey we've ever taken. We're lying on the floor, wrapped in our blankets, looking at the night light wavering at the end of the hallway, not sleeping. If we do drift off to sleep it's only for an instant. In the silent night we can hear the rustling of Mam's long white nightgown as she paces around the empty office. We hear her sigh, and when she goes back to sit in the easy chair next to the window we are able to go back to sleep.

At dawn my father comes back. He's brought a horse-drawn cart along and an Indian from Port Louis whom we don't know, a tall, thin man who looks like a seafarer. My father and the Indian load the furniture that was spared by the hurricane into the cart: some armchairs, kitchen chairs, tables, a wardrobe that was in Mam's room, her brass bed and her deckchair. Then the trunks that contain the treasure papers, and the clothing. For us it's not really a departure, since we don't have anything to take along. All of our books, all of our toys disappeared in the storm, and the bundles of journals no longer exist. We have no other clothes but the ones we're wearing, which are stained and torn from our long escapades in the underbrush. It's better this way. What could we have brought along? What we needed were the garden and its lovely trees, the walls of our house and its sky-coloured roof, Capt'n Cook's little hut, the hills of Tamarin and the Etoile, the mountains, and the dark valley of Mananava, where the two tropicbirds live. We stand in the sun while my father loads the last objects into the cart.

Shortly before one o'clock, without having eaten, we strike out. My father is sitting up front beside the driver. Mam, Laure and I are under the tarpaulin amid the teetering chairs and the crates with the rattling remnants of the dishes. We don't even try to peek out through the holes in the canvas to see the landscape growing gradually distant. That's how we leave Boucan, on that Wednesday, the 31st of August, that's how we leave our world, for we've never known any other, we're losing it all, the large house where we were born, the veranda where Mam used to read us the Holy Scripture, the story of Jacob and the Angel, Moses saved from the waters, and the garden, as luxuriant as the Garden of Eden, with the trees of the Intendance, the guava and mango trees, the ravine with the leaning tamarind tree, the tall chalta tree of good and evil, the alley of stars that leads to the place in the sky where there are the most lights. We're off now, leaving all that behind and we know that none of it will ever exist again, because it's like death — a one-way journey.

Forest Side

———————

That's when I began living in the company of the Mysterious Corsair, the Privateer, as my father called him. I thought about him, dreamt about him for so many years. He shared my life, my loneliness. In the cold, rainy shadows of Forest Side, then at Royal College in Curepipe, he was the one I really lived with. He was the Privateer, the man without a face or a name, who'd roamed the seas with his crew of pirates capturing Portuguese, English, Dutch ships and then one day disappeared without leaving a trace, except for these old papers, this map of an unnamed island, and a cryptogram written in cuneiform signs.

In Forest Side, far from the sea, life did not exist. Since we'd been driven away from Boucan, we'd never gone back to the coast. Most of my school friends would spend a few days in the 'campsites' around Flic-en-Flac or over on the other side of the island, near Mahébourg, or as far out as Poudre d'Or. Sometimes they'd go to Deer Island and would thoroughly relate their trip afterwards, a party under the palm trees, the luncheons, the teas which were attended by lots of young girls in light-coloured dresses with parasols. We were poor, we never took trips. For that matter, Mam wouldn't have wanted to. After the day when the hurricane passed, she hated the sea, the heat, the fevers. At Forest Side she'd been cured of that, even though an air of languor and abandon still hovered about her. Laure never left her side, never saw anyone. In the beginning she'd gone to school, like me, because she said she wanted to learn how to work so she would never have to marry. But she had to give up that idea because of Mam. Mam said she needed her at the house. We were so poor, who would help her with the housework? She had to accompany Mam to the market, cook the meals, clean. Laure didn't say anything. She gave up going to school, but she grew despondent, taciturn, oversensitive. She would only lighten up when I came back from the College to spend Saturday night and Sunday at the house. Sometimes on Saturday she would come to meet me on Route Royale. I recognized her from a distance, her long thin silhouette wrapped neatly in her blue dress. She wore no hat and had her black hair in a long braid folded up and knotted behind. When it was drizzling, she'd come with a large shawl around her head and shoulders like an Indian woman.

As soon as she'd catch sight of me, she'd start running towards me shouting, 'Ali! . . . Ali!' She'd hug me tight and start talking, saying all kinds of trivial things that she'd kept pent up inside all week long. Her only friends were Indian women who were poorer than she was and who lived in the hills of Forest Side, to whom she'd take a little food, some used clothing, or with whom she'd sometimes have long talks. Maybe that's why she'd ended up resembling them somewhat, with her slender silhouette, her long black hair and those large shawls of hers.

As for me, I would hardly listen to her, because back in those days my thoughts were exclusively occupied with the sea and the Privateer, his travels, his hideouts in Antongil, in Diego-Suarez, in

Monomotapa, his expeditions, swift as the wind, out as far as the Carnatic region in India, to cut off the route of the proud and heavy vessels of the British, Dutch and French East India Companies. At the time I used to read books dealing with pirates, and their names and exploits would resound in my imagination: Avery, dubbed the 'Little King', who'd ravished and kidnapped the Grand Moghul's daughter Martel, Teach, Major Stede Bonnet, who became a pirate due to a 'disorder of mind', Captain England, John Rackham, Roberts, Kennedy, Captain Anstis, Taylor, Davis, and the infamous Olivier Levasseur, known as La Buse, who, with the aid of Taylor, captured the viceroy of Goa and a vessel that contained a fabulous quarry of diamonds that belonged to the Golconda treasure. But the one I liked most was Misson, the pirate philosopher, who, with the aid of Cariccioli – a defrocked monk – founded the Republic of Libertalia in Diego-Suarez Bay, where all men were to live free and equal, regardless of origins or race.

I never talked to Laure about that, because she said it was just a bunch of pipedreams like the ones that had ruined our family. But I sometimes shared my desire to go to sea and my interest in the Corsair with my father, and I was able to pore over the documents concerning the treasure, which he kept in a case lined with lead under the table that served as his desk. Every time I was at Forest Side, closed up in that long, cold and humid room in the evening, by the light of a candle, I would examine the letters, the maps and the documents that my father had made notes on and the calculations he'd made based on indications left by the Privateer. I would carefully copy the documents and the maps and take them back to the College with me to fuel my dreams.

Years passed in that way, during which I was perhaps even more isolated than back in the days of Boucan, for life in the chill of the

College and its icy halls was dreary and humiliating. There was the
promiscuity of the other students, their odour, their contact, their
often obscene jokes, their penchant for foul words and their obsession
with sex. Until then I had heard nothing about such things and it all
began when we'd been driven away from Boucan.

There was the rainy season, not the violent storms of the coastal
regions, but a fine, monotonous rain that would settle over the town
and the hills for days, for weeks on end. In my spare time I'd go to
the Carnegie Library and read all the books I could find in French or
in English. *Les Voyages et aventures en deux îles désertes* by François
Leguat, *Le Neptune oriental* by d'Après de Mannevillette, *Voyages
à Madagascar, à Maroc et aux Indes Orientales* by l'Abbé Rochon,
and also Charles Alleaume, Grenier, Ohier de Grandpré, and I'd leaf
through the journals looking for illustrations, names, to nourish my
dreams of the sea.

Nights in the cold dormitory I would recite the names of the
navigators who'd sailed the oceans, fleeing squadrons, pursuing
myths, mirages, the elusive glitter of gold. Avery, as always, Captain
Martel, Teach – known as Blackbeard – who, when asked where
he'd buried his gold, answered, 'Nobody but me and the Devil know
where it be hid and the longest liver will get it all.' That is the way
Charles Johnson told it in his *General History of the Pyrates*. Captain
Winter and his adopted son England. Howell Davis, who one day
happened upon La Buse's vessel en route and, as they had both
hoisted the black flag, they decided to become allies and sail together.
Cochlyn, the pirate who helped them take the Fort of Sierra Leone.
Marie Read, disguised as a man, and Anne Bonny, John Rackham's
wife. Tew, who became Misson's ally and helped found Libertalia,
Cornelius, Camden, John Plantain, who became King of Rantabé,

John Falemberg, Edward Johner, Daniel Darwin, Julien Hardouin, François Le Frère, Guillaume Ottroff, John Allen, William Martin, Benjamin Melly, James Butter, Guillaume Plantier, Adam Johnson.

And all the seafarers who roamed the open seas in those days, inventing new lands. Dufouferay, Jonchée de la Goleterie, Charles Nicolas Mariette, Captain Le Meyer, who might have seen Taylor's pirate ship *Cassandra* sail right past him, 'rich to the tune of five or six million coming from China, where he had plundered those treasures', says Charles Alleaume. Jacob de Bucquoy, who sat with Taylor as he agonized and to whom the pirate might have entrusted his last secret. Grenier, who was the first to explore the Chagos Archipelago, Sir Robert Farquhar, De Langle, who accompanied La Pérouse to Alaska, and still yet, the man whose name I bear, l'Étang, who countersigned for Guillaume Dufresne, commander of the *Chasseur*, the act establishing French rule over Mauritius on 20 September 1715. These are the names I hear in the night, eyes wide open in the dark dormitory. I also dream of the names of the ships, the loveliest names in the world, written on the stern that traces the white wake on the deep sea, written for all time into the memory that is the sea, that is the sky and the wind. The *Zodiaque*, the *Fortuné*, the *Vengeur*, the *Victorieux* that La Buse commanded, and the *Galderland* that he captured, Taylor's the *Défense*, Surcouf's *Révenant*, Camden's *Flying Dragon*, the *Volant* that bore Pingré over to Rodrigues, the *Amphitrite*, and the *Grande Hirondelle*, commanded by the corsair Le Même, until he perished on the *Fortuné*. The *Néréide*, the *Otter*, the *Sapphire*, upon which, in September 1809, Rowley's Englishmen came sailing right up to the Pointe des Galets to conquer the Ile de France. There were also the names of the islands, fabulous names that I knew by heart, simple islets where explorers and privateers stopped in search of water or bird's eggs, hideouts in the crooks of bays, pirates' lairs where they established their towns, their palaces, their states: Diego-Suarez Bay, Saint Augustine Bay, Antongil Bay in Madagascar, Ile Sainte Marie, Foulpointe, Tintingue. The Comoros Islands, Anjouan, Maheli, Mayotte. The Seychelles and the Amirantes Archipelago, Alphonse Island, Coetivi, George, Roquepiz, Aldabra, Assumption Island, Cosmoledo, Astove, St Pierre, Providence, Juan de Nova, the Chagos group: Diego Garcia, Egmont, Danger, Eagle, Three Brothers, Peros Banhos, Solomon, Legour. The Cargados Carajos, the marvellous island of Saint Brandon, where women are forbidden; Raphael, Tromelin, Sand Island, the Saya de Malha Bank, The Nazareth Bank, Agalega . . . Those were the names I heard in the silence of the night, names so distant and yet so familiar, and even today as I write them my heart beats faster and I'm not sure any more whether I've been to them or not.

The moments of true life were when Laure and I would be reunited after being separated for a week. All along the muddy lane leading to Forest Side that ran parallel to the railway tracks as far as Eau Bleue, we'd talk, paying no attention to the people under their umbrellas, trying to recollect the days in Boucan, our adventures through the cane fields, the garden, the ravine, the sound of the wind in the she-oaks. We'd talk hastily and at times it all seemed like a dream. 'And Mananava?' Laure asked. I couldn't answer her, because there was a pain deep inside me and I thought of the sleepless nights, wide-eyed in the dark, listening to Laure's overly steady breathing, listening for the sound of the rising tide. Mananava, the dark valley where the rain was born, which we'd never dared to enter. I also thought of the sea breeze that bore the two very white tropicbirds along so slowly, like legendary spirits, and I could still hear, echoing through the valley, their grating calls like the sound of a rattle.

Mananava, where Old Cook's wife said the descendants of the black maroons lived, the ones who'd killed the masters and burned the cane fields. That was where Sengor fled to and it was there that the great Sacalavou had thrown himself from a cliff top to escape the white men who were pursuing him. And she would say that when a storm came you could hear a moan rising up from Mananava, an eternal complaint.

Laure and I would walk along, remembering, holding hands like two sweethearts. I repeated the promise I'd made to Laure, such a long time ago: we would go to Mananava.

How could the others have been our friends, our peers? No one in Forest Side knew of Mananava.

We'd learned to be indifferent to the poverty we lived in during those years. Too poor to have new clothing, we didn't know anyone, never went to birthday parties or festivities. Laure and I even took a certain pleasure in that solitude. To provide for us, my father had taken a job as an accountant in one of Uncle Ludovic's offices on Rempart Street in Port Louis, and Laure was indignant about the fact that the same man who was most responsible for our downfall and for our having to leave Boucan was feeding us, as if out of charity.

But we suffered less from poverty than from exile. I remember those dark afternoons in the wood-framed house at Forest Side, the damp chill of the nights, the sound of water trickling over the sheet-metal roof. There, the sea no longer existed for us. We barely caught a glimpse of it at times, when we accompanied our father to Port Louis on the train, or when we went with Mam over around Champ de Mars. Off in the distance, it was an expanse of steely sheen in the sunlight between the roofs of the docks and the crowns of the trees.

But we didn't go near it. Laure and I would turn away, preferring to burn our eyes gazing at the barren flanks of Signal Mountain.

Back in those days Mam used to talk about Europe, about France. Even though she didn't have any family over there, she talked about Paris as if it were a place of refuge. We would take the British-India Steam Navigation Company's liner coming from Calcutta and go to Marseilles. First we'd go across the ocean to the Suez Canal, and Laure and I enumerated all the cities we would be able to see, Monbaz, Aden, Alexandria, Athens, Genoa. Next we'd take the train to Paris where one of our uncles lived, one of my father's brothers, who never wrote and whom we knew by the name of Uncle Pierre, an unmarried musician, who, according to my father, had a nasty temperament but was very generous. He's the one who sent money for our education and who came to Mam's rescue after my father's death. That's what Mam had decided, we'd go live with him — at least at first — until we found lodgings. She even communicated the fever of that journey to my father and he would dream out loud about the plans. As for myself, I couldn't forget the Corsair or his hidden gold. Would there be room for a corsair over there in Paris?

So we were to reside in that mysterious city, where there were so many beautiful things and so many dangers as well. Laure had read the interminable serial novel *The Mysteries of Paris*, which related tales of bandits, child abductors, murderers. But the dangers were palliated in her eyes when she saw engravings in journals representing the Champ de Mars (the real one), the Vendôme Column, the wide boulevards, the fashions. During the long Saturday evenings we'd talk about the journey, listening to the rain drumming on the sheet-metal roof, and the sound of the gunnies' carts rolling through the mud in the lane. Laure spoke of the places we would visit, of the circus, especially, for she'd seen drawings in my father's journals of a huge circus tent under which tigers, lions, elephants parade, ridden by young girls wearing bayadère dresses. Mam would steer us back to more serious things: we would both study, law for me, music for Laure, we would go to the museums, maybe visit the large chateaus. We'd remain silent for long moments, having trouble imagining it all.

But best of all, for Laure and me, was when we'd talk about the evidently distant day when we would come back home to Mauritius like aged adventurers trying to find their way back to the land of their childhood. We would arrive one day, maybe on the same liner that we'd sailed away on, and we'd walk through the town's streets not recognizing a single thing. We'd go to a hotel somewhere in Port Louis, maybe down on the wharf, the New Oriental or else the Garden Hotel in Comedy Street. Or still yet we'd take the train, first class, and go to the Family Hotel in Curepipe, and no one would guess who we were. I'd write our names in the register:

Mister, Miss L'Étang
tourists.

And we would ride out through the cane fields on horseback, going west as far as Quinze Cantons, and even farther, and we would ride down the path that winds between the peaks of Trois Mamelles, then down the road to Magenta and it would be evening when we'd reach Boucan, and there nothing would have changed. Our house would still be there, leaning a bit to one side after the passage of the hurricane, with its roof painted the colour of the sky, and the vines would have overrun the veranda. The garden would be wilder, and near the ravine there would still be the tall chalta tree of good and

97

evil where the birds gather before nightfall. We'd even go out to the edge of the forest, facing the entrance to Mananava, where night always begins and, up in the sky, as white as sea spray, there would be the two tropicbirds that would wheel slowly above us, letting out their strange rattling calls, and then disappear into the shadows.

There would be the sea, the smell of the sea borne along on the wind, the sound of the sea and, shuddering, we would listen to its forgotten voice, saying: don't leave again, don't leave again . . .

———————

But the voyage to Europe never took place, because one evening in the month of November, just before the turn of the century, our father died, struck down by a heart attack. The news reached the College in the night, carried by an Indian messenger. They came to wake me in the dormitory and led me to the Principal's office, uncustomarily lit up at that hour. I was unceremoniously informed of what had happened, yet I felt nothing but an immense emptiness. First thing in the morning I was driven to Forest Side in a carriage and when I arrived, instead of the crowd I was dreading, I saw only Laure and our aunt Adelaide, and Mam, pale and prostrate on a chair in front of the bed where my father lay, fully dressed. For me, as well as for Laure, there was something incomprehensible and disastrous about this sudden death, coming after the ruin of the house we'd been born in, something that seemed like a punishment from heaven. Mam never quite got over it.

The first consequence of my father's death was even greater impoverishment, especially for Mam. Europe was now completely out of the question. We were prisoners on our island, with no hope of escaping. I began to hate that cold, rainy town, the roads crowded with the poor, the carts endlessly carrying loads of cane to the sugar train, and even the things I'd so loved in the past, those immense expanses of cane with the waves of wind running over them. Would I be forced to work one day as a gunny, load the sheaves of cane on to the ox carts, and then pitch them into the mouth of the mill every day of my life, with no hope, no freedom? That wasn't what came to be, but what did was perhaps even worse. My grant for the College having expired, I had to go to work, and it was in the post my father had occupied in the dreary offices of W. W. West, the export and insurance company controlled by my powerful uncle Ludovic.

So then I felt as if I were breaking the ties that bound me to Laure and to Mam, but more than anything else as if Boucan and Mananava were disappearing for ever.

Rempart Street was another world. I arrived every morning with the swarm of errand boys and Chinese and Indian merchants coming to do business. The important people, businessmen, lawyers, wearing dark suits, carrying their hats and canes came streaming from the first-class coaches. I was caught up in the flow of that crowd and swept over to the door of the offices of W. W. West, where the registers and piles of bills were awaiting me in the sultry half-light. I remained there until five o'clock in the evening, with a half-hour lunch break at noon. My colleagues went to eat at a Chinese place in Rue Royale, but to save money – and also because of my fondness for solitude – I would simply nibble on a few hot pepper cakes in front of the Chinese store, and sometimes, as a special treat, an orange from South Africa that I'd cut into sections, sitting on a low wall in the shade of a tree and watching the Indian peasants coming back from the market.

It was a routine life, with no surprises. And I often felt as if none of it was real, as if I was having a waking dream — all of it — the train, the figures in the registers, the smell of dust in the offices, the voices of the W. W. West employees who spoke in English and those Indian women walking slowly along the immense streets in the sunshine on their way back from the market carrying empty baskets on their heads.

But there were the boats. I would go down to the port to see them whenever I could, whenever I had an hour before the W. W. West offices opened, or after five o'clock, when Rempart Street was empty. On holidays, when other young men went strolling down the walkways of Champ de Mars with their fiancées on their arms, I preferred to hang around the wharves, surrounded by ropes and fishing nets, listening to the fishermen and watching the boats rocking on the heavy water, trying to follow the tracery of the riggings with my eyes. I was already dreaming of going away, but I had to make do with reading the names of the boats on the sterns. At times they were simply fishing barks bearing only a rudimentary drawing of a peacock, a rooster or a dolphin. I'd stare intently at the sailor's faces, old Indians, black men, turbaned Comorians, sitting in the shade of tall trees, barely moving, smoking their cigars.

Today I can still recall the names I used to read on the sterns of the ships. They're etched into my mind like the words of a song: *Gladys, Essalaam, Star of the Indian Sea, L'Amitié, Rose Belle, Kumuda, Rupanika, Tan Rouge, Rosalie, Poudre d'Or, Belle of the South.* To me they were the most beautiful names in the world, because they spoke of the sea, they told of the long waves out on the open seas, the coral reefs, the distant archipelagos, even the storms. When I read them I would suddenly be far from land, far from the city streets, and especially far from the dusty gloom of the offices and the registers filled with figures.

One day Laure came down to the wharves with me. We walked for a long time past the boats, past the indifferent looks of the seamen sitting in the shade of the trees. She's the one who brought up my secret dream first, saying, 'Will you be sailing away on a boat soon?' I laughed a little, surprised at her question, as if it were a joke. But she looked at me without laughing, her lovely dark eyes filled with sadness. 'Oh yes, I think you're quite capable of sailing away on any one of these ships, of going off any place, just like with Denis on the pirogue.' Since I didn't answer, she said, almost gaily, 'You know, I'd really like to do that too, just sail off to any old place on a ship, to India, to China, anywhere. But it's just so impossible! Do you remember the trip to France? I wouldn't want to go now,' said Laure. 'To India, to China, but not to France any more.' She stopped talking and we continued looking at the ships moored along the wharves, and I was happy, I knew why I was happy every time a boat raised its sails and sailed out towards the high seas.

That was the year I encountered Captain Bradmer and the *Zeta*. Now I wish I could remember every detail about that day, so I could relive it, because that was one of the most important days of my life.

It was a Sunday morning, I'd left the old house in Forest Side at the break of day and taken the train for Port Louis. I was wandering around as usual along the wharves among the fishermen, who were already coming in, their baskets filled with fish. The boats were still drenched from the high seas, weary, their sails hanging down on the masts to dry in the sun. I loved being there when they returned, hearing the creaking of the hulls, breathing in the smell of the sea that was still upon them. Then, amid the fishing barks, the luggers and the throng of pirogues with sails, I saw it: it was already an old boat, with the slender, graceful form of a schooner, two masts tilting slightly backwards and two lovely gaff sails snapping in the wind. On the long black hull, curving upward at the bow, I read its strange name in white letters: ZETA.

Surrounded by the other fishing boats, it looked like a thoroughbred prepared for a race, with its large, very white sails and its rigging sweeping from the topsail to the bowsprit. I stood still for a long time, admiring it. Where had it come from? Would it sail away again on some journey from which I imagined there would be no return? A sailor was standing on the deck, a black Comorian. I ventured to ask him where he'd come from and he responded, 'Agalega'. When I asked him to whom the ship belonged, he said a name that I misunderstood: 'Captain Bras-de-Mer', meaning 'arm of the sea' in French. Perhaps it was that name, evoking the days of pirates, that first sparked my imagination, drew me to that boat. Who was this 'Bras-de-Mer'? How might one go about meeting him? Those were the questions I would have liked to ask the sailor, but the Comorian had turned his back on me and sat down in a wooden armchair, at the back of the boat in the shade of the sails.

I returned several times that day to look at the schooner moored at the wharf, feeling anxious at the thought it might sail away on the evening tide. The Comorian sailor was still sitting in the wooden armchair shaded by the sail as it fluttered in the wind. Around three o'clock in the afternoon the tide began to rise and the sailor brailed up the sail to the yard. Then he carefully battened down the hatches with padlocks and made his way to the wharf. When he saw me standing in front of the boat again, he said, 'Captain Bras-de-Mer will be coming now.'

That afternoon spent waiting for him seemed terribly long. For quite some time I sat under the trees of the Intendance to keep out of the burning sun. As the day drew on, the activities of the seamen abated and soon there was no one about save a few beggars sleeping in the shade of the trees or gleaning leftovers from the market. With the rising tide the wind was blowing in from the sea, and off in the distance, between the masts, I could see the bright line of the horizon.

Near dusk I went back to stand in front of the *Zeta*. It was barely moving at the end of its mooring lines in the swell of the waves. Resting against the deck in the guise of a gangplank, a single board was squeaking in time to its sway.

In the golden light of evening in that deserted port where nothing was stirring but a few seagulls, with the tenuous sound of the wind whistling in the rigging and maybe also because of the long wait in the sun — just like in the old days when I used to go running through the fields — the ship took on something of a magical aura with its tall, tilted masts, its yards caught up in the network of lines, the sharp point of the bowsprit like a beak. On the shiny deck the empty wooden armchair placed in front of the helm heightened the feeling of otherworldliness. It wasn't a ship's chair, but rather an office chair made of turned wood, like the ones I saw every day at W. W. West! And there it was at the stern of the ship, weathered from sea spray, bearing the marks of travels out across the ocean!

I couldn't resist the temptation. In one leap I was up the board that served as a gangplank and found myself on the deck of the *Zeta*. I walked over to the armchair and sat down to wait in front of the large wooden wheel at the helm. I was so absorbed in the magic of the ship in that lonely harbour and the golden light of the setting sun that I didn't even hear the captain arrive. He walked straight up and looked at me inquisitively, without getting angry, and said with a strange look on his face, at once mocking and serious, 'Well, young man? When shall we be getting under way?'

I remember perfectly well the manner in which he asked me that question and the red flush that spread over my face, because I didn't know what to say in reply.

How did I apologize? Above all, I remember the impression the captain made on me at the time, his massive body, his clothing — as worn as his ship — covered with indelible stains like scars, his very ruddy skin, his stern, serious, Englishman's face that his black shiny eyes, the gleam of youthful mockery in his gaze, belied. He's the one who spoke first and I knew that 'Bras-de-Mer' was in truth Captain Bradmer, an officer in the Royal Navy who was nearing the end of his solitary adventures.

I think I knew immediately: I would sail on the *Zeta*, it would be my *Argo*, the vessel that would carry me over the sea to the place I had dreamt of, to Rodrigues, for my endless treasure hunt.

Heading for Rodrigues, 1910

———————

I open my eyes and see the sea. It's not the emerald sea that I used to see in the lagoons or the black water off the estuary of the Tamarin River. It's the sea as I have never seen it before, free, wild, of a dizzying blue, the sea that slowly lifts the hull of the ship, wave after wave, speckled with foam, crazed with sparkles.

It must be late, the sun is already high in the sky. I was sleeping so soundly I didn't even hear the ship casting off, going through the pass when the tide came in.

Yesterday evening I walked around the wharves late into the night, breathing in the smell of oil, of saffron, the smell of rotten fruit that hovers over the marketplace. I could hear the voices of seamen in the boats, the exclamations of dice-players, I could also smell the odour of 'arak', of tobacco. I went aboard the ship, lay down on the deck to avoid the suffocating hold, the dusty sacks of rice. I looked up at the sky through the mast rigging, my head resting on my trunk. I fought off sleep until after midnight, looking at the starless sky, listening to the voices, the creaking of the gangplank on the wharf and, in the distance, guitar music. I didn't want to think about anyone. Laure was the only one who knew about my departure, but she didn't say anything to Mam. She didn't shed a tear, on the contrary, there was an uncustomary gleam in her eyes. 'We'll see each other soon,' I said. 'Over there, in Rodrigues we'll be able to start a new life, we'll have a big house, with horses, with trees.' Was she able to believe me?

She didn't want me to reassure her. You're leaving, going away, maybe for ever. You have to go to the very end of your quest, the very end of the world. That is what she wanted to tell me as she stood there, looking at me, but I wasn't able to understand. Now I'm writing this for her, to tell her what that night was like, lying on the deck of the *Zeta*, surrounded by the lines, listening to the voices of seamen, and the guitar, tirelessly playing the same Creole song. At one point the voice grew louder, perhaps the wind rose or maybe the singer turned in my direction, in the dark harbour.

Vale, vale, prête mo to fizi	Bway, bway, len mi yuh rifle
Avla l'oiseau prêt envolé	Si waah bud deh, ready fi fly
Si mo gagne bonher touyé l'oiseau	If mi lucky fi kill di bud
Mo gagne l'arzent pou mo voyaze,	Mi wi mek di money fi my trip,
En allant, en arrivant!	Fi go and fi cum back!

I fell asleep listening to the words of the song.

And when the tide came in the *Zeta* silently set its sails and slipped out over the dark water, towards the forts of the pass, unbeknownst to me. I lay fast asleep on the deck next to Captain Bradmer, head resting on my trunk.

When I wake up and look around, dazzled by the sunlight, land no longer exists. I go all the way to the back of the ship, lean on the rail. I gaze at the sea as intently as I can, the long waves slipping under the hull, the wake like a sparkling path. I've been waiting for this moment for such a long time! My heart is pounding very hard, my eyes fill with tears.

The *Zeta* tilts slightly as the waves pass, then rights itself again. As far out as I can see, that is all there is: the sea, the deep valleys between the waves, the foam on their crests. I listen to the sound of the water hugging the hull of the ship, the stem ripping through a wave. The wind especially, billowing in the sails and making the stays moan. I'm quite familiar with that sound, it's just like the sound the wind used to make in the branches of the tall trees in Boucan, the sound of the rising tide that makes its way in as far as the cane fields. But it's the first time I've ever heard it like this, just that sound alone, with no obstacles, free from one end of the world to the other.

The sails are beautiful, puffed out in the wind. The *Zeta* is sailing close-hauled and the white canvas is rippling from top to bottom, making snapping sounds. Up front there are the three jibs, as finely tapered as the wings of seabirds, which seem to be guiding the ship out towards the horizon. Sometimes, after a sudden shift in the west wind, a fold in the canvas will suddenly tauten again with a deafening clap that thunders like a cannon blast. I feel dizzy from all the sounds of the sea, blinded by the light. Above all there's the blue hue of the sea, that deep, dark, powerful, sparkling blue. The wind is whirling around, inebriating me, and there's the salty taste of the sea spray when a wave crashes over the stem.

All the men are up on deck. They are sailors from India, the Comoros, I'm the only passenger on board. We're all feeling the giddiness of the first day at sea. Even Bradmer must be feeling it. He's standing on deck near the man at the helm, legs spread to counter the rolling of the ship. He hasn't budged in hours, hasn't taken his eyes off the sea. No matter how much I want to, I don't dare ask him any questions. I have to wait. Impossible to do anything but simply gaze out at the sea and listen to the sound of the wind, and nothing in this world could make me want to go down into the hold. The sun is burning down on the deck, on the dark seawater.

I go a little farther off to sit down on the deck at the end of the boom that is vibrating. The waves lift the prow of the ship, then let it fall heavily back down. It's an endless route, widening out towards the horizon behind us. There isn't a sign of land anywhere. There's nothing but the deep, light-filled water and the sky in which the clouds — thin wisps born of the horizon — seem to stand still.

Where are we going? That's what I want to ask Bradmer. Yesterday he didn't say a word, remained silent as if he were thinking it over or as if he didn't want to say. To Mahé maybe or Agalega, it all depends on the wind, so the helmsman tells me — he's an old man with brick-coloured skin, whose pale eyes gaze at you unblinkingly. The wind is east-south-east right now, steady, not gusting, and we're heading north. The sun is at the stern of the ship, the sails seem to be filled with its light.

The giddiness of the early morning doesn't subside. The black sailors and Indians remain standing on the deck, near the mizzen mast, hanging on the ropes. Now Bradmer has sat down in his wooden armchair, behind the helmsman, and is still looking straight out towards the horizon, as if he really were expecting something to appear. There's nothing but the waves lunging towards us like a herd of animals, heads high, crests sparkling, then smashing into the hull of the ship and slipping under it. When I turn I can see them fleeing with hardly a mark from the keel blade, out to the other end of the world.

My thoughts are knocking about in my head to the rhythm of the waves. I think I've changed, I'll never be the same again. The sea is already separating me from Mam and Laure, from Forest Side, from everything I used to be.

What day is it? It seems as if I've always lived here, at the stern of the *Zeta*, looking out over the rail at the vast sea, listening to it respiring. It seems as if everything I've been through since the day we were evicted from Boucan – at Forest Side, at the Royal College, then in the W. W. West offices – were nothing but a dream, and all I needed to do was open my eyes and look upon the sea for it all to vanish.

In the sound of the sea and the wind I can hear a voice deep within me, endlessly repeating: The sea! The sea! And that voice covers over all other words, all thoughts. Sometimes the wind that is driving us out towards the horizon comes in whirling gusts, making the boat rock. I can hear the clap of the sails, the whistle of the stays. Those sounds too are words bearing me away, distancing me from the land where I've lived all of this time. Where is it now? It's become very small, like a lost raft, while the *Zeta* is being pushed along in the wind and the light. It's adrift somewhere, out on the other side of the horizon, a thin trickle of mud lost in the blue immensity.

I'm so busy looking at the sea and the sky, at every dark hollow between the waves and the lips of the wake opening wider, I'm listening so intently to the sound of the water on the stem, the sound of the wind, that I haven't noticed the crewmen are eating. Bradmer walks over to me. He looks at me with that mocking glimmer in his little black eyes again.

'Well, sir? Has seasickness gotten the better of your appetite?'

I stand up immediately to show him I'm not feeling ill.

'No, sir.'

'So come and eat, then.' It's almost an order.

We go down the ladder into the hold below. In the bottom of the boat the heat is suffocating and the air is thick with the smells of cooking and merchandise. Despite the open hatches, it is dark. The inside of the boat is one large hold, the centre of which is filled with crates and bales of merchandise, and the back with mattresses set down on the bare floor where the crew sleeps. Under the front hatch the Chinese cook is busy distributing rations of curried rice that he's cooked on an old spirit stove, and pouring tea from a large pewter teapot.

Bradmer squats, Indian-style, his back propped against a rib, and I do likewise. Here in the bottom of the hold the pitching of the boat is dreadful. The cook gives us enamelled plates filled with rice, and two tin mugs of steaming tea.

We eat without speaking. In the half-light I can make out the Indian sailors also squatting as they drink their tea. Bradmer eats rapidly, using the dented spoon as one would a chopstick, pushing the rice into his mouth. The rice is greasy, smothered in fish sauce, but the curry is so strong you can hardly taste anything. The tea burns my lips and throat, but it's somewhat soothing after the spicy rice.

When Bradmer is finished, he stands and sets the plate and the tin mug on the floor next to the Chinese man. Just as he starts up the ladder towards the deck, he rummages about in his jacket pocket and draws out two odd-looking cigarettes made with a still green leaf of tobacco rolled up on itself. I take one of the cigarettes and light it with the captain's tinderbox. We climb up the ladder one after the other, and we're up on the deck again in the whipping wind.

After having been down in the hold for a few minutes I'm so dazzled by the light that my eyes fill with tears. Almost groping my way, hunched over the boom, I return to my place at the stern, sit down next to my trunk. As for Bradmer, he's gone back to his armchair screwed to the deck and is gazing out in the distance, not speaking to the helmsman, as he smokes his cigarette.

The smell of the tobacco is acrid and sweet, it makes me nauseous. To me it doesn't fit in with the pure blue of the sea and the sky, with the sound of the wind. I crush out the cigarette on the deck, but I can't bring myself to throw it into the sea. I can't allow this blemish, this foreign body to float on such beautiful, smooth, living water.

The *Zeta* is not a blemish. It has travelled so far over this sea and other seas as well, out beyond Madagascar, all the way out to the Seychelles or southward as far as Saint Paul. The ocean has purified it, made it resemble the great seabirds that glide along on the wind.

The sun is moving slowly down in the sky, it's lighting the other side of the sails now. I can see the shadow of the sails growing longer by the hour. By the end of the afternoon the wind has lost its breath. There's a light breeze that is barely pressing on the mainsails, smoothing over and rounding out the waves, making the surface of the water quiver like skin. Most of the sailors have gone down into the hold, they're drinking tea and talking. Some are sleeping on the mattresses placed directly on the floor, readying themselves for the night watch.

Captain Bradmer has remained in his armchair behind the helmsman. They're hardly speaking, just a few indistinct words. Tirelessly, they smoke those green tobacco cigarettes whose smell wafts over in my direction once in a while, when the wind swirls. I can feel my eyes stinging, maybe I have a fever? The skin on my face, my neck, my arms, my back is burning. The heat of the sun for so many hours has put its stamp on my body. All day long the sun beat down on the sails, on the deck, on the sea too, without my paying much heed. It fired sparkles on the crests of the waves, formed rainbows in the sea spray.

Now the light is coming from the sea, from the very depth of its hue. The sky is clear, almost colourless, and I gaze out at the blue expanse of sea and the blank sky until my head swims.

This is what I've always dreamt of. It's as if my life stopped long ago, sitting in the front of the pirogue that was drifting on the lagoon of the Morne, while Denis was inspecting the sea bottoms in search of a fish to spear. All of that, which I thought had vanished, been forgotten – the sound, the gaze of the sea with its fascinating depths – is now seething inside me, coming back as the *Zeta* clips along.

Slowly the sun is going down towards the horizon, lighting up the crests of the waves, opening up valleys of shadow. As the light declines and takes on a golden tint, the movement of the sea slows. The wind isn't gusting any more. The sails fall slack, hang loose between the yards. The heat grows suddenly oppressive, humid. All the men are up on deck, in the front part of the ship, or else sitting around the hatches. They're smoking, some are lying down bare-chested on the deck, eyes half-closed, daydreaming, perhaps under the influence of ganja. The air is calm now, the sea is barely lapping its slow waves against the hull of the ship. It has taken on a violet tinge that no longer emits any light. I can hear the voices, the laughter of the sailors very clearly, they're playing dice up in the front of the ship, and the monotone words of the black helmsman talking to Captain Bradmer without looking at him.

It's all very strange, like an uninterrupted dream from long ago, born of the shimmering sea when the pirogue had gone slipping along near the Morne, under the white void of the sky. I think about the place I'm going and my heart beats faster. The sea is a smooth route for discovering mysteries, discovering the unknown. There is gold in the light all around me, hidden under the mirror of the sea. I think about what is awaiting me at the other end of this journey, as if it were a land I'd already been to long ago and that I'd now lost. The ship is sliding over the mirror of memory. But will I be able to understand once I reach there? Here, on the deck of the *Zeta*, moving slowly along in the languid, dusk light, the thought of the future makes me dizzy. I close my eyes to shut out the glare of the sky, the unbroken wall of the sea.

THE FOLLOWING DAY ON BOARD

In spite of my loathing for it, I have to spend the night down in the hold. Captain Bradmer doesn't want anyone up on deck during the night. Lying on the bare floor (I don't much like the look of the sailors' mattresses), my head resting on my rolled-up blanket, I keep a firm grip on the handle of my trunk, because of the ship's constant rolling. Captain Bradmer sleeps in a sort of alcove built into the structure of the hull between two huge, rough-hewn, teak stanchions that support the deck. He even strung up a precarious curtain enabling him to close himself off, but it must stifle him, because at the break of dawn I see he's drawn the curtain away from his face.

Exhausting night, due mainly to the ship's rolling, but also to the promiscuous conditions. Men snoring, coughing, talking to one another, endlessly going back and forth from the hold to the hatches to get a breath of fresh air or to urinate overboard on the leeward side. Most of them are foreigners, Comorians, Somalians, who speak a guttural language, or Indians from the Malabar Coast with dark skin, with sad eyes. The fact that I haven't got any sleep tonight is also due to these men. In the oppressive darkness of the hold, which the flickering flame of the night light is barely able to pierce, with the hull groaning as it is tossed about in the waves, I feel an absurd and uncontrollable fear creeping over me. Among those men, perhaps there are mutineers, notorious pirates from East Africa, who were mentioned so often in the journals Laure and I used to read. Perhaps they plan on killing Captain Bradmer, myself, and the members of the crew who are not part of the plot, in order to take over the ship. Perhaps they believe I'm carrying money and precious objects in this old trunk, where I keep my father's papers locked up. Evidently I should have opened it in front of them, so they might see it holds nothing but old papers, maps, clothing and my theodolite. But then wouldn't they have thought there was a false bottom filled with gold pieces? As the ship rocks slowly I can feel the warm metal of the trunk against my shoulder and I keep my eyes open to watch over the dark hold. How different from the first night spent on the deck of the *Zeta*, when the ship had rigged out while I was sleeping and I'd awoken with a start in the morning, dazzled by the immense sea.

Where are we going? Seeing that we've been heading due north since our departure, there's no doubt now that we're heading for Agalega. To the inhabitants of that remote island Captain Bradmer is carrying the greater part of his disparate cargo: bales of cloth, spools of wire, barrels of oil, crates of soap, bags of rice and flour, beans, lentils and all sorts of pots and enamelled dishes wrapped in fishnets. It will all be sold to the Chinese shopkeepers, who supply the fishermen and the farmers.

The presence of the merchandise and its smell reassures me. Is this the type of cargo for pirates? The *Zeta* is a floating grocery store and the idea of a mutiny suddenly seems ludicrous.

But I'm still not able to sleep. Now the men have fallen quiet, but the insects have started in. I can hear the huge cockroaches scurrying around, sometimes flying across the hold, whirring. Between their scurries and their flights I can hear the high-pitched hum of mosquitoes near my ears. I'm watching out for them too, covering my arms and face with my shirt.

Unable to sleep, I walk over to the ladder and stick my head out of the open hatch. Outside it's a beautiful night. The wind has started blowing again, pulling on the sails that are about three-quarters out. It's a cold wind coming from the south that's driving the ship. After the oppressive heat of the hold the wind makes me shiver, but it feels pleasant. I'm going to break Captain Bradmer's rules. Armed with my horse blanket, a souvenir from the Boucan days, I'm up on the deck, walking towards the prow. In the back of the ship are the black helmsman and two sailors who are smoking ganja and keeping him company. I sit down all the way up at the front of the prow, under the wings of the jibs, and gaze out at the sea and sky. There is no moon and yet with my pupils dilated I can make out each wave, the night-coloured water, the patches of sea foam. The starlight is illuminating the sea. Never have I seen the stars like this. Even in the old days, in the garden at Boucan, when we'd walk with our father down the 'alley of stars', it wasn't this beautiful. On land the sky is eaten up by the trees, the hills, tarnished by that intangible mist rising like a breath from the streams, the grassy fields, the mouths of wells. The sky is distant, you see it as if through a window. But here, in the middle of the sea, the night is boundless.

There's nothing between me and the sky. I lie down on the deck, my head resting against the closed hatch, and look at the stars as intently as I can, as if I were seeing them for the first time. The sky rocks between the two masts, the constellations turn, stop for a moment, then fall back again. I don't recognize them yet. Here the stars are so bright – even the faintest ones – they seem new to me. There's Orion on the port side and over in the east – perhaps Scorpius, where Antarus is gleaming. The ones I can see very clearly at the stern of the ship when I turn around, so close to the horizon that I simply need to glance down in order to follow their slow swaying, are the stars of the Southern Cross. I recall my father's voice as he led us across the dark garden and asked us to pick it out, faint and fleeting above the line of hills.

I look at that cross of stars and feel as though I'm even farther away, because it truly belongs to the Boucan sky. I can't take my eyes from it, for fear of losing it for ever.

That's how I drift off to sleep, just before dawn, eyes fixed on the Southern Cross. Rolled up in the blanket, gusts of wind buffeting my face and hair, listening to the wind snapping in the jibs and the whishing sound of the sea against the stem.

ANOTHER DAY AT SEA

Up at the crack of dawn and from my post at the stern beside the black helmsman, I sit gazing at the sea, almost without moving. The helmsman is a Comorian who has an extremely dark face like an Abyssinian, but with luminous green eyes. He's the only one who really talks to Captain Bradmer, and my status as a paying passenger allows me the privilege of being able to sit near him and listen to him talk. He speaks slowly, choosing his words, in very pure French with barely any hint of a Creole accent. He says he was once enrolled in a Moroni Seminary and was to become a priest. One day he gave it all up, for no real reason, to become a seafarer. He's been sailing for thirty years now and he knows every port from Madagascar to the African coast, from Zanzibar to Chagos. He talks about the islands, the Seychelles, Rodrigues, and also more remote ones, Juan de Nova, Farquhar, Aldabra. The one he loves most is Saint Brandon, which belongs to the sea turtles and seabirds alone. Yesterday, tearing myself away from the spectacle of the waves rushing forwards and then forming again in the same place, I took a seat on the deck beside the helmsman and listened to him talking to

Captain Bradmer. I should say talking in front of Bradmer, for the captain — as any respectable Englishman — can remain sitting still for hours in his clerk's chair, smoking those little green cigarettes, while the helmsman talks, not responding save for a vague grunt of assent, a sort of 'ahem' that serves only as a reminder that he is still there. Strange stories of the sea that the helmsman tells in his slow melodic voice, his green gaze scanning the horizon. Stories of ports, of storms, of fabulous catches, of women, stories that are aimless and endless, like his life.

I like to hear him talk about Saint Brandon, because he speaks of it as if it were paradise. It is his favourite place, the one he always returns to in his thoughts, in his dreams. He's known a lot of islands, a lot of ports, but that is the place the sea routes always bring him back to. 'One day, I'll go there to die. Over there the water is as blue and clear as the purest of springs. In the lagoon it's transparent, so transparent that you slip over it in your pirogue, without seeing it, as if you were flying over the seabed. Around the lagoon there are quite a few islands, ten, I think, but I don't know their names. When I went to Saint Brandon I was seventeen years old, I was still a child, I'd just run away from the seminary. Back then I thought I'd reached paradise and now I still believe that is where earthly paradise once was, when mankind knew no sin. I named the islands as I fancied: there was Horseshoe Island and another the Claw, another the King, I don't know why. I'd come on a fishing boat from Moroni. The men had gone there to kill, to fish, like predatory animals. In the lagoon there were all the fish in creation, they swam slowly, fearlessly around our pirogue. And sea turtles that came up to see us as if there were no death on Earth. Seabirds flew about us by the thousands . . . They alighted on the deck of the boat, on the yards, to look at us, because I don't think

they'd ever seen humans before . . . Then we began killing them.'
The helmsman is talking, his green eyes are filled with light, his
face is straining towards the sea as if he could still see it all. I can't
keep from following his eyes, out beyond the horizon, all the way to
the atoll where everything is as new as it was in the very first days
of the world. Captain Bradmer puffs on his cigarette, says 'ahem-
hem', like someone who won't be easily taken in. Behind us two
black sailors, one of whom is from Rodrigues, are listening without
really understanding. The helmsman speaks of the lagoon that he
will never see again, except on the day of his death. He speaks of
the islands where the fishermen build huts of coral, long enough to
stock up on tortoises and fish. He speaks of the storm that comes
every summer, so furious that the sea covers the islands, sweeps
away all traces of life on land. Each time the sea erases everything
and that is why the islands are always new. But the water in the
lagoon remains lovely, clear, in that place where the most beautiful
fish in the world and the community of tortoises live.

The voice of the helmsman is gentle when he speaks of Saint
Brandon. I feel as if I am on this ship sailing along in the middle of
the sea just to be listening to him.

The sea has prepared this secret for me, this treasure. I take in
this sparkling light, I hunger for the colour of the depths, for this
sky, this boundless horizon, these endless days and nights. I must
learn more, take in more. The helmsman is speaking again, about
Table Bay off Cape Town, Antonia Bay, the Arab feluccas that prowl
along the African coast, the pirates from Socotra or Aden. What I
love is the sound of his melodious voice, his black face in which
his eyes shine, his tall figure standing at the wheel as he steers our
ship out towards the unknown, and it all melts in with the sound of
the wind in the sails, with the sea spray where a rainbow shimmers

every time the stem breaks through a wave. Every afternoon when the light begins to wane, I'm at the stern of the ship, watching the sparkling wake. It's the time of day I prefer, when everything is peaceful and the deck is deserted, except for the helmsman and a sailor keeping an eye on the sea. Then I think of land, of Mam and Laure so far away in their solitude in Forest Side. I can see Laure's dark look when I spoke to her of the treasure, of jewels and precious stones hidden by the Mysterious Corsair. Was she really listening to me? Her face was smooth and closed, and deep in her eyes shone a strange flame I didn't understand. That flame is what I want to see now in the infinite gaze of the sea. I need Laure, I want to think of her every day, because I know that without her I'll never be able to find what I'm looking for. She didn't say anything when we parted, she seemed neither sad nor happy. But when she looked at me on the platform of the train station in Curepipe I saw that flame in her eyes again. Then she turned around, she left before the train began to move away, I saw her walking through the crowd, down the road to Forest Side, where Mam — who knew nothing about it yet — was waiting for her.

That's why I want to remember every minute of my life, for Laure. I'm on this boat, making its way farther and farther out to sea for her. I have to defeat the destiny that drove us from our home, that destroyed us all, that made my father die. I feel as if something snapped when I left on the *Zeta*, as if I broke a circle. So when I go back everything will be changed, new.

That's what I'm thinking about and the dizzying light is filling me. The sun is almost touching the horizon, but at sea the night doesn't give rise to anxiety. On the contrary, there is a gentleness that settles over this land in which we are the only living creatures on the face of the water. The sky turns golden and is tinted with crimson.

The sea, which is so dark under the zenith sun, is now smooth and light like a purple mist mingling with the clouds on the horizon and veiling the sun.

I listen to the helmsman's lilting voice, talking perhaps to himself, standing in front of the wheel. At his side, Captain Bradmer's armchair is empty, because this is the time he retires to his alcove to sleep or write. In the horizontal light of the setting sun the tall form of the helmsman stands out against the bright sails, seeming unreal, as does the singing sound of his words filling my ears but which I don't understand. Night is falling and I think of the silhouette of Palinurus as Aeneas must have seen it, or even that of Typhus on the *Argo*, when he seeks to reassure his fellow travellers at nightfall. I still recall his words: '*Titan sank into the waters without a trace, confirming a good omen. Thus in the night the wind presses yet stronger upon the sails and sea: during those silent hours the vessel flies swifter. My eyes no longer follow the course of the stars leaving the sky and plunging into the sea, such as Orion that is now sinking or Perseus that is throwing the angry waves into uproar. My guide is the serpent enlacing seven stars in its coils that always hovers and never hides.*' I recite out loud the verses of Valerius Flaccus that I used to read in my father's library and for just a moment longer I can still believe I'm aboard the *Argo*.

Later, in the hush of twilight, the crew come up on deck. They are bare-chested in the warm breeze, they're smoking, talking or gazing out to sea, as I am.

Since the very first day I've been impatient to reach Rodrigues, where my journey will come to an end, and yet now I want this moment to go on for ever, for the vessel *Zeta*, like the *Argo*, to continue slipping endlessly over the buoyant sea, so close to the sky, its sail incandescent with sun like a flame against the already dark horizon.

YET ANOTHER NIGHT AT SEA

Having gone to sleep in my place in the hold, against my trunk, I'm awakened by the oppressive heat and the frantic activity of the cockroaches and rats. The roaches are whirring about in the thick air of the hold and the darkness makes their flight even more unsettling. You have to sleep with a handkerchief or a flap of shirt over your face if you don't want to have one of those monsters fall on your face. The rats are more circumspect, but more dangerous. The other evening a man was bitten on the hand by one of the rodents he'd disturbed while it was searching for food. The wound became infected in spite of the rags soaked in arak that Captain Bradmer used to clean it and I can now hear the man lying on his mattress, delirious with fever. The fleas and lice don't leave you any respite either. Every morning we scratch at the innumerable bites received during the night. The first night I spent in the hold I also underwent the assaults of battalions of bedbugs and that's why I declined the mattress reserved for me. I pushed it into the back of the hold and I sleep on the bare floor, rolled up in an old horse blanket, which has the advantage of allowing me to suffer less from the heat and sparing me the smell of sweat and brine that is ingrained in the bedding.

I'm not the only one who suffers from the all-pervasive heat in the hold. The men wake up one after the other, talk to one another, pick up their interminable game of dice where they had left off. What could they be playing for? Captain Bradmer, to whom I put the question, shrugged his shoulders and simply answered, 'Their wives.' Despite the captain's orders, the sailors have lit a small oil lamp up in the front of the hold, a Clarke night light. The orange flame flickering with the rocking of the ship lights up fantastically the black faces shiny with sweat. From a distance I can see the whites of their eyes shining, their sparkling teeth. What are they doing sitting around that lamp? They aren't playing dice, they aren't singing. They're talking, one after the other in whispers, a long conversation punctuated with laughter. Once again fear of a conspiracy, a mutiny, begins to creep over me. And what if they really did decide to take over the *Zeta*, what if they threw Bradmer, the helmsman and me overboard? Who would ever know? Who would go after them in the remote islands, in the Mozambique canal or on the coasts of Eritrea? I lie very still, waiting with my head turned towards them, watching the trembling flame to which careless red cockroaches and mosquitoes fly too close and get singed.

So then, just as I did the other night, without a sound, I climb up the ladder to the hatch where the sea breeze is blowing. Wrapped in my blanket I walk barefoot over the deck, delighted to be out in the night feeling the cool sea spray.

The night is so lovely out on the sea, with the vessel gliding almost noiselessly over the backs of the waves as if it were at the very centre of the world. It makes you feel as if you are flying rather than sailing, as if the firm wind pressing against the sails has changed the vessel into an immense bird with outstretched wings.

Tonight, once again, I lie down on the deck all the way up at the bow of the ship, against the closed hatch, sheltered by the rail. I can hear the lines of the jibs humming near my head and the steady whoosh of the sea opening out. Laure would love this sea music, the mixture of the high-pitched sound and the waves echoing deeply against the bow.

I'm listening to it for her, so I might send it back to her, all the way back to that dark house in Forest Side where I know that she too is lying awake.

I think again of the look in her eyes, before she turned away and strode off towards the road that runs along the railway tracks. I can't forget the flame that blazed in her eyes just as we parted, that tempestuous and angry flame. At the time I was so surprised I didn't know what to do, then — without thinking — I got on the coach. Now, on the deck of the *Zeta*, heading for an untold fate, I recall that look and feel the wrench of that parting.

Yet I had to go, it was the only hope. I think of Boucan again, of everything that might be able to be saved, the house with the sky-coloured roof, the trees, the ravine and the sea breeze that disturbed the night, awakening the moaning of the maroon slaves in the shadows of Mananava, and the flight of the tropicbirds before dawn. I don't want to stop seeing all of that, even far across the seas, when the hiding places of the Corsair have unveiled their treasures to me.

The vessel slips over the waves, ethereal, airy, in the starlight. Where is the serpent with seven lights that Typhus mentioned to the crew of the Argo? Is that Eridanus rising in the east, facing the sun Sirius, or is it Draco stretching northwards, bearing on its brow the gem Etamin? No, suddenly I can see it clearly under the Pole Star, it's the side of the Chariot, slender and precise, floating eternally in its place.

We too are following its sign, lost amid the whorling stars. The sky is traversed with that infinite wind that is filling our sails.

Now I understand where I'm going, and it so stirs me that I have to sit up to calm my racing heart. I'm heading out into space, into the unknown, I'm gliding through the middle of the sky towards an unknown end.

I think again of the two tropicbirds that circled, making their rattling sound over the dark valley as they fled the storm. When I close my eyes I can see them as if they were just above the masts.

A little before sunrise I fall asleep, while the *Zeta* endlessly wends her way towards Agalega. Now all the men are asleep. The black helmsman alone is keeping watch, his unblinking eyes fixed straight ahead in the night. He never sleeps. Sometimes, in the early afternoon, when the sun is beating down on the deck, he goes into the hold to lie down and smoke without saying anything, eyes open in the half-light, staring at the blackened planks overhead.

A DAY STEERING FOR AGALEGA

How long have we been travelling? While I'm sorting through the contents of my trunk in the stifling duskiness of the hold, that question is wracking my mind with disquieting insistence. What difference does it make? Why should I want to know? But I make a great effort to remember the date of my departure, to try to calculate the number of days at sea. It's a very long time, innumerable days, and yet it also seems quite fleeting. It's but one interminable day that I began when I boarded the *Zeta*, a day that is like the sea, in which the sky changes at times, turns cloudy and grows dark, in which starlight replaces sunlight, but the wind never stops blowing or the waves rolling onwards or the horizon encircling the ship.

As the journey draws on Captain Bradmer is growing friendlier with me. This morning he taught me to plot our position with the sextant and the method for determining the longitude and latitude. Today we're located at 12°38 S and 54°30 E, and calculating our position provides me with the answer to my question concerning the time, since it means we're two days navigating time from the island, just a few minutes too far east due to the trade winds that threw us off course during the night. When he finishes taking the bearing, Captain Bradmer carefully puts away the sextant in his alcove. I show him my theodolite and he looks at it, intrigued. I think he even says, 'What in the devil will you use that for?' I answer elusively. I can't tell him my father brought it back when he was preparing to lay claim to the Mysterious Corsair's treasures! Coming back up on deck again, the captain returns to sit in his armchair behind the helmsman. Since I'm standing beside him, he offers me — for the second time — one of those horrid cigarettes that I don't dare refuse and that I allow to go out on its own in the wind.

He says, 'Are you familiar with the Queen of the Islands?' He asks me the question in English and I repeat, 'The Queen of the Islands?' 'Yes, sir, Agalega. That's what it's called, because it's the most salubrious and most fertile island in the Indian Ocean.' I think he's going to pursue this, but he falls silent. He simply settles back in his armchair and repeats, 'the Queen of the Islands . . .' with a dreamy look in his eye. The helmsman shrugs his shoulders. He says, 'It should rather be called the Island of Rats.' Then he begins telling us about how the English declared war on the rats, because of the epidemic that was spreading from island to island. 'There was a time when there were no rats on Agalega. It too was like a little paradise, like Saint Brandon, because rats are animals of the Devil, there weren't any in paradise. And one day a boat from Grand Terre came to the island, no one can recall its name, an old boat that no one had ever seen. It sank in front of the island and the crates of cargo were salvaged, but there were rats in the crates. When the crates were opened they spread out over the island, they reproduced and became so numerous that they appropriated everything. They ate all of Agalega's provisions, the corn, the eggs, the rice. There were so many of them that people couldn't sleep any more. The rats even gnawed at the coconuts in the trees, they even ate the seabirds' eggs. So first they tried cats, but the rats grouped together and killed the cats and ate them, of course. So they tried traps, but rats are crafty, they avoided the traps. So then the English had an idea, they had boatloads of dogs shipped in – fox terriers, that's what they're called – and they promised to give a rupee for each rat. The children climbed up the coconut trees and shook the palm leaves to make the rats fall down and the fox terriers killed them. I was told that the people of Agalega killed more than forty thousand rats every year and there are still rats there! Most of them are in the north of the island. Rats are very fond of Agalega coconuts, they spend their lives up in the trees. There you have it, that's why your Queen of the Islands, should rather be called the Island of Rats.'

Captain Bradmer laughs loudly. This might be the first time the helmsman has told that story. Then Bradmer starts smoking again in his clerk's armchair, eyes squinted against the noon sun. When the black helmsman goes to stretch out on his mattress in the hold, Bradmer motions towards the helm.

'Try your hand at it, Mister?'

He says 'Missa', after the Creole fashion. He doesn't need to repeat the question. Now I've got a tight grip on the worn handles of the large wheel. I can feel the heavy waves against the rudder, the wind pressing against the large sails. It's the first time I've navigated a ship.

At one point a strong gust makes the ship heel, sails filled out tight enough to split, and I listen to the hull cracking under the pressure as the horizon tips up in front of the bowsprit. The vessel remains like that for a long time, balancing on the crest of the wave and I can't breathe. Then all of a sudden, I instinctively turn the wheel to port, yielding to the wind. Slowly the ship rights itself in a cloud of spray.

The sailors on deck shout, 'Whoa!'

But Captain Bradmer remains seated without saying a word, squint-eyed, the eternal green cigarette at the corner of his mouth.

That man would be capable of going down with his ship without even leaving his armchair.

Now I'm on my guard. I'm watching the wind and the waves and when both seem to be exerting too much pressure I ease up a little by turning the helm. I don't believe I've ever felt so strong, so free. Standing on the blistering deck, toes splayed to better keep my balance, I can feel the powerful movement of the water over the hull, on the rudder. I can feel the vibrations of the waves hitting the bow, the wind gusting in the sails. I've never experienced anything like this. It eclipses everything else, the land, time, I'm in the absolute future that is all around me. The future is the sea, the wind, the sky, the light.

For a long time, perhaps for hours, I remain standing in front of the wheel, with winds and sea spray whirling around me. The sun is burning my back, my neck, is reaching down along the left side of my body. It's almost touching the horizon already, it's casting its fiery dust over the sea. I'm so in tune with the gliding of the ship that I anticipate every pause in the wind, the trough of every wave.

The helmsman is beside me. He too is looking out to sea, not saying anything. I realize he wants to go back to the wheel. I savour the pleasure a little longer, just to feel the vessel slip along the curve of a wave, hesitate, then move on, pushed by the wind filling its sails. When we are in the trough of the wave I take a step to one side, without letting go of the wheel, and the helmsman's dark hand closes over the handle, gripping it forcefully. When he's not at the helm that man is even more taciturn than the captain. But no sooner have his hands touched the handles of the wheel than a strange change comes over him. It's as if he becomes another person, someone taller, stronger. His thin, sunburned face, as if it were sculpted in basalt, takes on a sharp, energetic expression. His green eyes shine out, become animated, and his entire face expresses a sort of well-being that I now understand.

So then he starts talking, in his chanting voice, launches out in an interminable monologue that is swept away in the wind. What is he talking about? I'm sitting on the deck now, to the left of the helmsman, while Captain Bradmer sits in his armchair, still smoking. The helmsman is talking neither to him nor to me. He's talking to himself, as others might sing or whistle.

He's talking about Saint Brandon again, where women are not allowed to go. He says, 'One day a young girl wanted to go to Saint Brandon, a young black girl from Mahé, tall and pretty, I don't think she was any older than sixteen. Since she knew it was forbidden, she asked her fiancé — a young man who worked on a fishing boat — "Please take me!" At first he didn't want to, but she would say, "What are you afraid of? No one will find out, I'll go disguised as a boy. You'll say I'm your little brother and there you have it." So he ended up accepting and she dressed up as a boy, put on a pair of worn trousers and a large shirt, she cut her hair and, because she was tall and thin, the other fishermen took her for a boy. So she left with them on the boat for Saint Brandon. Nothing happened during the whole journey, the wind was gentle as a breath and the sky was nice and blue and the boat reached Saint Brandon in a week. No one knew there was a woman on board, except for the fiancé, of course. But sometimes in the evenings he would whisper to her, saying, "If the captain learns of this, he'll get angry, he'll let me go." She would answer, "How could he ever find out?"

'So the boat entered the lagoon, the place that is like paradise, and the men began fishing the large tortoises that are so gentle they allow themselves to be caught without trying to flee. Up until then, still nothing happened, but when the fishermen landed on one of the islands to spend the night, the wind rose and the sea became furious. The waves came crashing over the coral reefs and rolled into the lagoon. Then there was a terrible storm all night long and the sea swelled over the rocks of the islands. The men left their cabins and sought refuge in the trees. Everyone prayed to the Virgin Mary and the saints to protect them and the captain bewailed the sight of his vessel beached on the shore, for the waves were going to batter it to pieces. Then one wave appeared that was taller than the others, it rushed towards the islands like a wild beast and when it arrived it ripped up a rock where the men had taken shelter. Then, suddenly, everything fell calm and the sun began to shine as if there had never been a storm. Then we heard someone weeping, saying, "Bhoo, bhoo, little brother!" It was the young boy who had seen the wave carry away his fiancée, but since he had disobeyed, bringing a woman on to the islands, he was afraid of being punished by the captain, and he was weeping, saying, "Bhoo, little brother!"'

When the helmsman finishes speaking, the light on the sea has taken on its golden colour, the sky is pale and blank down near the horizon. Night is already falling, another night. But twilight lasts a long time out at sea and I watch the daylight dwindling very slowly. Is this the same world I used to know? I feel as if I entered some other world when I crossed the horizon. It's a world that resembles that of my childhood, in Boucan, where the sound of the sea was all-pervasive, as if the *Zeta* were sailing backwards on the route that abolishes time.

As the daylight vanishes, little by little, I allow myself to slip into a daydream once again. I can feel the heat of the sun against my neck, on my shoulders. I can also feel the gentle evening wind that is swifter than our vessel. Everyone has fallen silent. Every evening it's like a mysterious ritual that we all observe. No one speaks. We listen to the sound of the waves breaking against the stem, the dull vibration of the sails and rigging. Like every evening the Comorian sailors kneel down on the deck in the front of the ship to say their prayer facing north. Their voices drift over to me in a muffled murmur, mingled with the wind and the sea. Never more than tonight have I so keenly felt – in the quick gliding and the slow rocking of the hull upon this limpid sea so like the sky – the beauty of that prayer, sent out to no particular place, lost in this immensity. I think how much I would like you to be here, Laure, at my side – you, who so love the muezzin's call to prayer that echoes in the hills of Forest Side – and for you to hear this prayer here, this susurration, while the vessel is swaying to and fro like a great seabird with dazzling wings. I would have liked to bring you with me like the fisherman of Saint Brandon, I too could have said you were my 'little brother'!

I know Laure would have felt the same way I do listening to the Comorian sailors' prayer in the sunset. We wouldn't have needed to talk about it. But just as I'm thinking of her, just as I feel that ache in my heart, I realize that no – on the contrary, I'm actually drawing nearer to her now. Laure is in Boucan, back in the large garden thick with vines and flowers near the house, or else she's walking along the narrow path in the cane field. She never left the place she loved. At the end of my journey the sea is rolling into the black beach of Tamarin, into the backwaters at the mouth of the two rivers. I went away to be able to get back there. But I'll have changed when I return. I'll go back as a stranger and this old trunk containing the papers my father left behind will be filled with the Corsair's gold and jewels, the treasure of Golconda or Aurangzeb's ransom. I'll go back redolent with the odour of the sea, browned with the sun, strong and hardened like a soldier, to win back our lost property. That's what I'm dreaming about in the still twilight.

One after the other the sailors go down below to sleep in the heat radiating from the hull that has been baking in the sun all day long. I go down with them, stretch out on the planks, head resting on my trunk. I listen to the sounds of the interminable game of dice that has been taken back up where the break of day had interrupted it.

SUNDAY

We've reached Agalega after a five-day journey.

The shoreline of the twin islands must have been visible very early this morning, at daybreak. I was sleeping heavily, down in the hold alone, my head rolling on the floor, oblivious to the agitation up on deck. I was awakened by the calm waters of the harbour, for I have grown so accustomed to the incessant rocking of the ship that the stillness disturbed me.

I go straight up on deck, barefoot, without going to the trouble of putting on my shirt. Before us the thin, grey-green strip, fringed with the foam of the reefs, is growing longer. To us, who for days have seen nothing but the vast blue expanse of the sea joining the blue immensity of the sky, that land, even so seemingly flat and desolate, is a source of wonderment. All the crew members are leaning over the rail up at the bow and watching the two islands avidly.

Captain Bradmer has given the order to douse and the ship remains adrift not far from the coast. When I ask the helmsman why, he simply answers, 'We have to wait for the right time.' Captain Bradmer, standing next to his armchair, explains: we must wait for the ebb tide in order to avoid being pushed up against the coral reefs by the currents. When we get close enough to the pass, we'll be able to drop anchor and lower the pirogue and make our way to shore. The tide won't begin till late this afternoon when the sun is going down. In the meantime we'll have to be patient and content ourselves with looking at the coast that is so near yet so very difficult to reach.

The sailors' enthusiasm has died down. Now they're sitting on the deck, smoking and playing dice in the shade of the sail that is stirring gently in the wind. Though the coast is quite near, the water is a dark-blue colour. Leaning over the rail at the prow, I watch the green shadows of large sharks passing.

The seabirds come out along with the tide. Small and large gulls, petrels that circle above and deafen us with their cries. They are famished and, mistaking us for one of the fishing boats from the islands, demand their share with shrill cries. When they realize their error, the birds fly off and return to the shelter of the coral reef. Only two or three large gulls continue tracing large circles above us, then dive towards the sea and fly skimming along over the waves. After all of these days spent scrutinizing the barren sea, I'm delighted at the sight of the gulls in flight.

Towards the end of the afternoon Captain Bradmer rises from his armchair, gives orders to the helmsman, who repeats them, and the crew hoist the large sails. The helmsman is standing at the wheel on his tiptoes in order to see better. We're going to go through the pass. Slowly, pushed along on the lazy wind of the rising tide, the *Zeta* nears the reef. Now we can clearly see the long waves crashing against the coral reefs, there is a constant roar in our ears.

When the ship is only a few fathoms from the reefs, the prow pointed straight for the pass, the captain gives the order to drop anchor. The main anchor along with its heavy chain falls into the water first. Then the crew drop three smaller frigate anchors: portside, starboard and at the bow. When I ask him why so many precautions, the captain tells me in a few words about the shipwreck of a one-hundred-and-fifty-ton, three-masted schooner, the *Kalinda*, in 1901: it had dropped anchor in this same spot, facing the pass. Then everyone had gone ashore, even the captain, leaving two green Tamil cabin boys on board. A few hours later the tide had risen, but was unusually strong on that particular day and the current that rushed into the unique pass was so powerful that the anchor chain broke. People on the shore had seen the ship drawing closer, high over the coral reef, where the rollers were breaking, as if it were going to take flight. Then it had suddenly plunged down on to the reefs and a receding wave engulfed it, pulling it down to the bottom of the sea. The next morning pieces of masts, bits of plank and a few bales of the cargo were found, but the two Tamil cabin boys never were.

Thereupon the captain gives the order to douse all sails and lower the pirogue. I gaze at the dark water – it's over ten fathoms deep – and I shudder, thinking of the green shadows of sharks slipping around, waiting perhaps for another shipwreck.

On the deck of the *Zeta* we're growing impatient. The sun is low when the pirogue returns, greeted by the joyous cries of the sailors. This time it's my turn. I follow the helmsman and slide down the cable to the pirogue, four other crew members also board. We are rowing, unable to see the pass. The helmsman is at the tiller, standing in order to steer better. The roar of the waves warns us that the reef is near. Indeed, I suddenly feel our skiff being lifted up by a swift wave and we make it through the narrow channel between the reefs riding high on its crest. Now we are already on the other side, in the lagoon, barely a few yards from the long coral barrier. The helmsman brings us to shore in the place where the waves come washing up to die, very near the sandy beach, and moors the pirogue. The sailors jump out on to the embankment, whooping, then disappear amid the crowd of inhabitants.

I disembark in turn. On the shore there are a good many women, children, black fishermen and Indians too. They all look at me curiously. With the exception of Captain Bradmer, who comes when he has a shipment of merchandise, these people must not see white people often. And what with my long hair and beard, my suntanned face and arms, my dirty clothes and bare feet, I must be quite a strange white man! It's mostly the children who examine me, laughing openly. On the beach there are dogs, a few scrawny black pigs, some young goats trotting around looking for salt.

The sun will soon be setting. The sky is a bright yellow above the coconut trees, behind the islands. Where am I going to sleep? I start to look for a spot somewhere on the beach between the pirogues when Captain Bradmer asks me to accompany him to the hotel. My astonishment at the word 'hotel' makes him laugh. In the guise of a hotel there's an old wooden house whose proprietress, an energetic woman – a mix of black and Indian – rents rooms to the rare travellers who venture out to Agalega. They say she even housed the chief justice of Mauritius during his sole visit in 1901 or 1902! For dinner the woman serves us a crab curry that is absolutely excellent, especially compared with the everyday fare of the Chinaman on the *Zeta*. Captain Bradmer is in top form, he questions our hostess about the inhabitants of the island and tells me about Juan de Nova, the first explorer to discover Agalega, and about a French colonizer by the name of Auguste Leduc, who organized the production of copra that was once the sole resource of the islands. Today the sister islands also produce rare wood, mahogany, sandalwood, ebony. He speaks of Guguel, the colonial administrator who founded the hospital and built up the island's economy in the beginning of this century. I promise myself to take advantage of the time we are in port – Bradmer has just informed me that he needs to load a hundred or so barrels of copra – to visit the forests which are, from what I've heard, the loveliest in the Indian Ocean.

After dinner I stretch out on my bed in the little room at one end of the house. Despite my weariness, I have trouble going to sleep. After all those nights in the suffocating hold, the tranquillity of this room unsettles me and I can't stop feeling the rolling movement of the waves. I open the shutters to breathe in the night air. Outside the smell of land is heavy and the song of toads punctuates the night.

How impatient I am already to get back to the desert of the sea, to the sound of the waves against the stem, the wind vibrating in the sails, to feel the quickness of the air and the saltwater, the power of the void, to hear the music of absence. Sitting on the old rickety chair in front of the open window, I inhale the fragrance of the garden. I can hear Bradmer's voice, his laughter, the laughter of the landlady. It sounds as if they're having a good time . . . Little matter! I think I fall asleep like that, with my forehead resting on the windowsill.

MONDAY MORNING

I walk across South Island, where the village is located. Together, the sister islands that make up Agalega are probably no larger than the Black River District. Nevertheless, it seems very large after the days on the *Zeta*, where the only activity consisted in going from the hold to the deck, from the stem to the stern. I walk across the groves of coconut trees and palmettos standing in straight rows as far as the eye can see. I walk slowly, barefoot in the sandy soil that is sapped with the burrows of land crabs. I'm also disoriented due to the silence. One can't hear the sound of the sea in these fields. There's only the murmur of the wind in the palms. Despite the early hour (when I left the hotel everyone was still sleeping) the heat is already oppressive. There is no one on the straight paths and if those ruled lines didn't signal a human presence I might think I was on a deserted island.

But I'm mistaken in saying there's no one here. Since I entered the grove I have been followed by anxious eyes. The land crabs are observing me along the path, they rise up at times, waving their threatening claws. At one point a group of them even block my passage and I have to make a long detour. At last I reach the other side of the plantation in the north. I'm separated from the sister island, poorer than this one, by the calm waters of the lagoon. There is a cabin on the shore and an old fisherman repairing his nets near his upturned pirogue. He lifts his head to look at me, then pursues his work. His black skin shines in the sunlight.

I decide to make my way back to the village by walking up the white beach that encircles almost the entire island. I can feel the sea breeze out here, but I no longer have the advantage of the shade of the coconut trees. The sun is so hot that I need to take off my shirt to cover my head and shoulders. When I reach the other end of the island, I can't wait any longer. I strip off all my clothes and dive into the clear water of the lagoon. I swim delectably towards the coral reefs until I come to the cold layers of water and the roar of the waves is very near. Then I go very slowly back to shore, drifting along, hardly moving. Eyes open under the water, I watch the fish of all different colours fleeing before me, I'm also looking out for the shadows of sharks. I can feel the cold flow of water coming from the pass, sweeping along fish and bits of seaweed.

When I'm on the beach I get dressed without drying off and walk barefoot over the burning sand. Farther along I encounter a group of black children going octopus-fishing. They are the same age as Denis and I were when we used to roam around Black River.

They gaze in astonishment at the '*burzois*' — which is Creole for bourgeois — clothes stained with seawater, hair and beard matted with salt. Maybe they take me for a castaway? When I walk over to them, they flee and hide in the shade of the coconut grove.

Before I enter the village I shake out my clothes and comb my hair, so I won't make too bad an impression. On the other side of the coral reefs I can see the two masts of Bradmer's schooner. The barrels of oil are lined up on the long coral embankment, waiting to be taken aboard. The sailors are coming and going with the pirogue. There are still some fifty barrels to be loaded.

Back in the hotel I have breakfast with Captain Bradmer. He's in a good humour this morning. He informs me that the crew will have finished loading the oil this afternoon and that we'll be leaving tomorrow at dawn. We'll sleep on board to avoid having to wait for the tide. Then, to my great astonishment, he speaks to me about my family, about my father, whom he'd known long ago in Port Louis.

'I learned of the misfortune that befell him, all of his problems, his debts. All of that is quite sad. You were in Black River, isn't that so?'

'In Boucan.'

'Yes, that's it, behind the Tamarin Estate. I went to your house a very long time ago, long before you were born. It was in the days of your grandfather, it was a lovely white house with a magnificent garden. Your father had recently married, I recall your mother, a very young woman with beautiful auburn hair and pretty eyes. Your father was very taken with her, he had organized a very romantic marriage.' After a silence, he adds, 'What a pity that it all ended in that way, happiness doesn't last.' He looks over past the other end of the veranda at the little garden where a black pig thrones, surrounded by pecking poultry. 'Yes, it's a pity . . . '

But he says nothing more. As if he regretted having revealed his feelings, the captain stands up, puts on his hat and walks out of the house. I hear him speaking to the landlady outside, then he reappears, 'This evening, sir, the pirogue will make its last trip at five o'clock, before the tide. Be on the embankment at that time.' It's more of an order than a piece of advice.

I am, therefore, standing on the embankment at the said hour, after having spent the day rambling around South Island, from the campsite to the eastern point, from the hospital to the cemetery. I'm impatient to be on board the *Zeta* again, to sail for Rodrigues.

In the pirogue that is moving away from the island it seems as if all the men are feeling the same thing, that desire for the high seas. This time the captain himself is at the tiller of the pirogue and I'm at the front. I see the barrier approaching, the long rollers crashing down, raising a wall of foam. My heart is racing when the front of the pirogue heaves up against the incoming wave. I'm deafened by the sound of the backwash, by the screeching birds circling overhead. 'Alley-oop!' cries the captain when the wave goes out, and along with the thrust of the eight oars the pirogue is precipitated into the narrow pass between the reefs. It leaps over the next wave. Not one drop of water has fallen into the pirogue! Now we are sliding over the deep blue, towards the dark silhouette of the *Zeta*.

Later, on board the ship, when the men have settled down in the hold to play dice or to sleep, I sit watching the night. Out on the island fires shine, pinpointing the campsite. Then the land fades out, disappears. There's nothing left but the void of night, the sound of the waves on the reefs.

Just like almost every other evening since this journey began, I'm stretched out on the deck of the ship, wrapped in my old horse blanket and looking up at the stars. The sea breeze whistling in the rigging heralds the tide. I can feel the first rollers slipping under the hull, making the frame of the ship crack. The anchor chains are groaning plaintively. Up in the sky the stars are shining in still brightness. I'm watching them attentively, looking for all of them tonight, as if their patterns would reveal the secrets of my fate to me. Scorpius, Orion and the faint shape of the Smaller Chariot. Near the horizon, the Argo with her narrow sail and her long stern, the Smaller Dog, the Unicorn. And tonight, above all, the ones that bring the lovely nights in Boucan to mind, the seven lights of the Pleiades, whose names our father made us learn by heart and that Laure and I used to recite like the words of a magic formula: Alcyone, Electra, Maia, Atlas, Taygeta, Merope . . . And the last one, that we would name hesitantly, Pleione, so small we weren't sure we'd really seen it. I still love to say their names today, half-whispering in the lonely night, because it's as if I knew they were appearing over there, in the sky over Boucan, through a rent in the clouds.

AT SEA, HEADING FOR MAHÉ

The wind changed during the night. Now it's blowing northwards again, making any attempt to turn back impossible. The captain decided to run before the wind, rather than resign himself to waiting in Agalega. The helmsman coolly informs me of this. Will we ever go to Rodrigues? That depends on the length of the storm. Thanks to it, we reached Agalega in five days, but now we have to wait for it to allow us to return.

I'm the only one who's worrying about our itinerary. The crewmen just go on with their lives and play dice as if nothing mattered. Is it because of their taste for adventure? No, that's not it. They don't belong to anyone, they don't come from anywhere, that's all. Their world is the deck of the *Zeta*, the airless hold where they sleep at night. I look at those dark faces, burnished by the sun and the wind, like shingles polished by the sea. Just as I had on the night we cast off, I begin to feel that vague, irrational anxiety again. These men belong to another way of life, another time. Even Captain Bradmer, even the helmsman, are with them, are on their side. They too are indifferent to places, to longings, to everything that's important to me. Their faces are as smooth as water, their eyes reflect the metallic glint of the sea.

The wind is whisking us north now, in full sail, with the stem slicing through the dark sea. We clip along, hour after hour, day after day. I have to get used to this, accept the rule of the elements. Every day when the sun is at its peak the helmsman goes down into the hold to rest without closing his eyes and I take the wheel.

Maybe this way I'll learn to stop asking questions. Can you question the sea? Ask the horizon for explanations? The only real things are the wind driving us forward, the rolling of the waves and, at nightfall, the still stars that guide us.

Yet today the captain talks to me. He tells me he hopes to sell his cargo of oil in the Seychelles, where he knows Mr Maury very well. Mr Maury is the one who will take care of having it loaded on cargo ships bound for England. Captain Bradmer talks to me about this with an air of indifference, smoking his green tobacco cigarette, sitting in his armchair screwed down to the deck. Then, when I'm not expecting it, he speaks of my father again. He'd heard of his experiments and his projects for bringing electricity to the island. He's also familiar with the disputes that had set him against his brother and caused his ruin. He talks to me about all of that calmly and without making any commentary. About Uncle Ludovic, he simply says, 'A tough man.' That's all. Out here, on such a blue sea, related in the captain's monotone voice, those events seem far away, almost foreign. And that is exactly why I'm on board the *Zeta*, as if suspended between the sea and the sky. Not in order to forget – can one forget? But rather to render the memory vain, inoffensive, so that it will slip along and pass away like a reflection.

After those spare words about my father and Boucan, the captain remains silent. Arms crossed, eyes closed as he smokes and I almost believe he's half-asleep. But he turns suddenly towards me and says, in his muffled voice that barely rises over the sound of the sea, 'Are you an only child?'

'Sir?'

He repeats his question without raising his voice, 'I'm asking you if you're an only child. Don't you have any siblings?'

'I have one sister, sir.'

'What's her name?'

'Laure.'

He seems to think that over, then, 'Is she pretty?'

He doesn't wait for my response, goes on for himself, 'She must be like your mother, pretty and, better yet, brave. And intelligent.'

It all sort of makes a vortex within me as I stand here on the deck of this ship, so far away from Port Louis and the high society in Curepipe, so far away! For such a long time I had thought that Laure and I lived in another world, unknown to the wealthy people of Rue Royale and Champ de Mars, as if – in the decrepit house in Forest Side, as in the wild valley of Boucan – we'd remained invisible. Suddenly it makes my heart start beating faster, from anger or shame, and I can feel my face growing red.

But where am I, after all? On the deck of the *Zeta*, an old schooner loaded with barrels of oil, full of rats and vermin, lost at sea between

Agalega and Mahé. Who cares about me or my blushing? Who can see my clothing, stained with grease from the hold, my sunburned face, my hair tangled with salt, who can see I've been barefoot for days? I look at Captain Bradmer, that old sea dog, his wine-coloured cheeks, his beady eyes closed against the smoke of his stinky cigarette, and the black helmsman standing in front of him, and even the forms of the Indian and Comorian sailors, some of whom are squatting on the deck smoking their ganja, while others are playing dice or daydreaming, and I don't feel ashamed any more.

The captain has already forgotten all about it. He says, 'Would you like to travel with me, sir? I'm getting old and I need a first mate.'

Surprised, I look at him. 'You've got your helmsman?'

'Him? He's old too. Every time I put into port I wonder whether he'll come back.'

Captain Bradmer's offer echoes through my mind for a moment. I imagine what my life would be like on the deck of the *Zeta* next to Bradmer's armchair. Agalega, Seychelles Amirantes or Rodrigues, Diego Garcia, Peros Banhos. Sometimes out as far as Farquhar or the Comoros, perhaps southwards down to Tromelin. The never-ending sea, longer than the road to travel down, longer than life. Is that what I left Laure for, what I broke my last tie to Boucan for? Then Bradmer's proposal sounds derisory to me, ridiculous. To avoid hurting his feelings, I say, 'I can't, sir. I must go to Rodrigues.'

He opens his eyes, 'I know, I've heard about that pipedream as well.'

'What pipedream, sir?'

'Well, the pipedream. The treasure. They say your father worked very hard on it.'

Does he say 'worked' ironically or is it just that I'm getting irritated?

'Who says that?'

'Everything comes out eventually, sir. But let's say no more about it, it's not worth it.'

'Do you mean to say that you don't believe the treasure exists?'

He shakes his head. 'I don't believe that in this part of the world,' he designates the horizon with a wide sweep of his arm, 'there has been any other treasure but that which man has torn from the land and the sea at the cost of the lives of his fellow human beings.'

For a moment, I want to talk to him about the Corsair's maps, the papers my father had compiled and that I'd copied and brought along with me in my trunk, everything that had helped and consoled me in the misfortune and loneliness of Forest Side. But to what avail? He wouldn't understand. He's already forgotten what he said to me and is letting himself be rocked by the swaying of the ship, eyes closed.

I too gaze out on the sparkling sea, to stop thinking about it all. I can feel the slow movement of the boat as it crests the waves like a horse leaping over an obstacle.

I add, 'Thank you for your offer, sir. I'll think it over.'

He cracks open his eyes. Maybe he doesn't know what I'm talking about any more. He growls, 'Ahem, yes, of course . . . Naturally.'

That's the end of it. We'll never mention it again.

The following days Captain Bradmer seems to have changed his attitude towards me. When the black helmsman goes down into the hold the captain doesn't ask me to take the wheel any more. He slips in front of the wheel himself, standing in front of his armchair that looks odd, abandoned in that way by its legitimate occupant. When he tires of steering, he calls one of the sailors randomly and surrenders the job to them.

I don't care. Here the sea is so lovely that no one can think of others for long. Maybe we become like the water and the sky, smooth, free of thought. Maybe we become free of reasoning, of time, of place. Each day resembles every other one, each night begins over again. Up in the blank sky, the burning sun, the still patterns of the constellations. The wind doesn't change: it is blowing northwards, driving the vessel onward.

Friendships crop up between the men, come undone. No one needs anyone. I met a Rodriguan sailor on the deck — for, ever since the barrels of oil were loaded, I can't bear to be closed up down below any more — he's an athletic and childish black man named Casimir. He speaks only Creole and Pidgin English that he learned in Malaysia. Using these two languages he informs me that he has sailed to Europe several times and has been to France and England. But he doesn't boast about it. I question him about Rodrigues, the names of the passes, the surrounding islands, the bays. Does he know of a mountain named the Commander? He recites the names of the main mountains: Patate, Limon, Quatre Vents, Piton. He doesn't speak of the 'Manafs', black people who live in the mountains, wild people who never go down to the coast.

Because of the heat the other sailors have settled in for the night on the deck, despite the captain's order against it. They aren't sleeping. They're stretched out with their eyes open, talking in low voices. They're smoking, playing dice.

One evening, just before we reach Mahé, an argument breaks out. An Indian, glassy-eyed with ganja, lays into a Muslim Comorian for some incomprehensible reason. They grab at each other's clothing, roll around on the deck. The others stand aside, make a circle, as if for a cock fight. The Comorian is small and thin, he's soon the underdog, but the Indian is so dopey he rolls over beside him and is unable to get back on his feet. The men watch the fight without saying anything. I can hear the hoarse panting of the combatants, the thud of clumsy blows, their groans. Then the captain comes up from the hold, watches the fight for a while and gives an order. Casimir, the gentle giant, separates them. He takes them both by the belt and lifts them up at the same time, as if they were merely bundles of laundry, and sets them each down at opposite ends of the deck. That way the matter is settled.

The next evening we are in sight of the islands. The sailors let out sharp cries when they glimpse the land, a barely visible line, like a dark cloud under the sky. A little later the tall mountains appear. 'It's Mahé,' says Casimir. He laughs with pleasure. 'Over there, Platte Island, and there, Frégate.' As the vessel approaches, other islands appear, sometimes so distant that a passing wave hides them from sight. The main island grows larger before us. Soon the first seagulls arrive and circle overhead, yapping. There are frigates too, the most beautiful birds I've ever seen, shiny black, spreading their immense wings, with their long, forked tails floating behind. They slip along on the wind above us, quick as shadows, clacking the red bags under their beaks.

It's the same every time we near new land. The birds come to get a closer look at these strangers. What are these men bringing? What kind of death threat? Or maybe food, fish, squid or even some cetacean lashed to the side of the ship?

The island of Mahé is in sight, a bare two miles from us. In the sultry dusk light I can make out the white rocks of the coast, the coves, the sandy beaches, the trees. We're sailing up the eastern coast to keep to the wind until we reach the northernmost point, passing near two small islands whose names Casimir tells me: Conception,

Theresa, and he laughs because they're women's names. The two mornes are just ahead with their peaks still in the sunlight.

After the small islands the wind weakens, becomes a light breeze, the sea is emerald-coloured. We are very near the coral reef, hemmed with foam. The village huts appear, like toys, amid the coconut trees. Casimir enumerates the villages for me: Bel Ombre, Beau Vallon, Glacis. Night falls and the heat is oppressive after so much wind. When we arrive in front of the pass on the other side of the island the lights of Port Victoria are already shining. In the harbour, sheltered by the islands, Captain Bradmer gives the order to douse the sails and drop anchor. The crewmen are already preparing to lower the pirogue into the sea. They're in a hurry to get ashore. I decide to sleep on deck, rolled up in my old blanket, in the spot I love, where I can see the stars in the sky.

The black helmsman and I, along with a silent Comorian, are the only ones on board. I love this solitude, this calm. The night is still, deep, land is near and invisible, it steals in like a cloud, like a dream would. I listen to the waves lapping against the hull and the rhythmic creaking of the anchor chain around which the vessel drifts first in one direction, then in the other.

I think of Laure, of Mam, so far away now across the sea. Is the same night blanketing them, the same silent night? I go down below to try to write a letter that I'll be able to send tomorrow from Port Victoria. By the dim glow of a night light I try to write. But the heat is stifling, there's the smell of the oil, the whirr of insects. My body, my face are streaming with sweat. The words won't come. What can I say? Laure warned me when I left, don't write unless it's to say: I'm coming back. If not there's no point in it. That's just like her: all or nothing. For fear of not having it all, she chose nothing, it's her pride.

Since I can't write to her to explain from a distance how beautiful everything is here, under the night sky, adrift on the smooth water of the harbour in this abandoned ship, what use is it to write? I put the paper and the writing case back into the trunk, which I lock, and go up on deck again to breathe. The black helmsman and the Comorian are sitting near the hatch, smoking and talking softly. Later the helmsman will stretch out on the deck, wrapped in a sheet that looks like a shroud, eyes wide. How many years has it been since he's slept?

PORT VICTORIA

I'm looking for a boat to take me to Frégate Island. It's more out of curiosity than genuine interest that I'm prompted to visit the island my father once believed he recognized as the one depicted on the hand-drawn map he kept among the papers dealing with the Corsair's treasure. In fact it was the map of Frégate that made it possible for him to understand that the Corsair's map was erroneously oriented east-west and had to be tilted 45° to attain its true orientation.

A black fisherman agrees to take me out there — some three or four hours sailing time, depending on the wind speed. We set sail immediately after I buy a packet of biscuits and some coconuts to ward off thirst at a Chinese store. The fisherman doesn't ask any questions. For provisions he brings only an old bottle of water. He hoists the lateen sail on the yard and fastens it to the long tiller, as Indian fishermen do.

As soon as we're through the pass we're out in the wind again and the pirogue moves along swiftly, listing over the dark sea. We'll reach Frégate in three hours. The sun is high in the sky, marking midday. Sitting on a stool up in the front of the pirogue, I watch the sea and the dark mass of the mornes growing distant.

We're heading east. On the horizon, drawn taut as a wire, I can see the other islands, the blue, ethereal mountains. Not a single bird is accompanying us. The fisherman is standing in the back, leaning on the long tiller.

As expected, we reach the coral reef of Frégate at approximately three o'clock. It's a small, flat island, surrounded by a band of sand where coconut trees and a few fishermen's huts stand. We go through the pass and touch land on a coral embankment, where three or four fishermen are seated. Children are swimming, running naked on the beach. Set a bit farther back, hidden in the vegetation, is a rundown wooden house with a veranda and some vanilla plants. The fisherman tells me it's Mr Savy's house. Indeed, that is the name of the family that is in possession of certain maps that my father copied and the island belongs to them. But they live on Mahé.

Walking across the beach I'm surrounded by black children laughing, calling to me, surprised to see a stranger. I take the path that borders Savy's compound and make my way across the whole width of the island. On the other side there is no beach or anywhere to land. Only rocky inlets. The island is so narrow that on stormy days the sea spray must blow right across it.

When I return to the embankment hardly an hour has gone by. There is no place to sleep here and I'm not keen to stay any longer. When the fisherman sees me come back, he unties the line and raises the angled yard up the mast. The pirogue glides out to sea. The waves of high tide are covering the embankment, flowing between the legs of the shouting children. They're waving their arms about, diving into the transparent water.

In his notes my father says that he ruled out the possibility that the Corsair's treasure was on Frégate, because of the small size of the island, the lack of water, of wood, of resources. From what I was able to see, he was right. There are no lasting landmarks here, nothing that can be used for plotting a map. The pirates that roamed the Indian Ocean in 1730 wouldn't have come here. They wouldn't have found what they wanted, the sort of natural mystery that would fit in with their scheme, that would defy time.

And yet, as the pirogue sails away from Frégate, skimming along westward, leaning over in the wind, I feel a little wistful. The clear water of the lagoon, the naked children running on the beach and that old abandoned wooden house among the vanilla plants all remind me of the days in Boucan. It's a world devoid of mystery and that's why I feel this longing.

What will I find in Rodrigues? And what if it's like this, what if there's nothing over there either, nothing but sand and trees? Now the sea is sparkling in the slanting rays of the setting sun. At the stern the fisherman is still standing up, leaning on the tiller. His dark face expresses nothing, neither impatience nor disinterest. He's simply watching the shapes of the two mornes – guardians of Port of Victoria – growing larger, already engulfed in darkness.

Port Victoria once again. From the deck of the *Zeta* I'm watching the comings and goings of the pirogues unloading the oil. The air is hot and languid, not a breath of wind. The light reverberating off the glassy sea fascinates me, plunges me into a dream state. I listen to the distant sounds of the port. At times a bird flies through the sky and its call makes me start. I've begun writing a letter to Laure, but will I ever send it? I'd rather she came, right now, to read it over my shoulder. Sitting cross-legged on the deck, shirt open, hair tousled, beard long and whitened with salt like an outlaw: that's what I'm writing to her now. I'm also telling her about Bradmer, about the helmsman who never sleeps, about Casimir.

The hours slip by without leaving a trace. I've stretched out on the deck in the shade of the mizzen mast. I put away the writing case and the piece of paper upon which I was able to write only a few lines. Later the heat of the sun on my eyelids awakens me. The sky is still just as blue and there is the same bird squawking as it circles. I take out the piece of paper and automatically write down the lines that came to mind while I was sleeping:

'Jamque dies auraeque vocant rursusque capessunt
Aequora, qua rigidos eructat Bosporos amnes . . .'

I take up the letter where I'd left off. But am I really writing to Laure? In the blistering silence of the harbour, surrounded with glitters and reflections, with the grey shoreline and the tall blue shadows of the mornes in front of the ship, other words pop into my mind: why did I leave everything behind, for what pipedream? Does the treasure I've been pursuing for so many years in my dreams really exist? Is it really in some vault, jewels and gems just waiting to reflect the light of day? Does it really hold the power to turn back time, to wipe away the misfortune and the ruin, the death of my father in the shabby house in Forest Side? But I am perhaps the only one who holds the key to the secret and I'm getting closer now. Out there at the end of my road is Rodrigues, where everything will at last fall into place. My father's former dream, the one that guided his research and haunted my entire childhood, at last I'll be able to fulfil it! I'm the only one who can do it. It's what my father wants, not me, for he'll never leave the earth of Forest Side. That's what I would like to write now, but not in order to send it to Laure. When I left, it was to stop the dream, so that life could begin. I'll go to the end of this journey, I know I have to find something.

That's what I wanted to tell Laure when we parted. But she saw it in my eyes, she turned away and left me free to leave.

I've been waiting for this journey for so long! It seems as if I've never stopped thinking about it. It was in the sound of the wind when the sea washed up the estuary in Tamarin, it was in the waves running over the green expanse of cane, in the plashing sound of the wind in the needles of the she-oaks. I remember the solid blue sky over the Tourelle and its dizzying drop down towards the horizon at twilight. In the evening the sea would turn purple, dappled with reflections. Now darkness is filling the harbour of Port Victoria and I feel as if I'm very near the place where the sky meets the sea. Wasn't that the sign the *Argo* followed in its quest for eternity?

Since night is falling, the watchkeeper has come up from the hold where he's been sleeping naked all afternoon in the muggy heat. He's simply wrapped a loincloth about his waist and his body is shiny with sweat. He squats down in the front, facing a scupper, and urinates into the sea for a long time. Then he comes over to sit by me, leans his back up against the mast and starts smoking. In the half-light his sunburned face is eerily lit by the whites of his eyes. We sit side by side for a long time without speaking.

FRIDAY, I BELIEVE

Captain Bradmer did the right thing in not trying to fight against the south wind. As soon as the cargo was unloaded at dawn the *Zeta* sailed through the pass and picked up the west wind that will enable us to return. Lighter, sails filled, the *Zeta* is faring along at a good speed, listing slightly like a true clipper. The dark sea is rough with long waves coming from the east, maybe from a distant storm on the shores of Malabar. They come crashing up against the stem and stream over the deck. The captain has battened down the fore-hatches, and the men who are not taking part in deck manoeuvres have gone below. I was able to obtain permission to stay on deck at the stern, maybe simply because I paid for my passage. Captain Bradmer doesn't seem worried about the waves that are washing over the deck all the way up to his armchair. The helmsman, legs spread, is holding the wheel and the sound of his words is lost in the wind and the crash of the sea.

For half of the day the ship rushes on in that way, listing under the wind, streaming with spume. My ears are filled with the sounds of the elements, they fill my body and vibrate deep down within me. I can no longer think of anything else. I glance at the captain clutching the arms of his chair, face reddened from the wind and sun, and it seems as if there's something foreign in his expression, something violent and stubborn, something disturbing like madness. Hasn't the *Zeta* reached the limits of her resistance? The heavy waves slamming the portside are making her heel dangerously, and in spite of the roar of the sea I can hear the entire framework of the vessel creaking. The men have taken shelter at the stern to avoid the high waves shipping onboard. They too are staring straight ahead, towards the bow, with a fixed gaze. We are all waiting for something, without knowing what, as if the act of turning our eyes away for a second could be fatal.

We remain standing there like that for a long time, for hours, clinging to the ropes, to the rail, watching the stem plunge into the dark sea, listening to the crashing of the waves and the wind. The sea is tugging so hard at the rudder that the helmsman has a hard time holding the wheel. The veins in his arms are swollen and there is a tense, almost painful expression on his face. Above the sails clouds of sea spray are roiling, steaming, glinting with rainbows. Several times

I think about getting up to ask the captain why we are pursuing in full sail like this. But the hard expression on his face and also the fear of losing my balance dissuade me from doing so.

Suddenly, for no reason, Bradmer gives the order to douse the jibs and the stay sails and reef. To make the manoeuvre possible the helmsman turns the wheel to portside and the ship rights itself. The sails fall slack, snap like banners. Everything has gone back to normal. When the *Zeta* returns to its heading, it's sailing slowly and no longer heeling. The powerful roar of the taut sails is replaced by the shrill whistling of the rigging.

And yet Bradmer hasn't moved. His face is still red, closed, his gaze hasn't faltered. Now the helmsman has gone to lie down in the hold to rest, eyes opened unblinkingly on the blackened ceiling. Casimir, the Rodriguan sailor, is at the helm and I can hear his sing-song voice speaking to the captain. On the drenched deck the crewmen have taken up their game of dice, their conversations again, as if nothing has happened. But has anything really happened? Just the madness of this blue sky, of this dizzying sea, of the wind that fills your ears, the solitude, the brute force.

The *Zeta* moves along easily, barely slowed by the waves. In the burning noonday sun the deck is already dry, covered with salt sparkles. The horizon is immobile, sharp, and the sea furious. Deep down inside me thoughts, memories are coming back to life and I realize I'm talking to myself. But who's paying any attention? Aren't we all the same, crazed with the sea, Bradmer, the black helmsman, Casimir and all the others? Who listens to us talk?

Deep within, memories are coming back, the secret of the treasure at the end of this road. But the sea wipes time away. These waves, what age are they coming from? Aren't they the same waves that existed two hundred years ago, when Avery fled the shores of India with his fabulous bounty, when Misson's white flag floated over this sea with gold letters reading:

Pro Deo et Libertate

The wind never grows old, the sea is ageless. The sun, the sky, are eternal.

I gaze out into the distance, at each crest of foam. I think I know now what I've come in search of. I think I can see inside myself like someone who's been visited by a dream.

SAINT BRANDON

After these days, these weeks of having nothing other to look at than the blue of the sea and the sky and the clouds slipping their shadows over the waves, the man on the lookout at the bow sights — barely distinguishes, rather than sights — the grey line of an island and a name is whispered around the deck: 'Saint Brandon . . . Saint Brandon!' And it's as if we'd never heard anything so important in our lives. Everyone leans over the rail, trying to see. Behind the wheel the helmsman squints his eyes, his face is tense, anxious. 'We'll be there before nightfall,' says Bradmer. His voice is filled with childish impatience.

'Is it really Saint Brandon?'

My question surprises him. He responds gruffly, 'What else do you think it could be? There's no other land less than four hundred miles from here, except Tromelin, which is behind us, and Nazareth, to the north-west, a pile of rocks lying at surface level.' He immediately adds, 'Yes, it's Saint Brandon all right.' The helmsman is the one who's peering most intently at the islands and I recall what he'd said, the sky-coloured water where the most beautiful fish in the world swim, the tortoises, the seabirds that people them. The islands where women never go and the legend of the girl the tempest swept away.

But the helmsman isn't talking. He's steering the ship towards the still dark line that can be seen in the south-east. He wants to get there before nightfall, go through the pass. We are all gazing impatiently in the same direction.

The sun is touching the horizon when we enter the waters of the archipelago. Suddenly the sea bottom is clearly visible. The wind dies down. The sunlight is soft-hued, diffused. The islands draw aside before the bow of the ship, they are as numerous as a pod of whales. In fact it is just one large circular island — a ring — from which a few barren coral islets emerge. Is this the paradise the Comorian spoke of? But gradually, as we enter the atoll, we can feel the strangeness of this place. The peacefulness, the languor that I've never felt anywhere else, that stems from the transparency of the water, from the purity of the sky, from the silence.

The helmsman steers the *Zeta* straight towards the line of the first reefs. The bottom is very close, dotted with coral and seaweed, turquoise-coloured, in spite of the deepening night. We slip between the black reefs where, from time to time, the open sea casts misty sprays. The rare islands are still far away, like so many sleeping marine animals, but suddenly I notice that we are in the middle of the archipelago. Without realizing it, we've reached the centre of the atoll.

Captain Bradmer is leaning over the rail as well. He's observing the bottom, which is so close we can make out each shell, each branch of coral. The sunlight that is fading out beyond the islands cannot dim the limpid sea. We've all fallen silent, so as not to break the charm. I hear Bradmer mumbling to himself. He says, 'Land of the Sea.'

Off in the distance we can hear the faint rumbling of the sea on the reefs. It must never stop, like in the old days around Tamarin, the sound of eternal toiling.

Night settles over the atoll. It is the gentlest night I've ever known. After the burning hot sun and the wind, night here is a reward, laden with stars piercing the purple sky. The sailors have taken off their clothes and are diving from the ship one after another, swimming silently in the light water.

I do likewise, I swim for a long time in the water, which is so soft I can barely feel it, like a soft flutter around me. The water in the lagoon cleanses me, purifies me of all longing, all anxiety. For a long time I glide along on the surface, smooth as a mirror, until the muffled voices of the sailors reach my ears, mingled with the cries of birds. Very near to me I see the dark shape of the island the helmsman calls La Perle, and a little farther off, surrounded by birds like a whale, Frégate Island. Tomorrow I'll visit their beaches and the water will be even lovelier still. The lights shining through the hatches of the *Zeta* guide me as I swim. When I climb up the knotted rope hanging from the bowsprit, the breeze makes me shiver.

No one is really sleeping tonight. On the deck the men sit up, talking and smoking all night long, and the helmsman remains seated at the stern, watching the reflections of the stars on the waters of the atoll. Even the captain stays up, sitting in his armchair. From my place next to the mizzen mast I can see the tip of his cigarette glowing from time to time. The sea breeze sweeps away the words of the sailors, mingling them with the rumbling of the waves on the reefs. Here the sky is immense and pure, as if there were no other land in the world, as if everything were about to begin.

I sleep a little, my head resting on my arm, and when I awaken it's dawn. The light is transparent, just like the water in the lagoon, azure-coloured, iridescent. I haven't seen such a beautiful morning since Boucan. The rumour of the sea has grown louder, it's as if it is the very sound of the broadening daylight. Casting a look around I see that most of the sailors are still sleeping, just as they had dozed off, lying on the deck or sitting with their backs against the bulwark. Bradmer is no longer in his armchair. Maybe he's writing in his alcove. The black helmsman alone is still standing in the same place at the stern. He's watching the day break. I draw nearer to him to speak, but he speaks first, saying:

'Is there any place more beautiful in the world?'

His voice is gruff, like that of a man who is deeply moved.

'When I came here for the first time I was still a child. Now I am an old man, but nothing has changed. You might think that not a day has passed.'

'Why did the captain come here?'

He looks at me as if my question doesn't make any sense.

'Why it was for you! He wanted you to see Saint Brandon, he was doing you a favour.'

He shrugs his shoulders and says nothing more. He undoubtedly knows I didn't accept the offer to stay aboard the *Zeta*, and that's why I no longer interest him. He sinks back into his contemplation of the sun rising over the immense atoll, of the light that seems to be springing from the water and rising up towards the cloudless sky. Birds are flitting around in the sky, cormorants grazing along the surface of the water where their shadows glide, petrels high up in the wind, tiny silvery specks whirling about. They loop up, pass one another, squawk and cackle so loudly they awaken the men on deck, who begin to chat in turn.

A little later I learn why Bradmer has made the stopover in Saint Brandon. The pirogue is lowered into the sea with six crew members.

The captain is at the tiller and the helmsman standing in the front, harpoon in hand. The pirogue slips noiselessly over the water in the lagoon, towards La Perle. Leaning over the front of the pirogue, near the helmsman, I soon glimpse the dark shapes of tortoises near the beach. We move silently nearer. When the pirogue is upon them, they see us, but it is too late. With a quick gesture the helmsman throws the harpoon that pierces the shell with a crunch and blood spurts out. With a savage cry the men pull on the oars and the pirogue lurches towards the shore of the island, with the tortoise dragging behind. When the pirogue is near the beach, two sailors jump into the water, pull the harpoon out of the tortoise and turn it on its back on the sand.

We are already heading back out into the lagoon, where the other tortoises await, fearlessly. Several times the helmsman's harpoon pierces the shells of tortoises. Blood flows in rivulets over the white sandy beach, clouds the sea. We must work quickly before the smell of blood attracts the sharks that will drive the tortoises towards the shoals. On the white beach the tortoises are finishing the process of dying. There are ten of them. Striking them with machetes, the sailors hack them into pieces, line up the hunks of meat on the sand. They load them into the pirogue to be smoked on board the ship, because there is no wood on the islands. Here the land is sterile, a place where creatures of the sea come to die.

When the slaughter is over, everyone gets back into the pirogue, hands covered with blood. I hear the sharp cries of the birds fighting over the tortoise shells. The light is blinding, I feel dizzy. I can't wait to get away from this island, this bloodstained lagoon. The rest of the day, on the deck of the *Zeta*, the men busy themselves around the brazier where the hunks of meat are grilling. But I can't forget what happened, I refuse to eat in the evening. Tomorrow morning at dawn the *Zeta* will leave the atoll and nothing will be left of our passage, only the broken shells that the seabirds have already picked clean.

SUNDAY, AT SEA

I've been away for so long! A month, maybe more? I've never been so long without seeing Laure, without Mam. When I said goodbye to Laure, when I spoke to her for the first time about my journey to Rodrigues, she gave me her savings to help me pay for my passage. But I saw that dark flash in her eyes, the gleam of anger that said, we might never see each other again. She said *adieu* to me and not *au revoir*, and she didn't want to go down to the harbour with me. I had to live through all of these days at sea, this light, the burning of the sun and wind, these nights, before I could understand. Now I know that the *Zeta* is carrying me away on an adventure of no return. Who can know what his destiny holds? The secret awaiting me, the one that I alone must discover, is written here. It's marked in the sea, in the foam capping the waves, in the bright midday sky, in the unchanging patterns of the constellations. How can I decipher it? I think of the *Argo* again, how it sailed on uncharted seas, guided by the serpent of stars. The vessel was fulfilling its own destiny, not that of the men on board. Of what matter were the treasures, the territories? Did they not have to find their own destinies — some in combat or in the glory of love, others in death? As I think of the *Argo*, the deck of the *Zeta* has suddenly changed, been transfigured. And the dark-skinned Comorian and Indian sailors, the helmsman always standing at the wheel with his lava-stone features and unblinking eyes, and even squint-eyed Bradmer with his drunkard's face, haven't they also been roaming from island to island for ever in search of their destinies?

Are the reflections of the sun glinting off the dancing waves making me lose my reason? I feel as if I'm outside time, in some other, very different world, so far away from everything I've ever known that I'll never again be able to find what I left behind. That's why I feel this dizziness, this nausea: I'm afraid of giving up what I once was and never being able to turn back. Each hour, each day that passes is like the waves of the sea that come running up against the stem, lift the hull briefly, then disappear in its wake. Each of them is taking me farther away from the time I love, from Mam's voice, from Laure's presence.

Captain Bradmer comes up to me this morning at the stern of the ship. 'Tomorrow or the day after, we'll reach Rodrigues.'

I repeat, 'Tomorrow or the day after?'

'Tomorrow if the wind keeps up.'

So the journey is coming to an end. That's undoubtedly why everything seems so different.

The men have finished the provisions of meat. As for myself, I ate only spiced rice, that flesh horrifies me. For several days now I've felt a fever coming over me in the evening. Rolled up in my blanket down in the hold I lie shivering in spite of the sweltering heat. What will I do if my body betrays me? In my trunk I find the phial of quinine, purchased before my departure, and swallow a pill with my saliva.

It has grown dark without my noticing.

Late in the night I wake up soaked in sweat. Next to me, sitting cross-legged with his back leaning against the hull, is a man whose black face is lit strangely by the lamplight. Raising myself up on one elbow, I recognize the helmsman, his fixed gaze. He speaks to me in his sing-song voice, but I can't really understand the meaning of his words. I hear him asking me questions about the treasure I am going to look for in Rodrigues. How does he know about it?

Captain Bradmer must have told him. He asks me questions and I don't answer, but that doesn't bother him. He just waits, then asks another question, and still another. Finally he grows disinterested in the subject and begins talking about Saint Brandon, where he says he will go to die. I imagine his body sprawled out among the tortoise shells. I drift back to sleep, lulled by his voice.

IN SIGHT OF RODRIGUES

The island appears out on the horizon. It wells up from the sea in the yellow evening sky, with its tall blue mountains against the dark sea. Perhaps the seabirds crying over our heads was what first alerted me. I go up to the bow to get a better look. The sails billowing in the west wind are causing the stem to skittle after the waves. The ship drops into the troughs, surges up again. The horizon is very clear, pulled taut. The island rises and falls behind the waves, and the peaks of the mountains seem to be born of the ocean depths.

Never has a landscape made such an impression on me: it resembles the peaks of Trois Mamelles, but higher still, it forms an impassable wall. Casimir is beside me at the front. He happily informs me about the mountains, tells me their names.

Now the sun is hidden behind the island. The tall mountains stand out aggressively against the pale sky.

The captain has the crew reduce sail. The men climb up to the yards to reach the reefs. We are heading towards the dark island at the same speed as the waves, the jibs shining in the twilight like the wings of seabirds. As the ship approaches the coast I can feel anxiety welling up inside. Something is coming to an end, freedom, the joy of the sea. Now I'll have to find shelter, talk, ask questions, be in contact with the land.

Night falls very slowly. Now we are in the shadows of the high mountains. At around seven o'clock we go through the pass and head for the red lantern lit at the end of the jetty. The ship sails along the reefs. I can hear the voice of a sailor taking soundings starboard, calling out the measures, 'Seventeen, seventeen, fifteen, fifteen . . .'

At the end of the channel the stone jetty begins.

I hear the anchor drop and the chain unreeling. The *Zeta* is at rest along the wharf and, without waiting for the gangplank, the men jump down from the ship, start talking loudly with the waiting crowd. I'm standing on deck and for the first time in days, in months maybe, I'm fully dressed, I've slipped on my shoes. My trunk is packed at my feet. The *Zeta* is leaving tomorrow, in the afternoon, when the tides have changed.

I say goodbye to Captain Bradmer, he shakes my hand, evidently doesn't know what to say. I'm the one who wishes him luck. The black helmsman is already down below, he must be stretched out, his fixed gaze watching the sooty ceiling.

On the wharf, the blasts of wind make me stagger under the weight of the trunk on my shoulder. I turn, take one last look at the silhouette of the *Zeta* against the pale sky, with its inclined masts and the network of its lines. Maybe I should turn around and go back on board. I'd be in Port Louis in four days, I'd take the train, I'd walk through the drizzling rain towards the house at Forest Side, I'd hear Mam's voice, I'd see Laure.

A man is waiting for me on the wharf. In the glimmer of the lantern I recognize Casimir's athletic shape. He takes my trunk and walks along with me. He's going to show me the only hotel on the island, near the Government House, a hotel run by a Chinaman, one can eat there too, apparently. I walk behind him in the darkness through the narrow streets of Port Mathurin. I'm in Rodrigues.

Rodrigues, English Bay, 1911

———————

That's how, one morning in the winter of 1911 (in August, I believe, or at the beginning of September) I find myself in the hills overlooking English Bay, where all of my explorations will be carried out.

For weeks, months now, I've wandered Rodrigues from the south, where the other pass opens facing Gombrani Island, all the way to the chaotic black lava of Malagache Bay in the north, by way of the high mountains in the middle of the island, through Mangues, Patate, Montagne Bon Dié. The notes copied from Pingré's book were my guide. 'To the east of the large harbour,' he writes in 1761, 'we find insufficient water to sustain our pirogues, or else the water communicating with the open sea was too rough to sustain such a fragile vessel. Monsieur de Pingré, therefore, sent the pirogues back along the same route they had been brought, with orders to join us the following day at the *Enfoncement des Grandes Pierres à Chaux* (Limestone Embayment) . . . ' And elsewhere: 'The Quatre Passes mountains are very steep, and as there are almost no coral reefs and the shore is directly exposed to the wind, the sea crashes so violently against the coast that it would be particularly imprudent to attempt to cross here.' Read in the wavering light of my candle, in the hotel

167

room in Port Mathurin, Pingré's account reminds me of the famous letter written by an old sailor imprisoned in the Bastille, who put his father on the trail of the treasure: 'On the west coast of the island, in a place where the sea crashes against the coast, there is a river. Follow the river, you will find a source, next to the source, a tamarind tree. Eighteen feet from the tamarind tree begins the stone work that hides an immense treasure.'

Very early this morning I walked along the coast with a kind of feverish haste. I crossed Jenner Bridge, which marks the city limits of Port Mathurin. Farther along, I waded across the Bamboo River in front of the little cemetery. After that point there are no more houses and the path along the coast grows narrower. To the right I take the road that leads up to the buildings of the Cable & Wireless, the English telegraph company, at the summit of Venus Point.

I skirt the telegraph buildings, perhaps out of fear of encountering one of those Englishmen that slightly frighten the people of Rodrigues.

Heart racing, I go all the way to the top of the hill. This is the place – I'm sure of it now – where Pingré came to observe the orbit of Venus in 1761, long before the astronomers, accompanying Lieutenant Neate who named Venus Point in 1874.

The strong easterly wind throws me off balance. At the foot of the cliff I can see the choppy waves coming from the ocean flowing through the pass. Just beneath me are the buildings of the Cable & Wireless, long wooden hangars painted grey with reinforcements like those of an ocean liner: bolted on plates of sheet metal. A little higher up, amid the screw pines, I notice the director's white house, its veranda with closed shutters. A lone black man sitting on the steps of a hangar is smoking without looking at me.

Pushing on through the underbrush I soon reach the edge of the cliff top and discover the vast valley. All at once I realize I've finally found the place I've been looking for.

English Bay opens out on to the sea from either side of the Roseaux River estuary. From where I'm standing I can see the entire stretch of the valley all the way up to the mountains. I can make out every bush, ever tree, every stone. There is no one in the valley, not a house, not a human trace. Only stones, sand, the thin trickle of the river, the tufts of desert vegetation. My eyes follow the course of a stream up to the back of the valley from where the tall, still dark mountains rise. For an instant I think of the time when Denis and I would stop at the Mananava ravine, as if on the threshold of a forbidden land, listening for the reedy call of the tropicbirds.

Out here, there isn't a bird in the sky. Only clouds that loom up from the sea in the north and scud over in the direction of the mountains, making their shadows scurry along the valley bottom.

I stand up on the cliff in the lashing wind for a long time. I look for a way to get down. From where I am, it's impossible. The rocks jut straight up over the estuary of the river. I go back towards the top of the hill, pushing my way through the underbrush. The wind blowing through the leaves of the screw pines makes a wailing sound that intensifies the lonely feeling of this place.

Just before reaching the top of the hill I find a passageway: a rockslide that drops all the way down to the valley.

Now I'm walking through the valley of the Roseaux River, not knowing which way to go. From here, the valley seems wide, bordered in the distance by the black hills and the high mountains. The north wind is coming in from the mouth of the river, bearing with it rumours of the sea, giving rise to little whirlwinds of sand, like ashes, that for a moment make me think there are people arriving on horseback. But there's a strange silence out here, due to all of this light.

On the other side of the hills of Venus Point there is the bustling life of Port Mathurin, the marketplace, the coming and going of pirogues in Lascars Bay. And here everything is silent like a desert island. What will I find here? Who is waiting for me?

I walk around haphazardly on the valley bottom until the end of the day. I want to understand where I am. I want to understand why I came all the way out here, what had spurred me, alerted me. In the dry sand of the river beach I trace a map of the valley using a twig: the entrance to the bay with large basalt boulders on the east and west. The bed of the Roseaux River leading up in almost a straight line to the south and then making a bend before entering the gorges, between the mountains. I don't need to compare it with the Corsair's map as it appears in my father's documents: I'm obviously in the very spot where the treasure is.

Once again I feel light-headed, dizzy. There's so much silence here, so much solitude! Only the wind blowing through the boulders and the underbrush, bearing along the distant rumbling of the sea on the reefs, but it's the sound of a world without humans. Clouds scurry across the dazzling sky, puff, disappear behind the hills. I can't keep the secret to myself any longer! I feel like screaming, as loud as I can, so that I'll be heard out beyond the hills, even farther out than this island, out on the other side of the sea, all the way out in Forest Side, and my scream will penetrate the walls and deep into Laure's heart.

Did I truly scream? I don't know, my life is already like those dreams in which longing and fulfilment are one and the same. I run along the bottom of the valley, leaping over the black rocks, over the streams, I run as fast as I can through the brush, past the sun-scorched tamarind trees. I don't know where I'm going, I'm running as if I were falling, listening to the sound of the wind in my ears. Then I fall to the grey earth, on the sharp stones, without even feeling any pain, breathless, my body streaming with sweat. I lie there on the ground for a long time, face turned towards the clouds that are still fleeing southward.

Now I know where I am. I've found the place I was looking for. After months of roaming I feel at peace, filled with new fervour. I spend the days following my discovery of English Bay, preparing for my explorations. At Jeremie Briam's on Douglas Street I buy the basic necessities: a pick, a shovel, rope, a storm lamp, sailcloth and food. The finishing touch to my explorer's kit is one of those large hats made of screw-pine fibre worn by Manafs, the black people in the mountains. As for the rest, I decide that the few pieces of clothing I have and my old blanket should suffice. I deposit the meagre sum of money I have left at Barclay's Bank, whose manager, an obliging Englishman with a parchment face, simply notes down that I've come to Rodrigues on business and, since he represents the Elias Mallac postal company, offers to keep my mail.

When I've finished all of my preparations I go to the Chinaman's place to eat rice and fish, as I always do at noon. He knows I'm leaving and comes over to my table after the meal. He doesn't ask any questions about my departure. Like most of the people I've met in Rodrigues, he thinks I'm going to pan for gold in the mountain streams. I've carefully refrained from denying those rumours. A few days ago, as I was finishing my dinner in this same room, two men asked to speak with me, two Rodriguans. Right off the bat they opened a small pouch in front of me and poured out on to the table some earth mixed with shiny bits. 'Is it gold, sir?' Thanks to my father's lessons, I immediately recognized copper pyrite, which has led so many prospectors astray and is called 'fool's gold'. The two men were looking at me anxiously in the light of the oil lamp.

I didn't want to disappoint them too badly. 'No, it isn't gold, but it might be a sign that you are going to find some.' I also advised them to obtain a phial of royal water to avoid errors. They went away, half-satisfied, with their leather pouch. I think that is how I earned the reputation of being a prospector.

After lunch I get in the horse-drawn cart I've rented for the journey. The coachman, a jovial old black man, loads up my trunk and the material I bought. I climb up next to him and we set off through the empty streets of Port Mathurin towards English Bay. We drive down Hitchens Street and past the Begué house, then we take Barclay's Street up to the Governor's house. After that we head west, past the protestant church and the Depot, through the Raffaut Estate. Black children run after the cart for a time, then grow weary of it and go back to swim in the harbour. We cross the wooden bridge over the Lascars River. Because of the sun, I've pushed my large Manaf hat down on my head and I can't help thinking about how Laure would burst out laughing if she could see me in this outfit, bumping around in this cart with the old black coachman shouting at the mule to make it keep going.

When we arrive at the top of the hill at Venus Point the coachman unloads my trunk and the other tools, as well as the burlap bags containing my provisions. Then, after having pocketed what I owe him, he drives off, wishing me luck (that tale of my being a prospector), and I'm left alone on the edge of the cliff with my load in the rustling silence of the wind with the odd impression of having been left on the shore of a deserted island.

The sun is descending over the hills in the west and the shadows are already stealing over the bottom of the Roseaux River Valley, making the trees grow taller, the pointed leaves of the screw pines sharper. Now there is a vague feeling of anxiety creeping over me. I dread going down into that valley bottom, as if it were some forbidden land. I stand there at the edge of the cliff, not moving, staring at the landscape just as I'd discovered it the first time.

The strong wind makes up my mind. I'd noticed a stone platform halfway down the incline that could protect me from the chill of night and the rain. That is where I decide to set up my first camp and I carry the heavy trunk down on my shoulder. Despite the late hour, the sun is beating down on the slope and I'm bathed in sweat when I reach the platform. I need to rest for quite some time before going back to get my equipment, the pick and shovel, the sacks of provisions and the canvas that will serve as a tent.

The platform is very similar to a balcony, supported by large blocks of lava fitted together over the precipice. It must certainly be a very old construction because large screw pines have grown on the platform, their roots are even splitting the lava walls. Farther away, towards the upper part of the valley, I can see other identical platforms on the sides of the hills. Who built these balconies? I think of the mariners of the past, of the American whale-hunters who came to smoke their catch. But I can't help imagining the Corsair I'm searching for coming here. Perhaps he's the one who had these outposts built so he might better observe the 'stonework' being done to hide his treasure!

Once again I feel a sort of dizziness creeping over me, a fever. As I come and go on the slope of the hill, carrying my belongings, suddenly, on the floor of the valley, among the withered trees and the forms of the screw pines, I think I see them: shadows walking in single file, coming from the sea, carrying heavy sacks and picks, heading for the shadows of the hills in the west!

My heart is pounding, sweat is trickling down my face. I have to lie on the ground at the top of the cliff and gaze out at the yellow twilit sky to calm myself down.

Night is setting in rapidly. I hurry to pitch my camp before everything grows dark. Left behind by the floodwaters, I find some tree branches and kindling for making a fire on the riverbed. I use the large branches to build a makeshift framework to which I attach the sailcloth. I consolidate the structure by means of a few large stones. When I've set everything up, I'm too weary to think about making a fire and I content myself with eating a few sea biscuits, sitting out on the platform. Night has fallen suddenly, drowning the valley beneath me, blotting out the sea and the mountains. It is a cold, mineral night, with no unnecessary sounds, nothing but the wind whistling in the brush, the cracking of stones contracting after the burn of day and, off in the distance, the roaring of the waves on the reefs.

Despite my weariness, despite the cold that is making me shiver, I'm happy to be here, in the place I've dreamt about for so long without knowing whether it really existed. Deep down inside I feel a persistent thrill and I sit, waiting wide-eyed, watching the night. Slowly the stars slip westward, descend towards the invisible horizon. The heavy wind is jerking at the sailcloth behind me, as if I had not yet come to the end of my journey. Tomorrow I'll be here, I'll see the shadows passing. Something, someone is waiting for me. That's why I've come all the way out here, to find it, that's why I left Mam and Laure. I have to be ready for what will appear in this valley out at the other end of the world. I fall asleep, sitting at the entrance to my tent, leaning up against a stone, eyes gazing at the dark sky.

I've been in this valley for a long time. How many days, months? I should have kept a calendar like Robinson Crusoe, whittling notches into a piece of wood. In this lonely valley I'm as lost as I was in the immensity of the sea. Days follow nights, each new day erases the preceding one. That's why I take notes in the tablets bought in the Chinaman's shop in Port Mathurin, so there will be a trace of the time gone by.

What else is there? There are repetitive gestures as I roam the valley bottom every day in search of landmarks. I rise before daybreak to take advantage of the cool hours. At dawn the valley is extraordinarily beautiful. At the first blush of day the blocks of lava and schist glitter with dew. The bushes, the tamarind trees and the screw pines are still dark, numb with the chill of night. There is barely a breath of wind and beyond the uniform line of coconut trees I can see the still sea, of a deep blue with no reflections, holding its roar in check. It's the moment I love most, when everything is suspended, as if in waiting. Always that very pure, blank sky, where the first seabirds pass, boobies, cormorants, frigates flying across English Bay and heading for the islands in the north.

They are the only living things I've seen since I arrived, except for a few land crabs that dig their holes in the dunes of the estuary and the throngs of tiny sea crabs that run over the silt. When the birds fly back over the valley I know it is day's end. I feel as if I know each one of them, and that they know me too, this ridiculous black ant crawling around on the bottom of the valley.

Every morning I start exploring again, using the plans I drew up the day before. I go from one landmark to another, measuring the valley with my theodolite, then I come back, plotting an ever larger semicircle in order to examine every inch of the terrain. Soon the sun is out, firing bright sparkles on the sharp rocks, delineating the shadows. In the noon sun the valley looks completely different. At that time of day it's a very harsh, hostile place, bristling with spines and thorns. Due to the reflecting sunlight it grows ever hotter in spite of the strong winds. The heat bounces back on my face like an oven and I stumble over the floor of the valley, eyes streaming with tears.

I have to stop, wait. I go over to the river to drink a little water out of the palm of my hand. I sit down in the shade of a tamarind tree, leaning against its roots, which the floodwaters have laid bare. I wait, sitting still, not thinking about anything, as the sun revolves around the tree and begins its descent towards the black hills.

Sometimes I still think I see those shadows, those fleeting figures on the hilltops. I walk along the riverbed, eyes stinging. But the shadows fade away, go back to their hiding place, melt in with the black trunks of the tamarind trees. This is the time of day I dread most, when the silence and the light bear down upon my head and the wind is like a red-hot knife.

I remain in the shade of the old tamarind tree by the river. It's the first thing I saw when I awoke up there on the promontory. I made my way over to it and maybe I was thinking of the letter about the treasure that mentions this tamarind tree, near the source. But at the time it seemed it was the true master of this valley. It isn't very tall and yet when you are in the shelter of its branches, in its shade, a profound feeling of peace comes over you. Now I'm very familiar with its gnarled trunk, blackened with time, with sun and with drought, its tortured branches decked with fine, lacey foliage, so very delicate, so very tender. Strewn about on the ground around it are the long golden pods swollen with seeds. Every day I come here with my notebooks and my pencils and I suck on the sour seeds as I think of new plans, far from the torrid heat filling my tent.

I try to situate the parallel lines and the five points that served as landmarks on the Corsair's map. The points were undoubtedly the mountain peaks that are visible at the entrance to the bay. In the evening, before nightfall, I go down to the mouth of the river and see the mountain peaks still lit up by the sun, and I feel that thrill of eagerness again, as if something were going to appear.

I keep drawing the same lines on the paper: the curve of the river that I'm familiar with, then the straight valley that penetrates deep into the mountains. The hills on either side are basalt fortresses above the valley.

Today, when the sun goes down, I decide to climb up the hill on the east, searching for the 'anchor ring' marks left by the Corsair. If he really did come here, as it seems to be becoming clearer and clearer, it would have been impossible for the seafarer not to leave these kinds of permanent marks on the side of the cliff or on some rock. The incline of the slope is easier to climb on this side but, the more I climb, the more the summit recedes. That which, seen from a distance, seemed to be a smooth rock face is a series of steps that disorient me. Soon I am so far away from the other side of the valley that it's difficult for me to make out the white splotch of sailcloth that serves as my shelter. The floor of the valley is a grey-and-green desert scattered with black blocks that hide the riverbed. At the entrance to the valley I see the high cliff of Venus Point. I'm so alone out here, even though there are people nearby! Perhaps that's what worries me the most. I could die here, no one would notice. Maybe some day someone fishing for octopuses would see the remains of my bivouac and come looking. Or maybe everything would be swept away in the water and the wind, mingled with the stones and the scorched trees.

I examine the western hill, facing me, attentively. Is it an illusion? I see a capital 'M' carved into the rock just above Venus Point. In the slanting twilight it appears very clearly, as if it had been etched into the mountain by some giant hand. Farther off, at the tip of a sharp peak, there is a half-tumbled-down stone tower that I hadn't seen when I set up camp just below it.

The discovery of these two landmarks exhilarates me. Without wasting a second I rush down the slope of the hill and run across the valley to reach there before nightfall. I cross the Roseaux River, making great splashes of fresh water, and climb up the hill on the west by way of the rock slide that I'd used the first time.

Once at the top of the hill I search in vain for the carved 'M': it has come undone before my very eyes. The spans of rock that formed the legs of the 'M' have grown farther apart and, in the centre there is a sort of plateau where wind-worn bushes grow. As I move forward, bent over, struggling against the gusting wind, the sound of tumbling stones alerts me. I believe I see some brown shapes fleeing between the euphorbia and the screw pines. They are goats, perhaps escaped from a Manaf herd.

I finally come up in front of the tower. It stands at the top of the cliff overlooking the valley already plunged in shadow. Why hadn't

I seen it when I first arrived? It's a tower made of large blocks of basalt assembled without mortar that has crumbled down on one side. On the other side there are the remnants of a door or a loop-hole. I go inside the ruin and squat down to get out of the wind. I can observe the sea through the opening. It stretches out infinitely in the twilight, its blue hue fraught with anger. Out on the horizon grey mists veil it, blending it in with the sky.

Up on the cliff top you can take in the seascape from the harbour of Port Mathurin all the way to the eastern point of the island. Then I realize that this hastily built tower was only here in order to keep a lookout on the sea and give the alert in case of an enemy approach. Who had built the watchtower? It couldn't have been the British Admiralty, which had nothing more to fear from the sea, since it controlled the route to the Indies. In fact, neither the English navy nor that of the King of France would have built such a precarious, isolated construction. Pingré doesn't mention the construction in his travel log when he made the first observation of the transit of Venus in 1761. On the other hand, I now recall the first English camp on Venus Point in 1810 set up on the site of the future observatory, exactly where I'm standing. The Mauritius Almanac, which I read at the Carnegie Library, spoke of a small 'outpost' built inside the gorge, overlooking the sea. As night falls, my mind races nervously, I'm in a state resembling the wakeful dreams that precede sleep. Just for myself, I recite out loud the sentences that I had read so often in Nageon de Lestang's letter, written in long, slanting script on a torn piece of paper:

'For the first sign, find a pgt stone
Take the 2nd V, have it run South-North,
it will look like the stern of a ship.

And from the source in the East trace an angle like an anchor ring
The mark on the sand of the source
For $\left|\frac{e}{w}\right|$ go to the left
From there, each one of the signs BnShe
There, rub against the pass, where you will find what to think.
Look for : : S
Calculate x — 1 do m of the diagonal in the direction of the
Commander's Garret.'

Right at the moment I'm sitting in the ruins of the watchtower of
the Commander's Garret as darkness fills the valley. I no longer feel
the exhaustion or the cold blasts of wind or the loneliness. I've just
discovered the Mysterious Corsair's first landmark.

The days following the discovery of the Commander's Garret, I roam the floor of the valley consumed with a feverishness that sometimes slips into delirium. I remember (though it grows blurry and elusive like a dream) those burning hot days in the April sun during the cyclone season, I remember it as you would a sudden fall through a vertical void, and the burn of the air when my chest lifts laboriously. From dawn to dusk I follow the path of the sun in the sky, from the solitary hills in the east all the way out to the mountains overlooking the centre of the island. I move, as does the sun, in a semicircle, with the pick on my shoulder, measuring the relief of the terrain — my only point of reference — with the theodolite. I see the shadows of the trees wheel slowly round, grow longer on the ground. The heat of the sun burns through my clothing and continues burning throughout the night, preventing me from sleeping, mingling with the cold rising from the earth. On some evenings I'm so weary from walking that I lie down wherever I am at nightfall, between two blocks of lava, and sleep until morning, when hunger and thirst awaken me.

One night I wake up in the middle of the valley, I can feel the breath of the sea upon me. There is still the blinding spot of the sun in my eyes, on my face. It's a dark moon night as my father used to say. The sky is filled with stars and, in the grip of that madness, I contemplate them. I talk out loud, saying: I can see the pattern, it's there, I can see it. The Corsair's map is none other than the pattern of the Southern Cross and its 'followers', the *Belles de nuit*. Over the vast stretch of the valley I can see the lava stones shimmering. They are lit up like stars in the dusty darkness. I walk towards them, keeping my eyes wide, I can feel their gleaming light on my face. Thirst, hunger, loneliness are whirling around inside me, faster and faster. I can hear someone speaking in the same tone of voice as my father. At first it reassures me, but then makes me shudder, for I realize I'm the one who is speaking. To avoid falling I sit on the ground, near the big tamarind tree that shelters me during the day. The waves of the shudder continue to move over my body, I feel the chill of the earth and of space penetrating me.

How long have I remained sitting here? When I open my eyes, first I see the foliage of the tamarind tree above me and the dappled sunshine through the leaves. I am lying between the roots. A child and a young girl with dark faces, dressed in rags like Manafs, are sitting beside me. The young girl is holding a piece of cloth in her hands that she is twisting to make drops of water fall on my lips.

The water runs into my mouth, over my swollen tongue. Every swallow I take is painful.

The child walks away, comes back carrying a piece of cloth soaked with water from the river. I drink some more. Every drop awakens my body, awakens a pain, but it is good.

The young girl talks to the little boy in a Creole I barely understand. I'm alone with the young Manaf girl. When I attempt to lift myself, she helps me to sit up. I want to talk to her, but my tongue still refuses to move. The sun is already high in the sky, I can feel the heat rising in the valley. Beyond the shade of the tamarind tree, the landscape is blinding, cruel. Just the thought that I will have to cross that sunlit area makes me nauseous.

The child comes back, he's carrying a hot pepper cake in his hand, he offers it to me with such ceremony that it makes me want to laugh. I eat the cake slowly and the hot pepper feels good in my sore mouth. I share out what is left of the cake, offer some to the young girl and to the boy, but they refuse.

'Where do you live?'

I didn't speak in Creole, but the young Manaf girl seems to understand. She points to the high mountains at the back of the valley.

I think she says, 'Up there.'

She's a true Manaf, quiet, guarded. Since I have sat up and begun talking, she's backed away, she's poised to turn and go. The child has also stepped back, he's watching me furtively.

All of a sudden they're off. I want to call out to them, hold them back. They're the first human beings I've seen in months. But what good would it do to call to them? They're moving away unhurriedly, but without turning back, jumping from stone to stone, they disappear into the underbrush. I see them a moment later on the flank of the hill to the west, just like two young goats. They disappear high up in the valley. They saved my life.

I remain in the shade of the tamarind tree until evening, almost without moving. Large black ants run tirelessly along the roots in vain. Near the end of the day I hear the cries of the seabirds flying over English Bay. The mosquitoes are dancing. As cautiously as an old man, I set off across the valley, go back to my camp. Tomorrow I'll go to Port Mathurin to wait for the first boat to sail out. Maybe it will be the *Zeta*?

There were the days in Port Mathurin, far from English Bay, the days in the hospital — the Head Doctor, Camal Boudou, who said only these words to me, 'You could have died of exposure.' *Exposure*, it's a word that has stuck in my mind, it seems like none other could better express what I felt on that night, before the Manaf children gave me the water to drink. Yet I can't make up my mind to leave. It would be a terrible failure; the house in Boucan, Laure and I would be losing our whole life.

So this morning, before daybreak, I leave the hotel in Port Mathurin and go back to English Bay. I don't need a cart this time: all my things have remained at my camp, wrapped in the sailcloth, secured with a few stones.

I've decided to hire a man to help me with my explorations. In Port Mathurin I was told about the Castel farm, behind the Cable & Wireless buildings, where I could certainly find someone.

I arrive before English Bay as the sun is rising. In the morning crispness, with the smell of the sea, everything seems new, transformed. The sky over the hills in the east is a very soft shade of pink, the sea is shining like an emerald. In the dawn light the forms of the trees and screw pines seem unfamiliar.

How could I have forgotten this beauty so quickly? The exaltation I feel today has nothing to do with the fever that drove me mad and made me go running around in the valley. Now I understand what I've come in search of: it is a force much greater than my own, a memory that began before I was born. For the first time in months it seems as if Laure has drawn nearer, as if the distance between us doesn't count any more.

I think of her, prisoner to the Forest Side house, and I gaze at the dawn landscape in order to send this beauty and serenity to her. I remember the game we used to play sometimes up in the attic of the Boucan house; each of us at one end of the dark attic with an issue of the *Illustrated London News* open in front of us, we would try our best to send each other images or words by telepathy. Will Laure win at the game once again, just as she used to? I send her all of this: the pure line of the hills standing against the pink sky, the emerald-green sea, the wind, the slow flight of the seabirds coming from Lascars Bay and heading towards the rising sun.

Around noon, having climbed up to the Commander's Garret in the Corsair's ruined watchtower, I discover the ravine. At the upper end of the valley. It hadn't been visible because of a rockslide that is hiding its entrance. In the light of the sun at its zenith I can clearly see the dark gash it makes in the flank of the hill to the east.

I carefully note its location in regard to the trees in the valley. Then I go and talk to the farmer, near the telegraph buildings. His farmhouse, as I was able to see when I arrived on the road from Port Mathurin, is a rather precarious shelter from the wind and rain, half-hidden in a declivity in the land. As I draw near a great dark shape stands up, grunting, a half-wild pig. Then it's a dog, fangs bared. I recall Denis's lessons in the old days, out in the fields: a stick, a stone are useless. You need two stones, one you throw and the other you threaten with. The dog backs away, but defends the door to the house.

'Mister Castel?'

A man appears, bare-chested, wearing fishermen's trousers. He's a tall, strong black man with a scarred face. He pushes the dog aside and invites me to come in.

The inside of the farmhouse is dark, smoke-filled. The furniture consists of a table and two chairs. At the back of the only room, a woman dressed in a faded dress is cooking. At her side is a little girl with light skin.

Mr Castel invites me to sit down. He remains standing, listens to me politely as I explain what I've come for. He nods his head. He'll come and help me from time to time, and his adopted son Fritz will bring me a meal every day. He doesn't ask me why we are going to dig up the ground. He doesn't ask a single question.

This afternoon I've decided to continue my explorations further south at the upper end of the valley. I leave the shelter of the tamarind tree, where I've now set up camp, and follow the Roseaux River upstream. The river winds along on the sandy bed, forms meanders, islands, a narrow stream of water that is only the exterior aspect of an underground river. Higher up, the river is a mere trickle running over a bed of black shingles in the middle of the gorge. I am already very near the foothills of the mountains. The vegetation is even sparser, thorn bushes, acacias and the ever-present screw pines with leaves like cutlass blades.

The silence is heavy up here and I try to walk, making as little noise as possible. At the foot of the mountains the stream splits into several sources in schist and lava gullies. Suddenly the sky grows dark, it's going to rain. The drops come large and cold. In the distance, down at the very bottom of the valley, I notice the sea veiled in the storm. Standing under a tamarind tree I watch the rain making its way up the narrow valley.

Then I see her: it's the young girl who saved me the other day when I was delirious with thirst and fatigue. She has a child's face, but she is tall and svelte, wearing a short skirt, as is the custom for Manaf women, and a ragged shirt. Her hair is long and curly like that of Indian women. She's walking along the valley, head down because of the rain. She's coming towards my tree. I know she hasn't seen me yet and I'm apprehensive about what will happen when she notices me. Will she cry out in fear and run away? She walks silently along with the supple movements of an animal. She stops to glance at the tamarind tree, she sees me. For an instant her smooth, handsome face betrays wariness. She stands still, balanced on one leg, leaning on her long harpoon. Her rain-soaked clothes are clinging to her body and her long black hair makes her copper skin seem more luminous.

'Good day!'

I say that first, to drive away the anxious silence that reigns up here. I take a step towards her. She doesn't move, just stares at me. The rain is running down her forehead, her cheeks, down her long hair. I notice she's holding a vine bandolier strung with fish in her left hand.

'Have you been fishing?'

My voice rings out oddly. Does she understand what I'm saying? She goes as far as the tamarind tree and sits on one of its roots, sheltered from the rain. She keeps her face turned towards the mountains.

'Do you live in the mountains?'

She nods her head. In a lilting voice she says, 'Is it true you're looking for gold?'

I am less surprised by the question than by the language. She speaks French with hardly any accent.

187

'Have you been told that? Yes, it's true, I am looking for gold.'

'Have you found any?'

I laugh.

'No, I haven't found any yet.'

'And do you really believe there's gold around here?'

I find her question amusing.

'Why? Don't you believe so?'

She looks at me, her face is smooth, fearless, like that of a child.

'Everyone is so poor here.'

Again she turns her head towards Mont Limon, which has vanished in the cloud of rain. For a moment we watch the rain falling without saying anything. I look at her wet clothing, her slender legs, her bare feet resting nice and flat on the ground.

'What's your name?'

The question has slipped out almost in spite of myself, maybe so I can hold on to something about this strange young girl who will soon disappear into the mountains. She looks at me with her deep, dark eyes, as if thinking about something else.

Finally she says, 'My name is Ouma.'

She stands, picks up the vine on which the fish are strung, her harpoon, and leaves, walking quickly along the stream in the slackening rain. I see her nimble silhouette leaping from stone to stone, just like a young goat, then it fades into the underbrush. It all happened so fast that it's difficult for me to believe I haven't imagined that apparition – that beautiful, wild, young girl who saved my life. The silence is making my head reel. The rain has stopped altogether and the sun is shining brightly in the blue sky. The mountains seem even higher, more inaccessible, in the sunlight. In vain I scan the slopes of the mountains, over in the direction of Mont Limon. The young girl has disappeared, she's blended in with the walls of black stone. Where does she live, in which Manaf village? I think of her strange name, an Indian name, whose two syllables she'd made ring out clearly, a name that troubles me. I end up running back down to my camp under the old tamarind tree at the bottom of the valley.

In the shade of the tree I spend the rest of the day studying the maps of the valley and marking the places I'll need to probe with a red pencil. When I go out to locate them on the terrain, not far from the second point, I can clearly make out a mark on an immense boulder: four regular holes chiselled into the rock in the shape of a square. Suddenly I recall the formula in the Mysterious Corsair's letter: 'Look for : :'. My heart starts beating faster when I turn to the west and discover that the watchtower of the Commander's Garret does indeed lie on the diagonal of the north–south axis.

Late in the day I find the first mark of the anchor ring on the slope of the hill on the eastern side.

As I'm trying to establish the east–west axis that cuts across the Roseaux River at the edge of the old swamp, I find the anchor ring.

Walking along with compass in hand, my back to the sun, I pass over a dip in the ground that I think is the bed of a former tributary. I reach the cliff on the east side, very sheer in that particular place. It is almost a vertical wall of basalt that is partially crumbled down. On one of the rock faces, up near the top, I see the mark.

'The mooring ring! The mooring ring!'

Repeating these words in a hushed voice I try to find a way to reach the top of the cliff. The stones roll out from underfoot, I grab hold of shrubs to pull myself up. Once near the top I have a hard time finding the rock wall with the mark. Seen from below, the sign was clear, in the shape of an inverted equilateral triangle, exactly like anchor rings in the days of the corsairs. As I'm searching for that sign, I can feel my blood beating in my temples. Could I have been the victim of an illusion? I see angular marks caused by past fractures on all the rock faces. I examine the edge of the cliff several times, slipping on the loose rocks.

Down below in the valley young Fritz Castel, who's come to bring me my meal, has stopped at the foot of the cliff and is looking up. I understand my error when I see the direction in which he's looking. The rock faces all resemble one another and I'm sure the ones I'd spotted are higher up. I climb higher and reach a second level that is also where the vegetation stops. There, before my eyes, on a large black rock, shines the magnificent triangle of the mooring ring, etched into the hard rock with a regularity that only a chisel could achieve. Trembling excitedly, I step up to the stone, brush my fingertips across it. The basalt is warm with light, soft and smooth as skin and I can feel the sharp edge of the triangle that is inverted, like this:

I will surely find the same sign on the other side of the valley by following a line running east-west. The other slope is at quite a distance, even with a telescope, I wouldn't be able to see it. The hills on the western side are already in shadows and I put off the search for the other mooring ring until tomorrow.

When young Fritz has left I climb back up. I stay there, sitting on the crumbling rock, gazing out on the expanse of English Bay being overtaken by the night. For the very first time I have the feeling that I'm not seeing it with my own eyes, but with those of the Mysterious Corsair who came here a hundred and fifty years ago, who drew up the plan of his secret in the grey sand of the river and then allowed it to fade away, leaving only the marks carved in the hard stone. I imagine how he must have held the hammer and chisel in order to engrave this sign and how the pounding of the hammer must have rung out all the way to the other end of the deserted valley. In the serenity of this bay, where a quick ruffle of wind passes from time to time, bearing along with it snatches of the rumbling sea, I can hear the sound of the chisel chipping at the stone echoing in the surrounding hills. Tonight, lying on the bare ground between the roots of the tamarind tree, wrapped in my blanket just as I used to be out on the deck of the *Zeta*, I dream of a new life.

Today at the crack of dawn I'm standing at the foot of the western cliff. There is barely enough light to make out the black rocks and in the crook of the bay the blue of the sea is translucent, lighter than the sky. Like every morning I hear the cry of seabirds flying over the bay, squadrons of cormorants, gulls and boobies calling out hoarsely on their way to Lascars Bay. I've never been so happy to hear them. It seems as if their cries are greetings they are sending to me as they pass over the bay, and I too cry out to them in answer. A few birds fly right over me, sterns with vast wings, fast-flying petrels. They circle round near the cliff, then go off to join the others out at sea. I envy their lightness, the speed with which they slip through the air, free of all ties to the earth. Then I see myself glued to the floor of this sterile valley, spending days, months scouting out territories that the birds' eyes have scanned in an instant. I love watching them, I partake in a bit of their beauteous flight, a bit of their freedom.

Do they need gold, riches? The wind is enough for them, the morning sky, the sea abounding in fish and the emerging rocks, their sole shelter from storms.

Guided by my intuition I make my way over to the black cliff where I'd noticed crevices from the hill on the other side of the valley. As I pull myself up with the aid of shrubs, the wind buffets, inebriates me. All at once the sun appears above the hills in the east — magnificent, dazzling, lighting sparkles on the sea.

I examine the cliff bit by bit. I can feel the burn of the sun growing steadily hotter. Around midday I hear someone call. It's young Fritz waiting for me below, near the camp. I climb back down to rest. The enthusiasm I felt in the morning has waned considerably. I feel weary, discouraged. In the shade of the tamarind tree I eat the white rice in Fritz's company. When he's finished eating, he sits waiting in silence, gazing out into the distance with that impassive attitude that is characteristic of the black people from here.

I think of Ouma, so wild, so lithe. Will she come back? Every evening before sunset I walk along the Roseaux River until I reach the dunes, looking for traces of her. Why? What could I say to her? Even so, I think she's the only one who understands what I've come here in search of.

Tonight, when the stars appear one by one in the sky, to the north, the Smaller Chariot, then Orion, Sirius, I suddenly understand where I've gone wrong: when I plotted the east-west axis, starting from the mark of the mooring ring, I was using the magnetic north as my compass indicated. The Corsair, who drew up his maps and marked off the rocks, didn't use a compass. He undoubtedly used the northern star as a reference point and it is in relation to that direction that he established the east-west perpendicular. Since the difference between the magnetic north and the stellar north is 7°36, that would mean a discrepancy of nearly one hundred feet at the base of the cliff — that is to say on the other rock face which forms the first spur of the Commander's Garret.

I'm so shaken by this discovery that I can't convince myself to wait until morning. Armed with my storm lamp, I walk barefoot out to the cliff. There is a heavy wind blowing, sweeping along clouds and sea spray. In the shelter of the roots of the old tamarind tree I hadn't heard the storm. But out here I can barely stand up, it's whistling in my ears and making the flame of my lamp flicker.

Now I'm at the foot of the black cliff and I'm searching for a route to climb up. The cliff wall is so sheer that I need to hold the lamp between my teeth to scale up. I reach a ledge about halfway to the top in this manner and start looking for the mark along the crumbling cliff wall. In the light of the lamp the basalt rock face takes on an eerie, diabolic aspect. Each pock mark, each crack, makes me cringe. I work my way along the length of the ledge like this until I reach a crevice that separates this part of the cliff from the rocky bluff hanging over the sea. I'm numb from the cold, lashing winds, from the roaring of the sea directly below me, from the water streaming over my face. Just as I'm preparing to go back down, exhausted, I notice a large boulder just above me and I know the sign must be there, I'm certain of it. It's the only boulder visible from all points in the valley. To reach it I have to make a detour, follow a path over a shifting rockslide. When I finally find myself before the boulder, holding the storm lantern between my teeth, I see the mooring ring. It's engraved so clearly that I could have seen it without the lantern. Under my fingers its edges are as sharp as if they'd been carved yesterday. The black rock is cold, slippery. The triangle is drawn with the summit pointing upwards, contrary to the mooring ring on the east. On this rock, it seems like a mysterious eye staring out from the other end of time, contemplating the opposite side of the valley unfalteringly, day after day, night after night. A shudder runs through my body. I've found my way into a secret that is more powerful, more durable than I am. Where will it lead me?

After that I live in a sort of waking dream in which Laure's voice and that of Mam out on the veranda in Boucan mingle with the Corsair's message and with the fleeting vision of Ouma slipping through the brush high up in the valley. Loneliness has closed in upon me. With the exception of young Fritz Castel, I don't see anyone. Even he doesn't come as regularly as he used to. Yesterday (or the day before, I'm not sure any more) he set the pot of rice down on a stone in front of the camp, then left, climbing the hill in the west without answering my calls. As if I frightened him.

At dawn I go down to the estuary of the river, as I do every morning. I take my toiletry bag with a razor, a bar of soap and a brush, as well as the laundry that needs washing. I put the mirror on a stone and begin by shaving my beard, then I cut my hair that now reaches down to my shoulders. In the mirror I look at my thin face, darkened from the sun, my eyes shiny with fever. My nose — which is thin and aquiline, as is that of all males who bear the name L'Étang — accentuates the lost, almost ghostly expression on my face. I sincerely believe that by dint of following in his footsteps I've begun to resemble the Mysterious Corsair who once lived in this valley.

I truly enjoy being here at the Roseaux River estuary, in the place where the dunes begin, where you can hear the sea so close, its slow respiration as the wind comes gusting in amid the euphorbia and the reeds, setting the palms to creaking. Here, at daybreak, the light is so soft, so calm, and the water is as smooth as a mirror. After I've finished shaving, bathing and washing my clothes, just as I'm preparing to go back to my camp, I see Ouma. She's standing in front of the river, holding her harpoon and staring at me openly with a somewhat mocking look in her eyes. I've often hoped to meet her here on the beach at low tide, on her way back from fishing, and yet, surprised, I just stand there, stock still, my wet laundry dripping on my feet.

By the side of the water in the nascent light of day, she's even lovelier, her cotton skirt and shirt are soaked with seawater, her face the colour of copper, the colour of lava, glittering with salt. She's just standing there, one leg extended and her torso leaning over her cocked left hip, holding the reed harpoon with the ebony tip in her right hand, her left hand resting on her right shoulder, draped in her wet clothing, like an antique statue. I stare at her without daring to speak and, in spite of myself, I think of the beautiful and mysterious Nada, as she used to be pictured in the illustrations of the old journals in the dusk light of our attic at Boucan. I take a step forward and I feel as if I've broken a spell. Ouma turns, she strides away along the riverbed.

'Wait!' I've shouted without thinking, running after her.

Ouma stops, she looks at me. I can see mistrust, wariness in her eyes. I want to say something to hold her back, but I haven't spoken to a living soul in such a long time, the words don't come. I want to tell her about the marks I've searched for on the beach, in the evening before the tide comes in. But she's the one who speaks to me.

She asks me in her chanting, mocking voice, 'Have you found gold at last?'

I shake my head and she laughs. She sits on her heels at the top of a dune, a slight distance away. To sit down, she pulls her skirt between her legs with a gesture I've never seen any other woman make. She leans on the harpoon.

'And you, have you caught anything?'

She shakes her head in turn.

'Are you going back to your place in the mountains?'

She looks at the sky.

'It's still early. I'm going to try again, over by the point.'

'Can I come with you?'

She stands without answering. Then she turns towards me. 'Come along.'

She sets off without waiting for me. She walks quickly over the sand with that animal-like gait, the long harpoon on her shoulder.

I throw the bundle of wet laundry in the sand, not worrying that the wind might blow it away. I run after Ouma, catch up with her near the sea. She's walking along the waves that are washing in, eyes fixed on the open sea. The wind is blowing her wet clothing against her slender body. In the still, grey morning sky, my bird-companions pass by, yelping and making that rattling sound of theirs.

'Do you like the seabirds?'

She stops, one arm lifted towards them. Her face is shining in the light. She says, 'They're beautiful.'

At the end of the beach the young girl bounds agilely, effortlessly, barefoot over the sharp rocks. She goes out to the point facing the deep water, colour of blue steel. When I come up next to her, she motions me to stop. Her long silhouette is leaning over the sea, harpoon raised, she's searching the depths down near the coral reefs. She remains in that position for a long time, perfectly still, then suddenly leaps forward and disappears into the water. I search the surface, looking for escaping bubbles, a ripple, a shadow. When I no longer know where to look, the young girl surfaces a few arm's lengths from me, gasping. She swims slowly over to me, throws a speared fish on to the rocks. She gets out of the water with the harpoon, her face is pale with cold.

She says, 'There's another one over there.'

I take the harpoon and, in turn, dive into the sea, fully clothed.

Under the water I see the murky bottom, the sparkling flakes of seaweed. The waves breaking on the coral reef make a shrill, grating sound. I swim underwater towards the coral, clasping the harpoon close to my body. I swim twice around the reefs without seeing anything. When I go back to the surface Ouma is leaning over me, shouting, 'There, over there!'

She dives in. Under the water I see her dark shadow slipping along near the bottom. In a cloud of sand the grouper comes out of its hiding place and moves slowly past me. Almost of its own accord the harpoon leaps out of my hand and pins the fish. The blood makes a cloud in the water around me. I go up to the surface immediately. Ouma is swimming next to me, she climbs up on the rocks before I do. She's the one who takes the harpoon and kills the fish, beating it against the black rock. Short of breath, I remain sitting on the rocks, shivering with cold. Ouma pulls me by the arm.

'Come on, you need to get moving!'

Holding the two fish by the gills, she's already bounding from rock to rock in the direction of the beach. She looks in the dunes for a creeper vine on which to string the fish. Now we're walking together towards the bed of the Roseaux River. In the place where the river makes a deep, sky-coloured pool she lays the fish on the bank and dives into the fresh water, splashing her head and body like a bathing animal. On the edge of the river I look like a large wet bird and it makes her laugh. I jump into the water too, sending up great sprays, and we spend a good long time splashing each other and laughing. When we get out of the water I'm surprised not to feel cold any longer. The sun is already high in the sky and the dunes near the estuary are burning hot. Our wet clothes are sticking to our skin. Kneeling in the sand, Ouma wrings out her skirt and shirt, from top to bottom, taking one sleeve off at a time. Her copper-coloured skin shines in the sunlight and trickles of water run down from her heavy, soaked hair along her cheeks, down her neck. The wind is blowing in gusts, riffling over the river water. We're not talking any more. Out here, standing by this river in the harsh sunlight, listening to the mournful sound of the wind in the reeds and the rumble of the sea, we're all alone on Earth, perhaps the very last inhabitants, having come from nowhere, brought together by a chance shipwreck. Never would I have thought that this could happen to me, that I could feel anything like this. There is a new strength awakening in me, spreading through my body, a desire, a burning feeling. We remain sitting in the sand for a long time, waiting for our clothes to dry. Ouma isn't moving either, sitting on her heels as she knows how to, in the manner of the Manafs, her long arms wrapped about her legs, face turned towards the sea. The sun is shining on her tangled hair, I can see her flawless profile, her straight forehead, the bridge of her nose, her lips. Her clothing is stirring in the wind. I feel as if nothing else is of any importance now.

Ouma decides it's time to leave. She suddenly stands up, without steadying herself with her hands, gathers up the fish. Squatting on the riverbank, she prepares them in a way I've never seen before. With the tip of her harpoon she splits open the bellies of the fish and guts them, then washes their insides with sand and rinses them in the river. She throws the innards out towards the army of waiting crabs.

She's done all of this quickly, silently. Then she erases the traces left on the riverbank with water. When I ask her why she does that, she answers, 'We Manafs are maroons.'

A little farther on, I collect my laundry, almost dry, covered with white sand. I walk behind her until we reach the camp. When she gets there, she lays the fish that I speared on a flat rock and says, 'It's yours.'

When I protest, trying to give it back to her, she says, 'You're hungry, I'll cook for you.'

She hurriedly gathers some dry twigs. With a few green reeds she builds a sort of rack that she sets up over the twigs. I hand her my tinderbox, but she shakes her head. She prepares a heap of dry lichen and, squatting, back to the wind, strikes two flints against one another, very rapidly, not stopping until sparks rain from the hot stones. The pile of lichen begins to smoke at its centre. Ouma takes it very carefully in her hands and slowly blows on it. When the flame bursts forth she puts the lichen under the dry branches and soon a fire is crackling. Ouma straightens up. Her face is lit with infantile joy. On the reed rack the fish is roasting and I can already smell the delicious fragrance. Ouma's right, I'm famished.

When the fish is cooked, Ouma lays the rack on the ground. Each in turn, burning our fingers, we take mouthfuls of flesh. I truly believe I've never eaten anything better than that unsalted fish grilled on that rack of green reeds.

When we've finished eating, Ouma stands up. She carefully puts out the fire, covering it with black sand. Then she takes the other fish that she'd rolled in the dirt to protect it from the sun. Without saying a word, without looking at me, she walks away. The wind describes the shape of her body under the garments faded from saltwater and sun. The light is shining on her face, but her eyes are two dark shadows. I understand that she must not speak. I understand that I must remain here, that's part of her game, the game she's playing with me.

Lithe and nimble as an animal, she makes her way through the bushes, leaping from rock to rock high into the valley. Standing by the old tamarind tree, I can still see her for another minute, scaling up the mountainside like a wild goat. She doesn't turn around, doesn't stop. She walks up into mountains, in the direction of Mont Lubin, disappears in the shadows covering the western slopes. I can hear my heart beating, my thoughts are sluggish. Loneliness creeps back into English Bay, ever more frightening. Sitting near my camp, facing the setting sun, I watch the shadows inching closer.

And so these last few days I've been led even further into my dream. Each day a little more of what I'm searching for is unveiled and it is so powerful it fills me with joy. From dawn to dusk I tramp through the valley looking for landmarks, for clues. The dazzling light that precedes the winter rains, the cries of the seabirds, the gusts of wind from the north-west, fill me with a sort of giddiness.

At times, between the blocks of basalt, halfway up the slope, on the banks of the Roseaux River, I catch a glimpse of a furtive shadow, so fleeting that I'm never sure I have really seen it. Ouma, come down from her mountain, is observing me, hiding behind a boulder or in the stands of screw pines. Sometimes she comes accompanied by a young boy of extraordinary beauty, whom she says is her half-brother and who is mute. He stays at her side, not daring to come near, looking at once cautious and curious. His name is Sri, according to what Ouma says, it's a nickname her mother gave him because he's like a messenger from God.

Ouma brings me food, strange dishes wrapped in bitter melon leaves, rice and dried octopus cakes, manioc, hot pepper cakes. She sets down the food on a flat stone at the entrance to my camp, like an offering. I tell her of my discoveries and it makes her laugh. In a notebook I've drawn the signs I've found as the days go by. She likes me to read them to her out loud: stones marked with a heart, with two round punch marks, with a crescent moon. Stone marked with the letter M in keeping with the Key of Solomon, stone marked with a cross. The head of a serpent, the head of a woman, three round indentation marks forming a triangle. Stone marked with a chair or a 'Z', evoking the Corsair's message. Truncated boulder. Boulder sculpted into a roof. Stone embellished with a large circle. Stone whose shadow represents a dog. Stone marked with an 'S' and two round punch marks. Stone marked with a 'Turkish dog' (crawling, with tips of paws missing). Boulders with a row of round punch marks indicating south-south-west. Broken and burned boulder.

Ouma also wants to see the signs I've brought back, lava in strange shapes, obsidian, stones with embedded fossils. Ouma takes them in her hands and looks at them carefully as if they were magic. Sometimes she brings me strange objects that she's found. One day she brings me a smooth, heavy stone the colour of iron. It's a meteorite and my hands coming in contact with that object fallen from the sky perhaps thousands of years ago gives me a thrill like a secret.

Now Ouma comes to English Bay almost every day. She waits in the shade of a tree, high up in the valley while I measure the distances and also when I dig probe holes, because she's afraid the noise might attract people in the vicinity. Several times young Fritz and farmer Begué come out to see me and help me dig holes near the estuary of the river. On those days Ouma doesn't show herself, but I know she's somewhere nearby, hiding behind the trees, in some nook where the colour of her skin blends in with the surroundings.

Fritz and I place the markers. They are reeds I've prepared for this very purpose which must be planted every hundred paces to trace straight lines. So I go up to the top of the valley, up among the signs I've recognized, stones engraved with punch marks, marked angles, piles of rocks forming a triangle, etc., and I plot the extension of the straight lines using the theodolite, in order to transcribe them upon the initial diagram (the Corsair's grid). The sun is beating down, making the black stones sparkle. Every now and again I shout to young Fritz to come and join me and he plants a new marker at my feet. Squinting my eyes, I can see all the lines meeting on the bed of the Roseaux River, and the knots — where I will be able to dig probe holes — appear.

Later Fritz and I dig holes near the hill in the west, at the foot of the Commander's Garret. The earth is hard and dry and our picks strike basaltic rock immediately. Every time I begin a new probe hole I'm filled with impatience. Will we finally find a sign, a trace of the Corsair's passage, perhaps the beginning of the 'stone work'? One evening, in the guise of a treasure, as Fritz and I are digging in the sandy soil at the foot of the hill, I suddenly feel, rolling under my pick, a light ball that — in my folly — I take for the skull of some seafarer buried there. The object rolls over the sand and suddenly unfolds its legs and claws! It's a large land crab that I've surprised in its sleep. Young Fritz, swifter than I, clubs it with his shovel. He gleefully stops his work to go fetch some water in the stewpot and, having lit a fire, he prepares a court bouillon with the crab!

In the evening, when the light wanes and the valley is silent and calm, I know that Ouma is near. I can feel her observing me from high up in the hills. At times I call out to her, I shout and listen to the echo repeating her name deep into the valley: 'Ou-ma-a!'

Her gaze is at once near and distant like that of a gliding bird whose shadow we don't notice until it makes the sun blink out. Even if I go for long periods without seeing her, because of Fritz Castel or Begué (for no Manaf woman ever shows herself to the inhabitants of the coast), I love feeling her gaze upon me, upon the valley.

Perhaps all of this belongs to her and she and her people are the true masters of this valley. Does she even believe in the treasure I'm searching for? Sometimes, when the daylight is still uncertain, I think I see her walking among the blocks of lava in the company of Sri, and stooping to examine the stones, as if she were following an invisible trail.

Or else she walks along the river down to the estuary, on to the beach where the sea is unfurling. Standing before the transparent water, she gazes out to the horizon, out beyond the coral reef. I walk up to her, contemplate the sea as well. Her face is tense, almost sad.

'What are you thinking about, Ouma?'

She starts, turns her face towards me and her eyes are filled with sadness.

'I'm not thinking about anything, I only think about impossible things,' she says.

'What's impossible?'

But she doesn't answer. Then the sunlight appears, throwing everything into sharp contrast. Ouma is standing still in the cold wind with the river water running between her feet, pushing back the lip of the wave. Ouma shakes her head as if she wanted to drive away something uncomfortable, she takes my hand and pulls me over towards the sea.

'Come on, let's go octopus-fishing.'

She takes up the long harpoon that she'd thrust into the dune among the other reeds. We walk eastwards, heading for the coast that is still in the shadows. The bed of the Roseaux River bends behind the dunes and reappears very close to the black cliff. There are tufts of reeds all the way down to the waterline. When we walk through them, swarms of tiny, silver-coloured birds suddenly flush, twittering: 'weeet! weeet!'

'This is where the octopuses come, the water is warmer.'

She walks over near the reeds, then suddenly takes off her shirt and skirt. Her long, slender body shines in the sunlight, the colour of dark copper. She steps over the rocks into the sea and disappears under the water. Her arm rests at the surface for an instant, holding the long harpoon, then there's nothing but the water, the choppy waves. After a few moments the water parts and Ouma comes slipping out, just as she went in. She walks up to me on the beach, takes the octopus dripping with ink from the harpoon and goes back. She looks at me. There is nothing affected about her, nothing but wild beauty.

'Come on!'

I don't hesitate. I undress too and plunge into the cold water. Suddenly I remember what I lost so many years ago, the sea at Tamarin when Denis and I swam naked through the waves. It's a feeling of freedom, of happiness. I swim underwater very close to the bottom, eyes open. I catch sight of Ouma over by the rocks searching with the tip of her harpoon in the crevices and the cloud of ink floating up. We swim together on the surface. Ouma throws the second octopus up on to the beach after having turned it inside out. She holds out the harpoon to me. A smile shines upon her face, her breathing is a bit hoarse. I dive down towards the rocks in turn. I miss a first octopus and I spear a second one on the sand at the bottom just as it leaps backwards, releasing its ink.

We swim together in the transparent water of the lagoon. When we're very near the reefs Ouma dives in front of me, disappears so quickly that I can't follow her. She reappears an instant later with a grouper on the end of her harpoon. But she unhooks the still live fish and tosses it back towards the shore. She motions me not to say anything. She takes my hand and together we allow ourselves to sink under the water. Then I see a threatening shadow swimming back and forth in front of us: a shark. It passes — two or three times, then swims away. We come up to the surface, gasping for breath. I swim to shore, while Ouma dives again. When I reach the beach I see she has captured the fish again. We run, side by side, over the white sand. Her body sparkles like basalt in the sun. With quick, precise movements, she scoops up the octopuses and the grouper and buries them in the sand near the dunes.

'Come on. Let's go dry off.'

I'm stretched out on the sand. Kneeling, she takes dry sand in her hands and sprinkles it over my body from my neck down to my feet.

'Put sand on me too.'

I take the light sand in my hands and let it run down on her shoulders, her back, her chest. Now we look exactly like two Pierrots smothered in powder and that makes us laugh.

'When the sand falls off, we're dry,' says Ouma.

We remain on the dune near the reeds, dressed in white sand. There's nothing but the sound of the wind in the reeds and the rumbling of the sea drifting over to us. Not another living thing but the crabs that come out of their holes, one after the other, brandishing their uplifted claws. The sun is already at its zenith in the sky, it's burning down in the middle of this solitude.

I look at the sand drying on Ouma's shoulder and back, trickling down in little rivulets, uncovering the glowing skin. Ardent desire rises within me, burning like the sun on my skin. When I put my lips on Ouma's skin, she quivers, but doesn't move away. With her long arms wrapped about her legs, she is resting her head upon her knees and gazing into the distance. My lips move down along her neck, over her soft, shiny skin, where the sand is slipping off in a cascade of silvery particles. My body is trembling now and Ouma raises her head, looks at me anxiously.

'Are you cold?'

'Yes . . . No.' I'm not really sure what's happening to me. I'm shivering nervously, it's difficult for me to breathe.

'What's wrong?'

Ouma gets up suddenly. She dresses with rapid gestures. She helps me put on my clothing, as if I were ill.

'Come rest in the shade, come on!'

Is it a fever, exhaustion? My head is spinning. With great difficulty I follow Ouma through the reeds. She's walking very straight, carrying the octopuses on the end of her harpoon like pennants, holding the fish by its gills.

When we reach the camp I lie down in the tent, close my eyes. Ouma has remained outside. She's making a fire to cook the fish. She also cooks the bread patties that she brought this morning in the coals. When the meal is ready, she brings it to me in the tent and watches me eat without having anything herself. The grilled fish is exquisite. I eat with my fingers, hurriedly, and drink the cool water that Ouma has gone to fetch upriver. Now I'm feeling better. Wrapped in my blanket, despite the heat, I observe Ouma, her profile turned towards the outside as if she were keeping a lookout. Later it begins to rain, at first a drizzle, then large drops. The wind is jerking at the sailcloth above us, making the branches of the tamarind tree creak.

When the daylight is waning, the young girl tells me about herself, about her childhood. She speaks hesitantly in her melodious voice, with long silences, and the sound of the wind and the rain on the tent blend in with her words.

'My father is Manaf, a Rodriguan from the mountains. But he left here to sail on a British-India ship, a large ship that went all the way to Calcutta. He met my mother in India, he married her and brought her back here, because her family was against the marriage. He was older than she was and died of fever during a journey when I was eight years old, so my mother placed me in a convent in Ferney on Mauritius. She didn't have enough money to bring me up. I also think she wanted to remarry and feared I would be a hindrance to her . . . At the convent I liked the Mother Superior very much and she liked me a lot too. When she had to go back to France, since my mother had abandoned me, she took me with her to Bordeaux, then to somewhere near Paris. I studied and worked in the convent. I think the Mother wanted me to become a nun and that's why she took me with her. But when I was thirteen I fell sick and everyone thought I was going to die, because I had tuberculosis . . . Then my mother wrote from Mauritius, she said she wanted me to come back and live with her. At first I didn't want to, I cried, I thought it was because I didn't want to leave the Mother Superior of the convent, but it was because I was afraid of going back to my real mother and the poverty on the island, in the mountains. The Mother Superior of the convent cried also, because she truly liked me, and also because she'd hoped I'd become a nun too, and since my mother isn't Christian — she kept the Indian religion — the Mother Superior knew I would be turned away from a religious life. And then I left anyway, I took a long journey alone on the boat, through the Suez Canal and the Red Sea. When I arrived in Mauritius I went back to my mother, but I didn't remember her any more and I was surprised to find that she was so small, draped in her robes. Next to her stood a little boy and she told me he was Sri, God's messenger on Earth . . . '

She stops talking. Night is very near now. Outside the valley is already in shadows. The rain has stopped, but we can hear water dripping on the tent when the wind shakes the branches of the old tamarind tree.

'In the beginning it was hard living here, because I didn't know anything about life with the Manafs. I didn't know how to do anything, I couldn't run or fish or make a fire, I didn't even know how to swim. And I couldn't talk, because no one spoke French, and my mother spoke only Bohjpuri and Creole. It was dreadful, I was fourteen years old and I was like an infant. In the beginning the neighbours made fun of me, they said my mother would have done best to leave me with the bourgeois. I wanted to leave, but I didn't know where to go. I couldn't go back to France, because I was a Manaf and nobody would have wanted me. And also, I liked my little brother Sri a lot, he was so gentle, so innocent, I think my mother was right to say he was God's messenger . . . So I started learning everything I needed to know. I learned how to run barefoot over the rocks, to run after and catch goats, to make a fire, and to swim and dive for fish. I learned how to be a Manaf and live like the maroons, hiding in the mountains. But I truly like being here with them, because they never lie, they never harm anyone. People from the coast in Port Mathurin are the same as the others from Mauritius, they lie and trick you, that's why we stay hidden in the mountains . . . '

Now it's completely dark. Cold settles in over the valley. We're lying close against one another, I can feel the warmth of Ouma's body against mine, our legs are intertwined. Yes, it's exactly as if we were the only living beings on Earth. The valley of English Bay is lost, it's drifting away in the cold sea wind.

I'm not trembling any more, I don't feel hurried or fearful at all now. Ouma too has forgotten that she must constantly be fleeing, hiding. Just as she had a little while ago in the reeds, she takes off her clothing and helps me get undressed too. Her body is smooth and warm, still covered with sand in places. She laughs as she brushes off the patches of sand on my back, my chest. Then we are inside one another, I'm not sure how. Her face is tilted backwards, I can hear her breathing, I can feel the beating of her heart and her warmth is within me, vast, more powerful than all of the burning days spent out at sea and in the valley. Now we are gliding, soaring, free of all thoughts, out into the night sky among the stars that hover silently, listening to us breathing in unison like two people deep in sleep. We lie holding one another close, so as not to feel the cold stones.

———————

At last I've found the ravine where a spring once flowed, but has now run dry. It's the one I'd glimpsed when I first arrived in English Bay and that I'd judged too far from the riverbed to appear on the Corsair's map.

But as I plant more and more markers extending the straight lines from the first signs, I am led over to the eastern side of the valley. One morning while I'm out alone, surveying in English Bay, not far from the western mark of the mooring ring, I decide to explore along the line that stretches from the mooring ring to the stone with the four punch marks that I found on the first spur of the eastern cliff and that, in the Corsair's document, is noted down as 'Look for :: S'.

Having nothing but the lengths of reeds planted at irregular intervals as markers, I move slowly forwards along the floor of the valley. A little before noon I arrive at the top of the eastern cliff, having measured and marked over a thousand king's feet. At the same time as I reach the top of the cliff I notice the crack of the ravine and the stone marking it. It is a block of basalt around six feet high, stuck in the powdery earth of the hillside in such a manner that it must be visible from the original estuary at the bottom of the valley. It's the only one of its kind, fallen from the basalt overhang that culminates above the cliff. I'm certain it was brought here by human means, perhaps rolled on logs and then stood upright in the manner of druid stones. On its sides the notches made to wrap ropes around it are still clear. But what catches my eye is the mark the rock bears at its top, exactly in the middle: a straight groove, approximately six inches long, carved by means of a chisel. The groove is precisely aligned with the extended straight line I followed from the western mooring ring, and indicates the opening of the ravine. Heart pounding, I step nearer and see the ravine for the first time. It's a corridor of erosion that runs through the width of the cliff and grows narrower towards English Bay. A rockslide obstructs its entrance and that is why it still hadn't dawned on me to explore it. Seen from the valley the entrance to the ravine blends in with all the other rockslides on the cliff. And from the top of the eastern hill as I first saw it, the ravine resembles a shallow depression in the land.

There is only one path that could have led me to it and that's the line I followed that began at the western mooring ring, ran across the Roseaux riverbed at point 95 (the exact intersecting point of the north–south line), passed through the middle of the stone with the four punch marks (point 'S' on the Corsair's document) and then led me to the block of basalt, where it converges with the groove carved by the Corsair's chisel.

I'm so excited by this discovery that I need to sit down and collect myself. The cold wind brings me back to my senses. Hurriedly, I climb down the slope to the bottom of the ravine. There, I'm in a sort of open well in the shape of a horseshoe, about twenty-five king's feet large, which runs some hundred feet down to the rockslide that closes off the entrance.

This is the place – I have no doubt about it – where the key to the mystery is to be found. This is the place, somewhere here under my feet, where the vault must be and also the sea chest, once solidly fixed to the front part of the ship where the Corsair kept his fabulous riches locked up, safeguarding them from the English and the cupidity of his own men. What better hiding place could he have found than this natural fault in the cliff, invisible from both the sea and the valley and closed off by the natural obstacle of the rockslide and silt from the torrent? I'm too impatient to wait until I can find help. I go to the camp and come back with everything I'll need: the pick, the shovel, the long iron-probe rod, a rope and a supply of drinking water. Till evening, without stopping, I probe and dig on the floor of the ravine in the place that I believe the groove in the block of basalt indicates.

Near the end of the day, when the shadows begin to darken the bottom of the ravine, the rod penetrates the earth diagonally, revealing the opening to a cache half-filled with dirt. Furthermore, the dirt is of a lighter colour, proof, in my view, that it was put there to plug up this cavity.

Using my hands to clear the blocks of basalt, I enlarge the opening. My heart is pounding in my temples, my clothes are drenched in sweat. The hole grows larger, uncovering an old chamber fortified by means of a drystone structure built in a half-circle. I am soon inside the cellar up to my waist. I don't have enough room to work with the pick and I have to dig with my hands, clear away the blocks by pushing on the rod like a lever. Then the metal rod rings on rock. I can't go any further, I've touched bottom: the hiding place is empty.

It's already night. The blank sky over the ravine is slowly growing dark. But the air is so hot that it's as if the sun were still beating down on the stone walls, on my face, on my hands, inside my body. Sitting in the bottom of the ravine, facing the empty cache, I drink all the water that's left in the canteen, hot, tasteless water that doesn't quench my thirst.

For the first time in a long time I think of Laure, I feel as if I'm coming out of my dream. What would she think of me if she saw me like this, covered with dust at the bottom of this ditch, hands bloody from digging? She'd look at me with her dark, shiny eyes and I'd feel ashamed. Right now I'm too tired to move, to think, to feel anything at all. I await the coming of night avidly, longingly, and I stretch out right where I am at the bottom of the ravine, head resting on one of the black rocks I've torn from the earth. Above me, between the high stone walls, the sky is black. I see the stars. They are bits of broken constellations, whose names I no longer remember.

In the morning, when I come out of the ravine, I see Ouma's silhouette. She's sitting near the camp, in the shade of a tree, waiting for me. Sri is beside her, watching me walk up, without moving.

I go over to the young girl, sit down beside her. In the shade her face is dark, but her eyes are shining bright.

'There's no more water in the ravine, the fountain has dried up,' she says.

She says 'fountain' for spring, Creole-style. She says it calmly, as if I'd been searching for water in the ravine.

The morning light is shining on the stones, in the foliage of the trees. Ouma has gone to fetch water in the river with the stewpot and now she's preparing the porridge, called *kir*, that Indian women make with flour. When the porridge is ready, she serves me on an enamel plate. As for her, she dips her fingers directly into the pot.

In her calm, chanting voice she tells me again about her childhood in France, in the nun's convent, and about her life when she came back to live with her mother, in Manaf country. I like the way she talks to me. I try to imagine her, the day she got off the huge ocean liner, wearing her black uniform, squinting against the light.

I too tell her about my childhood, in Boucan, about Laure, lessons with Mam under the veranda in the evenings and the adventures with Denis. When I tell her of our journey in the pirogue, out to the Morne, her eyes light up.

'I'd really like to go out to sea too!'

She stands, looks over towards the lagoon.

'On the other side there are lots of islands, islands where the seabirds live. Take me over there to fish.'

I love it when her eyes shine like that. I've made up my mind, we'll go out to the islands, to Booby Island, to Baladirou, maybe even down south to Gombrani. I'll go to Port Mathurin to rent a pirogue.

A storm was blowing for two days and two nights. I lived huddled up under my tent, eating only salt biscuits, hardly going out. Then on the morning of the third day the wind stops. The sky is a brilliant colour of blue, cloudless. I find Ouma standing on the beach, as if she hadn't budged the whole time.

When she sees me she says, 'I hope the fisherman will bring the pirogue today.'

One hour later, in fact, the pirogue comes running up on the beach. We embark, with the water supply and a tin of biscuits. Ouma is at the prow, holding her harpoon, watching the surface of the lagoon.

We leave the fisherman at Lascars Bay and I promise to bring the pirogue back the next day. We set off, sail blown taut in the east wind. The tall mountains of Rodriques tower behind us, still pale in the morning light. Ouma's face is lit with joy. She points out to me the mountains: Limon, Piton, Bilactère. When we go through the pass, the swell makes the pirogue lurch and we are enveloped in sea spray.

But further out we're back in the lagoon, sheltered by the reefs. Even so, the water is dark, traversed by mysterious reflections.

An island appears in front of the prow: it's Booby Island. Even before seeing them, we hear the calls of the seabirds. It's a constant, regular chatter, filling the sea and sky.

The birds have seen us, they fly out over the pirogue. Sterns, albatrosses, black frigates and the huge boobies, circling and squawking.

The island is now only some fifty yards from us, starboard side. On the lagoon side it is a band of sand and, facing the ocean, a rocky shore upon which the waves come crashing down. Ouma has made her way over to me at the tiller, she says in a low voice next to my ear, 'It's beautiful . . . !'

Never have I seen so many birds. There are thousands of them on the rocks which are white with guano, they dance, take flight and come to rest, and their wings make a rushing sound like the sea. The waves come thundering over the reefs, covering the rocks with a dazzling white roil, but the boobies aren't frightened. They open their powerful wings and raise themselves up in the wind over the water flowing past, then drop back down on to the rocks.

A flight of birds flying in tight formation passes over us, screeching. They circle around our pirogue, darkening the sky, flying against the wind, their immense wings outstretched, their black heads with the cruel eye turned towards the strangers, whom they hate. Now there are more and more of them, their strident cries are deafening. Some of them attack, swooping down upon the stern of the pirogue and we are forced to protect ourselves. Ouma is afraid, she huddles close to me, covers her ears with her hands.

'Let's get out of here! Let's go!'

I push the tiller starboard and, snapping, the sail fills with wind again. The boobies understand. They fly off, gain altitude and continue circling, keeping an eye on us. On the rocks of the island the bird population continues jumping over the swirling foam.

Ouma and I are still shaken. We're skipping along on the wind and for a long time after having left the waters around the island we can hear the sharp cries of the birds and the swift beating of their wings. One mile from Booby Island we find another islet on the coral reefs. To the north, the waves from the ocean break upon the rocks with a thundering sound. Here there are almost no birds, except for a few sterns gliding over the beach.

As soon as we've landed, Ouma takes off her clothes and dives in. I see her dark body shine under the water, then disappear. She comes up to the surface several times to catch her breath, her harpoon pointing skyward.

I undress too and dive in, swimming with my eyes open close to the bottom. In the coral there are thousands of fish I don't even know the names of, silver-coloured, striped with yellow, with red. The water is very soft and I slide along effortlessly near the coral. I search for Ouma in vain. When I come back to shore I stretch out in the sand and listen to the sound of the waves behind me. The sterns are hovering in the wind. There are even a few boobies come over from their island to stare at me, shrieking.

A long time afterwards, when the white sand has already dried on my body, Ouma comes up out of the water in front of me. Her body is shining in the light like black metal. She's wearing a string of braided creeper vines around her waist, where she's hung her prey: four fish, one thumbprint emperor, one spangled emperor and two silver sea bream. She sticks the harpoon into the sand, tip pointing upward, undoes the belt and puts the fish in a hole in the sand that she covers with wet seaweed. Then she sits down on the beach and sprinkles sand over her body.

By her side I can hear her breath, still heaving with the effort. On her dark skin the sand glitters like gold dust. We don't speak. We look at the water in the lagoon, listening to the powerful sound of the sea behind us. It's as if we've been here for days, having forgotten everything about the world. Off in the distance, the tall mountains of Rodrigues are slowly changing colour, the indentations of the bays are already in shadows. The tide is high. The lagoon is swollen, smooth, a deep shade of blue. The stem of the pirogue, with its arching bow that looks like a seabird, is barely touching the beach.

Later on, when the sun has gone down, we eat. Ouma gets up, the sand slips from her body in a fine spray. She gathers dried kelp, pieces of wood left by the tides. With my tinderbox I set fire to the twigs. When the flame springs forth Ouma's face is lit with a wild joy that draws me to her. Ouma makes a rack with some wet twigs, she cleans the fish. Then she smothers the fire with handfuls of sand and lays the rack directly on the coals. The smell of grilled fish fills us with a feeling of well-being and soon we are eating hurriedly, burning our fingers.

A few seabirds have arrived, drawn by the scraps. They trace large circles against the sun, then land on the beach. Before eating, they look at us, head tilted to one side.

'They won't harm us now, they're used to us.'

The boobies don't land on the sand. They dive towards the offal and catch it up in mid-flight, making sudden puffs of dust rise into the air. There are even crabs that come out of their holes, looking at once cowardly and ferocious.

'There's quite a crowd!' says Ouma, laughing.

When we've finished eating, Ouma hangs our clothing on the harpoon and we lie down in the hot sand, in the shade of that makeshift parasol. We bury ourselves beside one another in the sand. Perhaps Ouma falls asleep like that as I observe her face and closed eyes, her smooth, handsome forehead where her hair stirs gently in the wind. When she breathes, the sand slips off her chest, making her shoulder glint in the sun like a stone. I caress her skin with my fingertips. But Ouma doesn't move. She's breathing slowly, head resting on her crooked arm as the wind sweeps the sand from her immense body in tiny rivulets. Before me I see the blank sky and Rodrigues in a haze on the mirror of the lagoon. The seabirds fly over, alight on the beach a few yards from us. They're not afraid any more, they've become our friends.

I think this day is endless, like the sea.

Yet evening comes and I walk down the beach, surrounded by swooping birds letting out worried cries. It's too late to envisage going back to Rodrigues. The tide is going out, laying bare the coral plateaus in the lagoon, and we'd be in danger of running aground or wrecking the pirogue. Ouma has just joined me at the point of the island. We've put our clothes back on, because of the breeze. The seabirds fly out after us, alight on the rocks in front of us, giving strange cries. Out here the sea is free. We can see the waves breaking at the end of their journey.

When I sit down next to Ouma she wraps her arms around me, lays her head on my shoulder. I can smell her odour, sense her warmth. There is a twilight breeze blowing in, ushering in the darkness. Ouma shivers against me. The wind is what's troubling her, it's troubling the birds as well and making them leave their roosts and sail high into the sky, calling to the last glimmers of sunlight over the sea.

Night is settling quickly. Already the horizon is vanishing and the sea foam has stopped gleaming. We go back to the other side of the island, the leeward side. Ouma prepares a pallet for the night.

She lays out dried kelp on the dune above the beach. We roll up in our clothes to keep out the humidity. The birds have ceased their anxious flight. They've settled on the beach not far from us and in the darkness we can hear their cackling, the snapping of their beaks. Huddled close to Ouma, I breathe in the odour of her body and her hair, I can smell the taste of salt on her skin and lips.

Then I can feel her breathing growing calmer and I lay still, eyes open on the night, listening to the crashing of the rising waves behind us, drawing closer and closer. The stars are so numerous, they're as beautiful as they were when I lay on the deck of the *Zeta*. Before me, near the dark shapes of the mountains on Rodrigues, is Orion and the Summer Triangle and at the very zenith, near the Milky Way, just like back in the old days, I search for the shiny specks of the Pleiades. Like in the old days, I try to make out the seventh star, Pleione, and at the extremity of the Greater Chariot, Alcor. Low down on the left I recognize the Southern Cross and slowly I see the great ship Argo appear, as if it were truly sailing out on the dark sea. I would like to hear Ouma's voice, but I can't bring myself to wake her. I can feel the slow movement of her chest against me as she breathes and it blends in with the rhythmic crashing of the sea. After this very long day, filled with light, we are plunged in the deep, slow night that is penetrating and transforming us. That's why we're here, to live this day and night, far from other human beings, at the entrance to the open seas, among the birds.

Did we actually sleep? I'm not sure now. I lay still for a long time with the wind blowing over me, feeling the terrific pounding of the waves on the coral shelf, and the stars wheeled slowly round until dawn.

In the morning Ouma lies with her back nestled into my body, she's sleeping in spite of the bright sunlight shining on her eyelids.

The sand, damp with dew, is sticking to her dark skin, slipping down in little trickles along her neck, mixing with the wallow of clothing. Before me, the water in the lagoon is green and the birds have left the beach: they've started their rounds again, wings spread in the wind, sharp eyes searching the sea bottom. I can see the mountains of Rodrigues standing out very sharply, Piton, Bilactère and Diamant — all by itself on the shore. There are pirogues gliding along with full sails. In a few minutes we'll have to put on our clothes, gritty with sand, we'll get into the pirogue and the wind will pull upon the sail. Ouma will remain half-asleep, lying up in front on the bottom of the pirogue. We'll leave our island, set off, we'll head for Rodrigues, and the seabirds won't come with us.

MONDAY, 10 AUGUST (1914)

This morning, alone at the back of English Bay, I'm counting the days. I started several months ago, following the example of Robinson Crusoe, but not having a stick to notch I make marks on the covers of my notebooks. That's how I've arrived at this date, which to me is extraordinary, since it means that it has been exactly four years since I first came to Rodrigues. The discovery has got me so worked up that I can't stay put. Hastily, I put on my dusty shoes barefooted, for it's been a good while that I haven't had any socks. From the trunk I take out the grey jacket, a souvenir from my days in the offices of W. W. West in Port Louis. I button my shirt all the way up to the collar, but it's impossible to find a tie, mine having served to tie down the side flaps of the sailcloth I use as a tent one stormy night. Hatless, my long hair and beard looking like those of a castaway, my face all sun-browned and wearing this bourgeois jacket and these old boots, I would have been the laughing stock of the Rempart Street crowd in Port Louis. But here in Rodrigues people aren't so fussy and I go almost unnoticed.

The offices of the Cable & Wireless are still empty at this hour. A sole Indian employee looks at me indifferently, even when, as politely as possible, I put my absurd question to him.

'Excuse me, sir, what day is it today?'

He seems to think it over. Without moving from the place he's standing on the stairs, he says, 'Monday.'

I insist, 'But what's the date?'

After another silence, he announces, 'Monday, the tenth of August, 1914.'

As I walk down the path between the screw pines towards the sea I feel sort of light-headed. I've been living in this lonely valley in the company of the ghost of the Mysterious Corsair for such a long time! Alone with Ouma's shadow, which sometimes disappears for such a long time I'm no longer certain she really exists. I've been far away from home, from the people I love, for so very long. My heart wrenches at the memory of Laure and Mam, like a presentiment. The blue sky is blinding, the sea seems to be on fire. I feel as if I'm from some other world, some other time.

When I reach Port Mathurin I'm suddenly surrounded by a crowd. They're fishermen going back to their homes in Lascars Bay or farmers from the mountains who've come to the market. Black children run along beside me, laughing, then hide when I look at them. From having lived so long in the Corsair's lair I think I've begun to resemble him a bit. Quite an odd sort of Corsair, without a boat, coming out of his hideout all dusty and raggedy.

Once past the Portalis cabin I'm in the middle of town, in Barclay's Street. At the bank, while I'm withdrawing my last savings (enough to buy some sea biscuits, cigarettes, oil, coffee and a harpoon tip to fish for octopuses), I hear the first rumours of the war towards which the world seems to be hurtling frantically. A recent copy of the *Mauritian* tacked on the wall of the bank reveals the news received by telegraph from Europe: Austria has declared war on Serbia after the assassination in Sarajevo, France and Russia are mobilizing, Great Britain is making preparations for war. The news is already ten days old!

For a long time I wander through the streets of the city, where no one seems to realize the destruction that is threatening the world. The crowd throngs around the stores on Duncan Street, the Chinese shops on Douglas Street, along the wharf. For an instant I think about going to talk to Doctor Camal Boudou at the dispensary, but I'm ashamed of my ragged clothing and my overly long hair.

A letter is awaiting me in the offices of the Elias Mallac Company. I recognize the handsome, slanted writing on the envelope, but I can't bring myself to read it right away. There are too many people in the post office. I keep it in my hand as I walk down the streets of Port Mathurin, all the while I'm doing my shopping. Not until I am back in English Bay, sitting in my camp under the old tamarind tree, do I open it. I read the date postmarked on the envelope: 6 July 1914. The letter is only a month old.

It's written on a piece of India paper — light, thin and opaque — that I recognize simply from the way it crackles between my fingers. It's the paper our father used to enjoy using for writing or drawing his maps. I thought all of that paper had disappeared when we'd moved away from Boucan. Where had Laure found it? I think she must have kept it all this time, as if she'd set it aside for writing to me. Seeing her slanted, elegant handwriting so disconcerts me that I'm unable to read for a moment. Then I read her words, half-whispering to myself.

My dear Ali,

    You see, I am incapable of keeping my word. I had sworn to write to you to say only one thing: come back! And here I am writing to you without even knowing what I shall say.

    First, I will give you some news, which as you might guess is not excellent. Since you left, everything here has grown even bleaker. Mam has stopped all activity, she does not even want to go to town any more to attempt to sort out our affairs. I have gone there several times to try to make our creditors take pity on us. One Englishman, a certain Mr Notte (one could not invent a name like that!), is threatening to seize the few pieces of furniture left to us at Forest Side. I succeeded in stopping him, but for how long? Enough of that. Mam is quite weak. She still talks of taking refuge in France, but news from there is all about war. Yes, everything is quite gloomy these days, the future is hardly promising.

My heart sinks as I read those lines. Where is Laure's voice, she who never complained, who refused to take part in what she called 'whining and moaning'? The worry I'm feeling is not about the war that is threatening the world. But rather about the gap that has deepened between me and the people I love, that separates me from them irrevocably. I press on and read the last line in which I feel I briefly recognize Laure's voice, her mockery.

I think constantly about the time when we were happy in Boucan, about those unending days. I hope that for you, wherever you may be, there are also lovely days and, for want of treasures, happiness.

She signs with only her initial, 'L', with no closing words of goodbye. She never did like handshakes or hugs. What remains of her in this old piece of India paper that I'm holding in my hands?

I carefully fold the letter and put it away with my papers next to the writing case in my trunk. Outside, the noon light is glaring, making the stones on the floor of the valley glitter brightly, sharpening the leaves of the screw pines. The sound of the rising tide is floating in on the wind. The gnats are dancing at the entrance to the tent, maybe they feel a storm coming? It seems as if I can still hear Laure's voice speaking to me from across the sea, calling out for me to help her. Despite the sound of the sea and the wind, silence is everywhere out here, the light is blinding with loneliness.

I walk haphazardly through the valley, still wearing my grey jacket that is too big for me, my feet are being rubbed raw from the dried-out leather of my ankle boots. I walk on familiar paths, along the lines of the Corsair's map and his clues, a large hexagon ending in six points, none other than the star of Solomon's seal, which echoes the two inverted triangles of the mooring rings.

I traverse English Bay several times, my eyes wandering over the ground, listening to the sound of my footsteps resounding. I see every familiar stone, every bush and, on the sand dunes at the estuary of the Roseaux River, my own footprints that no rain has washed away. I lift my head and see the blue, inaccessible mountains at the back of the valley. It's as if I wanted to remember something very remote, forgotten, maybe the deep, dark ravine of Mananava, the place where night began.

———————

I can't wait any longer. This evening when the sun is going down towards the hills over Venus Point I walk to the entrance of the ravine. Feverishly, I scramble up the blocks of rock that close off the entrance and dig, swinging my pick into the walls of the ravine, running the risk of being buried in a rockslide. I don't want to think about my calculations, my markers any more. I can hear the pounding of my heart, the hoarse sound of my laboured breathing and the crashing of slabs of earth and schist tumbling down. I feel relieved, freed from my anxiety.

Furiously, I throw blocks of rock weighing a hundred pounds against the basalt walls at the bottom of the ravine, the smell of saltpetre is floating in the overheated air. I believe I'm drunk, drunk with loneliness, drunk with silence, and that's why I'm shattering the rocks, why I'm talking to myself, why I'm saying, 'Here! Here . . . ! There! Over there again . . . !'

In the bottom of the ravine I tackle a group of basaltic boulders so huge and so old that I'm certain they were rolled down from the black hills. It would take several men to move them, but I can't bring myself to wait for the black men from the farms, Raboud, Adrien Mercure or Fritz Castel. With a great deal of effort, having dug out a probe hole under the first basaltic rock, I am able to slip the point of my pick into it and I push on the handle like a lever. The block moves slightly, I can hear dirt falling into a deep cavity. But the handle of the pick cracks off and I fall heavily against the rock wall.

I'm left half-dazed for a long time. When I come back to my senses I feel something warm running through my hair, down my cheek: I'm bleeding. I'm too weak to stand and I remain lying at the bottom of the ravine, leaning on one elbow, pressing my handkerchief against the back of my head to stop the bleeding.

A little before nightfall I'm drawn from my torpor by a noise at the entrance to the ravine. Delirious, I grab the pick handle to defend myself in case it's a wild dog or a starving rat. Then I recognize Sri's slim, dark figure against the blinding light of the sky. He's walking at the top of the ravine and when I call him he comes down the slope.

There's a wary look in his eyes, but he helps me get up and walk to the entrance of the ravine. Although wounded and weak, I say, like a frightened animal, 'Come on, get on with it!' Together we walk through the valley to the camp. Ouma is waiting for me. She brings some water in the pot and dips it out in the hollow of her hand to wash the wound where the blood has matted my hair.

'Are you really all that fond of gold?' she asks.

I tell her about the cache I found under the basalt rock, the signs that point to those rocks and that ravine, but I'm belligerent and confused and she must think I'm crazy. For her, the treasure is meaningless, she scorns gold as do all Manafs.

Head wrapped in my bloody handkerchief, I eat the meal she's brought me, dried fish and *kir*. After the meal she sits beside me and we remain silent for a long time, facing the translucent, twilit sky. The seabirds are flying across English Bay in flocks towards their roosting place. Now I don't feel impatient or angry any more.

Ouma rests her head against my shoulder like she used to when we first met. I can smell the odour of her body, of her hair.

I tell her about the things I love, the fields in Boucan, Trois Mamelles, the dark and dangerous valley of Mananava, where the two tropicbirds always fly. She listens without stirring, she's thinking of something else. I can sense that her body is no longer at ease. When I try to reassure her, caress her, she moves away, puts her arms around her long legs, as she does when she's alone.

'What's the matter? Are you cross?'

225

She doesn't answer. We walk down to the dunes together in the gathering night. The air is so balmy, so soft at summer's start, the cloudless sky begins to light up with stars. Sri has stayed back near the camp, sitting up straight and as still as a guard dog.

'Tell me about when you were a child again.'

I talk slowly, smoking a cigarette, smelling the honey-like odour of English tobacco. I talk about all of that, about our house, about Mam who read the lessons under the veranda, about Laure, who went to hide in the tree of good and evil, about our ravine. Ouma interrupts me to ask questions about Mam, about Laure mostly. She questions me about her, about her outfits, about her likes, and I believe she's jealous. I find it amusing that this wild girl should pay so much heed to a young girl from the bourgeoisie. I don't believe I can understand, even for an instant, what she's going through, what's tormenting her, making her vulnerable. In the darkness I can barely make out her silhouette sitting next to me in the dunes. When I make to get up and go back to camp, she holds me back by the arm.

'Stay a little longer. Talk to me some more about over there.'

She wants me to tell her more about Mananava, the fields of cane where Denis and I used to run, the ravine that opened in the mysterious forest, and the slow flight of the dazzlingly white birds.

Then she talks to me about herself again, about her journey to France, the sky so dark and so low that you'd think the light would be extinguished once and for all, the prayers in the chapel and the songs she loved. She talks of Hari and Govinda, who is growing up amid the herd animals back there in her mother's country. One day Sri made a flute out of a reed and started playing it all alone in the mountains and that's how her mother had realized he was the Lord's messenger. When she came back to live with the Manafs he was the one who taught her to chase after and catch goats, who led

226

her down to the sea for the first time to fish for crabs and octopuses. She also speaks of Soukha and Sari, the two birds of light who can speak and who sing for the Lord in the land of Vrindavan, she says they were the birds I saw back in the old days at the entrance to Mananava.

Later we go back to the camp. Never before have we talked in that way, gently, in hushed tones, without being able to see each other, in the shelter of the tall tree. It's as if time as well as everything else in the world except this tree, these stones, has ceased to exist. When we've talked far into the night, I lie down on the ground to sleep in front of the entrance to the tent, my head resting on my arm. I wait for Ouma to come and join me. But she remains sitting still where she is, looking at Sri, who is perched on a stone off to one side, and their silhouettes outlined against the sky are like two night watchmen.

———————

When the sun rises in the sky, above the mountains, I'm sitting cross-legged in my tent in front of my trunk, which I use as a desk, drawing a new map of English Bay, upon which I trace all the lines between the markers, thereby making a sort of spider web appear whose six anchoring points form the large Star of David that was first represented by the two inverted triangles of the mooring rings to the east and west.

Today I'm not thinking about the war any more. Everything seems new and pure to me. Lifting my head I suddenly see Sri, who is looking at me. I don't recognize him immediately. At first I think he's one of the children from the Raboud farm who's come down with his father to fish. It's the look in his eyes that I recognize, wild, wary, but also gentle and bright, a look that comes straight over to me, unaverted. I leave my papers there and walk slowly in his direction, to avoid frightening him. When I'm ten steps away, the young boy turns and takes off. He goes jumping leisurely over the rocks, turning around to wait for me.

'Sri! Come here!' I've shouted, even though I know he can't hear me. But he continues to make his way to the back of the valley. So I follow on the path without trying to catch up to him. Sri bounds lightly over the black rocks and I see his lithe shape, which seems to be dancing out in front of me, then he disappears in the underbrush. I believe I've lost him, but there he is standing in the shade of a tree or in the hollow of a rock. I only just catch sight of him when he starts walking again.

For hours I follow Sri through the mountains. We are high up, above the hills, on the bare flank of the mountain. Below me I see the rocky slopes, the dark patches of the screw pines and bramble bushes. Up here everything is barren, mineral. The sky is magnificently blue, the clouds coming from the east are skittering across the sea, passing over the valley, casting swift shadows. We continue climbing. At times I can't even see my guide any more and when I do catch sight of him, far out ahead, dancing along swift and light, I'm not sure I haven't seen a goat, a wild dog.

At one point I stop to look out at the sea, far in the distance, as I've never seen it before: immense, sparkling and hard in the sunlight, traversed by the long silent hem of breakers.

The wind is blowing in cold bursts that bring tears to my eyes. I sit down on a rock to catch my breath. When I start walking again, I fear I've lost Sri. Squinting, I search up around the top of the mountain, on the dark slopes of the valleys. Just as I'm about to give up trying to find him, I see him surrounded by other children with a herd of goats on the other side of the mountain. I call to him, but the echo of my voice makes the children flee and they disappear with their goats among the brush and the stones.

I can see traces of human beings up here: some sort of circular, drystone walls, much like those I found when I first arrived in English Bay. I also notice barely visible footpaths through the mountains, but I can make them out because the life out in the wild I've been living for the past four years in English Bay has taught me to spot signs of human presence. As I'm preparing to go down to the other side of the mountain to look for the children, I suddenly see Ouma. She walks up to me and, without saying a word, takes me by the hand and leads me over to the cliff top, to a place where the land makes a sloping overhang. On the other side of the shallow valley, on the arid mountainside, along a dried-up stream, I can see huts made of stone and branches, a few tiny fields, protected from the wind by low walls. Dogs have picked up our scent and are barking. It's the Manaf village.

'You shouldn't go any farther,' says Ouma. 'If a stranger came, the Manafs would have to move farther out into the mountains.'

We walk along the cliff top all the way to the northern slope of the mountain. We're facing the wind. Down below, the sea is infinite, dark, spotted with white horses. Over in the east is the turquoise-coloured mirror of the lagoon.

'At night you can see the lights of the city,' says Ouma. She points to the sea. 'And over in that direction you can see boats coming in.'

'It's beautiful!' I say that almost in a whisper. Ouma has squatted down on her heels, as she does, wrapping her arms about her knees. Her dark face is turned towards the sea, the wind is tousling her hair. She turns westward, in the direction of the hills.

'You should go back down, night will be falling soon.'

But we just sit there very still in the whipping wind, unable to tear ourselves away from the sea, like birds gliding very high up in the sky. Ouma doesn't talk to me, but I have the feeling I can sense everything within her, her longing, her despair. She never puts it into words, but that's why she so loves to go down to the shore, dive into the sea, swim out to the breakers armed with her long harpoon and, hiding behind the rocks, observe the people from the coast.

'Do you want to go away with me?'

The sound of my voice or else my question makes her start. She looks at me angrily, her eyes blazing.

'Go away? Where? Who would have me?'

I try to find words to appease her, but she says vehemently, 'My grandfather was a maroon, along with all the black maroons from Le Morne. He died when they crushed his legs in the cane mill because he'd joined Sacalavou's people in the forest. Then my father came to live here, on Rodrigues, and he became a sailor so he could travel. My mother was born in Bengal, and her mother was a musician, she sang for Govinda. Where would I be able to go? To a convent in France? Or to Port Louis to wait on the people who killed my grandfather, the people who bought and sold us like slaves?'

Her hand is ice-cold, as if she has a fever. All of a sudden, Ouma stands up, walks over to the slope in the west, over to the place where the paths separate, the place where she was waiting for me a little while ago. Her face is calm again now, but her eyes still glare with anger.

'You have to go now. You can't stay here.'

I'd like to ask her to show me her house, but she's already walking away without looking back, she's going down into the dark, shallow dip in the land where the Manafs' huts stand. I can hear the voices of children, the barking of dogs. The darkness settles in rapidly.

I climb down the slopes, run through the thorn bushes and the screw pines. I can no longer see the sea or the horizon, only the shadow of the mountains growing larger in the sky. When I reach the valley of English Bay it is dark and a fine rain is falling gently. Under my tree, in the shelter of my tent, I curl up and lie still, feeling the cold, the loneliness. Then I think about the sound of destruction that is growing louder every day, that is rolling around like a rumbling thunderstorm, the sound that is now hanging over the entire world and that no one can forget. That night I decide to go off to war.

They are all standing together this morning at the entrance to the ravine: there are Adrien Mercure, a tall black man with herculean strength, who was once a foreman in the copra plantations on Juan Nova, Ernest Raboud, Celestin Prosper and young Fritz Castel. When they learned I'd found the cache they dropped everything and came immediately, each with a shovel and a piece of rope. Anyone seeing us walking across English Bay like that, them with their shovels, wearing their large vacoa hats, and me leading with my long beard and hair and my torn clothing, my head still bandaged with a handkerchief, might have thought it was a parody of the Corsair's men coming back to retrieve their treasure!

We're encouraged by the cool morning air and begin digging around the blocks of basalt at the bottom of the ravine. The earth, crumbly on the surface, becomes as hard as rock as we dig deeper. Taking turns, we heave at it with our picks, while the others busy themselves clearing the rubble over to the wider part of the ravine. That is when the idea dawns upon me that the boulders and earth piled up at the entrance to the ravine that I had taken for a natural obstruction caused by water runoff in the old torrent bed, are in reality the material that the Corsair's men cleared away after having excavated the caches in the bottom of the ravine. Once again I have the strange impression that the entire ravine is of human creation. Starting with a simple crevice in the basaltic cliff, those men dug, excavated, until they attained the appearance of this gorge which the rainwater has remodelled for almost two hundred years. It's a strange feeling, almost awesome, like the one explorers must experience when they uncover the ancient tombs of Egypt in the silence and the ruthless light of the desert.

Around noon the base of the largest basalt block has been sapped to such an extent that a simple nudge ought to be enough to send it tumbling into the bottom of the ravine. Together we all push on the same side of the rock, which rolls a few metres, causing an avalanche of dust and small stones. Before us, exactly in the place indicated by the groove engraved on the boulder at the top of the cliff, is a gaping hole still hidden by the dust floating in the air. Without waiting another minute I lie flat on my belly and drag myself through the opening, it takes several seconds for my eyes to adjust to the darkness: 'What's in there? What's in there?' I hear the voices of the impatient black men behind me. After a very long time I back up, pull my head out of the hole. I feel sort of giddy, my blood is beating in my temples, in my jugular veins. This second cache is clearly empty as well.

Using my pick, I enlarge the opening. Little by little we uncover a sort of well that reaches all the way down to the base of the cliff that dead-ends the ravine. The bottom of the well is of the same rust-coloured rock that alternates with the outcrops of basalt on the bottom of the ravine. Young Fritz goes down into the well, where he disappears entirely, then comes back up.

He shakes his head. 'There's nothing down there.'

Mercure shrugs his shoulders derisively.

'It's the goat fountain.'

Is it really one of those old troughs for the herds? Then why would anyone have gone to so much trouble, since Roseaux River is so near? The men saunter away with their shovels and ropes. I hear their laughter fading out as they pass through the entrance to the ravine. Only young Fritz Castel has remained at my side, standing before the gaping cache, as if waiting for my instructions. He's ready to go back to work, plant new markers, dig new probe holes. Perhaps he's been infected with the same fever as I have, the one that makes you forget everything, the world and human beings, in quest of a mirage, a gleam of light.

'There's nothing more to be done here.' I speak to him in a hushed voice, as if talking to myself. He looks at me with his shiny eyes, not understanding.

'All the caches are empty.'

We come out of the burning trench of the ravine in turn. At the top of the slope I contemplate the vast valley, the dark-green tufts of the tamarind trees and the screw pines, the fantastic forms of the basaltic rock and especially the thin stream of sky-blue water that snakes towards the swamp and the dunes. The latanias and coconut trees form a moving screen in front of the sea and when the wind blows I can hear the sound of the breakers, a sluggish respiration.

Where to search now? Down there by the dunes in the marsh-lands where the sea once raged? In the caves on the other bank at the foot of the ruined tower of the Commander's Garret? Or else high up, deep in the wild mountains of the Manafs, at the source of the Roseaux River where the herds of goats live in cracks hidden by thorn bushes? Now I feel as if all the lines on my maps are fading away, as if the signs inscribed on the rocks are merely the traces of storms, the bite of lightning bolts, the abrasion of the wind. A sense of despair is creeping over me and draining my strength.

I feel like saying to Fritz, 'It's all over, there's nothing more to find here, let's go.'

The young man is looking so insistently at me, his eyes shining so brightly, that I can't bring myself to reveal my despair to him. As firmly as I can, I stride across the floor of the valley to my camp under the tamarind tree.

'We're going to explore the area over there to the west. We'll need to probe, plant new markers. You'll see, we'll find it in the end. We'll search everywhere on the other side and then high up in the valley too. We won't leave an inch of terrain unturned. We'll find it!'

Does he believe what I'm saying? My words seem to have put his mind at ease.

'Yes, sir, we'll find it, if the Manafs haven't found it before us!' he says.

The idea of the Corsair's treasure being in the hands of the Manafs makes him laugh. But growing suddenly serious, he adds, 'If the Manafs found the gold, they'd throw it into the sea!'

And what if that were true?

———————————

That feeling of anxiety I've been having for weeks now, the sound that is rumbling out beyond the seas like thunder and which I cannot forget, either by day or by night, today suddenly — the full measure of its violence has dawned upon me.

Having left for Port Mathurin early this morning in the hopes of getting a new letter from Laure, I come up through the underbrush and the screw pines in front of the buildings of the Cable & Wireless at Venus Point and I see the gathering of men in front of the telegraph house. The Rodriguans are waiting at the foot of the veranda, some are standing up, conversing, others are sitting in the shade, on the steps, with blank looks on their faces, smoking cigarettes.

In these past few days of madness in the bottom of the ravine, trying to find the Corsair's second cache, I hadn't really thought of the gravity of the situation in Europe. And yet the other day, when passing in front of the Mallac & Co. building, I read, along with the crowd, the communiqué tacked up by the door that had arrived from Port Louis on the postal ship. It spoke of a general mobilization for the war that had begun over there in Europe. Britain and France have allied and declared war on Germany. Lord Kitchener is calling upon all volunteers, in the colonies and the dominions, in Canada, in Australia, and also in Asia, the Indies, Africa. I read the public notice, then I went back to English Bay, maybe in the hope of finding Ouma, of talking to her about it. But she didn't come and later the noise of the work at the bottom of the ravine must have frightened her off.

As I walk up to the telegraph building, no one pays any attention to me, despite my torn clothing and my overly long hair. I recognize Mercure, Raboud and, a little off to one side, the giant Casimir, the sailor on the *Zeta*. He recognizes me as well and his face lights up. Eyes bright with pleasure, he explains to me that they're waiting here for instructions on how to enlist. That's why there are only men here! Women are repelled by war.

Casimir talks to me about the army, warships that he hopes will take him on, poor gentle giant! He's already talking about the battles he will wage in countries he's never seen against an unknown enemy. Then a man, an Indian telegraph employee, appears on the veranda.

He begins reading a list of names, the ones that will be communicated to the recruitment bureau in Port Louis. With his ringing, nasal voice and his English accent which deforms the syllables, he reads out the names very slowly in the silence that now lies heavily over the men.

'Hermitte, Corentin, Latour, Lamy, Raffaut . . .'

He reads those names, and the wafting wind sweeps them away and strews them over the hills amid the blades of screw pines and the black rocks, those names that already have a strange ring to them, like the names of dead men, and suddenly I want to flee, go back to my valley, to the place where no one can find me, disappear into Ouma's world among the reeds and the dunes without leaving a trace. The slow voice enumerates the names and I shudder. Never have I felt this before, as if the voice would pronounce my name among those names, as if the voice had to say my name among those of the men who are going to leave their world to fight against our enemies.

'Portalis, Haouet, Céline, Bégué, Hitchen, Castor, Pichette, Simon . . .'

I can still leave, I think about the ravine, about the lines that intersect on the valley bottom and make the landmarks shine out like beacons, I think about everything I've experienced in all of these months, all of these years, that light-filled beauty, the sound of the sea, the fancy-free birds. I think of Ouma, of her skin, her smooth hands, her body of black metal slipping under the water of the lagoon. I can go away, there's still time, far from this insanity, where the men laugh and rejoice when the Indian pronounces their name. I can leave, find a place where I could forget all of this, where I wouldn't hear the sound of the war in the sound of the sea and the wind any more. But the sing-songy voice continues to pronounce the names, those names that are already unreal, the names of men from here who will die over there, for a world they know nothing about.

'Ferney, Labutte, Jeremiah, Rosine, Medicis, Jolicoeur, Victorine, Imboulla, Ramilla, Illke, Ardor, Grangourt, Salomon, Ravine, Roussety, Perrine, Perrine the younger, Azie, Cendrillon, Casimir . . .'

When the Indian pronounces his name, the giant stands up and jumps up and down, shouting. There is an expression of such naive contentment on his face one might think he'd just won a bet or that he'd learned some good news. And yet it's the name of his death that he's just heard. Maybe that's why I didn't flee to English Bay, didn't try to find a place where I'd be able to forget the war. I think it's because of him, because of his joy at hearing his name called.

When the Indian has finished reading the names on his list, he stands still for a moment with the paper fluttering in the wind and asks in English, 'Are there any other volunteers?'

And almost in spite of myself I climb up the cast-iron stairs to the veranda and give him my name to add to the list. A little while ago Casimir set the tone for a celebration and now most of the Rodriguans are dancing and singing right on the spot. When I go down the stairway, some of them circle around me and grasp my hands. The jubilation draws out all along the road that follows the coast to Port Mathurin, and we go through the streets of the town in a boisterous crowd, to reach the hospital where the medical exam-ination is to be carried out. The examination is simply a formality that only lasts a minute or two. Each in turn — bare-chested — we enter the torrid office where Camal Boudou, flanked by two nurses, examines the volunteers and hands them a stamped travel author-ization. I'm expecting him to ask me some questions, but he just checks my eyes and teeth. He hands me the paper and, as I'm going out, he merely says in that deep and gentle voice of his, his Indian face remaining expressionless, 'You are going out to the Front too?' Then he calls in the next person without waiting for an answer. On the paper I read my departure date: 10 December 1914. The name of the ship is left blank, but the destination of the journey is filled in: Portsmouth. There you have it, I'm enlisted. I won't even see Laure and Mam before leaving for Europe, since we'll be departing from somewhere around the Seychelles.

Yet I go back to the ravine every day, as if I would at last be able to find what I'm searching for. I can't tear myself away from that crack in the side of the valley, with not a blade of grass, not a tree, nothing that moves or is alive, with only the light reverberating on the rusty slopes of the mountain and the basalt rocks. In the morning, before the sun gets too hot, and in the evening twilight, I walk down to the bottom of the dead-end ravine and look at the holes I discovered at the foot of the cliff. I stretch out on the ground, run my fingers over the mouth of the well, over the wall worn smooth by the waters of another era, and dream. All around on the bottom of the ravine there are furious pick marks and the earth is full of craters that are already beginning to fill with dust. When the wind pushes its way into the ravine, wailing, blustering violently up at the top of the cliff, little avalanches of black dirt run into those holes, echo on the stones at the bottom of the caches. How long will it take for nature to close up the Corsair's well which I've laid bare in this way? I think of those who will come after me, in ten years, perhaps, in a hundred years, and it's for them that I decide to seal up the caches again. Down in the valley I find large, flat stones that I carry with great difficulty to the mouths of the wells, I use other smaller rocks gathered right in the ravine to fill up the cracks and with my shovel I throw red earth on top that I tamp down by pounding it with the shovel. Without understanding, young Fritz Castel helps me with this work. But he never asks any questions. For him, from the very beginning this whole thing will have been nothing but a series of incomprehensible and somewhat frightening rituals.

When everything is finished I contemplate with satisfaction the mound that hides the Corsair's two caches in the bottom of the ravine. I feel as if, in accomplishing this job, I've made a new step forward in my quest, as if — in a way — I've become the accomplice of the mysterious man whose trail I've been following for such a long time.

I like being in the ravine, especially in the evening. When the sun is drawing near the jagged line of the hills in the west, over by the Commander's Garret, the sunshine reaches almost all the way to the back of the long stone corridor, lighting up the slabs of rock in a strange way, igniting the flakes of mica in the schist. I just sit there at the entrance to the ravine, watching the shadows creep over the silent valley. I observe every detail, every movement in this stone-laden, thorny land. I await the arrival of my friends the seabirds, who leave every evening from the southern shores, Pierrot Island, Gombrani, and fly to their roosts in the north, where the sea breaks on the coral reefs.

Why do they do that? What secret command guides them every evening along their way over the lagoon? At the same time as I'm waiting for the seabirds I'm also waiting for Ouma, I'm waiting to see her walking in the riverbed, slender and dark, carrying the octopuses on the end of her harpoon or a necklace of fish.

Sometimes she comes, sticks her harpoon in the sand near the dunes, as if it were the signal for me to join her. When I tell her I found the Corsair's second cache and that it was empty, Ouma bursts out laughing, 'So there's no more gold, there's nothing at all here!' It irritates me at first, but her laughter is contagious and I'm soon laughing with her. She's right.

When we discovered that the wells were empty, we must have looked pretty comical! Ouma and I run through the reeds out to the dunes and swarms of silver birds fly up in front of us, twittering. We hurriedly take off our clothes and dive together into the transparent water of the lagoon, so mild that we hardly feel it when our bodies enter the other element. We glide along underwater near the coral for a long time without coming up for breath. Ouma isn't even trying to catch fish. She's just having fun chasing them underwater, flushing out the red groupers from their dark crannies. Since we learned that the treasure caches are empty, we've never been so happy! One evening, as we're watching the stars appearing above the mountains, she says, 'Why are you looking for gold here?'

I want to tell her about our house in Boucan, about our infinite garden, about everything we lost, because that is what I'm looking for. But I don't know how to tell her and she adds in a whisper, as if talking to herself, 'Gold is worthless, one mustn't be afraid of it, it's like scorpions, they only sting those who are afraid.'

She says that simply, not braggingly, but in a hard voice, like someone who is sure of herself.

She also says, 'You people from the upper crust believe that gold is the most powerful, most desirable of all things, and that's why you go to war. People everywhere are going to die just to have gold.'

Her words make my heart race, because I think about my enlistment. For a second I feel like telling Ouma everything, but I get a lump in my throat. I have only a few more days left to live here with her in this valley, so very distant from the world. How can I talk to Ouma about the war? To her it's evil, she would probably never forgive me, would run away immediately.

I can't tell her. I hold her hand very tightly in mine in order to fully feel her warmth, I drink in the breath from her lips. The night is balmy, a summer night, and the wind stopped when the tide went slack, the stars are countless and lovely, everything is filled with joy and peace. I believe that for the very first time I'm savouring the hours that are passing with no feelings of impatience or longing, but with sadness, thinking that none of this can ever be again, that it is going to be destroyed. Several times I'm on the verge of confessing to Ouma that we will never see each other again, but it's her laughter, her breath, the odour of her body, the taste of salt on her skin that stop me. How can I disturb this peace? I can't hold on to what will be inevitably broken, but I can still believe in a miracle.

Every morning, like most Rodriguans, I go and stand in front of the telegraph building in search of news.

The communiqués are posted on the veranda beside the door to the telegraph office. Those who know how to read, translate into Creole for the others. In the shuffle I am able to read a few lines: there is talk of French's and Haig's armies and of de Langle's and Lanrezac's French troops; about battles in Belgium, threats on the Rhine, the front lines on the Oise near Dinant, those in the Ardennes near the Meuse. I know those names from having learned them in the Royal College, but what could they mean to most Rodriguans? Do they think of the names like some sorts of islands, where the wind sways the palms of the coconut trees and the latanias, where you can hear the endless sound of the waves on the reefs, as you can here? I feel angry, impatient, because I know that in no time — maybe just a few weeks — I'll be over there on the banks of those unfamiliar rivers, in the middle of that war that negates all names.

This morning, when Fritz Castel came, I made something that resembles a testament. Armed with my theodolite I calculated for the last time the east-west line that passes exactly through the two mooring-ring signs on the two shores of the valley, and I identified the place in which this line intersects the north-south axis, as indicated by the compass, with the slight difference as calculated by the stellar north. At the point of intersection of the two lines, which is the centre of the valley of the Roseaux River, at the edge of the marshland that forms a tongue of land between the two arms of the river, I set down a heavy basalt rock shaped like a boundary stone. To get the rock there I had to slide it, with the help of the young black boy, over a path along the riverbed laid with reeds and round branches. I tied a rope around the boulder and, each of us pushing and pulling in turn, we brought it from the other side of the valley over a distance of more than a mile, all the way to the point that I'd marked 'B' on my maps, and placed it on a small mound of earth that extends into the estuary and is surrounded by water at high tide.

All of this work kept us busy for most of the day. Fritz Castel helped me without asking any questions. Then he went back to his place.

The sun is low in the sky when, wielding a cold chisel and a large stone in the guise of a mallet, I begin engraving my message for the future. At the top of the boulder I cut out a three-inch-long groove that converges with the line linking the east-west mooring rings. On the southern face of the stone I make marks corresponding to the Corsair's principal points of reference. First there is the capital 'M' representing the peaks of the Commander's Garret, the point of the : : punched into the rock, the groove indicating the ravine, and a round punch mark standing for the northernmost stone at the entrance to the estuary. On the northern face of the stone I chisel out five punch marks for the Corsair's five main landmarks: the peaks of Charlot, Bilactère, Quatre Vents that form the first south-south-east alignment, and that of Commander and of Piton that form a second, slightly divergent alignment.

I would also like to engrave the triangles on the Corsair's grid, which are inscribed in the circle that passes through the points of the mooring rings and the northernmost stone, and the centre of which — I now realize — is this boulder. But the surface of the stone is too rough to be able to chisel out such a precise drawing with my dull tool. At the base of the stone I simply mark my initials in capital letters, 'AL'. Under that, the date in Roman numerals.

X   XII   MCMXIV

This afternoon, undoubtedly the last I'll be spending here in English Bay, I feel like taking advantage of the full-blown summer heat and having a long swim in the lagoon. I undress in the reeds facing the deserted beach where Ouma and I used to go. Today everything seems even more silent, remote, abandoned. No more do swarms of silver-coloured birds flush up, letting out their sharp cries. There are no more seabirds in the sky. There are only the soldier crabs that go fleeing over to the mud in the marshland with their claws raised skyward.

I swim for a long time in the very still water, brushing up against the coral that the sea is beginning to uncover. Eyes wide open under the water, I see the shallow-water fish go by, boxfish, pearl-coloured needlefish, and even a stonefish, magnificent and venomous, its dorsal fins bristling like rigging. Very close to the coral reef I flush out a grouper that stops to look at me before fleeing. I don't have a harpoon, but, if I did, I don't think I'd have the heart to use it against any of these silent creatures and then see their blood clouding the water red!

Back on shore in the dunes I cover myself with sand and wait for the setting sun to make the little trickles run over my skin, like when I used to be with Ouma.

I sit watching the sea for a long time, I'm waiting. Maybe I'm waiting for Ouma to appear on the beach, in the twilight, holding her ebony harpoon in her hand, carrying octopuses like trophies. Darkness is filling the valley as I walk back to my camp. Anxiously, hopefully, I look up at the tall, blue mountains at the back of the valley, as if today I would at last see a human shape appear in this stone-filled land.

Did I call out, 'Ouma-ah'? Perhaps, but if so, in such a weak, strangled voice that no echo rose from it. Why isn't she here tonight, of all nights? Sitting on my flat stone under the old tamarind tree I smoke and watch the night creeping into the crook of English Bay. I think of Ouma, of how closely she listened when I talked to her about Boucan. I think of her face hidden by her hair, of the taste of salt on her shoulder. So, she knew everything, she knew my secret, and when she came to me on that last night, it was to say goodbye. That's why she was hiding her face and her voice was hard and bitter when she spoke to me about gold, when she said, 'you people from the upper crust'. Now I feel angry at not having understood, angry at her, at myself. I walk around in the valley feverishly, then come back to sit under the tall tree where the night has settled in, I crumple up the papers and maps in my hands. None of it matters to me any more! Now I know that Ouma will never come back. I've become like all the others, like the people from the coast that the Manafs keep a watchful eye on from a distance, waiting until the coast is clear.

In the wavering dusk light I go running across the valley, climb up the hills to get away from the gaze that is coming from all sides at once. I trip over stones, cling to blocks of basalt, I can hear the earth shifting under my feet, tumbling all the way down to the valley bottom. In the distance, outlined against the yellow sky, the mountains are dense and black, not a light, not a fire. Where do the Manafs live? On Mont Piton, Mont Limon in the east, or on Bilactère up above Port Mathurin? But they never spend more than two nights in the same place. They sleep in the warm ashes of their fires which they smother at twilight, like the black maroons used to do in the mountains of Mauritius, above the Morne. I want to go higher up, all the way to the foothills of the mountains, but night has fallen and I'm bumping against the rocks, tearing my clothing and my hands apart. I call to Ouma again, with all my might this time, 'Ou-maaa', and my cry echoes through the night, through the ravines, makes a strange bellowing sound, an animal-like moan that horrifies even me. So then I stop, lie down, propped on my elbows on the slope, and wait for silence to settle over the valley again. Then everything is smooth and pure, invisible in the darkness, and I don't want to think about what tomorrow will bring any more. I want to be the same as I used to be, as if nothing had ever happened.

Ypres, winter 1915
Somme, spring 1916

———————

We're no longer neophytes, any of us. We've all had our share of hardships, faced danger. All of us — the French Canadians of the 13th Infantry Brigade, Indians of the 27th and 28th Colonial Divisions — have experienced the winter in Flanders, when the beer froze in the casks, the battles in the snow, the fog and the poison fumes, the endless bombardments, the fires in the shelters. So many men have died. We hardly even feel fear any more. We are indifferent, as if in a dream. We are the survivors . . .

For months now we've been burrowing in the dirt of the river-banks, in the mud, day after day, with no idea of what we're doing, not even wondering about it ourselves. We've been in this dirt for so long now, listening to the rumbling of cannon and the song of the death crows, time is utterly foreign to us now. Do days, weeks, months exist? Or is it rather just one identical day that constantly returns to find us sleeping in the cold dirt, weak with hunger, weary, one sole and identical day that is slowly wheeling round with the pale sun behind the clouds?

It's still the same day when we responded to Lord Kitchener's call to arms so long ago now, we don't know when it all began any more or even if there was a beginning. Boarding a steel castle, the *Dreadnought*, in the fog of Portsmouth. Then the train across the north, the convoys of horses and men marching through the rain along the railway towards Ypres. Did I live through all of that? When was it? Months ago, years? The men who were with me on that winter road in Flanders, Remy from Quebec, Le Halloco from Newfoundland, and Perrin, Renouart, Simon, whose origins I don't know, all of the men who were there in the spring of 1915 to relieve the British Expeditionary Force decimated in the battle of La Bassée . . . We don't know anyone now. We shovel this clay earth, dig the trenches, creep towards the Ancre River day after day, yard by yard, like horrid moles, towards the dark hills overlooking this valley. At times, in the silence that lies heavily over these empty fields, we shudder upon hearing the rat-a-tat of a machine gun, a mortar explosion off in the distance beyond the line of trees.

When we speak, it's in whispers, words that come and go, orders being repeated, contradicted, deformed, questions, news of newcomers. At night, when the cold prevents us from sleeping in our dugouts, a song that suddenly stops, and no one thinks to tell him to go on, that the silence is more painful.

We lack water, in spite of the rain. We're being devoured by lice, by fleas. We're covered with a layer of mud mixed with filth, with blood. I think about the early days when — in the streets of London, amid the red-clad foot soldiers, the squadrons of grenadiers, of lancers of the 27th and 28th Indian Army, sporting tunics and wearing their tall, white turbans in the biting cold air and the December sun — we proudly showed off the light beige Overseas Volunteers uniforms, the felt hats. I remember the endless festivities around St Paul's during the first days of the New Year, the cavalcades in the frost-covered gardens, the excitement of the last nights and then the joyous boarding on the wharves of Waterloo and the misty dawn on the deck of the enormous *Dreadnought*. The men in their khaki greatcoats, covered with sea spray, volunteers from the four corners of the Earth, filled with hope, searching the horizon for the dark coast of France.

All of that is so distant now, we're not even sure it really happened. Exhaustion, hunger, fever have blurred our recollections, worn away the marks etched on our memories. What are we doing here today? Buried in these trenches, faces blackened with smoke, clothing in rags, stiff with dried mud, surrounded for months now with the stench of latrines and of death.

We've become familiar with, indifferent to death. Little by little, it decimated the ranks of the men I learned to know in the early days, when we rode in armoured railway carriages towards the train station in Boves. An immense crowd, glimpsed from time to time through the boards covering the windows, marching through the rain in the direction of the Yser River Valley, scattered along the roads, branching apart, coming back together, branching apart again. Morland's 5th Division, Snow's and Bulfin's 27th and 28th Divisions, Alderson's 1st Canadian Division, October veterans whom we were to join along with the Territorial Army and the British Expeditionary Force. Back then we all still thought about death, but a glorious death, the death we spoke of to each other in the evenings, in the bivouacs: the Scottish officer, who, armed with a sword at the head of his men, had led the charge against the German machine guns. On the Comines Canal the impatient, excited men awaited the order to attack, listening to the sound of the cannon thundering day and night like an underground storm. When the order came, when we knew that General Douglas Haig's troops had begun their march on Bruges, there was a childish outburst of joy. The soldiers were shouting 'Hurrah!', throwing their caps into the air, and I thought of the men in Rodrigues who were waiting in front of the telegraph office. The cavalry from the French Squadrons came to join us on the bank of the Lys River. In the dusky winter light their blue uniforms seemed unearthly, like the fine feathers of colourful birds.

Then we began our long march up the Ypres Canal heading north-west in the direction of Hooges Wood, where the thunder was rumbling. We passed troops every day. They were French and Belgians who'd escaped the Dixmude massacre, who were coming back from Ramskappelle, where the Belgians had provoked vast floods by opening the sluice gates. Bloody, in tatters, they related terrifying stories, frenetic bellowing hordes of Germans endlessly moving forward, hand-to-hand combat in the mud, with bayonets, with daggers, bodies scattered along the river, hung up in the barbed wire, stuck in the reeds.

Those tales keep ringing in my ears. Then, all around us, the circle of fire is closing in to the north over by Dixmude, by Saint Julien, in Houthulst Forest, to the south on the banks of the Lys, in the direction of Menin, Wervicq. Then we move forwards through a deserted landscape gutted by mortar shells, where the only things standing are the branchless trunks of charred trees. We move forwards so very slowly, as if crawling on our bellies: some mornings, at the other end of the field, we can see the ravine, the ruined farm that we know we won't reach until evening. The earth is heavy, it weighs upon our legs, clings to the soles of our shoes and makes us fall facedown in the mud. Some never get up again.

We crawl through the trenches we dug before sunrise, listening to the rumbling of cannon – very near now – and the clattering of machine guns. Far away, on the other side of the hills, around Ypres, the French are fighting too. But we don't see any soldiers: only the dirty black smudges they're making in the sky.

In the evenings Barneoud, who comes from Trois Rivières, talks about women. He describes their bodies, their faces, their hair. He talks about all of that in a strange voice, hoarse and sad, as if the women he's describing are all dead. We laugh at first, because it's so incongruous, all those naked women in the middle of the war with us. War doesn't have anything to do with women, on the contrary, it's the most sterile gathering of men that could exist. Then all of those women's bodies in the mud, surrounded by the smell of urine and putridity, with the circle of fire burning day and night around us, makes us shudder, fills us with horror. Then we tell him in English, in French: that's enough, shut up, *tais-toi*! Stop talking about women, shut up! One evening when he starts raving again, a tall English devil beats him savagely with his fists and might well have killed him if the officer, the second lieutenant, hadn't come up with his service pistol in hand. The next day Barneoud had disappeared. They say he was sent to join the 13th infantry brigade and died in the fighting near Saint Julien.

At that time I think we'd already grown indifferent to death. Every hour of every day the sounds of the dead filled our ears, the dull thud of shells exploding in the earth, the spurts of machine-gun fire and the strange rumour that immediately followed. Voices, the sound of men running in the mud, orders shouted by officers, the rout before the counter-attack.

23 April: following the first release of poison gas over the French lines, we counter-attack under the orders of Colonel Geddes, joining the 13th Brigade and the battalions of the 3rd Canadian Brigade. All day long we march north-west in the direction of Houthulst Forest. In the

middle of the plain the exploding bombs, leaving craters nearer and nearer to us, force us to find shelter for the night. Hastily, we open up ten-foot ditches in which six or seven of us ensconce ourselves, packed in as tight as crabs. Huddling, steel helmet pushed down over our heads, we await the following day, hardly daring to move. We can hear the British cannon countering German cannon. In the morning, as we sleep leaning against one another, the whistling of a mortar shell awakens us with a start. The explosion is so powerful that we are sent sprawling, despite the narrowness of the ditch. Crushed under the weight of my comrades, I feel a warm liquid running over my face: blood. I'm wounded, dying maybe? I push away the bodies that have fallen on me and see that my comrades are the ones who've been killed, it's their blood spilling on me.

I crawl over to the other holes filled with men, calling out to survivors. Together we pull the wounded back behind the lines, to find shelter. But where? Half of our company has been killed. The second lieutenant who arrested Barneoud was decapitated by a mortar shell. We reach the rear. At five in the evening we launch another assault with General Snow's Englishmen, advancing in sallies of five yards. At five-thirty, when the twilight is growing dimmer, a large, yellowish-green cloud rises suddenly in the sky some fifty yards ahead of us. The light breeze pushes it slowly southwards, fans it out. Other, still closer explosions, cause new poisonous plumes to rise.

My heart stops beating — horror-stricken — I'm unable to move! Someone cries, 'The gas! Turn back!' We run for the trenches, hurriedly improvise masks with handkerchiefs, bits of torn coats, tatters of ripped cloth that we wet with our meagre provisions of water. The cloud is still moving towards us, light, menacing, copper-coloured in the dusk light. Already the acrid smell is entering our lungs, making us cough. The men turn, looking over their shoulders with expressions of hatred, of terror on their faces. When the order to fall back to Saint Julien comes, many have already begun to run, doubled over towards the ground. I think of the wounded who've been left in their holes, over whom death is now passing. I too am running across the shell-pocked field, through charred stands of trees, clamping the handkerchief dampened with muddy water to my face.

How many have been killed? How many are still able to fight? After what we've seen — that deadly cloud wafting slowly towards us, yellow and golden brown like a sunset — we remain hunkered down in our holes, tirelessly scrutinizing the sky, day and night. We count our ranks, maybe in the hopes of making those who are absent, whose names no longer belong to anyone, reappear: 'Simon, Lenfant, Garadec, Schaffer . . . and Adrien, and the little redhead — Gordon, that was his name, Gordon . . . and Pommier, Antoine who was from Joliette, but whose family name I've forgotten, and Léon Berre and Raymond, Dubois, Santeuil, Reinert . . .' Are they really names? Did they really exist? We thought of death differently when we first arrived from so far away: glorious death out in broad daylight, a star of blood on one's chest. But death is deceitful and insidious, it sneaks up, whisks men away in the night while they're sleeping, unbeknownst to others. It drowns men in the bogs, in the muddy pools at the bottom of ravines, it smothers them in the earth, it spreads its icy fingers into the bodies of those who are lying in lazarettos, under torn tents, those with livid faces and emaciated chests, wasted from dysentery, from pneumonia, from typhus. Those who die vanish and one day we notice their absence. Where are they? Maybe they've been lucky enough to have been sent to the rear, maybe they've lost an eye, a leg, maybe they'll never go back to war. But something tells us, something about their absence, about the silence that surrounds their names: they're dead.

Thus, it's as if some monstrous animal came in the night, during our precarious slumber, to seize certain men among us and carry them off to devour them in its den. It makes a pain, a burning feeling deep down in our bodies that we can never forget, no matter what. We haven't moved since the gas attack on 24 April. We've remained in the trenches, the same ones we began digging six months ago when we first arrived. Back then the landscape before us was still intact, undulating woodland, rusty with winter, farms in their fields, pastures dotted with ponds, fences, rows of apple trees, and off in the distance the silhouette of the town of Ypres with its stone steeple rising out of the mist. Now all I can see through the machine-gun sights is a chaos of churned earth, burned trees. The shells have gouged out hundreds of craters, destroyed the forests and the hamlets, and Ypres's steeple is leaning over like a broken branch. Silence, solitude have taken the place of the hellish din of the bombardments of the early weeks. The circle of fire has waned, like a wildfire that has consumed everything in its path and is dying out for want of anything to burn. Now we can just barely make out the rumbling of artillery from time to time, barely glimpse puffs of smoke in the places where allied shells have struck.

Is everyone dead? One night when I'm on guard, sitting on a crate behind the shield of the machine gun, that thought crosses my mind. To stave off the urge to smoke, I'm chewing on a licorice root given to me by a Canadian soldier whose name I don't even know. The night is cold, cloudless, another winter night. I can see the stars, some that I'm not familiar with that belong to the northern skies alone. In the light of the rising moon the shell-torn earth seems even stranger, more deserted. In the silent night the world seems bereft of men and beasts, like a remote, high plateau in some region that has been for ever abandoned by all life. The feeling of death that has come over me is so powerful I can't stand it any longer. I walk over to a comrade who's asleep, sitting with his back propped against the wall of the trench. I shake him. He looks at me in a daze as if he doesn't remember where he is any more. 'Come and see! Come on!' I drag him over to the lookout post, I show him the frozen landscape in the moonlight, looking through the peephole in the gun shield. 'Look, there's not a soul out there. It's all over with! The war's over!' I'm speaking in a low voice, but the tone of my voice, the look in my eyes must be disturbing, because the soldier pulls away. He says, 'You're crazy!' In the same strangled voice, I repeat, 'But look! Look! I'm telling you there's no one out there, they're all dead! The war is over!' Other soldiers come over, having been roused from their sleep. The officer is there, he says in a loud voice, 'What's going on here?' They say, 'He's crazy! He says the war's over.' Still others add, 'He says everyone's dead.' The officer looks at me, as if trying to comprehend. Maybe they'll realize that it's true, that everything is over now, since everyone is dead. The officer seems to be listening to the silence of the night all around us. Then he says, 'Go back to sleep! The war isn't over. We'll have plenty to do tomorrow!' To me, he says, 'You go to bed too. You're tired.' Another man stands guard and I go down into the trench. I listen to the breathing of the men who have already gone back to sleep, the only living beings on earth, buried in the gutted earth.

SOMME, SUMMER 1916

Like so many ants, we're walking across this plain on the banks of the great muddy river. Endlessly, we follow the same paths, the same grooves, dig up the same fields, making countless holes, not knowing where we're going. Digging out underground galleries, corridors, tunnels through the heavy black earth, the damp earth that slides down all around us. We don't ask any more questions, we have no desire to know where we are, why we're here any more. Day after day, for months now, we've been ploughing through, digging up, raking the earth along the river, facing the hills. In the beginning, when we arrived on the banks of the Ancre, shells would fall, to the left, to the right, and we'd throw ourselves on our bellies in the mud, listening to the sinister whistling of the projectiles at the end of their trajectory. The shells exploded in the earth, blew up trees and houses and the fires burned throughout the night. But there was no counter-attack. We waited, and then went back to digging trenches, and the convoys of mules continued to bring wooden stanchions and cement, sheet metal for the roofs. In the spring a drizzling rain falls, a mist dispelled by the sun. Then the first planes appear, flying under the clouds. Odilon and I look up at them, blinking our eyes, trying to see who they are. They veer round and fly off southward. 'They're French,' says Odilon. On the Kraut's side they've only got dirigibles. Sometimes we see them rising in the dawn sky like large ribboned slugs. 'Just wait, the French planes will gouge their eyes out!'

Odilon is my comrade. He's a Jerseyman, who speaks with a funny accent that I don't always understand. He's an eighteen year old with an angelic face. He hasn't got a beard yet and the cold makes his skin ruddy. We've been working side by side for months now, we share the same nooks to eat and sleep in. We never really talk, except to say a few words, just the bare minimum, a few questions and answers. He enrolled in the army after I did, and since I was named corporal after the Battle of Ypres, I chose him to be my orderly. When they wanted to send him to the front lines in Verdun, I requested that he stay with me. Ever since I met him I feel as if I need to look after him in this war, as if I am his older brother.

Warmer weather has set in, nights are clearer, with deep, star-filled skies. In the evening, when everything is asleep, we listen to the song of the toads in the marshes, on the banks of the river. That is where the men from our contingent are building barricades of barbed wire, lookout towers, laying cement platforms for the cannon. But at night, when you can't see the barbed wire or the trenches gaping like open graves, you can forget there is a war, thanks to the gentle songs of toads.

The train brought the horse carcasses to the station in Albert. They were carried in carts along muddy roads to the banks of the Ancre. Every day carts bring mountains of horse carcasses and dump them in the grassy fields near the river. We can hear the shrieking of the ravens and crows following the carts. One day we're walking along the shore of the Ancre to work in the trenches and we cross a large field of oats and stubble where the cadavers of horses killed in the war lie. The bodies are already black and stinking, and flights of crows fan out, squawking. We aren't neophytes, we've all seen death, comrades suddenly doubling over as if from an invisible punch and being thrown backwards by machine-gun bullets. Those who've been disembowelled or had their brains blown out by mortar fire. But when we go across that field where hundreds of horse carcasses have been left, our legs grow wobbly and nausea rises in our throats.

That was the very beginning of the war and we didn't know it. At the time we thought the fighting would soon be over, that all around us the countryside was deserted like these open graves where they dumped the dead horses.

Stretching out before us like the sea: those hills, those forests, so very dark in spite of the bright summer light, almost unreal, over which only the crows have the right to fly. What lies out there? Our enemies, silent, invisible. They are living over there, conversing, eating, sleeping like we are, but we never see them. From time to time the sound of machine guns in the distance to the north-west or to the south tells us they still exist. Or else the high-pitched humming of an aeroplane slipping between two clouds that we never see again.

So we work at building roads. Every day trucks bring loads of stones that they dump in piles along the banks of the Ancre. The soldiers from the Territorial Army and the New Army join us in the road construction, in preparing the railway that will cross the river to reach Hardecourt. No one would recognize this land after these past few months. In the place where, in the beginning of winter, there was nothing but pasture, fields, woods, a few old farms, now stretches a network of stone roads, railways, with their sheet-metal shelters, their hangars for trucks and aeroplanes, tanks, cannon, munitions. Over all of that, the camouflage teams have strung great brown tarps, tent cloths that imitate the scabby prairies. When the wind blows the tarps snap like the sails of a ship and you can hear a metallic hum in the barbed wire. The heavy cannon have been buried in the centre of large craters, looking like giant antlions, wicked land crabs. The carts come and go endlessly, bringing loads of artillery shells: the Navy's 37- and 47 mm-calibre shells, but also 58-, 75-calibre shells. Beyond the railway the men are digging trenches on the banks of the Ancre, pouring concrete platforms for cannon, building fortified shelters. In the plains south of Hardecourt, near Albert, Aveluy, Mesnil, where the valley grows narrower, props in trompe l'œil have been set up: fake ruins, fake wells that hide machine-gun positions. With old uniforms we make figures stuffed with straw that look like the bodies of soldiers sprawled on the ground. With bits of sheet metal and branches we set up fake hollow trees to shield lookouts, machine guns, artillery. On the roads, the railway, the bridges, we've put up large grass-coloured raffia screens, bales of hay. With an old barge brought from Flanders, the British Expeditionary Corps has prepared a river gunboat that will sail down the Ancre all the way to the Somme.

Now that summer is here, bringing such long days, we feel new strength, as if everything we were witnessing being prepared here were nothing but a game, and we don't think about death any more. After the despair of the long winter months spent in the mud of the Ancre, Odilon has become gay and self-confident. After days of working on the roads and railways he drinks coffee and talks with the Canadians before curfew in the evenings. Nights are starry and I recall the nights in Boucan, the sky over English Bay. For the first time in months we allow ourselves to confide in one another. The men talk about their parents, their fiancées, their wives and children. Photographs are passed around, dirtied, mouldy old bits of cardboard upon which, in the flickering light of the lamps, smiling faces appear, distant, fragile figures, like spectres. Odilon and I don't have any photographs, but in my coat pocket I have the last letter I received from Laure, in London, before boarding the *Dreadnought*. I've read and reread it so many times I could recite it by heart, with those half-mocking and somewhat melancholy words I so love. She mentions Mananava, where we'll be reunited one day, when all this is over. Does she really believe that? One night I can't keep from talking to Odilon about Mananava, about the two tropicbirds that circle over the ravine at twilight. Has he listened to me? I think he's gone to sleep with his head on his bag in the underground shelter that serves as a barracks. It doesn't matter. I need to go on talking, not for him, but for myself. So that my voice will reach out beyond this hellhole, all the way out to the island where Laure is surrounded by the night silence, eyes wide, listening to the rustling of the rain, as in the old days in the house in Boucan.

We've been working on setting up this scenery for so long that we don't believe in the reality of war any more. Ypres, the forced marches in Flanders, are far behind. Most of my comrades didn't live through that. At first this trompe l'œil work made them laugh, they who'd been expecting the smell of gunpowder, the thundering of cannon. Now they don't understand any more, they're growing impatient. 'Is this what war is all about?' asks Odilon after a harrowing day spent digging out mine galleries and trenches. The sky above us is leaden, heavy. The storm breaks with a sudden downpour and when it's time for the relief guard we are drenched, as if we'd fallen in the river.

Evenings, in the underground shelter, the men play cards, dreaming out loud as they await curfew. News is passed around, the fighting in Verdun, and for the first time, we hear those strange names that will be repeated so often: Douamont, *le ravin de la Dame* or the Lady's Ravine, Fort Vaux, and the name that makes me shudder in spite of myself, *le Mort-Homme* or Dead Man's Hill. One soldier, an English-speaking Canadian, tells of the Tavannes Tunnel, where the wounded and dying are piled, while shells explode overhead. He relates the lurid incandescence of explosions, the smoke, the ripping sound of 370 mm mortar shells, of all the men that are being mutilated and burned at this very moment. Can it be summer already? On some evenings the sunset over the trenches is extraordinarily beautiful. Huge violet and crimson-coloured clouds hovering in the grey, golden sky. Can those who are dying at Douamont see it? I imagine life up in the sky, soaring so high above the earth as if on the wings of the tropicbirds. You wouldn't see the trenches, the shell marks any more, you'd be far away.

We all know that combat is near now. The preparations we've been working on since the beginning of winter have come to an end. The teams don't go down to the river any more, the trains have almost stopped running. In the shelters under the tarps, the cannon are ready, the light machine guns are in the circular dugouts at the ends of the trenches.

Around mid-June Rawlinson's soldiers begin to arrive. Englishmen, Scots and battalions from India, South Africa, Australia, divisions coming back from Flanders, from Artois. We've never seen so many men before. They turn up on all sides, march along the roads, the railways, settle into the kilometres of trenches we've dug. They say the attack will take place on 29 June. The cannon start firing as early as the 24th. All along the bank of the Ancre to the south, along the bank of the Somme, where the French forces are entrenched, the deafening blasts of cannon roll. After so many days of silence, after this long, huddled wait, we feel giddy, feverish, we're trembling with impatience.

All day, all night long, the cannon boom, a red glow lights up the sky over the hills around us.

Out there, on the other side, they remain silent. Why don't they respond? Have they vanished? How can they resist this deluge of artillery fire? We don't sleep for six days and six nights, constantly combing the landscape in front of us. On the sixth day the rain begins to fall, a torrential rain that turns the trenches into streams of mud. The cannon fall silent for several hours, as if the sky itself has joined in battle.

Crouching in the shelters, we watch the rain falling all day until evening and we're seized with anxiety, as if the rain will never stop. The Englishmen talk about the flooding in Flanders, hordes of green uniforms swimming in the swamped waters of the Lys. Most of us feel disappointed that the attack has been put off. We study the skies and, as evening is approaching, Odilon announces that the clouds have grown thinner, that you can even see a patch of sky, and everyone cries, 'Hurrah!' Maybe it's not too late. Maybe the attack will take place during the night. We watch the darkness creeping slowly into the Ancre Valley, drowning the forests and the hills facing us. It is a strange night that has fallen, not one of us is really sleeping. Near dawn, just as I'm dozing off with my head resting on my knees, I'm startled awake by the brouhaha of the attack. The light is already bright, blinding, the wind blowing in the valley is hot and dry, the sort of wind I haven't felt since Rodrigues and English Bay. From the still damp riverbanks a glowing, gossamer mist is rising, and the odour that I perceive just then, the odour that penetrates and disconcerts me: the smell of summer, of earth, of grass. And also what I glimpse between the stanchions of the shelter, the gnats dancing in the light, buoyed by the wind. There is such peace in that moment, everything seems to be suspended, stopped.

All of us are standing in the muddy trench, helmets pushed down tight, bayonets fixed to the barrels of our rifles. We're peering over the embankment at the blue sky where white clouds, light as down, fluff. We are tense, we're listening to the sounds of summer, the water flowing in the river, the chirping insects, the singing of a lark. We're waiting with painful impatience in the peaceful silence, and when the first rumblings of cannon come from the north, the south and the east, we flinch. Soon the heavy English artillery begins to thunder behind us, and in response to their powerful blasts the earth-shaking boom of the shells hitting the ground on the other side of the river echoes out. The bombardment is nerve-rattling — after that long rainy day — to us it seems incomprehensible that it should be rumbling around in that utterly clear blue sky and that beautiful bright summer sunlight.

After an eternity the din of explosions comes to an end. The silence that follows is filled with pain and dazedness. At exactly seven-thirty the order to attack is passed down from trench to trench, repeated by sergeants and corporals. When it's my turn to shout it out, I look at Odilon's face, I catch the last expression on his face. Now I'm running, leaning forwards, clutching my rifle in both hands, towards the bank of the Ancre, where the pontoons are covered with soldiers. I can hear the spitting of machine guns in front of me, behind me. Where are the enemy bullets? Still running, we make it across the moored pontoons in a racket of boots on the wooden planks. The river water is heavy, blood-coloured. Men slip in the mud on the other bank, fall, do not get up again.

The dark hills are above me, I can feel their threat like a penetrating gaze. Black plumes of smoke are rising on all sides, smoke with no fire, the smoke of death. Isolated rifle shots ring out. Spurts of machine-gun fire come up out of the ground in the distance, without our being able to tell from where. I run behind the group of men, not trying to find shelter, towards the objective that has been pointed out to us for months: the hills that lay between us and Thiepval. Men are running, joining us on the right, in a shell-torn field: they're from the 10th Corps, the 2nd Corps, and Rawlinson's division. In the middle of that vast and empty field the bushes burned by the gases and shells look like scarecrows. The sound of light machine-gun fire bursts forth all of a sudden, straight ahead of me at the end of the field. Barely a light cloud of bluish smoke floating here and there at the edge of the dark hills; the Germans are buried in the mortar craters, their LMGs are spraying the field. Men are already falling, cut down, puppets with no strings, crumpling up in groups of ten, of twenty. Were any orders given? I didn't hear anything, but I throw myself on the ground, I'm looking around for shelter, a crater, a trench, a muddy tree stump. I'm crawling over the field. All around me I can see shapes crawling like I am, like huge slugs, their faces hidden behind their rifles. Others are lying still, faces in the muddy earth. And the cracking of rifles resounding in the still air, the spurts of LMG fire, in front, behind, everywhere, leaving their small blue, transparent clouds floating in the warm breeze. After crawling like that through the loose earth, I finally find what I'm looking for: a block of stone, hardly larger than a boundary stone, left in the field. I stretch out against it, my face so close to the stone I can see every crack, every moss stain. I remain there, not moving, my body racked with pain, ears ringing with the blasts of the bombs that have stopped falling now. I think, say out loud, now's the time to let them have it! Where are the other men? Are there still men on this earth or only these pathetic, ridiculous larvae, crawling along and then stopping, disappearing in the mud? I lie there for so long, my head against the stone, listening to the LMGs and the rifles that my face grows as cold as stone. Then I hear the cannon behind me. Shells explode in the hills, black clouds from fires rise into the hot sky.

I hear officers shout out the order to attack, just as they had a little while ago. I'm running straight out ahead again, towards the mortar craters where the LMGs are buried. There they are all right, like huge burned insects, and the bodies of the dead Germans look like their victims. The men run in close ranks towards the hills. The LMGs hidden in other craters spray the field, killing dozens, scores of men at a time. Along with two Canadians I roll, head over heels, into a crater occupied by German bodies. Together we heave the cadavers overboard. My comrades are pale, their faces stained with mud and smoke. We stare at each other, saying nothing. In any case the noise of the battle would drown out our words. It even drowns out our thoughts. Protected by the gun shield of the LMG, I examine the objective: the hills of Thiepval are still just as dark, just as distant. We'll never make it.

Around two o'clock in the afternoon I hear the retreat being sounded. The two Canadians immediately leap out of the shelter. They run towards the riverbank so fast I can't keep up with them. I can feel cannon blasting ahead of me, hear the howling of heavy mortar sailing over us. We've only got a few minutes to get back to the base, back to the shelter of the trenches. The sky is filled with smoke, the sunlight that was so beautiful this morning is smirched now, tarnished. When I finally get to the trench, breathless, I look at the men who are already there, I attempt to recognize their eyes in their exhausted faces, in the blank, absent look of men who have narrowly escaped death. I look for Odilon's eyes and my heart is pounding in my chest because I don't recognize them. I move hurriedly through the trench, all the way to the night bunker. 'Odilon? Odilon?' The men look at me in bewilderment. Do they even know who Odilon is? There are so many missing. For the rest of the day, as the bombardments continue, I keep hoping – irrationally – that I will finally see him appear at the edge of the trench with his calm, child's face, his smile. The officer calls roll in the evening, puts an 'X' in front of the names of the absentees. How many of ours are missing? Twenty, thirty men, maybe more. Slumped against the banking, I smoke and drink bitter coffee, looking up at the beautiful night sky. The next day and those that follow, the rumour goes around that we've been beaten at Thiepval, as well as at Ovillers, at Beaumont-Hamel. They say that Joffre, commander-in-chief of the French army, had requested Haig to take Thiepval at any cost and that Haig refused to send his troops into another massacre. Have we lost the war?

No one talks. Everyone eats hastily in silence, drinks the tepid coffee, smokes, without looking at his neighbour. What disturbs the living, what worries them, are the men who didn't come back. At times, in my half-sleep, I think of Odilon as if he were alive, and when I wake up I look around for him. Maybe he's wounded, at the infirmary in Albert, sent back to England? But deep down inside I know very well, despite the glorious sunshine, that he fell face down in the muddy field within sight of the dark line of the hills we were unable to reach.

Now everything has changed. Our division, which was decimated during the Thiepval attack, has been divided up between the 12th and 15th Corps, to the south and north of Albert. We are fighting under Rawlinson's orders, using the 'hurricane' technique. Every night the columns of light infantry advance from one trench to the next, crawling noiselessly across the wet fields. We penetrate deep into enemy territory and if it weren't for the magnificent, star-filled sky I wouldn't know that we are going further south each night. Thanks to my experience on board the *Zeta* and during the nights in English Bay I'm able to take note of this.

Before daybreak the cannon begin the bombardment, burning the forests, the hamlets, the hills before us. Then, as soon as the sun appears, the men mount the attack, take up positions in the mortar craters, fire at the enemy lines with their rifles. A moment later the retreat is sounded and we all fall back, safe and sound. Fourteenth of July, after the attack, the British cavalry breaks cover for the first time and charges between the bomb holes. Along with the Australian Corps, we enter Pozières, which is nothing but a heap of ruins.

Summer simmers on, day after day. We sleep wherever the attack has led us, anywhere, lying on the bare ground, shielded from the dew with a scrap of canvas. We can't think of death any more. Every night we move forwards, under the stars, in single file through the hills. From time to time the flash of a flare shines out, we hear the haphazard cracking of shots. Warm, empty nights with not an insect, not an animal.

In the beginning of September we meet General Gough's 5th Army and, along with those who remained under the orders of Rawlinson, we march further south, towards Guillemont. Under cover of night we make our way back north-east, going up the railway in the direction of the woods. Now they're on all sides, darker and even more menacing: the Trônes Woods behind us, the Leuze Woods to the south, and before us the Birch Woods. The men aren't sleeping, just waiting in the calm of night. I don't think any of us can help but dream about what this place used to be like before the war; the beauty of it, these stands of still birches where the hooting of barn owls, the purling of streams, the leaping of wild rabbits could be heard. These woods where lovers would go after the dance, the grass — still warm with the day's sunlight — where bodies would roll and enlace one another, laughing. The woods at evening time, when blue plumes of smoke would rise so peacefully from the villages and on the paths, the silhouettes of little old women gathering firewood. Not one of us is sleeping, we're staring wide-eyed into the night — maybe our last. We've got our ears pricked up, our senses alert to the slightest vibration, the slightest sign of life that seems to have completely vanished. In pained apprehension, we await the moment when the first blasts of 75 mm-calibre cannon will come tearing through the night behind us, making the 'hurricane' of fire rain down upon the tall trees, disembowel the earth, lay open the dreadful path of the attack.

It begins to rain before dawn. A fine drizzle that penetrates our clothing, wets our faces and makes us shiver. And so, almost with no fire support, the men launch into the attack of the three woods, in successive waves. Behind us the night lights up eerily over in the direction of the Ancre, where the 4th Army is mounting a diversionary attack. But for us it is a silent, cruel, often hand-to-hand combat. One after the other the waves of infantrymen pass over the trenches, capture the LMGs, pursue the enemy into the woods. I hear shots cracking very near to us, in the Birch Wood. Lying in the damp earth we shoot haphazardly into the underbrush. Soundlessly, flares light up above the trees, fall back to earth in a rain of sparks. As I'm running towards the wood I stumble over something: it's the body of a German lying on his back in the grass. He's still holding his Mauser, but his helmet has rolled several feet away. The officers shout, 'Cease fire!' The wood is ours. Everywhere, in the grey light of dawn, I see the bodies of the Germans lying in the grass in the fine rain. There are dead horses all over the fields and the cawing of crows is already echoing out grimly. Despite their exhaustion, the men are laughing, singing. Our officer, a red-faced, jovial Englishman, tries to explain to me. 'Those bastards, they weren't expecting us . . . !' But I turn away and I hear him repeating the same thing to someone else. I feel so intensely exhausted it makes me stagger and feel nauseous. The men settle in for the night in the underbrush, in the German camps. Everything was ready for them to wake up, they say that even the coffee was already brewed. The Canadians are the ones to drink it, laughing. I'm stretched out under the tall trees, my head leaning against the cool bark, and I fall asleep in the lovely morning light.

Winter's heavy rains are here. The Ancre and the Somme are flooding their banks. We are prisoners of the conquered trenches, stuck in the mud, huddled in makeshift shelters. We've already forgotten the exhilaration of the battles that brought us this far. We captured

Guillemont, the Falfemont farm, Ginchy, and, during the day of 15 September alone, Morval, Gueudecourt, Lesboeufs, pushing the Germans back to their rear-line trenches atop the hills near Bapaume or Transloy. Now we're prisoners of the trenches on the other side of the river, prisoners of the rain and mud. Days are grey, cold, nothing happens. At times the boom of cannon fire resounds in the distance over by the Somme, in the woods around Bapaume. At times we're awakened in the middle of the night by bright lights suddenly illuminating the sky. But they aren't lightning flashes. 'On your feet!' the officers shout. We pack our bags in the dark, set out, stoop-backed in the icy, sucking mud. We're advancing southward on worn paths along the Somme, unable to see where we're going. What do all these rivers everyone talks about so much look like? The Yser, the Marne, the Meuse, the Aisne, the Ailette, the Scarpe? Rivers of mud under the low-hanging sky, heavy waters washing along the remains of forests, burned rafters, dead horses.

Near Combles we meet the French Divisions. They are paler, more battered than we are. Sunken-eyed faces, ragged, mud-stained uniforms. Some don't even have shoes, only bloody rags around their feet. In the convoy is a German officer. The soldiers are roughing him about, insulting him, because of the gases that have killed so many of our men. Very proud in spite of his tattered uniform, he suddenly pushes them away. He shouts in perfect French, 'Why you're the ones who used the gases first! You're the ones who forced us to fight in that manner! You!' A striking silence follows. Each of us looks away and the officer goes back to his place among the prisoners.

Later we enter a village. I have never learned the name of that village, in the drab dawn, the streets are deserted, the houses in ruins. Our boots echo out strangely in the rain, as if we'd reached the end of the world, out at the very edge of the void. We pitch camp in the ruins of the village and convoys, Red Cross vans, file by all day long. When the rain stops a cloud of dust veils the sky. Farther away, in the trenches that are extensions of the village streets, we can hear the rumbling of cannon again and, off in the distance, the thud of shells.

Sitting in front of a fire of burning boards, beside piles of rubble, Canadian, Territorial and French soldiers fraternize, exchange names. There are others who aren't asked any questions, who don't say anything. They roam the streets endlessly, unable to stop. Exhaustion. Off in the distance we hear faint rifle shots, like schoolboys playing with firecrackers. We're drifting along in a strange land, steering out into incomprehensible time. The same day, the same endless night, are forever tormenting us. We haven't spoken in such a long time. Haven't spoken a woman's name in such a long time. We hate the war with every fibre of our beings.

All around us, bombed-out streets, ruined, gutted houses. Bodies like ragdolls hanging from machines. In the fields around the village there are dead horses as far as you can see, bloated and black like dead elephants. The crows dip and swoop over the carcasses, their piercing cries make the living wince. Cohorts of pitiful prisoners come into the town, wasted with disease and wounds. With them, mules, lame horses, emaciated donkeys. The air is foul, the fumes, the smell of cadavers. Effluvia of a musty, cellar-like odour. A German shell has sealed up a tunnel where some French soldiers had sought shelter for the night. A man is lost, searching for his company. He clings to me, repeating, 'I'm from the 110th Infantry. The 110th. Do you know where they are?' In a mortar crater, at the foot of the ruins of the chapel where the dead and dying are piled one on top of the other, the Red Cross has set up a table. We sleep in the Frégicourt trench, then the following night in the Iron Doors trench. We pursue our march across the plain. At night the tiny lights of the artillery posts are our sole points of reference. Sailly-Saillisel is ahead of us, enveloped in a black cloud like that of a volcano. Cannon thunder very nearby, to the north, on the hills of Batack, to the south, in the Saint-Pierre-Vaast Wood.

Battles in the village streets by night, with grenades, rifles, revolvers. Blackened basement windows, the LMGs spray the intersections, cutting down men. I listen to the heavy pounding, breathe in the smell of sulphur, of phosphorous, shadows dance in the clouds. 'Hold on! Don't shoot!' Along with men I don't know (French? Haig's Englishmen?) I'm huddled up in a ditch. Mud. We've been short on water for days. Fever is burning in my body, I'm seized with a fit of vomiting. The acrid smell fills my throat, in spite of myself, I shout, 'The gas! The gas is coming . . . !' I believe I see blood gushing out incessantly, filling the holes, the ditches, rushing into the toppled houses, trickling into the ravaged fields just at daybreak.

Two men are carrying me. They drag me, holding me up by the shoulders, over to the Red Cross shelter. I lie on the ground for such a long time I feel as if I've turned into a hot stone. Then I'm in the van that is bumping along, zigzagging to avoid the bomb craters. In the lazaretto in Albert the doctor looks like Camal Boudou. He checks my temperature, palpates my stomach. 'Typhus,' he says. And then adds (but I think I must have dreamt that), 'It's lice who win the wars.'

Heading for Rodrigues,
summer 1918–1919

———————

Freedom at last: the sea. For all of these grim, lifeless years, this is what I've been waiting for: the moment I would be on the deck of the liner with the crowd of demobilized soldiers heading back to India, to Africa. We gaze out to sea from dawn to dusk, and even at night, when the moon lights our wake. Once past the Suez Canal, nights are so very mild. We sneak out of the holds to sleep on deck. I roll up in my army blanket, one of the only souvenirs I'm bringing back from the army, along with my khaki jacket and the canvas duffel bag my papers are in. I've been sleeping out of doors, in the mud, for such a long time that the wooden deck and the star-filled dome above me seem like paradise. The other soldiers and I talk in Creole, in Pidgin, we sing, tell each other interminable stories. The war is already a legend, transformed by the storyteller's imagination. On deck with me there are Seychellois, Mauritians, South Africans. But not a single one of the Rodriguans who answered the call to arms with me in front of the telegraph office. I remember Casimir's joy when his name was called. Could I be the only survivor, having escaped the massacre only by the grace of lice?

*

Now I'm thinking about Laure. When it's authorized, I go all the way up to the end of the prow, near the capstan and look out at the horizon. I think of Laure's face as I gaze at the dark-blue sea, at the clouds. We're just off Aden, then we'll be sailing around Cape Guardafui, towards the large ports whose names Laure and I used to dream of back in the days of Boucan: Mombasa, Zanzibar. We're heading for the equator and the air is already searing, nights are dry, illuminated with stars. I keep an eye out for flying fish, for albatrosses, for dolphins. Each day it seems as if I can see Laure more clearly, can hear her voice more clearly, see her ironic smile, the light in her eyes. In the Sea of Oman a magnificent tempest comes upon us. Not a cloud in the sky, a furious wind pushing the waves against the liner, a moving cliff wall that the wild rams of the sea are battering up against. Pushed sideways, the vessel is tossing violently, waves are sweeping across the lower deck, where we're standing. Whether we like it or not we're forced to abandon our holiday spot and descend into the nauseating, oven-hot holds again. The crewmen inform us that it's the tail end of a storm passing over Socotra and, sure enough, that very evening torrential rains come driving down upon the ship, flooding the holds. We relay one another to pump out the water as rivers wash through the holds between our legs, sweeping garbage and trash along with them! But when the sea and the sky have grown calm again, they are so resplendent! On all sides the blue immensity of the sea with the long waves trimmed in foam moving slowly along with us.

Stopovers in the ports of Mombasa, Zanzibar, the journey out to Tamatave, have all gone by very quickly. I hardly left my spot on the deck, except when the sun grew too hot in the afternoons or when there were showers. I almost never took my eyes off the sea, I watched it change colours and moods, sometimes smooth, without a wave, riffling in the wind, other times so very hard, horizonless, grey with rain, roaring, heaving its billows at us. I think about the *Zeta* again, about the journey to English Bay. It all seems so far away, Ouma slipping over the sand in the river, harpoon in hand, her body sleeping close against mine, under the glittering sky. Here, thanks to the sea, I've finally found the rhythm, the colour of dreams again. I know I must go back to Rodrigues. It's a part of me, I have to go. Will Laure understand?

When the long pirogue that makes its way to and fro in the harbour of Port Louis finally moors at the wharf, I'm dazed by the crowd, the smells, just as I was in Mombasa, and for a second I feel like going back on board the big liner that will cast off and pursue its journey. But suddenly, in the shade of the trees of the Intendance, I see Laure's silhouette. The next instant she's hugging me in her arms, dragging me through the streets to the train station. Even though we're both very moved, we're talking quietly, as if we'd parted only yesterday. She asks me questions about the journey, the military hospital, she talks about the letters she wrote to me. Then she asks, 'But why have they cut your hair like a convict's?' At that I can answer, 'Because of the lice!' And there is a moment of silence. Then she starts questioning me again about England, about France, as we walk towards the station through the streets that I no longer recognize.

After all these years Laure has changed, and I don't think I would have recognized her if she hadn't been standing off to one side, wearing the same white dress she had on when I left for Rodrigues. In the second-class passenger carriage, heading for Rose Hill and Quatre Bornes, I notice her pale complexion, the rings under her eyes, the bitter wrinkles on either side of her mouth. She's still pretty, with that flame in her eyes, the wary alertness that I love, but with an added touch of weariness, weakness.

I feel my heart sink when we near the house at Forest Side. In the rain that seems as if it's been falling for years, it is even darker, sadder. At first glance I notice the veranda that is collapsing, the little garden overrun with weeds, the broken window panes that have been replaced with oil-paper. Laure follows my gaze and says very quietly, 'We're poor now.' My mother comes out to meet us, she stops on the steps of the veranda. Her face is tense, worried, unsmiling, she's shading her eyes as if trying to see us. Yet we're only a few yards away. I realize she's almost blind. When I am next to her, I take her hands. She hugs me very close to her breast without saying anything for a long time.

In spite of the hardship, the neglected state of the house, that evening and the days that follow I am happier than I have been in a good while. It's as if I've found myself at last, as if I've become my old self again.

December: despite the rain that falls every afternoon on Forest Side, this summer is the finest and the freest I've spent in a long time. Thanks to the bundle I was given on the day we were demobilized – along with the Military Medal and the DCM (the medal for Distinguished Conduct in the Field), and the rank of First Class Warrant Officer – we won't be in need for some time and I can roam the region as I will. Laure often comes with me and we set out across the cane fields on bicycles that I bought in Port Louis, headed for Henrietta, for Quinze Cantons. Or else we take the road to Mahébourg, crowded with carts, out to Nouvelle France, then follow the muddy paths to Cluny, or cross the tea fields to Bois Chéri. Mornings, when we've come out of the mist around Forest Side, the sun shines down on the dark foliage, the wind makes the cane fields ripple. Carefree, we ride along, zigzagging between the puddles, me wearing my uniform jacket and Laure in her white dress and sporting a large straw hat. In the fields the women in gunny cloth stop working to watch us go by. Around one o'clock we pass the women coming back from the fields on the road to Quinze Cantons. They walk along slowly, long skirts swinging, hoes balancing on their heads. They call out to us in Creole, make fun of Laure, who's pedalling with her dress bunched between her legs.

One afternoon Laure and I are riding out beyond Quinze Cantons and we cross the Rempart River. The path is so difficult we need to abandon our bicycles, which we hide hastily in the cane. Despite the burning sun, the path is like a torrent of mud and we have to take off our shoes. Just like back in the old days, we're walking barefoot in the warm mud and Laure has hitched up her white dress to look like the loose pants Indian women wear.

With my heart racing, I head for the peaks of Trois Mamelles towering above the cane fields like strange termite mounds. The sky, so clear a little while ago, has filled with large clouds. But we pay no heed. Driven by the same desire, we are walking as fast as we can through the sharp cane leaves, without stopping. The cane fields end at the Papaya River. After that there are the vast, grassy fields with, here and there, those piles of black stones that Laure calls martyrs' graves, in honour of the people who died working in the cane fields. Then, at the end of that steppe, between the peaks of Trois Mamelles, we come out before the stretch of coast land that runs from Wolmar all the way down to Black River. When we reach the pass, the sea wind hits us. Huge clouds are rolling over the sea. The wind is exhilarating after the heat in the cane fields. We remain standing still for a moment, taking in the view stretching before us as if no time has gone by, as if we'd left Boucan only yesterday. I glance at Laure. Her face is closed and hard, but her breathing is laboured, and when she turns towards me, I see tears shining in her eyes. It's the first time she's come back to see our childhood landscape. She sits in the grass and I settle down beside her. Not talking, we gaze out at the hills, the shaded streams, the rise and fall of the land. In vain, I look for our house near the banks of the Boucan River, behind the Tourelle de Tamarin. But all signs of an edifice have disappeared and in place of the thickets there are large swathes of burned land. Laure speaks out first, as if to answer the questions I'm asking myself.

'Our house isn't there any more, Uncle Ludovic demolished everything long ago, while you were in Rodrigues, I think. He didn't even wait for the court to make a ruling.'

Anger strangles my voice, 'But why, how could he?'

'He said he wanted to use the land for cane, that he didn't need the house.'

'What a dirty trick! If I'd known that, if I'd been here . . .'

'What would you have done? We couldn't do anything. I hid everything from Mam, to keep from upsetting her even more. She wouldn't have been able to bear such ruthless determination to destroy our house.'

Blurry-eyed, I look at the magnificent stretch of land before me, the sea sparkling as the sun draws near, and the shadow of the Tourelle de Tamarin growing longer. From having scanned the banks of the Boucan so thoroughly I believe I've spotted something like a scar in the brush, in the place where the house and garden once were, and the dark patch of the ravine where we used to go and daydream, perched in the old tree. Laure goes on talking, to console me. Her voice is calm, her pain has eased now.

'You know it doesn't matter any more that the house is gone. That was all so long ago now, it was another life. What counts is that you've come back, and anyway Mam is quite old, we're all she's got. What's a house, after all? An old karya-eaten shack full of holes that let in the rain? There's no reason to regret that it doesn't exist any more.'

'No, I can't forget it, I'll never forget it!' Unrelentingly, I examine the still landscape under the skittering sky. I scrutinize every detail, every water hole, every stand of trees, from the Black River Gorges all the way to Tamarin. Fires are smoking on the shore, over by Grande Rivière Noire, by Gaulette. Maybe Denis is over there — like in the old days, in Old Cook's cabin — and from having searched for so long in the golden light illuminating the shore and the sea, it seems as if I'll soon be able to make out the shadows of the children we once were, running through the tall grasses barefoot with scratched faces, tattered clothing, in that limitless world, waiting in the dusk light for the flight of the two tropicbirds over the mystery of Mananava.

The elation of homecoming soon passes. First of all there is the post in the offices of W. W. West, the post I'd occupied long ago, which they feigned belief that I'd left in order to go to war. Once again the dusty smell, the moist heat that filters through the shutters along with the brouhaha of Rempart Street. The indifferent employees, the clients, the merchants, the accountants . . . For all of those people, nothing has changed. The world hasn't budged. Yet Laure told me that one day in 1913, while I was in Rodrigues, crowds of starving people, reduced to poverty by cyclones, had gathered in front of the train station, a throng of Indians, of blacks from the plantations, women in gunny cloth with their children in their arms, they'd all come together there — not shouting, not making any noise — in front of the station, and they waited for the arrival of the train from the highlands, the one that brings the whites, the owners of the banks, the shops and the plantations from Vacoas, from Curepipe. They waited for them a long time, patiently at first, then gradually — as time went by — with growing resentment, growing despair. What would have happened had the whites come that day? Having been warned of the danger, they hadn't taken the train for Port Louis. They'd stayed home and waited for the police to take care of the problem. So the crowd was dispersed. There were perhaps a few Chinese shops looted, stones thrown at the windows of Crédit Foncier or even those of W. W. West. And then everything blew over.

My cousin Ferdinand, Uncle Ludovic's son, lords over the office. He pretends he doesn't know me, treats me like his servant. I feel anger mounting within me and the only reason I resist the temptation to lay into him is because of Laure, who would so like me to stay. As in the past, I spend every free second walking around the wharves among the sailors and dockers, by the fish market. What I would like more than anything else is to see the *Zeta*, Captain Bradmer and the Comorian helmsman again. I wait for a long time in the shade of the trees of the Intendance, hoping to see the schooner arrive with its armchair screwed down to the deck. It's already inside me, I know I'll go away again.

Every evening in my room in Forest Side I open the old trunk, rusted from its days in English Bay, and look at the treasure papers, the maps, the sketches and the notes I accumulated and sent back from Rodrigues before leaving for Europe. When I look at them I see Ouma, her body diving suddenly into the sea, swimming free, holding her long harpoon with its ebony tip.

Every day the desire to return to Rodrigues grows stronger, the longing to get back to the silence and peace of that valley, the sky, the clouds, the sea that belongs to no one. I want to flee the 'upper crust', spitefulness, hypocrisy. Ever since the *Cernéen* published an article about 'Our World War Heroes', in which my name is cited and I am credited with purely imaginary acts of bravery, Laure and I are suddenly on all the invitation lists for parties in Port Louis, in Curepipe, in Floréal. Laure accompanies me, wearing the same worn white dress, we converse and dance. We go to the Champ de Mars or have tea at the Flore. I think about Ouma all the time, about the cries of the birds that fly over the bay every morning. The people from here are the ones who seem imaginary, unreal to me. I'm fed up with these false honours. One day, without telling Laure, I leave my grey clerk's suit at Forest Side and dress in my old khaki jacket and trousers that I brought back from the war, stained and torn from life in the trenches. I also put on my officer's insignia and decorations – the MM and the DCM – and after the offices of W. W. West have closed in the afternoon, still in the same accoutrement, I go sit in the tearoom at the Flore, after having had a few glasses of arak. From that day on, as if by magic, I stopped receiving invitations from the chic set.

Yet the boredom I feel and the yearning to flee are so intense that Laure can't be blind to them. One evening she's waiting for me when the train arrives at Curepipe, as in the old days. The thin drizzle in Forest Side has dampened her white dress and her hair and she's standing under a large leaf for shelter. I tell her she looks like Virginie and that makes her smile. We walk along the muddy road together among the Indians, who are returning home before nightfall.

'You're going away again, aren't you?' Laure asks suddenly.

I cast about for an answer that will reassure her, but she repeats, 'You're going away soon, aren't you? Tell me the truth.'

Without waiting for my answer or because she already knows it, she gets angry.

'Why don't you ever tell me anything? Why must I learn everything from others?'

She hesitates before saying this, but then, 'That woman you live with over there like a savage! And that stupid treasure you're bent on finding!'

How does she know about that? Who told her about Ouma?

'We'll never be able to be like we were before, there'll never again be a place for us here!'

Laure's words hurt me, because I know they're true.

'But that's why I have to go away. That's why I have to succeed.'

How can I explain it to her? She's already gained control of herself again. She wipes away the tears running down her cheeks with the back of her hand, blows her nose in a childish manner. The Forest Side house is in front of us, dark, atop its hills like a boat run aground in the aftermath of a flood.

This evening, after dinner with Mam, Laure is more cheerful. On the veranda we talk about the journey, the treasure.

In a sprightly tone Laure says, 'When you've found the treasure, we'll join you over there. We'll have a farm, we'll work the land ourselves like the Transvaal pioneers.'

Then, gradually, we begin dreaming out loud, like in the old days up in the attic in Boucan. We talk about that farm, the animals we'll have, for everything will begin all over again, far from the bankers and lawyers. Among my father's books I found François Leguat's journal and I read the passages that deal with the flora, the climate and the beauty of Rodrigues.

Drawn by the sound of our voices, Mam emerges from her room. She comes all the way outside and her face in the light of the storm lantern on the veranda seems as young, as lovely, as it was back in the days of Boucan, when she gave us grammar lessons or read us passages of Bible History. She listens to our preposterous ravings, our projects, then kisses us, hugs us tight. 'All of that is nothing but dreams.'

On this night the old, dilapidated Forest Side house is truly a ship sailing across the sea, rocking and creaking as it goes in the soft pattering of the rain, on its way to the new island.

Being back on the *Zeta* is like being alive again, being free again, after all those years in exile. I'm back in my old place, at the stern, next to Captain Bradmer, who's sitting in his armchair which is screwed to the deck. We've been running downwind, heading north-east along the 20th parallel for two days. When the sun is high, Bradmer rises from his armchair and, just as in the old days, turns towards me, 'Would you like to try your hand at it, sir?'

As if we'd been sailing together all this time.

Standing barefoot on the deck, hands clutching the wheel, I am happy. There's no one on deck except for two Comorians, wearing their white headdresses. I love hearing the wind in the stays again, seeing the prow lift up against the waves. It's as if the *Zeta* were sailing all the way out to the horizon, out to where the sky is born.

I believe it was only yesterday that I was heading for Rodrigues the first time and, standing on the deck, I felt the ship moving like an animal, the heavy waves passing under the stem, the taste of salt on my lips, the silence, the sea. Yes, I don't believe I've ever left this place at the wheel of the *Zeta*, sailing on a journey whose end is constantly receding, all the rest was only a dream. The dream of the

Mysterious Corsair's gold in the ravine in English Bay, the dream of Ouma's love, her body the colour of lava, the water in the lagoons, the seabirds. The dream of the war, the freezing nights in Flanders, the rain of the Ancre, of the Somme, the clouds of gas and the flashes of bombs.

When the sun goes back down behind us and we can see the shadow of the sails on the sea, Captain Bradmer takes the wheel again. Standing up, his red face creased from the reflections on the waves, he hasn't changed. Without my asking, he tells me of the helmsman's death.

'It was in 1916 or maybe the beginning of '17 ... We'd almost reached Agalega, he fell ill. Fever, diarrhoea, he was delirious. The doctor came, he ordered that he be put into quarantine, because it was typhus ... They were afraid of contagion. He was already unable to eat or drink. He died the next day, the doctor didn't even come back ... And so I grew angry, sir. Since they didn't want to have anything to do with us, I had all the merchandise thrown into the sea off Agalega and we sailed south, heading for Saint Brandon ... That was where he'd said he wanted to die ... So we put a weight on his feet and threw him into the sea, in front of the reefs where the sea is a hundred fathoms deep, where it is so very blue ... When he sank, we said some prayers and I said, "Helmsman, my friend, now you are home forevermore. May peace be with you." And the others said, "Amen" ...We stayed anchored off the atoll for two days, the weather was so fine, not a cloud, and the sea so calm ... We stayed and watched the birds and the tortoises swimming close to the boat ... We caught a few tortoises, for smoking, and then we left.'

His voice is hesitant, drowned out by the wind. The old man is gazing straight ahead, beyond the wind-filled sails. In the light of the dying day his face is suddenly that of a weary man, apathetic about the future. Now I understand the illusion I've been under: history has run its course, here as it has elsewhere, and the world is not the same any more. There have been wars, crimes, violations, and because of it life has come undone.

'Now it's funny I haven't found another helmsman. That man, he knew everything about the sea, out as far as Oman . . . It's like the boat doesn't really know where it's going any more . . . Funny, isn't it? He was the master, had the boat in the palm of his hand . . .'

Then, looking out on the sea that is so beautiful, the wake tracing a route on the impenetrable water, I feel anxious again. I'm afraid of arriving in Rodrigues, afraid of what I will find there. Where is Ouma? The two letters I sent her, the first from London, before leaving for Flanders, the second from the military hospital in Sussex, remain unanswered. Did they even arrive? Can you write to a Manaf?

Nights, I don't go down in the hold to sleep. In the shelter of the bales secured to the deck, I sleep rolled up in my blanket, head resting on my duffel bag, listening to the rhythm of the sea and the wind in the sails. Then I wake up, go and urinate over the rail, then walk back and sit down to contemplate the star-filled sky. Time is so slow out at sea! Every hour that passes cleanses me of the things I need to forget, brings me closer to the eternal figure of the helmsman. Isn't he the one I must find at the end of my travels?

Today – the wind having changed directions – we are sailing close-hauled, the masts leaning at sixty degrees, while the stem rams at the rough sea, sending up clouds of spray. The new helmsman is black with an imperturbable face. Beside him, despite the lean of the deck, Captain Bradmer is sitting in his old armchair screwed down to the deck, gazing at the sea, smoking. All of my attempts at starting a conversation have come up against two words which he grumbles without looking at me: 'Yes, sir.' 'No, sir.' The wind is gusting against us and most of the men have sought refuge in the hold, save the Rodriguan merchants, who don't want to leave their merchandise, which is out on the deck. The crew has hurriedly spread a waxed tarpaulin over the bales and closed the front hatches. I've slipped my duffel bag under the tarp and, in spite of the sunshine, wrapped myself in my blanket.

The *Zeta* is struggling hard to work her way up the waves and I can feel the creaking of the hull, the groaning of the masts deep in my body. Powerful, spuming waves come rushing up to knock against the *Zeta*, which is heeling over on its flank. At three o'clock the wind is so strong I think it's a cyclone, but there aren't many clouds, only pale cirrus streaking the sky with immense trails. It's not a hurricane sky.

The *Zeta* is having difficulty staying on course. Bradmer is at the wheel, bracing himself on his short legs, grimacing against the sea spray. Despite reduced sail area, the weight of the wind is making the ship moan. How long can it go on like this?

Then, suddenly, the gusts grow gentler, the masts of the *Zeta* right again. It is near five o'clock in the evening and in the glowing warm light above the vehement horizon the looming shapes of the Rodriques mountains appear.

Immediately everyone is on deck. The Rodriguans sing and shout, even the taciturn Comorians are talking. I'm at the stern with the others, contemplating the blue line, as illusory as a mirage, and it is making my heart pound.

This is exactly the way I dreamed of returning for so many years, while I was in the hell of war, in the trenches amid the mud and garbage. I'm living my dream now as – in a shower of sparkling sea foam – the *Zeta* lifts up like a gondola over the sphere of dark waters, towards the transparent mountains of the island.

That evening, in the company of frigates and sterns, we sail past Gombrani, the point of Plateau, and the sea becomes glassy. The beacons are already shining off in the distance. Night has fallen on the northern slopes of the mountains. I'm not afraid any longer. Now I'm in a hurry to disembark. The ship is gliding along at full sail and I'm watching the sea wall drawing nearer. I'm leaning over the rail with the Rodriguans, holding my bag, ready to jump ashore. Just as everyone is disembarking and the children are already coming aboard, I turn to catch a glimpse of Captain Bradmer. But he's given his orders and I see only his face dimly lit by the beacons, his profile marked with fatigue and solitude. Without turning around, the captain goes down into the hold to smoke and sleep, and maybe think about the helmsman, who never left the ship. I walk towards the lights of Port Mathurin with that disturbing vision in my mind, and I don't know yet that it will be the last one I will have of Bradmer and his ship.

———————

At dawn I reach my former domain, the Commander's Watchtower, the spot where, long ago, I glimpsed English Bay for the first time. Here, nothing seems to have changed. The large valley is still dark and lonely, facing out to sea. As I am climbing down the slope, between the blades of screw pines, causing the earth to slide out from under my feet, I try to recognize all of the things I used to live around, that were once familiar: the dark patch of the ravine on the right bank with the tall tamarind tree, the blocks of basalt where the signs are engraved, the narrow stream of the Roseaux River snaking through the bushes until it reaches the swamp, and, off in the distance, the peaks of the mountains that served as landmarks. There are trees I'm not familiar with, umbrella trees, coconut trees, hyophorbes.

When I get to the middle of the valley I look in vain for the old tamarind tree under which I'd once pitched camp and that had sheltered Ouma and me on mild nights. In the place where my tree grew I see a mound of earth upon which thorn bushes are growing. I realize the tree is there, lying under the earth, in the place where it was felled by a hurricane, and from its roots and trunk this mound — like a tomb — has sprung. In spite of the sun that is burning my back and neck, I sit there on that mound amid the underbrush, trying to find traces of my old life. There, in the place where my tree once stood, I decide to build my shack.

I don't know anyone in Rodrigues any more. Most of the people who left with me, answering Lord Kitchener's call, didn't come back. During the war years there had been a famine. Due to the blockade, the boats no longer brought any supplies, no rice or oil or canned goods. Diseases decimated the population, especially typhus, which killed the people in the mountains, for want of medicine. There are rats everywhere now. They run through the streets of Port Mathurin in broad daylight. What has become of Ouma, what has become of her brother, up in those arid, destitute mountains? What has become of the Manafs?

Fritz Castel is the only one who stayed behind, in the isolated farm near the telegraph office. Now he's a young man of seventeen or eighteen with an intelligent face, a deep voice in which I have a hard time recognizing the child who helped me set the markers. The other men, Raboud, Prosper, Adrien Mercure, are gone, like Casimir, everyone who answered the call. 'Plumb dead,' Fritz Castel repeats when I say their names.

With Fritz Castel's help I've built a hut of branches and palms in front of the grave of the old tamarind tree. How long will I stay? I now know the days are numbered. Money isn't lacking (the army bonus is still almost intact), but time is the thing I'll run short of. It's the days and the nights that have been taken out of me, weakened me. I know that immediately, as soon as I'm back in the Bay, in this silence, surrounded by the power of the tall basalt walls, hearing the unbroken sound of the sea. Is there really anything I might still hope for from this place, after everything that has destroyed the world? Why have I come back?

Every day I sit still, as do those blocks of basalt strewn about the floor of the valley like the remains of a lost city. I don't want to move. I need this silence, this stupor. Mornings, at dawn, I go down to the beach among the reeds. I sit in the place where Ouma used to cover me with sand to let me dry in the wind. I listen to the rumbling of the sea on the semicircle of the coral reef, I wait for the moment when it comes up through the bottleneck of the pass, blowing its clouds of spume into the air. Then I listen to it go out again, slipping over the smooth bottom, uncovering the secrets of the pools. Every evening, every morning, the flight of the seabirds traversing the bay, marking the boundaries of day. I think of how lovely the nights that crept so simply, so fearlessly into the valley used to be. The nights when I waited for Ouma, the nights when I didn't wait for anyone, the nights when I watched for the stars, each appearing in its place in the cosmos, tracing their eternal figures. Now the coming of night disturbs me, makes me anxious. I feel the bite of cold, I listen to the sounds of the stones. Most nights I am curled up in the back of the hut, eyes wide, shivering, unable to sleep. Sometimes the anxiety is so intense I have to go back to the city to sleep in the narrow room of the Chinese hotel after having barricaded the door with the table and chair.

What's happened to me? Days in English Bay are long. Young Fritz Castel comes to sit on the tumulus of the tree in front of my hut. We smoke and talk, or rather I talk — about the war, hand-to-hand combat in the trenches, the flashing of the bombs. He listens to me, saying, 'Yes, sir,' 'No, sir,' quietly. Trying not to disappoint him, I send him out to dig holes for markers. But the old maps I drew don't make sense to me any more. The lines grow blurry before my eyes, the angles grow wider, the landmarks melt into one another.

When Fritz Castel has gone, I sit down under the tall tamarind tree at the entrance to the ravine and smoke, gazing down at the valley where the light changes so quickly. Sometimes I go into the ravine to feel, as in the old days, the burn of the sunlight on my face and chest. The ravine is exactly as I left it: the rocks obstructing the first cache, the pick marks, the large notch in the shape of a gutter on the basalt above. What have I come in search of out here? Now I feel surrounded by emptiness, abandonment. It's like a body left drained by a fever, in which everything that was once burning, throbbing, is now only shivering, weakness. Yet I love this light in the ravine, this solitude. I also love the sky, so blue, the shape of the mountains above the valley. Maybe I came back because of that.

Evenings, in the dimming twilight, sitting in the sand dunes, I dream of Ouma, of her metallic body. With the tip of a piece of flint I've drawn her body on a block of basalt in the place where the reeds begin. But when I want to write the date, I realize I don't know what day or what month it is. For a minute I think of running to the telegraph office to ask — as I once did — what's the date today? But it immediately strikes me that it wouldn't mean anything to me, that the date is no longer of any importance.

This morning I struck out for the mountains at the break of dawn. At first I believe I'm following a familiar path through the shrubs and the screw pines. But soon the reverberations of the sunlight burn my face, make my vision blurry. Beneath me stretches the hard, blue sea surrounding the island. If Ouma is up here somewhere, I'll find her. I need her, she's the one who holds the key to the secret of the prospector. That's what I think and my heart is pounding in my chest as I scale up the rockslides on Mont Limon. Is this the way I came the first time, when I was following the elusive figure of Sri, as if I were climbing up to reach the sky? The sun is above me at its zenith, it's swallowing up the shadows. No place to hide, no way to orient oneself.

Now I'm lost in the middle of the mountains, surrounded by stones and shrubs that all look alike. The charred peaks rise up on all sides against the bright sky. For the first time in years I cry out her name: 'Ou-ma-ah!' Standing up, facing the ochre mountain, I shout: 'Ou-ma-ah!' I can hear the sound of the wind, a burning, blinding wind. A lava-and-screw-pine wind that deadens the mind. 'Ou-ma-ah!' Again, facing north this time, towards the heaving sea. Climbing up to the summit of Mont Limon, I see other mountains surrounding me. The valley bottoms are already in shadows. The sky is growing dim in the east. 'Ou-ma-ah!' It seems as if I'm calling my own name in this deserted landscape, to awaken the echo of the life I lost during so many years of destruction. 'Ouma! Ou-ma-ah!' My voice cracks as I wander around the high plateau, searching in vain for the trace of a dwelling, a goat corral, a fire. But the mountain is empty. There are no human traces, not a broken branch, not a furrow on the dry earth. Only, here and there, the mark of a centipede between two stones.

Where am I? I must have wandered for hours without realizing it. When night falls it's too late to envisage going back down. I glance about, looking for a shelter, a crack in the rocks to protect me from

the chill of night, from the rain that is beginning to fall. On the mountainside, already engulfed in darkness, I find a sort of embankment
of scruffy grass, and that's where I settle in for the night. The wind
blows over my head, whistling. Exhausted, I fall asleep immediately.
I'm awakened by the cold. The night is pitch-black, before me, the
crescent moon is shining with an eerie gleam. The beauty of the
moon stops time.

At daybreak I am gradually able to make out the shapes around
me. Then with great relief, I slowly understand that, without realizing it, I've slept in the remnants of an old Manaf campsite. Digging
into the earth with my bare hands, I discover among the stone, the
traces I was looking for: bits of glass, rusted cans, shells. Now I can
clearly see the circles of the corrals, the bases of the huts. Is this all
that is left of the village where Ouma lived? And what became of
them? Did they all die of hunger and fever, abandoned by everyone?
If they went away, they didn't have time to cover their traces. They
must have fled the death that was swooping down upon them. I
stand still in the middle of these ruins feeling utterly discouraged.

When the sun is again burning high in the sky, I go back down
through the thorn bushes on the slope of Mont Limon. Soon the
screw pines, the dark foliage of the tamarind trees, appear. Out at
the end of the long Roseaux River Valley I can see the sea gleaming
like steel, the vast stretch of sea that holds us prisoners.

Summer, winter, then the rainy season again. I've been dreaming all of this time in English Bay, with nothing to go by, unable to understand what is going on inside me. Little by little I've begun my explorations again, measuring the distance between rocks, tracing new lines in the invisible network that covers the valley. I live and move around on that spider web.

Never have I felt so close to the secret. Now I no longer feel the febrile impatience I did in the beginning, seven or eight years ago. Back then I would discover a new sign or symbol every day. I'd go back and forth between the banks of the valley, leaping from rock to rock, digging probe holes everywhere. I was burning with impatience, with impetuosity. Back then I couldn't hear Ouma, couldn't see her. I was blinded by this stony landscape, I was waiting for a shift in the shadows that would reveal a new secret.

Today all of that is past. There is a faith within me that I wasn't aware of. Where did it come from? Faith in those blocks of basalt, in this ravined earth, faith in the thin trickle of the river, in the sand dunes. Perhaps it comes from the sea, the sea that encircles the island and makes its deep sound, the sound that breathes. All

298

of that is in my body, I've finally understood that in coming back to English Bay. It's a power that I believed was lost. So now I'm no longer hurried. Sometimes I sit still for hours in the dunes near the estuary, looking at the sea on the coral reefs, watching for the mangrove herons and the gulls to fly over. Or else in the shelter of my hut, when the sun is at its place in the noonday sky, after having had a few boiled crabs and a little coconut milk for lunch, I write in the school notebooks that I bought at the Chinaman's store in Port Mathurin. I write letters to Ouma or to Laure, letters they won't read, in which I talk about things of little importance, the sky, the shape of the clouds, the colour of the sea, ideas that pop into my head out here deep in English Bay. Nights also, when the sky is cold and the swollen moon prevents me from sleeping, sitting with my legs crossed in front of the door, I light the storm lamp and smoke, while I draw exploration maps in other notebooks to keep track of my progress towards the secret.

As I walk aimlessly along the beach of the Bay, I collect odds and ends that have been washed up on the sand, seashells, fossil sea urchins, shells of tek-tek shrimp. I tuck these things very carefully away in my empty biscuit tins. I'm collecting them for Laure, and I remember the things Denis used to bring back from his treks. Fritz Castel and I are sounding the sand in the back of the bay and I find strangely shaped stones, mica schist, flints. One morning, as we're taking turns digging with our picks, in the place where the Roseaux River makes a bend to the west, following the course of its original outlet to the sea, we uncover a large, soot-black basalt rock that has, at its top, a series of notches made with a chisel. Kneeling before the rock, I try to decipher the marks. My companion is observing me with a look of curiosity, of fear on his face: what in God's name have we brought out of the sand in the river?

'Look! Look close!'

The young black man hesitates. Then he kneels down beside me. On the black stone I show him each of the notches, which correspond to the mountains that are before us here on the floor of the valley.

'Look, this is Mont Limon. That's Mont Lubin, Patate. This is the towering Mont Malartic. Here, the two Charlots, and there, the Commander's Garret with the watchtower. Everything is marked on this stone. This is where he landed back then, he used this stone to tie up his pirogue, I'm certain of it. These are all the landmarks he used to draw up his secret plan.'

Fritz Castel straightens up. The same expression of curiosity mingled with fear is still on his face. What, whom is he afraid of? Of me or of the man who marked this stone so long ago?

Since that day Fritz Castel hasn't come back. Isn't it for the best? In this solitude I can better understand the reasons for my being in this sterile valley. Now I feel as if nothing is separating me from the stranger that came to leave his secret here before dying almost two hundred years ago.

How could I have lived without noticing what was around me, seeking only gold here, planning to flee once I'd found it? The soundings in the earth, the heavy work of moving boulders around, was all a profanation. Now, in my solitude and abandonment, I understand that, I see. This entire valley is like a grave. It is mysterious, wild, it's a place of exile. I recall Ouma's words, when she spoke to me for the first time, her ironic, hurt tone when she was dressing the wound to my head.

'Are you really all that fond of gold?'

At the time I hadn't understood, I was amused by what I took for naivety. I didn't think there was anything else to be had in this harsh valley, it never occurred to me that the strange, wild girl knew the secret. Isn't it too late now?

Alone amid these stones, with nothing to fall back on but these bundles of documents, these maps, these notebooks in which I've written down my life!

I think back on the time when I was gradually discovering the world around Boucan Embayment. I think of the days when I would run through the grass, chasing the birds that circle eternally over Mananava. I've started talking to myself again, just like I used to. I sing the lyrics to 'The Taniers River', the refrain we used to sing with Old Cook as he slowly rocked us.

Waï, waï, mo zenfant,   Yeh, yeh mi pickney,
Faut travaï, pou gagne so pain . . .   Haffi wuk fi get yuh bread . . .

That voice is inside me once again. I watch the water in the Roseaux River flowing out to the estuary as everything melts into the dusk. I forget about the burn of day, the fretfulness of the exploration at the foot of the cliff, the probe holes I've dug for nothing. When night settles with that barely perceptible rustling of the reeds, that gentle murmur of the sea. Wasn't this the way it used to be over by the Tourelle de Tamarin, when I'd watch the shallow valleys being drowned in shadow, when I'd try to spot the wisp of smoke over by Boucan?

At last I have found the freedom of night again, when lying on the bare earth, eyes open, I used to communicate with the centre of the sky. Alone in the valley, I watch the world of stars opening out and the still cloud of the Milky Way. One by one I recognize all the patterns of my childhood, Hydra, the Lion, the Larger Dog, proud

Orion wearing his jewels on his shoulders, the Southern Cross and its followers and, as always, the Argo, drifting in space, its stern to westward, lifted on the invisible wave of night. I remain lying in the black sand near the Roseaux River, not sleeping, not dreaming. I can feel the soft light of the stars on my face, I can feel the rotation of the earth. In the peaceful summer silence, with the distant lowing of the breakers, the patterns of the constellations are legends. I see all of the routes in the sky, the points that shine brighter, like beacons. I see the secret trails, the dark wells, the traps. I think of the Mysterious Corsair, who might have slept on this beach so very long ago. Maybe he'd known that old tamarind tree that now lies dead under the ground. Did he not avidly study this sky, which guided him out to the island? Stretched out on the soft sand after violent battles, murders, this is where he was able to savour peace and repose, sheltered from the sea winds by the coconut trees and the hyophorbes. I've leapt over time, vertiginously, in gazing at the stars in the sky. The Corsair is here, he is breathing within me, and I'm contemplating the sky through his eyes.

How can it be I didn't think of it earlier? The lay of English Bay mirrors the universe. The very simple layout of the valley never stopped expanding, filling with signs, with landmarks. Soon that crisscrossing hid the truth of this place from me. Heart racing, I jump to my feet, run over to my hut, where the night light is still burning. In the flickering light of the flame I look through my bag for the maps, the documents, the grids. I take the papers and the lamp outside and, sitting facing southwards, I compare my maps with the patterns in the night sky. In the centre of the map, the place where I put the boundary stone long ago, the intersection of the north-south line with the axis of the mooring rings corresponds with the Cross that is shining before me with its magical glow. To the east, above the ravine whose shape it describes exactly, Scorpius curls its body with red Antares at its heart, throbbing in the very place where I discovered the Corsair's two caches. Looking westwards, above the three points that form the 'M' of the Commander's Watchtower, I see the Three Marys of Orion's Belt that have just appeared over the mountains. Northwards, in the direction of the sea, there is the Chariot, light, elusive, showing the entrance to the pass, and, farther out, the curve of the Argo, which depicts the form of the bay and whose stern reaches up the estuary to the edges of the olden shore. I need to close my eyes against the reeling. Am I the victim of another hallucination? But these stars are living, eternal, and the earth beneath them mirrors their patterns. Thus, the secret I've been seeking has always been inscribed in the heavens, where no error is possible. Without realizing it, I've been seeing it ever since I used to look up at the stars, back in the Alley of Stars.

Where is the treasure? Is it in Scorpius, in Hydra? Is it in the southern triangle that joins the points 'H', 'D', 'B' that I located in the middle of the valley in the very beginning? Is it at the stem of the Argo or at the stern, marked by the lights Canopus and Miaplacidus, which gleam every day in the form of the two basalt rocks on either side of the bay? Is it in the gem Fomalhaut, the solitary star whose brightness is disconcerting – like a sharp stare – the star that rises to the zenith like a night sun?

I've been keeping watch all night, haven't slept a minute, tingling from head to foot with this heavenly revelation, examining each constellation, each sign. I remember the starry nights in Boucan, when I used to slip noiselessly out of the hot bedroom, seeking the coolness of the garden. Back then, like now, I thought I could feel the patterns of the stars on my skin and when it was daylight I would copy them in the dirt or in the sand of the ravine, using little pebbles.

Morning has come, paling the sky. Just like in the old days I've finally fallen asleep in the daylight, not far from the mound were the old tamarind tree lies.

Ever since I unlocked the secret of the Corsair's map I no longer feel hurried in the least. For the first time since I came back from the war it seems as if my quest has taken on a different meaning. Before, I didn't know what I was looking for, *who* I was looking for. I was stuck in an illusion. Now I've been relieved of a great weight, I can live freely, breathe. Now, just as I used to when I was with Ouma, I'm able to walk, swim, dive into the water of the lagoon to fish for sea urchins. I made a harpoon with a long reed and an ironwood point. As Ouma taught me, I dive naked into the cold, dawn sea just when the current of the rising tide is running through the opening in the reefs. Swimming flush with the coral, I look for fish, for breams, groupers, emperors. Sometimes I see the blue loom of a shark and I remain motionless, not letting any air out, turning to face it. Now I can swim just as far as Ouma, just as fast. I know how to grill fish on the beach, on racks of green reeds. Near my hut I've planted some corn, some fava beans, sweet potatoes, christophines. I put a young papaya tree that Fritz Castel gave me in a tin pot.

In Port Mathurin people are beginning to wonder. One day when I go in to withdraw some money, the director of Barclay's says, 'Well there? You don't come into town very often any more, do you? Does that mean you've lost all hope of finding your treasure?'

I look at him, smiling and answer firmly, 'On the contrary, sir. It means I've found it.'

I went out without waiting for any further questions.

*

In fact, I go down to the sea wall every day, hoping to see the *Zeta*. It's been months since it came into Rodrigues. The transporting of goods and passengers is now provided by the *Frigate*, a steamer from the all-powerful British India Steamship of which Uncle Ludovic is the representative in Port Louis. That's the boat that brings the mail, the letters Laure has been sending me for several weeks in which she talks of Mam's illness. Laure's last letter, dated 2 April 1921, is even more pressing. I keep the envelope in my hand, not daring to open it. I wait under the awning of the landing stage, surrounded by the agitation of sailors and dockers, looking at the clouds gathering over the sea. There's talk of a storm coming, the barometer is falling by the hour. Around one o'clock in the afternoon, when things have calmed down again, I finally open Laure's letter, in reading the first words, I'm grief-stricken:

> My dear Ali, when this letter reaches you, if it ever reaches you, I don't know whether Mam will still be alive . . .

My eyes grow blurry. I know that this is the end of everything now. Nothing can keep me here, since Mam is so ill. The *Frigate* will be here in a few days, I'll sail with it. I send a telegram to Laure to inform her of my return, but silence has crept into me, it accompanies me everywhere.

The storm starts blowing during the night and I'm awakened by a feeling of anxiety: at first it's a slow, persistent wind in the oppressively dark night. In the morning I see the torn shreds of clouds darting rapidly over the valley, the sun casting quick flashes between them. In the shelter of my hut I hear the roaring of the sea on the coral reefs, a terrifying, almost animal sound, and I realize a hurricane is sweeping down upon the island. I don't have a second to lose. I take my duffel bag and, leaving my other belongings in the hut, climb up the hill to Venus Point. The only place to seek refuge from the hurricane is in the telegraph buildings.

When I come up in front of the large grey hangars, I see the neighbouring inhabitants that have gathered there: men, women, children, even dogs and pigs that the people have brought with them. An Indian employee of the telegraph company announces that the barometer is already below 30. Around noon the howling wind reaches Venus Point. The buildings begin to shake, the electric lights go out. Torrential rains come pelting down on the sheet metal of the walls and roof like a waterfall. Someone has lit a storm lamp that lights up the faces grotesquely.

The hurricane lasts all day long. In the evening we fall asleep, exhausted, on the floor of the hangar, listening to the howling wind and the creaking metal framework of the buildings.

At dawn the silence awakens me. Outside the wind has died down, but we can hear it roaring out on the reefs. The people are gathered on the headland in front of the main telegraph building. When I draw near I see what they are looking at: on the coral reef in front of Venus Point is a shipwrecked vessel. At less than a mile from shore, we can clearly make out the broken masts, the gouged-out hull. Only half of the ship is left, the upright stern, and the furious waves are breaking on the wreck, tossing up clouds of foam. The name of the ship is on everyone's lips, but at the very moment I hear it I've already recognized it: it's the *Zeta*. On the stern I can see the old armchair screwed down to the deck where Captain Bradmer used to sit. But where is the crew? No one knows anything. The shipwreck took place during the night.

I run down to the shore, walk along the devastated coast strewn with branches and stones. I hope to find a pirogue, someone who can help me, but in vain. There's no one on the shore.

Maybe in Port Mathurin, the lifeboat? But I'm just too anxious, I can't wait. I take off my clothing, enter the water, slipping on the rocks, slapped by the waves. The sea is raging, washing over the coral reef, the water is troubled like that of a flooding river. I swim against the current that is so strong I make no headway. The roaring of the breaking waves is directly in front of me, I can see curtains of foam thrown up into the dark sky. The wreck is barely a hundred yards away, the sharp teeth of the reefs have cut it in two where the masts rose from the deck. The sea is covering the deck, swirling around the empty armchair. I can't get any closer without running the danger of being crushed against the reefs myself. I want to shout, call 'Bradmer . . . !' But my voice is drowned out by the thundering of the waves and even I can't hear it! For a long moment I swim against the sea, which is sweeping over the reef. The wreck is lifeless, it looks like it ran aground here centuries ago. Shivers are running through my body, cutting short my breath. I have to give up, turn back. Slowly I allow myself to be carried along on the waves with the debris from the storm. When I reach shore I am so weary and desperate I can't even feel that my knee has been injured from having knocked against a rock.

In the beginning of the afternoon the wind stops completely. The sun shines down on the ravaged land and sea. It's all over. Staggering, on the verge of fainting, I walk towards English Bay. Near the telegraph buildings, everyone is outside, laughing, talking loudly: having escaped unscathed with nothing but a good fright.

When I am just above English Bay I see the ruined landscape. The Roseaux River is a dark torrent of mud crashing loudly down into the valley. My hut has disappeared, the trees and screw pines have been uprooted and nothing is left of the vegetables I planted. On the floor of the valley there is nothing but gullied-out land and blocks of basalt that have sprung up from the earth. Everything I left in my cabin has vanished: my clothes, my cooking pots, but especially my theodolite and most of the documents concerning the treasure.

Day is rapidly waning in this apocalyptical setting. Once again I'm walking around in the back of English Bay in quest of some object, some trace that might have escaped the hurricane. I look everywhere, but everything has already completely changed, become unrecognizable. Where is the pile of stones that mirrored the Southern Triangle? And these basalt rocks near the slope, are they the ones that first led me to the mooring rings? The dying day is the colour of copper, the colour of molten metal. This will be the first time that the seabirds will not fly across the bay to go back to their roosts. Where have they gone? How many of them survived the hurricane? This will also be the first time the rats have come down into the valley bottom, driven from their nests by the mudslides. They are bounding about me in the dusk light letting out sharp little alarming cries.

In the middle of the valley, near the river that has broken its banks, I find the tall slab of basalt upon which, before leaving for the war, I engraved the east-west line and the two inverted triangles of the mooring rings that form the star of Solomon. The slab has resisted the wind and the rain, it's simply sunken a little deeper into the ground, and standing in the middle of this ravaged landscape it looks like a monument from the origins of the human race. Who will find it one day and understand what it signifies? The valley of English Bay has clapped its secret shut, closed the doors that had opened momentarily for me alone. On the cliff to the east, lit by the beams of the setting sun, the entrance to the ravine draws me over one last time. But when I get closer I see that, with the heavy water runoff, part of the cliff has collapsed, barring access to the corridor. The torrent of mud that poured out of the ravine devastated everything in its path, uprooting the old tamarind tree, whose soothing shade I so loved. In a year there will be nothing left of its trunk, only a mound of earth topped with a few thorn bushes.

I stay up there for a long time, until nightfall, listening to the sounds of the valley. The river rushing down, hauling earth and trees along with it, the water trickling from the schist cliffs and, far away, the constant thundering of the sea.

I spend the two days I have left gazing out over the valley. Every morning I leave the narrow room in the Chinese hotel early and go up to the Commander's Watchtower. But I don't go down into the valley any more. I just sit in amid the underbrush, near the ruins of the tower, and contemplate the long red-and-black valley, where all traces of me have already disappeared. Out at sea, hanging on the coral reef, the unearthly stern of the *Zeta* remains motionless amid the crashing waves. I think of Captain Bradmer, whose body hasn't been found. They say he was alone aboard his ship and did not try to save himself.

It's the last image I'm taking away with me from Rodrigues, as I stand on the deck of the new *Frigate* heading out to sea with all of its iron plating vibrating in time to its straining engines. The *Zeta* stands facing the tall, barren mountains shimmering in the morning sun, as if it were balancing for all time on the brink of the deep water. A few seabirds are circling over it, exactly as if it were the carcass of a whale washed up by the storm.

Mananava, 1922

—————

Since my return, everything at Forest Side has grown to be unfamiliar, silent. The old house — the shack, as Laure calls it — is like a ship taking on water everywhere, patched up as best as possible with bits of sheet metal and tarpaper. The humidity and the karyas will soon get the better of it. Mam doesn't speak, doesn't move, hardly even eats any more. I admire Laure's perseverance, she stays at Mam's side night and day. I haven't got the strength. So I walk out along the paths through the cane fields, over by Quinze Cantons, over where you can see the peaks of Trois Mamelles and what the sky looks like on the other side.

I have to work and, following Laure's advice, I've mustered up the courage to apply for a job at W. W. West again, which is now managed by my cousin Ferdinand. Uncle Ludovic has grown old, he's withdrawn from the business and lives in the house he had built near Yemen, where our lands once commenced. Ferdinand welcomes me with scornful derision, which would have made me angry in the past. Now it just doesn't faze me.

When he says, 'So you've come back to your old . . . '

I suggest, 'Haunts?'

And even when he speaks of 'war heroes the likes of which we see every day', I don't bat an eye. In the end he offers me a job as foreman on their Médine plantation and I have to accept. Now I've become a sirdar!

I live in a cabin over by Bambous and every morning I ride around the plantation on horseback to oversee the work. I spend the afternoons in the racket of the sugar mill, supervising the arrival of the cane, the bagasse, the quality of the syrups. It's exhausting work, but I prefer it to the suffocating offices of W. W. West. The manager of the sugar mill is an Englishman by the name of Pilling, sent from the Seychelles by the Agricultural Company. In the beginning Ferdinand had tried to pit him against me. But he's a fair man and our relationship is excellent. He talks about Chamarel, where he hopes to go. If he's sent over there he promises to try to have me come along.

Yemen is lonely. Mornings, the field workers and women wearing gunny cloth move through the immense fields like a ragged army. The whooshing sound of the cane knives makes a slow, regular rhythm. At the edge of the fields, over by Walhalla, men are breaking 'teeth' or heavy stones to make the pyramids. I ride across the plantation, heading southwards, listening to the sound of the cane knives and the yapping of the sirdars. I'm streaming with sweat. In Rodrigues the burn of the sun made my head reel, I saw sparks firing on the stones, on the screw pines. But here the heat just adds to the loneliness in the dark-green stretch of the cane fields.

I think about Mananava now, the only place left to me. It's been within me for so long, ever since the days when Denis and I would walk up to the entrance of the gorges. Suddenly, as I ride along the paths of the cane fields, I glance southwards and imagine caches at the source of rivers. I know that's where I must go in the end.

I saw Ouma today.

They've started cutting the virgin cane, high up in the plantations. The men and women have come from all parts of the coast, with anxious faces, because they know that only a third of them will be hired. The others will have to go back home with hungry bellies.

On the way to the sugar mill a woman in gunny cloth is standing to one side. She turns halfway towards me, looks at me. In spite of her face being half-hidden by the long white veil, I recognize her. But she's already disappeared in the crowd that is separating on the paths between the fields. I try to run over to her, but bump into field hands and women who've been turned away, and everything is covered with a cloud of dust. When I get to the fields all I can see is the thick, green wall undulating in the wind. The sun is burning down on the dry earth, burning down on my face. I start running along one of the paths, shouting, 'Ouma! Ouma . . . !'

Scattered women in gunny cloth raise their heads, stop cutting the grass between the cane. A sirdar calls out to me in a harsh voice. Looking somewhat disoriented, I question him. Are there Manafs here? He doesn't understand. People from Rodrigues? He shakes his head. There are some, but they're in the refugee camps down by the Morne, at Ruisseau des Créoles.

I look for Ouma every day on the road that brings the gunnies and in the evening in front of the accountant's office at pay time. The women have already caught on, they make fun of me, call out to me, jeer at me. So now I don't venture out on the paths in the cane fields any more. I wait for night and cross the fields. I pass children gleaning. They aren't afraid of me, they know I won't turn them in. How old would Sri be now?

I spend my days riding around the plantation in the dust, in the sun that makes my head spin. Is she really here? All the women in gunny cloth resemble her, frail figures stooped over their shadows, working with their sickles, their hoes. Ouma has only shown herself to me once, as she used to by the Roseaux River. I think about the first time we met, when she fled between the shrubs in the valley, when she climbed into her mountains as agile as a young goat. Did I dream all of that?

That's how I make the decision to give everything up, get it all out of my system. Ouma showed me what I need to do, she told me, in her own way, simply by appearing before me like a mirage, in the middle of all those people who come to work on land that will never belong to them: black people, Indians, half-breeds, every day hundreds of men and women here in Yemen, in Walhalla or Médine, in Phoenix, Mon Désert, in Solitude, in Forbach. Hundreds of men and women who pile rocks atop walls and pyramids, who rip out tree stumps, plough, plant young cane stalks, then, throughout the seasons, strip the leaves from the stalks, crop off the tops, clean the land, and when summer comes, move through the fields, patch by patch, and cut, from morning to night, stopping only to sharpen their cane knives, until their hands, their legs are bleeding, lacerated by the sharp leaves, until the sun makes them nauseous and dizzy.

Almost without realizing it I've gone all the way across the plantation to the southern end, where the smokestack of an abandoned sugar mill stands. The sea isn't far, but you can't see or hear it. You can, however, get glimpses of seabirds circling, freely, up in the blue sky. There are men working here, clearing new land. In the heat of the sun they're loading black rocks on to carts, they're digging at the earth, striking it with their hoes. When they see me they stop working, as if they are afraid of something. So then I walk over to the cart and start digging up stones too and throwing them on to the pile. We work without stopping, while the sun descends towards the horizon, burning our faces. When one cart is full of stones and stumps, another replaces it. The old walls stretch far into the distance, maybe as far as the seashore. I think of the slaves who built them, the people Laure calls the 'martyrs', who died in these fields, the ones who escaped into the mountains to the south, to the Morne . . . The sun is very near to the horizon. Today, just like back in Rodrigues, I feel as if its burn has purified me, has freed me.

A woman in gunny cloth walks up. She's an old Indian woman with a shrivelled face. She's brought sour milk for the workers to drink, dipping it from a pot with a wooden bowl. When she reaches me, she hesitates, then extends the bowl to me. The sour milk cools my throat, burning from the dust.

The last cartload of rocks rolls away. In the distance the sharp whistle of the boiler announces the end of the workday. The men take up their hoes and saunter off.

When I get to the sugar mill Mr Pilling is waiting for me in front of his office. He looks at my sunburned face, my dusty hair and clothing. When I tell him that I want to work in the fields from now on, harvesting, clearing, he interrupts me, snapping, 'You aren't capable of doing that, and at any rate it's impossible, no white man ever works in the fields.' He adds in a calmer voice, 'In my view, you are in need of rest and you have just turned in your resignation.'

The discussion is closed. I walk slowly down the dirt road, deserted at this hour. In the light of the setting sun the cane fields seem as vast as the sea and, scattering into the distance, the smokestacks of other sugar mills resemble ocean liners.

The rumour of a riot has once again brought me over to the arid lands around Yemen. They say the fields are burning in Médine, in Walhalla, and that men who are out of work are threatening the sugar mills. Laure tells me the news without raising her voice, so she won't worry Mam. I dress hastily. Despite the morning drizzle I go out wearing my military shirt, without a jacket or hat, barefooted in my shoes. When I'm up on the plateau, near Trois Mamelles, the sun shines down on the wide-open fields. I can see columns of smoke rising from the stands of cane around Yemen. I count four fires, maybe five. I start to climb down the cliff, cutting through the underbrush. I think of Ouma, who's undoubtedly down there. I remember the day when I saw the Indians throw the field manager into the bagasse furnace and the silence of the crowd when he disappeared into its flaming mouth.

I reach Yemen around midday. I'm soaked with sweat and covered with dust, my face scratched from the underbrush. The people are crowded around the sugar mill. What's going on? The sirdars have contradictory stories. Some men have fled in the direction of Tamarin after having set the hangars on fire. The mounted police are on their trail.

Where is Ouma? I move closer to the refinery buildings surrounded by the police, who refuse to let me in. In the courtyard, guarded by militiamen armed with rifles, men and women are squatting in the shadows, hands on their heads, waiting for their fate to be decided.

So I start running across the plantation again, heading for the sea. If Ouma is here, I'm sure she would seek refuge by the sea. Not far from me, in the middle of the cane field, heavy smoke is wafting up into the sky and I can hear the cries of the men fighting the fire. Somewhere, deep in the field, rifle shots ring out. But the cane stalks are so high I can't see over the leaves. I run through the cane, not knowing where I'm going, first one way, then another, listening to the crash of rifle shots. Suddenly I trip, stop, out of breath. I can hear my heart skipping in my chest, my legs are trembling. I've reached the boundary of the property. Everything is silent here.

I climb up a pyramid of rocks, I can see that the fires have already gone out. Only one column of light smoke is rising over by the sugar mill, indicating that the bagasse furnace is functioning again.

It's all over with now. When I get to the beach of black sand I stand still among the tree trunks and branches washed up by the storm. I do this so that Ouma will see me. The coast is deserted, wild, like English Bay. I walk along Tamarin Bay in the light of the setting sun. I'm sure that Ouma has seen me. She's following me without making a sound, without leaving a trace. I mustn't try to see her. It's her game. One day when I told her about Ouma, Laure said, in her mocking voice, 'Yangue-catéra! She put a spell on you!' Now I believe she's right.

I haven't been here in so long. It's as if I were walking in my own footprints, the ones I left when I used to watch the sun slip into the sea with Denis.

At nightfall I'm on the other side of the Tamarin River. I can see the twinkling lights of the fishing village across the river. Bats are flying around in the pale sky. It's a warm, calm evening. For the first time in a very long time I'm preparing to sleep outdoors. In the black sand of the dunes, at the foot of some tamarind trees, I make my pallet and lie down, hands behind my head. I lie there with my eyes open, watching the sky growing more beautiful. I listen to the gentle sound of the Tamarin River mingling with the sea.

Then the moon appears. It moves through the middle of the sky, the sea is sparkling below. Then I see Ouma, sitting not far from me in the glowing sand. She's sitting like she always does, arms around her legs, face in profile. My heart is beating very hard, I'm trembling, from the cold perhaps? I'm afraid that it's only an illusion, that she'll disappear. The breeze is rising, awakening the sounds of the sea. So then Ouma comes over to me, takes my hand. Just like in the old days in English Bay, she takes off her dress, walks down to the sea without waiting for me. Together we dive into the cool water, swim against the waves. The long rollers coming from the other side of the world pass over us. We swim for a long time in the dark sea, under the moon. Then we come back to shore. Ouma pulls me over to the river, where we wash the salt from our bodies and hair, stretched out on the pebbles of the riverbed. The air coming from the open sea makes us shiver and we talk in whispers, so we won't wake up the dogs in the vicinity. As in the old days we sprinkle black sand on each other and wait until the wind makes it slip off our stomachs, our shoulders, in little rivulets. I have so many things to say, I don't know where to begin. Ouma talks to me too, she tells me about death coming to Rodrigues with typhus, her mother's death on the boat that was taking the refugees to Port Louis. She tells me about the camp in Ruisseau des Créoles, the salt fields in Black River, where she worked with Sri. How had she learned I was in Yemen, by what miracle? 'It's not a miracle,' says Ouma. Suddenly her voice is almost angry. 'I waited for you every minute of every day, in Forest Side or I went to Port Louis, to Rempart Street. When you came back from the war I'd waited so long I could wait a little longer and I followed you everywhere, all the way out to Yemen. I even worked in the fields, until you saw me.' I feel a sort of dizziness coming over me and my throat tightens. How could it have taken me so long to understand?

Now we aren't talking any longer. We're lying close to one another, holding each other tightly, so we won't feel the chill of night. We're listening to the sea and the wind in the needles of the she-oaks, for nothing else exists in the world.

The sun rises over Trois Mamelles. As in the past, back in the days when Denis and I would go roaming, I see the blue-black volcanoes against the bright sky. I remember I always loved the southernmost peak, the one that looks like a fang, the one that's the axis around which the sun and the moon turn.

I wait, sitting in the sun, facing Le Barachois, watching the river flow peacefully along. The seabirds are skimming slowly along the surface of the water — mangrove herons, cormorants, quibbling seagulls — flying out to meet the fishing pirogues. Then I go up the Boucan River until I reach Panon, walking very slowly, carefully, as if over a minefield. In the distance, through the leaves, I can see the Yemen chimney that is already smoking and I can smell the mellow odour of cane juice. A little higher up, on the other side of the river, I also see Uncle Ludovic's very white, new house.

I feel something aching deep down inside, because I know where I am. This is where our garden began and, a little farther up — at the end of the pathway — I would have seen our house, its blue roof shining in the sunlight. I walk through the tall weeds, getting scratched by the thorn bushes. There's nothing left here.

Everything's been destroyed, burned, pillaged, for so many years. Perhaps this is where our veranda began? I think I recognize a tree, then another. But at the same time I notice ten more that look just like it, tamarind, mango trees, she-oaks. I trip over unfamiliar rocks, stumble into holes. Is this really where we lived? Wasn't it in some other world?

I keep going, feverishly, feeling the blood pounding in my temples. I want to find something, a bit of our land. When I talked about it to Mam, her eyes lit up, I'm sure of it. I was holding her hand very tightly in mine, trying to give her my life, my strength. I talked about it all as if our house still existed. I talked to her as if nothing ever had to end, as if the years that were lost would be reborn in our sweltering garden in the month of December, when Laure and I would listen to her lilting voice reading Bible History.

I want to hear her voice now, here in this place in the wild underbrush, among these piles of black rocks that were the foundations of our house. Walking up in the direction of the hills I suddenly catch sight of the ravine where we spent so many hours perched on the main branch of the tree, watching the water in the nameless stream flow by. It's difficult to recognize. While everywhere else the terrain has been overrun with weeds and underbrush, here everything is barren, arid, like after a wildfire. My heart is beating very hard, because this is where our — Laure's and my territory, our secret place really was. But now it's nothing but a ravine, a dark, ugly, lifeless crevice. Where is the tree, our tree? I think I recognize it, an old blackened trunk with broken branches, sparse leaves. It is so ugly, so small I can't imagine how we could have climbed it back then. When I lean out over the ravine, I see that wondrous branch upon which we would lie and it is like an emaciated arm extended over the void. Below, at the bottom of the ravine, water is flowing among the debris of branches, bits of sheet metal, old boards. The ravine was used as a dump when our house was demolished.

I didn't tell Mam any of that. It was no longer important . I talked to her about everything that used to be, that was even more true, more real, than this ravaged land. I talked to her about what she loved most, the garden filled with hibiscuses, with poinsettias, arums, and her white orchids. I talked to her about the large oval pond in front of the veranda where we could hear the toads singing. I also talked to her about the things I loved, that I would never forget, her voice when she used to read us a poem or when she recited the evening prayers. The path we would all walk solemnly down together to look at the stars, listening to our father's explanations.

I stay until nightfall, wandering through the underbrush, searching for traces, clues, searching for smells, for memories. But it's a dry, broken land, the irrigation ditches have been stopped up for years now. The remaining trees have been burned by the sun. There are no more mango or medlar or jackfruit trees. The tamarind trees, tall and scrawny as in Rodrigues, are still there and the banyans that never die. I'm trying to find the chalta tree, the tree of good and evil. I have the feeling that, if I succeed in finding it, something from the old days will have been saved. I recall it being at the end of the garden, on the edge of the fallow lands, where the path leading to the mountains and the Black River Gorges began. I walk through the underbrush, hastily climb up to the high end of the property, where you can see Terre Rouge and the Brise-Fer mountains. Then, suddenly, I see it right in front of me, in the midst of the under- brush, even taller than before, with its dark foliage making a lake of shade. I walk up to it and recognize its smell, a subtle, disquieting fragrance that used to make our heads swim when we would climb in its branches. It hasn't surrendered, hasn't been destroyed. To it,

323

the whole time I was away, far from the shelter of its leaves, far from its branches, was but a moment. The storm waters have passed, the droughts, the wildfires, and even the men who demolished our house, who trampled on the flowers in the garden and let the water in the pond and the irrigation ditches dry up. But it has remained the tree of good and evil that knows all, sees all. I look for the marks Laure and I made on it with a knife, to write our names and how tall we were. I look for the wound of the branch the cyclone ripped off. Its shade is deep and cool, its odour inebriates me. Time has stopped its course. The air is vibrating with insects, with birds, the earth under it is damp and alive.

Here the world knows no hunger or misfortune. War doesn't exist. The chalta tree holds the world at bay by the strength of its branches. Our house was destroyed, our father is dead, but nothing is hopeless because I've found the chalta tree. I'll be able to sleep under it. Outside, night comes, obliterates the mountains. Everything I've ever done, ever searched for, was simply to bring me here, to the entrance to Mananava.

———————

How long has it been since Mam died? Was it yesterday or the day before? I'm not sure any more. During the days and nights that we stayed by her side, taking turns, me during the day, Laure at night, so that she would constantly have a hand to hold in her thin fingers. Every day I told her the same story, the story of Boucan, where everything is always young and beautiful, where the sky-coloured roof shines. It's a make-believe land, it only exists for us three. And I think that, from having talked about it so much, a bit of that immortality is within us, unites us against death, which is so near.

As for Laure, she doesn't talk. On the contrary, she's silent, obstinate, but that's her way of struggling against oblivion. I brought back a small branch of the chalta tree for her and when I gave it to her I saw she hadn't forgotten. Her eyes shone with pleasure when she took the branch, which she laid on the nightstand or rather tossed there, as if inadvertently, because that's the way she acts with objects she loves.

There was that terrible morning when Laure came to wake me up, standing in front of the cot with canvas webbing where I sleep in the empty dining room. I remember how she looked, hair tangled, that hard, angry gleam in her eye.

'Mam's dead.'

That's all she said, and I followed her, still sluggish from sleep, into the dark room where the night light shone. I looked at Mam, her thin, regular face, her lovely hair spread out upon the very white pillow. Laure went to lie down on the cot in turn and fell asleep immediately, arms crossed over her face. And I remained alone in the dark room with Mam, dazed, bewildered, sitting on a creaking chair in front of the quivering night light, ready to start telling my story again any minute, talking in hushed tones about the large garden where we used to walk together in the evenings to explore the heavens, talking about the paths strewn with tamarind hulls and hibiscus petals, about listening to the shrill song of mosquitoes that danced around our hair and, when we turned around, the joy of seeing the large window of the office where my father sat smoking and looking at his nautical charts lit up in the blue night.

And this morning, standing in the rain in the cemetery near Bigara, I'm listening to the earth fall on to the coffin, and looking at Laure's pale face, her hair covered tightly with Mam's black shawl, drops of water running down her cheeks like tears.

*

How long has Mam been gone? I can't believe it. It's all come to an end, there will never again be the sound of her voice talking in the dusk light on the veranda, never again the smell of her perfume, the warmth of her gaze. When my father died it seems as if I began sliding downhill backwards, towards a forgetfulness I can't accept, which is pulling me away once and for all from what used to be my strength — youth. The treasures are inaccessible, impossible. They are the 'fool's gold' that the black prospectors showed me when I arrived in Port Mathurin.

Laure and I are now alone in this old empty, cold shack with closed shutters. In Mam's room the wick of the night light has drowned and I light another one on the night stand, among the pointless phials, beside the bed with livid sheets.

'Nothing would have happened if I'd stayed . . . It's all my fault, I shouldn't have left her.'

'But you had to go, didn't you?' Laure is asking herself the question. I look at her worriedly.

'What are you going to do now?'

'I don't know, stay here, I suppose.'

'Come with me!'

'Where?'

'To Mananava. We can live on the *pas géométriques*.'

She looks at me ironically, 'All three of us, along with *Yangue-catéra*?' That's what she calls Ouma.

But her eyes grow cold again. Her expression is one of weariness, of remoteness.

'You know very well that's impossible.'

'But why?'

She doesn't respond. She looks straight through me. I suddenly realize that, during my years of exile, I lost her. She followed a different

326

path, became a different person, our lives don't fit together any more. Her life is with the nuns of the Visitation, where penniless, homeless women err. Her place is by the side of the hydropsical, cancer-ridden Indian women, who beg for a few rupees, a smile, words of consolation. By the side of feverish children with bloated bellies, for whom she cooks pots of rice, for whom she niggles a little money from her fellow 'bourzois'.

For an instant there's a note of solicitude in her voice, as in the old days when I would walk barefoot across the room to slip out into the night.

'And you, what are you going to do?'

I boast, 'Well, I'm going to pan in the river like they do in the Klondike. I'm sure there's gold in Mananava.'

Yes, for an instant, her eyes shine again with amusement, we're close again, we're 'sweethearts', as people used to say when they saw us together.

Later, I look at her while she's packing her little suitcase to go and live with the sisters of Loreto. Her face is calm, indifferent once again. Only her eyes are bright with a sort of anger. She wraps her lovely black hair in Mam's shawl and walks away without looking back, carrying her little cardboard suitcase and holding her large umbrella up high and straight, and from now on nothing can hold her or turn her from her course.

All day long I remain at the estuary of the rivers, facing the Barachois, watching the tide going out, uncovering the black sand of the beaches. When it is low tide some tall, black adolescents come to fish for octopuses, and they look like wading birds in the copper-coloured water. The bravest ones come over to see me. One of them, having taken me for a British soldier because of my army shirt, addresses me in English. So as not to disappoint him, I answer in English as well and we talk for a moment, he standing, leaning on a long harpoon, me sitting in the sand, smoking a cigarette in the shade of some velvet soldierbushes.

Then he goes back to the other young boys and I hear their voices and their laughter dying out on the other side of the Tamarin River. Now there are only the fishermen standing in their pirogues, sliding slowly over the water that is reflecting their image.

I wait for the first thrust of the tide to send a wave up on to the sand. The wind is coming in, just like back in the old days, the sound of the sea makes me shudder. Then, with my duffel bag over my shoulder, I walk back up the river towards Boucan. Before reaching Yemen, I veer off into the underbrush where our lane used to start, that wide path of red earth that ran between the trees straight up to our very white house with its azure-coloured roof. I remember us walking down that lane such a long time ago, when the bailiffs and Uncle Ludovic's lawmen drove us away. Now the lane has disappeared, swallowed up by the weeds, and, along with it, the world it once led to.

How beautiful and ashen the light is here, just like the light that used to envelop me out on the veranda as I watched evening creep over the garden! The light is the only thing I recognize. I walk through the underbrush and don't even try to see the chalta tree or the ravine again. Like the seabirds, I'm feeling hurried, fretful at the coming of night. Now I'm walking quickly southwards, guided by Mont Terre Rouge. Suddenly, in front of me, a pool flashes with light from the sky: it's the Bassin aux Aigrettes, the place where my father had set up his generator. Overrun with weeds and reeds, the pond is now abandoned. Nothing is left of my father's construction work. The dams, the metal frames supporting the dynamo, were carted off long ago, and the dynamo was sold to pay debts. The water, the mud, have erased my father's dream. Birds fly up, squawking, as I walk around the pond to take the path to the gorges.

Once past Brise-Fer Mountain I can see the Black River Valley beneath me and, off in the distance, between the trees, the sea glittering in the sunlight. Here I am, facing Mananava, drenched with sweat, breathless, apprehensive. As I start into the gorge I feel a pang of anxiety. Is this where I am to live now, a castaway? In the blazing light of the setting sun, the shadows cast by Machabé and Pied de la Marmite mountains make the gorges seem even darker. Up above Mananava the red cliffs form an insurmountable barrier. To the south, in the direction of the sea, I can see the smoke from the sugar mills and the villages, Case Noyale, Black River. Mananava is the end of the world, where one can see without being seen.

I'm in the very heart of the valley now, in the shade of the tall trees, night has already begun. The wind is blowing in from the sea and I can hear the sound of the leaves, those invisible movements, those sudden dashes, those dances. I've never been this far into the heart of Mananava. As I walk through the shadows under the still very bright sky, the forest opens out before me, boundless. Everywhere there are ebony trees with smooth trunks, turpentine and colophony trees, wild fig trees, sycamores. My feet sink into the carpet of leaves, I breathe in the stale odour of the earth, the humidity of the sky. I walk up the bed of a torrent. As I go, I gather dasheen, red guavas, coromandel. This freedom fills me with a feeling of exhilaration. Isn't this the place where I was always meant to be? Isn't this the place that the Mysterious Corsair's maps pointed to, this valley forgotten to everyone, with the same orientation as the lines of the

Argo constellation? Just like long ago in English Bay, as I'm walking through the trees, my heart starts pulsing in my ears. I'm aware that I'm not alone in Mananava. Somewhere, close by, someone is walking in the forest, following a path that is going to intersect mine. Someone is slipping noiselessly through the leaves and I can feel a gaze upon me, a gaze that is penetrating everything and shining upon me. Soon I emerge facing the cliff, still lit up in the sun. I'm above the forest, near the sources of the rivers, and I can see the foliage undulating all the way out to the sea. The sky is stunning, the sun slips behind the horizon. This is where I will sleep, facing westwards, among the blocks of lava, warm with light. This will be my house, from where I will always see the sea.

Now I see Ouma coming out of the forest towards me with her light step. At the same time I see the two white birds appear. Very high in the colourless sky, they are gliding in the wind, circling Mananava. Have they seen me? Silently, one beside the other, almost without moving their wings, like two white comets, they are gazing at the halo of the sun on the horizon. Thanks to them the world has stopped, the course of the stars has been suspended. Their bodies alone are moving in the wind . . .

Ouma is near me. I can smell the odour, sense the warmth of her body. I say in a soft whisper, 'Look! They're the ones I used to see, it's them . . . !' Their flight carries them towards Mont Machabé, as the sky begins to change, grow grey. Suddenly they disappear behind the mountains, plunge towards Black River, and it is night.

———————

We dream days of happiness in Mananava, far from human beings. We live a wild life, busied only with trees, berries, herbs, water from the sources that spring from the red cliff. We catch crayfish in an arm of the Black River, and near the estuary, shrimp, crabs, under flat stones. I remember the stories that old Capt'n Cook used to tell me, with Zako the monkey who went fishing for shrimp with his tail.

Here everything is simple. At dawn we slip quietly into the forest — quivering with dew — to gather red guavas, wild cherries, Madagascar plums, wild sweetsop, or to pick dasheen, wild christophines, bitter melons. We live in the same place the maroons did back in the days of the great Sacalavou, in Sengor's time. 'Over there, look! Those were their fields. And that's where they kept their pigs, their goats, their chickens. They grew fava beans, lentils, yams, corn.' Ouma shows me the tumbled-down, low walls, piles of stones covered with brush. Up against a lava cliff a thorn bush hides the entrance to a cave. Ouma brings me sweet-smelling flowers. She puts them in her heavy mane of hair, behind her ears. 'Blackcurrant flowers.'

She's never been so beautiful, her black hair framing her smooth face, her svelte body in her faded and patched gunny-cloth dress.

So I never think about gold, I have no desire for it any more. I've left my pan by the stream near the source, and I roam the forest, following Ouma. My clothing has been torn by branches, my hair and beard have grown long just like Robinson's. With strips of screw pine Ouma weaves a hat for me and I don't think any one would recognize me in this accoutrement.

We've gone down to the mouth of Black River several times, but Ouma is afraid of being seen, because of the gunny revolt. All the same, we did go out as far as the Tamarin River estuary once at daybreak and walked over the black sand. At that time of day everything is still covered with the dawn mist and there is a cold wind blowing. Half-hidden among the screw pines, we watched the choppy sea, filled with waves spitting up foam. There's nothing more beautiful in the world.

Sometimes Ouma goes fishing in the lagoon, over around the Tourelle or out by the salt fields to see her brother. She brings back fish for me in the evening and we grill it in our hiding place near the sources.

Every evening, when the sun goes down towards the sea, we sit very still in the rocks, waiting for the tropicbirds to arrive. They appear very high up in the light-filled sky, soaring slowly along like stars. They've built their nest in the cliffs, around Machabé. They are so lovely, so white, they glide through the sky on the sea breeze for such a long time that we no longer feel hungry or fatigued or worried about tomorrow. Are they not eternal? Ouma says they're the two birds that sing the praise of God. We watch for them every day at twilight, because they make us happy.

And yet when night falls I sense something troubling. Ouma's handsome face, the colour of dark copper, has a blank expression, as if nothing around us is real. Several times she says in a soft voice, 'One day, I'll go away . . .'

'Where will you go?' But she says nothing more.

The seasons have passed, a winter, a summer. It's been such a long time since I've seen other people! I don't know what it was like before, at Forest Side, in Port Louis. Mananava is vast. The only person tying me to the outside world is Laure. When I talk about her, Ouma says, 'I wish I knew her.' But she adds, 'That's impossible.' I talk about her, I remember when she went begging for money from the rich people in Curepipe, in Floréal, for the indigent women, the wretched sugar-cane outcasts. I talk about the rags she collected in the wealthy houses to make shrouds for the old Indian women on the verge of death. Ouma says, 'You should go back to live with her.' Her voice is clear and it hurts and troubles me.

*

Tonight is cold and pure, a winter night like those in Rodrigues when we would lie in the sand of English Bay, looking up at the sky being peopled with stars.

Everything is silent, stopped, time on Earth is the same as that of the universe. Lying on the screw-pine mat, curled up with Ouma in the army blanket, I look up at the stars: Orion to the west and, close up against Argo's sail, the Larger Dog, where Sirius — the night sun — shines. I love talking about the stars (and I never miss the chance to), I say their names out loud, as I used to when I would recite them for my father, walking down the Alley of Stars.

'Arcturus, Denebola, Bellatrix, Betelgeuse, Acomar Antares, Shaula, Andromeda, Fomalhaut . . . '

All of a sudden, above us in the vaulted heavens, a sprinkle of stars falls. On all sides trails of light streak through the night, then blink out, some very brief, others so lengthy they leave their marks on our retinas. We have sat up to see them better, heads thrown back, spellbound. I can feel Ouma's body trembling against mine. I try to warm her, but she pushes me away. Touching her face, I realize she's crying. Then she runs towards the forest, hides under the trees, so as not to see the fiery trails that are filling the sky. When I join her, she speaks in a hoarse voice, filled with anger and weariness. She speaks of tragedy and of war that must return, once again, of her mother's death, of the Manafs, who are always driven away from everywhere, who must now go away again. I try to calm her, I want to tell her, but they're only aerolites! But I can't tell her that, and for that matter, are they really aerolites?

Through the foliage I see the shooting stars slipping silently across the icy sky, dragging other stars, other suns, along in their wake. Perhaps war will return, the sky will once again be lit with the flash of bombs and fires.

We stand there for a long time, holding tightly to one another under the trees, sheltered from the signs of fate. Then the sky grows still and the stars begin to shine again. Ouma doesn't want to go back to the rocks. I wrap her in the blanket and fall asleep, sitting at her side, like a useless watchman.

Ouma's gone. Under the canopy of branches where the evening dew is pearling, all that is left is the screw-pine mat where the mark of her body is already fading. I want to believe she'll come back and, to avoid thinking about it, I go down to the stream to wash sand in my pan. Mosquitoes dance all around me. The mynahs flit about, calling to one another with their mocking cries. At times, in the thick of the forest, I think I see the silhouette of the young woman leaping through the bushes. But it's only a monkey that flees when I approach.

I wait for her every day, near the source where we used to bathe and pick red guavas. I wait for her, playing a grass harp, for that is how we agreed to communicate. I remember the afternoons when I used to wait for Denis and I would hear the signal squeaking deep in the tall grass, a strange insect repeating: veenee, veenee, veenee . . .

But out here no one answers. Night falls, blanketing the valley. Only the mountains that surround me — Brise-Fer, Machabé — remain floating above it. And off in the distance, looking out over the metallic sea, the Morne. The wind is blowing in on the tide. I remember what Cook used to say when the wind would echo through the gorges. He'd say, 'Listen! It's Sacalavou moaning, because the white men pushed him off the top of the mountain! It's the voice of the great Sacalavou!' I listen to the complaint as I watch the light fading. Behind me the red rock of the cliffs is still burning hot, and down below stretches the valley steeped in its mists. I feel as if, any minute now, I'll hear Ouma's footsteps in the forest, I'll smell the odour of her body.

*

The English soldiers are surrounding the refugee camp in Black River. Rolls of barbed wire have been around the camp for several days to prevent anyone from going in or out. Those who are in the camp, Rodriguans, Comorians, people from Diego-Suarez, from Agalega, Indian or Pakistani coolies, are waiting to be screened. Those whose papers are not in order must go back to their homes on their islands. An English soldier breaks the news to me when I try to go into the camp in search of Ouma. Behind him, in the dust between the shacks, I see children playing in the sun. It is poverty that sets the cane fields afire, makes anger flame, makes your head reel.

I wait for a long time in front of the camp, in the hope of seeing Ouma. In the evening I don't want to go back to Mananava. I sleep in the ruins of our old property in Boucan, in the shelter of the chalta tree of good and evil. I listen to the toads singing in the ravine before falling asleep and I feel the sea breeze rise along with the moon and the waves running all the way into the grassy fields.

At dawn some men come with a sirdar and I hide under my tree in case they've come for me. But they're not looking for me. They're carrying *machabées*, those heavy, cast-iron pliers that are used for digging up tree stumps and large rocks. They've also got picks and mattocks, axes. With them is a group of women in gunny cloth, balancing their hoes on their heads. Two men on horseback accompany them, two white men, I know that from the way they give orders. One of them is my cousin Ferdinand, the other is an Englishman I don't know, a field manager probably. From my hiding place under the tree I can't hear what they're saying, but it's easy to understand. The last acres of our land are going to be cleared for sugar cane. I look on with indifference. I remember the despair all of us felt when we'd been driven out and were riding slowly away in the carriage loaded with furniture and trunks through the dust on the wide straight road. I remember the anger that rang in Laure's voice when she kept repeating, 'I wish he were dead!' Meaning Uncle Ludovic — and already, Mam no longer protested. Now it's as if all of that were part of some other life. The two horsemen have left and from my hiding place — a bit muffled by the leaves of the trees — I can hear the sound of the pick hitting the earth, the *machabées* grating against the rocks, and the slow and sad song of the black men as they work.

When the sun reaches its zenith, I feel hungry, I walk over to the forest in search of guavas and coromandel. There's a pang in my heart when I think of Ouma in the prison of the camp where she's chosen to join her brother. From up on the hill I can see the trails of smoke coming from the camp in Black River.

Near evening I notice the dust on the road — the long convoy of trucks heading for Port Louis. I reach the road just as the last trucks are passing. Under tarpaulins, half-opened due to the heat, I glimpse dark, weary, dust-streaked faces. I realize they're being taken away, Ouma is being taken away, to some other place, anyplace, somewhere to be loaded into the holds of ships headed for their homelands, so they won't ask for water, for rice, for work any more, so they won't burn the white men's fields any more. I run down the road for a moment in the dust that is covering everything, then stop, breathless, with a burning pain in my side. The people, the children all around are staring at me in incomprehension.

I roam around on the shore for a long time. Above me stands the Tourelle with its ragged rock like a watchtower before the sea. Climbing up through the brush to the Etoile, I'm in the very same spot I was when, thirty years ago, I saw the great hurricane that destroyed our house coming. Behind me is the horizon from where the clouds, the plumes of smoke, the sweeping trails filled with lightning flashes and rain came. Today I believe I can truly hear the howling of the wind, the rumbling of the catastrophe that is brewing.

———————

How did I reach Port Louis? I walked in the sun until I was utterly exhausted, following the tracks of the military trucks. I ate whatever I found on the wayside, pieces of sugar cane that had fallen from carts, a little rice, a bowl of kir porridge in an Indian woman's hut. I avoided the villages for fear of the children mocking me or because I was afraid the police were still looking for the people who started the fires. I drank water from ponds, slept in the brush on the edge of the road or hidden in the dunes at Sables Point. At night, as if I were still with Ouma, I bathed in the sea to cool my feverish body. I swam in the waves, very slowly, and it was just like sleeping. Then I sprinkled my body with sand and waited for it to run off in little trickles with the wind.

When I come out upon the harbour I see the ship with the people from Rodrigues, the Comoros, from Agalega already on board. It's a large, new ship that belongs to Abdool Rassool, the *Union La Digue*. It's far out in the water and no one can go near it. The English soldiers are guarding the customs buildings and the warehouses. I spend the night waiting under the trees of the Intendance, along with the tramps and drunken sailors. The grey light of morning awakens me. There isn't a soul on the wharves. The soldiers have gone back to Fort George in their trucks. The sun rises slowly, but the wharves remain deserted, as if it were a holiday. Then the *Union La Digue* lifts its anchors and, puffing smoke, starts to slip over the calm sea with the seabirds flying around its masts. First it heads westwards until it becomes a tiny speck, then it veers and slips over to the other side of the horizon, to the north.

Once again I'm going back to Mananava, the most mysterious place in the world. I remember I used to think it was where night was born and that it later flowed down along the rivers to the sea.

I'm walking slowly through the damp forest, following the streams. I can feel Ouma's presence all around me, in the shade of the ebony trees, I can smell the odour of her body mingling with the fragrance of the leaves, I can hear the pad of her feet in the wind.

I stay close to the sources. I listen to the sound of the water trickling over the pebbles. The wind is making the crowns of the trees glitter. Through the gaps between the leaves I can see the dazzling sky, the clear light. What can I expect from this place? Mananava is a place of death and that's why people never come here. It's the domain of Sacalavou and the black maroons, who are nothing but phantoms now.

Hastily, I gather the few objects that make up the traces of me in this world, my khaki blanket, my duffel bag and my prospecting tools, pan, sieve, phial of royal water. Carefully, as Ouma taught me to do, I erase my tracks, the marks left by my fires, I bury my waste.

The landscape is luminous in the west. Far away, on the other side of Mont Terre Rouge, I can see the dark notch of Boucan Embayment, where the land has been cleared and burned. I think of the path that leads through the *chassés* up to the top of Trois Mamelles, I think of the dirt road that runs through the cane fields to Quinze Cantons. Laure is waiting for me, maybe, or else she's not waiting for me. When I get there she'll pick up some ironic or comical sentence, as if it were only yesterday that we'd parted, as if time doesn't exist for her.

I reach the Black River estuary at the end of the day. The water is dark and smooth, there isn't a breath of wind. On the horizon a few pirogues are slipping along, their triangular sails fixed to the tillers, in search of a wind current. The seabirds are beginning to come up from the south, down from the north, they pass each other, skimming over the water, letting out worried cries. I take the papers I still have concerning the treasure out of my bag, maps, sketches, notebooks I'd written here and in Rodrigues, and burn them on the beach. The wave that washes up on the sand sweeps away the ashes. Now I know that this is what the Corsair did after having taken his treasure out of the caches in the ravine in English Bay. He destroyed everything, threw everything into the sea.

So one day, after having lived through so much killing and so much glory, he retraced his steps and undid what he'd created, in order to be free at last.

I walk along the black beach in the direction of the Tourelle, I have nothing left.

———

Before reaching the Tourelle I settle in for the night up on the Etoile. To the right is the Boucan Embayment, already in shadow, and a little farther away, the smoking chimney of Yemen. Have the labourers finished clearing the land where our property used to be? Maybe they've taken their axes and cut down the tall chalta tree, our tree of good and evil. If so, there must be nothing left of us on this Earth, not a single thing to refer to.

I think of Mam. It seems as if she must still be sleeping somewhere, alone in her big brass bed, under the cloud of the mosquito net. I want to talk with her about the things that never end, about our house and its azure roof, so fragile, as transparent as a mirage, and the bird-filled garden where the night is creeping in, the ravine, and even the tree of good and evil at the gates of Mananava.

Here I am again in the very place where I saw the great hurricane coming when I was eight years old, when we were driven away from our home and cast out into the world like a second birth. Up on the Etoile I can feel the sound of the sea swelling within me. I'd like to talk with Laure about Nada the Lily, whom I found in lieu of the treasure and who has now gone back to her island. I'd like to talk with her about travels and see her eyes light up as they used to back when we would glimpse, from atop a pyramid, the vast stretch of the sea where one is free.

I'm going to go down to the harbour to choose my ship. This is the one: it's slender and light, it's just like a frigate with immense wings. Its name is *Argo*. It slips slowly towards the open seas over the dark, twilit waters, surrounded by birds. And soon it is sailing through the night in the starlight, heading for its destiny in the sky. I'm up on deck, at the stern, the wind swirling around me, I'm listening to the waves slapping against the stem and the snapping of the wind in the sails. The helmsman is singing his endless monotone song all to himself, I can hear the voices of the crew playing dice in the hold. We're alone at sea, the only living beings. Then Ouma is with me again, I can feel the warmth of her body, her breath, I can hear the beating of her heart. How far will we travel together? Agalega, Aldabra, Juan de Nova? The islands are innumerable. Perhaps we'll defy the taboo and sail out to Saint Brandon, where Captain Bradmer and his helmsman have found refuge. To the other side of the world, to a place where neither the signs in the sky nor the wars men wage are feared any longer.

Now night has fallen, deep within I can hear the living sound of the sea rolling in.